ON VIEWSCREEN

from the ship *No Return* Hilaire Gowdy spoke. "This is a savage night, Tregare."

"Not by my choosing."

"I suppose not. Well, what do you want of me?"

"What do you offer, Gowdy?"

"Peralta's dead, isn't he? For you to be alive, he has to be. All right—I'll open my ship to you and bring my people groundside. None armed, of course."

"Gowdy—why do you offer so much?"

"We've both had our fill of treachery. I offer only what I'd ask, in your place."

Tregare nodded. "I accept." He turned to Rissa. "There could still be trouble. You want to come along?"

"Did you think, Tregare, that I would stay behind?"

Berkley Books by F. M. Busby

THE RISSA KERGUELEN SAGA

THE SECOND BOOK IN THE
3-PART SAGA OF RISSA KERGUELEN

RISSA AND TREGARE

F. M. BUSBY

BERKLEY BOOKS, NEW YORK

To Benjamin

Young Rissa, Rissa and Tregare, and
The Long View were originally published
in two volumes as *Rissa Kerguelen* and
The Long View. They were also published
in one volume as *Rissa Kerguelen.*

RISSA AND TREGARE

A Berkley Book / published by arrangement with
the author

PRINTING HISTORY
Berkley Medallion edition / June 1977
Berkley edition / June 1984
Second printing / September 1984
Third printing / May 1985
Fourth printing / November 1986

ISBN: 0-425-10140-1

A BERKLEY BOOK ® TM 757,375
Berkley Books are published by The Berkley Publishing Group,
200 Madison Avenue, New York, NY 10016.
The name "BERKLEY" and the stylized "B" with design
are trademarks belonging to Berkley Publishing Corporation.

PRINTED IN THE UNITED STATES OF AMERICA

PRELUDE

IN the 21st century, the United Energy and Transport conglomerate is the most powerful government on Earth. Beginning with control of North America, UET has begun to expand its reign, not only on the planet but out to star colonies.

UET did not develop star travel. When the alien Shrakken visited Earth they were slain by treachery; UET's labs copied the captured ship and began the exploration of interstellar space. Not all their ships return: dissidents speak of Escaped Ships and the rebel colonies known as Hidden Worlds.

UET's rule is harsh. At the age of five, Rissa Kerguelen and her older brother Ivan Marchant are consigned to a Total Welfare Center, after their parents were murdered by UET's Committee Police. Basically, Total Welfare is slavery with UET as the slaveowner. Eleven years later, by a quirky backlash of a Welfare supervisor's corruption, the man buying Official lottery tickets with Clients' money, she is not only freed but made rich. Escaping to Argentina, she undergoes survival training at the Establishment of Erika Hulzein; then, in disguise, she buys her way off of Earth. At the minor UET colony world Far Corner she makes contact with a Hulzein agent and secures passage on the ship *Inconnu*, for the Hidden World called Number One.

Inconnu is the only armed ship ever to Escape; its captain, Bran Tregare, is called pirate and suspected of worse things; his behavior is arbitrary and arrogant. The battle of wills between him and Rissa ends short of affection but with mutual respect.

Arriving at Number One, Rissa falls afoul of the Provost, one Stagon dal Nardo, but finds haven at Hulzein Lodge, property of Erika Hulzein's younger sister Liesel and of Liesel's husband Hawkman Morey. Their daughter Sparline is also in residence. Rissa learns that Tregare the pirate is the son of Liesel and Hawkman, estranged from his family and embittered that, when they enrolled him (at age 13) in "the Slaughterhouse", UET's Space Academy, they were unable to rescue him from that grim environment.

Rissa Kerguelen, product of Erika Hulzein's survival training, has little option but to accept a death-duel with Stagon dal Nardo. By her choice, both fight weaponless and nude. The man is twice her weight and inflicts painful injuries to her, but Rissa kills him. Dazed, she accepts Sparline Moray's word that it is necessary, for "political reasons," to marry an unnamed man—but even though he is masked, she recognizes Bran Tregare. She accepts the marriage.

Hulzeins never make any move that serves only one purpose. Rissa has made a bet, with a slightly shady business tycoon named Alsen Bleeker, on her survival in the duel with dal Nardo. The bet is for ten million Weltmarks (from "welt," the Deutscher word for "world"), five of Rissa's and five of Liesel Hulzein's. But that bet is still to be collected.

Rissa is still playing her disguised role under the name of Tari Obrigo. Only the Hulzeins know her true identity.

Rissa and Tregare

SEATED, looking to his wife Rissa and his mother Liesel, Bran Tregare said, "Where's Hawkman and Sparline? Something I want to explain."

"Busy elsewhere," said Liesel. "They'll be calling in sometime this day. Why not tell me, and I'll pass it along?"

"All right—it's this. Rissa told you I've been slave trading." He raised a hand. "No, don't blame her—from what she heard, I *was*. But the whole story . . ."

When he had told it, Liesel grinned. "A good Samaritan, at a profit. You relieve my mind—on both counts. Hawkman and Sparline will like hearing this, too."

"I notice you didn't ask me about it."

"Anything you want me to know, I expect you'll tell me." She turned to Rissa. "Now, then—first, are you in good enough shape to go collect your bet from Bleeker?"

"I suppose so—but is there any hurry about it?"

"As a matter of fact, yes. I don't know how much longer— well, never mind that, for now. And are you fit to drive an air-car?"

Before she could answer, Tregare said, "No need for that. I'll take her."

"You think she's still in danger?"

"After yesterday? Peace, no! I have my own reasons."

Liesel nodded. "Good ones, I'm sure. All right—Rissa, when Bleeker tries to stall you, and he will—he can't help himself just now—there's something I want you to do. You don't have to—the bet's all in your name though I covered half of it—but if you don't, it's a great waste." Her eyebrows rose.

"Of course—I knew the bet was part of a larger plan. Tell me what you wish."

Liesel explained. "You understand it?" Rissa nodded. "Just don't let him talk you out of any part of it."

"Bleeker? He could not talk me out of a mud puddle, if I wished to stand in it!"

A laugh. "No, I suppose not. Well, then—ready to go?"

"I must go up for a jacket, and of course I do not have the Tari Obrigo accessories applied yet—"

Tregare rose. "I'll get the jacket—the green one all right? For the rest—you won't have to thumbprint anything, and the shape your face is in, pardon my saying so, nobody's going to notice any details you can't hide with sun goggles." He turned to leave.

"All right, but bring a cap. The fuzzy one, that matches the jacket—so I can tuck my hair up under it."

"Done." She heard his steps, running upstairs, then a pause and more fast clatter as he descended and returned. "Here you are."

As Rissa arranged her appearance, Liesel said, "Call me if anything unforeseen happens. Otherwise, I'll expect you in a few hours."

"Yes. Tregare? I am ready now."

THEY rode in silence. Rissa, thinking only of Liesel's instructions and what they implied, did not ask Tregare's thoughts. He landed alongside Bleeker's building and they proceeded to the fifth floor.

This time the receptionist said, "Ms. Obrigo? Mr. Bleeker was not expecting you so soon. He—"

"I am sure he will be pleased to see how quickly I have recovered." As before, she did not pause, but walked in to confront Bleeker unannounced. Tregare followed; in a side glance she saw him suppress a smile.

Behind his desk, Bleeker rose. "Ms. Obrigo! I—" Then; "Tregare! Look, man—I didn't know! You can't—"

Tregare waved a hand. "My wife's business comes first. Get on with it."

Bleeker sat slowly and looked at Rissa. "I didn't expect you today."

"As I told you before, I imagine many things happen, that you do not expect. At any rate I am here—for my ten million Weltmarks."

"But—" Bleeker shook his head. "I don't have—I don't have *time* right now. An appointment—it's urgent—I must go—"

"In less time than you have already wasted, you can prepare the necessary certificate. If your appointment is indeed urgent, I suggest you do so—for until you do, you will not leave this room."

Unspeaking, Bleeker looked to one side, then the other, as if seeking an answer. Rissa answered for him. "What you mean, Bleeker, is that you cannot raise the money within five days. Correct?"

"That devil! She has me stretched thin as kite string. Tied up here, tied up there—how did she do it? It all *seemed* to be working. Now—"

"Now to pay me would cost you twice the bet in forced liquidations. Is that true?"

His brow wrinkled. "Not that much—but crucial holdings, control—oh, never mind. I can't pay you today, and that's all there is to it."

"Is it, now?" She paused. "Tell me—what happens to your shaky financial structure when I announce on public viewscreen that you have welshed on a recorded, bonded wager?"

"You can't!"

"If it is true, I certainly can. Write me the certificate."

"You'll ruin me!"

"If you are ruined, it is through your own greed and poor judgment. But . . . perhaps you are not."

His eyes narrowed. "What are you up to?"

"This bet—it is not large, is it, in comparison to your overall holdings?"

"No—of course not. It's just that everything's tied up."

"Then you have no difficulty. Write—and immediately, before leaving this room, I will exercise my option to convert the certificate into twelve million in shares of your interests. You will lose a sliver of your frozen moneys instead of having to liquidate much more under harsh circumstances." He hesitated; she pitched her voice to ring. "Write! Or I leave and have it announced that you welshed."

Sweating, he nodded and obeyed. "There. Are you satisfied?"

"To this point, yes. Let us get on with the conversion."

"Of course. Let me see—I can let you have three million in shares of the spaceport warehouse complex, two in waterborne transport, and—"

"Oh, no! It is *my* choice, Bleeker. You know that; do not deny it." She heard Tregare chuckle—now she would set the hook.

"What do you want?"

"The entire twelve million in shares—voting shares—of the parent company, Bleeker, Ltd."

"Control! You—she—that's what you're after." He scribbled on a pad, then laughed. "Well, you won't get it."

"You are breaking our agreement?"

He shook his head. "Of course not. Your twelve million won't swing it, that's all. Not with—I'll have to retrench, once this squeeze is off, but—now if I'd bet fifteen the way you wanted, I'd be in tight. No, you get your shares. The market price is—let me see—" He punched viewscreen buttons for data. "Here—come look for yourself. Will you take conversion as of now?"

She moved and stood beside him, watching. The quotation gained a fraction, held there a few seconds, then dropped back to the original value. Perhaps half a minute she watched, and it did not change again. "All right. Two-thirty-nine it is. Fifty thousand shares and a little over." Then; "No, wait—I will convert also the half-million you paid me earlier. So that will be—fifty-two thousand, seven hundred twenty shares—less eighty Weltmarks, which I shall pay you in cash."

He looked at her, then punched the figures into his desk

calculator. "You're right. Let's see the eighty."

When the transaction was completed, she put the share certificates in her shoulder bag. "Thank you, Bleeker. Dealing with you has been . . . interesting."

"Yes, I'm sure." His shoulders sagged. "Is there anything else?"

Tregare spoke. "A while ago you were bloody anxious to talk with *me*. I'm still here."

"Why—I'd forgotten! Look—at the port, that was just a business thing. If I'd known who you were—Tregare, you got away with my goods at the price you intended. Can't you let it go at that? So many difficulties—"

"Our little argument? Is that what worried you? Bleeker, that's garbage out the airlock—forget it. Just don't let me catch you trying it again, is all."

"You mean that? Why didn't you tell me?"

"Tari's business had priority—I didn't want to distract you." And this time it was Rissa who had to hide her amusement. Bleeker did not answer. Tregare said, "Well, good day to you," and they left.

NOT until he had the aircar at cruising altitude did either speak. Then he said, "I wish we had that scene recorded, for Liesel. Granted, she gave you the bones of it—but Rissa!—the way you improvised!"

"And it was most helpful, Bran—the way you *refrained* from distracting Bleeker." They laughed together. "We work well in concert, do we not?"

He reached to squeeze her shoulder. "Yes. I should have you with me on *Inconnu*—but you'll do better for yourself here."

She turned to him. "Bran! What kind of marriage is that—to sit and grow old while you are gone? I *will* go with you. I—"

"Not this time—maybe later. And no point in talking, now —I don't know my own plans yet. When I do, then we'll talk."

She made no answer; if he wanted silence, he could have it. Sidelong, she saw him turn to watch her occasionally, but he said nothing. Then it was time to land; still silent, they entered the Lodge and went to Liesel's office.

"Well! You two look as if you lost the argument. What happened? Did Bleeker have an extra string to his kite after all?"

Rissa shook her head. "No, nothing like that. It is merely that Bran and I—no, never mind. Here is the paper for the shares you wished me to obtain. Give me the proper form and I will sign your part over to you as agreed."

"Then it went according to plan?"

"You should have been there," Tregare said. "When she pulled his string tight, I thought he'd melt down to a puddle!"

"But," said Rissa, "if it was control you wanted, we did not succeed. Bleeker thought of that, scribbled a few figures, then laughed and said he could safely part with these shares. I am sorry, Liesel, but I did carry out your plan."

Liesel's palm slapped the desk; she grinned. "You did enough—Bleeker's wrong. Assuming you vote with us, we have control—he'll find that out at his next board meeting." She looked at Rissa. "You don't understand? Ever hear of sleeper dummies? A lot of my stock's been voting Bleeker's way, up to now, to keep him off guard until I could grab the decisive block without his knowing."

She nodded. "No, Rissa—you didn't fail. Bleeker's about to go down the drain."

"What will happen to him?"

"He'll just have to face the fact that he's working for *us* now. He may even gain by it, financially—he's a rotten manager, Bleeker is—if I hadn't put him under, someone else would have. We just got there first. But if he can follow instructions he'll be all right."

Rissa frowned. "Do you consider him a dependable employee? He is too easily confused."

"He won't be making decisions without our approval. But we need him as a figurehead, nominally still an oligarch, to use his vote in Council." She smiled. "That makes seven in direct control, not counting allies. We're getting there . . ."

Rissa stared. "You intend to control the entire planet?"

"That bothers you?"

"No—if anyone can, it would be you, I think. You are capable—even ruthless—yet not cruel. And without direction, this world will tear itself apart, as Earth was doing when I left it.''

''Yes—that's about how I see it. But there'll be hell to pay when some get their first sniff of what I'm up to. Right now, everyone suspects everyone else, so I'm covered. But if I make a definite move too soon—crash landing! They'd gang up.''

Tregare said, ''Liesel, we need to talk, you and I. Not just now—but it takes me that your plans and mine, rubbed together, might strike a spark or two.''

''Your plans? Yes—I've been curious, but you keep your kite on a short string. Sure—we'll talk. Anytime you like.''

Rissa stood. ''Talk now, if you wish. I will go and rest.''

''Here—I'll go with you,'' said Tregare.

''No. Not now—and not tonight. I will manage by myself.''

''What the hell—'' But leaving, Rissa did not answer Liesel. Upstairs, she thought this was the closest to sulks that she had had for years. Childish? Perhaps. Reaction from the duel, or —she pursued the thought no further. Closing the mind-compartment that held Bran Tregare, she lay down and, without undressing, slept.

THE sound of a landing aircar woke her. Outside, shadows lengthened and sunset neared. Lying quietly she searched her feelings and found herself relaxed, the tensions gone. All right —she would go to dinner and behave to Tregare with friend-ship; certainly he had earned that much. And if she were patient, perhaps he would explain . . .

She bathed and dressed, curled her hair in the Tari Obrigo fashion, and pinned all but the backfall into a topknot cluster. She had soaked the bandage off her cheek; the cut was closed and makeup disguised it well enough. The swelling at her eye, she decided, added such grotesquerie that it would be a shame to tamper with its coloring. She smiled into the mirror and turned to go downstairs.

AT a table set for five, she found only Sparline and Tregare. They broke off conversation; Sparline said, ''You know what, Rissa? Bran and I figured it out—he used to be a year the older of us, but now he's traveled so much more, he's a year or two younger!''

Tregare grinned; suddenly his cheek tattoo seemed out of place. "That's as close as we can calculate," he said. "My early trips with UET, I don't have exact data."

To Rissa, the lines at his eyes spelled anxiety. She smiled and said, "Relativity makes strange agemates, does it not? Yes, I suppose you two—separated for so long—have found much to discuss and compare."

Sparline laughed. "Oh, yes! And it's so *good*—after all the grim stories we'd heard—to find that the ogre Tregare is still my brother Bran!"

His finger pushed the tip of her nose. "Hey—remember how I used to do that when you got stubborn, to make you laugh? You were four, maybe," Then he sobered. "But the ogre's not all make-believe. I've done things you wouldn't like to hear."

"Haven't we all?" She spoke quietly. "Life here—it's no maypole dance. But to be harsh when you don't need to— that's not only cruel, but foolish. So we don't—and I bet you don't, either."

After a pause, he said, "Funny thing about need—it's what you think it is. I've been rougher at times than might have been strictly necessary, to impress some folks who thought Tregare was maybe a soft touch. Well, Tregare wasn't."

"I would imagine," said Rissa, "that you averted much trouble. As to whether your harshness was justified, I was not present."

"Yeah. Well, UET taught me the iron-fist trick; it took a while to learn that easier ways work, too. I'm still learning."

Rissa touched his hand. "So are we all—to stop learning is to stop living. I am not at all prepared for that, so soon."

"You're telling me something," he said, "but I'm not sure what."

"Neither am I—except that this afternoon I spoke in anger, and I wish to retract what I said. If you would like, again, the unrewarding role of simply helping me to keep warm . . ."

Sparline's laugh rang. "Now *that's* a polite way to say you're still too sore to spread for pleasure! Your answer, Bran?"

He scowled. "You know our history. Husband or no, it's

fitting that bed games, now, wait on *her* decision." He slanted an eyebrow. "Of course, if she takes too long, I can help myself elsewhere."

Sidelong, he looked at Rissa. She said, "What you do outside our bed is your concern—as what I do is mine. Need we belabor the point?"

Sparline, hands to face, shook with laughter. Then, "Bran —if you haven't learned yet not to bait this one, you're slow."

She looked at Tregare; he smiled. "Given time enough, I think we'll make a good match."

Liesel and Hawkman entered from one door, food-laden servitors from another. Between seating and greetings and serving, a new conversation began—skipping, as they ate, from one subject to another. Tregare recapitulated the Bleeker interview; Hawkman, laughing, slapped the table hard enough to upset his wine. Rissa only partially understood the talk of how to consolidate the Windy Lakes situation after Fennerabilis' withdrawal. Even less could she follow Tregare's cryptic mentions of other Escaped Ships. "I'll know in a few weeks what's realistic to plan for, and what isn't," he said.

Before Rissa could frame a question, Liesel spoke to her. "I've got a figure on your share from dal Nardo—nearly thirty million. With the rest, it's as I said; you're well up in the middle oligarchal ranks. If you don't mind discussing it now, I've got some ideas to sell you—how to invest as much as you choose, here, to benefit the whole family interest. All right?"

"Of course. Liesel, you need not be a salesperson to me. Tell me your wishes, and I will see how far I can agree with you."

Liesel rubbed her forehead. "Black eye and all, you look so baby-face young I keep forgetting you trained with Erika. All right—Bleeker's warehouse complex that he tried to fob off as part of the bet. The way he runs it, he's losing money. But look—" With stylus on paper she sketched rapidly. "Here's the way he has it set up. You see?"

"Yes. His routings. Here—and here—blockages, and much time wasted." She pointed. "Is this building of importance?"

"No—a catchall for things he buys and can't sell."

"Then remove it, contents and all, at salvage prices." She took the stylus and sketched new routings. Brow wrinkled, muttering, she corrected her first efforts. ". . . smooth flow

. . . separate access in and out from dockside . . . a gate *here*, to do the same for the spaceport . . . load in and out without undue delay . . ."

Liesel waved a hand. "Enough—you see it perfectly. Now, then—you'll take it?" Rissa nodded. "All right; let me do the dickering, though—I can do it quicker than I could coach you on the details." She brought out another paper. "Now, then—"

With elaborate ostentation, Tregare yawned. "Liesel, with all due respect, you'd stop in mid-fuck to modify a contract. Enough of business, I say! Who votes with me?"

Laughter answered him, and Hawkman said, "If your mother's not insulted—and I see she isn't—I'll forgive your underestimation of *me*. And you have my vote!"

Sparline lit a drugstick. "Shall we relax, then?" Each, except Rissa, took one. She thought, then shook her head.

"I am still tuned to utilize tension for survival. In a few days, perhaps, but not now." She watched the euphoria take them, and knew their time-senses were expanding as hers had done under adrenaline shock. But it is so different, she thought—the one time-dilation so diffuse and relaxed, the other so tense and concentrated. In her own way she, too, relaxed, and enjoyed the vague strands of conversation as the others went deeper into pleasant drug-hazed introversion.

When, much later, the group dispersed, she steadied Tregare's path to the stairs and up them. Drug or no drug, she thought, if necessary, he could act. But here there was no need. She helped him out of clothing and into bed, and fell asleep against his warmth.

NEXT morning, she woke first. Seeing that Tregare still slept heavily, she did not wake him as she dressed and prepared for the day. Downstairs she found Liesel with papers, some coffee-stained, spread among her breakfast debris.

"Morning, Rissa. Sit here; clear yourself a space. Just shuffle that stack together; my clerk can sort them later."

"Good morning." But Liesel's attention was back to her work. Not until Rissa had been served her breakfast and eaten it, and was thinking of taking coffee to Tregare as a wake-up bonus, did Liesel speak again.

"The warehouses—I'll offer six, and eight is tops. All right?"

"You know the values; I do not. Liesel, something bothers me. Even with the poor routing, that complex should make a profit. Tell me—how does Bleeker base his charges?"

Liesel shoved papers at her. "Look it over. If you see any changes to make, note them down." And she went back to her own chores, reading, muttering, marking and underlining in red slashes.

Rissa puzzled at the tariff sheets; finally she saw what was wrong. Depending on weight and bulk, storage was charged by a flat daily rate. ". . . nothing separate for loading in and out, and that is where his costs are greatest." The charges were disproportionate, with longer-storage items paying far more than their fair share.

She wrote. A base fee for having a given weight and bulk on the premises at all. Then—she was surprised at how much the daily rates could be reduced—longer storage, which meant less work and more profit, would become considerably more attractive. Finished, she handed the sheets back to Liesel and waited.

After a moment, the older woman nodded. "You've caught it—except one point you couldn't know. Only about a tenth of what Bleeker stores rates special security. But the damn fool installed and maintains it for the whole complex."

"I see. We cut costs by maintaining the extra precautions only where needed, and sell the excess equipment—cheaper than new, but not by much—as demand arises."

"I was hoping you'd see that one. Now, then—here's a list of things you could invest in or buy outright. For instance—"

As the talk continued, Rissa approved most items. When she demurred, it was on the grounds that the enterprise was outside her field of knowledge. Until they came to the question of land, Liesel agreed, but that matter she refused to pass.

"No. To be taken seriously, Rissa, you've *got* to have some. And this peninsula's ideal. It's Fennerabilis' last toehold near Windy Lakes, distant from his other areas; he'll be glad to sell."

"But I know nothing of agriculture."

"You don't have to; there's not enough to notice. Or logging—someday the upland timber will be worth considerable, but not until the area's more settled. For now, North Point's mostly good for grazing; the herds prosper. But where you can make profit is in offshore fishing rights, out to the edge of the Shelf. Lease them out; sit back and collect. Fennerabilis hasn't done well because he's too cheap to commission a patrol boat against poachers, so very few bother to pay him."

"All right—as you explain it, it sounds manageable." Rissa leaned back and stretched. "It is hardly mid-morning but I feel we have done a day's work. Yet there is one more thing."

"Yes?"

"I have noted the sums we propose to spend, adding on the normal operating expenses, and I think we have reached my limit."

"Why, we've hardly gone past half!"

"I have not yet mentioned the moneys I wish to send to Earth—and in lesser degree, to Far Corner." She named the amounts.

Liesel whistled. "On top of what's already tied up off-planet, that's a lot to risk at such distances, over so many years. Why stretch yourself so thin and so far?"

Rissa shrugged. "A feeling—that I have not seen the last of Earth. Far Corner, of course, is my liaison. But on Earth I would not like to be short of assets—particularly, of holdings in UET. In writing Erika—her Establishment—I have stressed that point. This time I will devote the entire sum to that one purpose."

"Whatever you say. Maybe it wouldn't hurt if *I*—not that it'll do me any good, personally—but in the long view . . ."

"The long view, yes—I am only beginning to appreciate its power." She smiled and stood. "I will take coffee up, and wake Tregare if he still sleeps."

In the kitchen, after an enthusiastic greeting ("Hey! It's our champion!"), she obtained a pot of coffee and two cups. She needed no tray; the pot had hooks on the side for cups and accessories. Upstairs, as she entered the room, the door banged against a chair. From the bathroom Tregare called, "Set it down in there! It sure took long enough!"

Rissa pitched her voice to the high tones of Lysse Harnain. "Oh, I'm sorry, sir—I was busy kissing one of the stewards."

"You what?" Scowling, holding a towel around him,

Tregare emerged. He stared, then shook his head and laughed. "That's one on me. How long you been up?"

"For hours." She poured the coffee and set the additives handy to their reach. "Liesel and I have been dividing Number One between us and deciding which is to be my half."

"Yeah, I can imagine—just as well I slept in, for once." Haphazard, he slung the towel into the bathroom, then sat naked across from her and sampled his cup.

Again she noted the scars and welts that marred his skin. "Bran—I have never asked before and, if you wish, I will not again. But I *am* curious—how is it that you are so scarred? In battles, or—"

His face tensed almost to snarling. Then he shook his head and made visible effort to relax. "Mostly not. This, and this—at Escape, when we first took the ship. This, and a few others, in various hassles since then. But most of it—" He shuddered. "—most of it at UET's Academy, before I ever got into space."

"They—"

"Some of it they called 'discipline,' but the worst was called 'training.' They'd send a group of us—officer candidates— into the arena to fight free-for-all, every hand against every other. Usually unarmed, sometimes with clubs or knives. The fight went on until someone was killed."

"What if all *refused*?"

"All died. One example taught us that. Then a group tried to be smart—ganged up on the smallest and killed him fast. It didn't work; the rest had to do it all over again." He put his hands to his face, then looked up. "I hadn't known it was possible to live in such constant fear. *Any* day they could—"

Her hand was to her mouth; she had drawn blood from a knuckle, unheeding the pain of her loosened teeth. "Tregare! That first day on *Inconnu*—when I asked if you were— afraid—"

He nodded. "Yes. I'd fought fear for so many years, the very word set me off. I'd thought I was done with that, but coming into Far Corner, two of my officers were down sick and I had to stand double watches. Got so tired that when I did sleep I had nightmares—and guess what about? Right the first time!"

She squeezed his hand once and let it go. "And to think

—when I goaded you until you hit me—I thought you were a weak man hiding behind hardness.''

His lips twitched but no smile came. "Who knows? Maybe I am.''

"You, Tregare—Bran? No. If you were, you would not be here. You would not be alive." She went to him and clasped his head against her. "Bran? If you wish—perhaps today I am not really so sore after all.''

Through her clothing she felt his lips move against her upper belly, below her breasts. Then, gently, he moved free of her and looked up. "No, Rissa—I can wait until you're truly healed. But you're quite a healer yourself—you know?" He stood, stretched and sat again, and refilled his cup.

She, too, sat. He looked better now, more like himself. She said, "What are your immediate plans? Can you tell me yet?"

"I'm waiting for information I can't move without. How long? I don't know—too many factors—except that whether a certain ship gets here or not, there'll be a day when I go to *Inconnu* or she comes here. And then I'll have to decide things.

"For now—first I have business in One Point One. When that's done, you'll have the tape off your ribs and be chewing again. And you and I go across the Hills to my scoutship for a while, if you like the idea . . .''

"Yes. I do like it.''

"Good.'' Careful of her damaged mouth, he kissed her. "All right—I'd better get dressed and go.''

"If I could accompany you, you would have said so. Very well—when shall I expect you to return?''

He was pulling a shirt over his head; the mesh fabric muffled his voice. "Two-three days maybe—I'll call you sometimes.'' Now his head came free of the garment. "Or you call me. If I'm not at Maison Renalle, I'll code relay, when I can, to reach me.''

"All right. If I am not here, I will arrange for relay also.''

"What? Where are *you* going?''

"How can I say? My plans are no more firm than yours.''

"Plans? I didn't know you had any. I mean—''

"All my life, Bran Tregare, I have had plans. But only in the past two years have I had the scope to implement them.''

Fully clothed, he met her in a brief kiss and made his foot-clattering way downstairs and out of her hearing. And to herself Rissa thought, *We will be a time, he and I, learning the limits of each other—and how to loosen them.*

AFTER she heard the aircar leave, she dressed for outdoors, took a snackbag from the kitchen and set out walking. She started slowly, but as her muscles limbered she turned uphill and lengthened her pace; soon she was sweating freely, panting against the tape that restricted her breathing. She stopped at a minor summit and turned to look down at the Lodge, and past it. The valley below fell into blue distances before it reached its lighter-colored floor, flecked with yellows.

Breeze cooled her; she found a sunlit, sheltered clearing and sat to eat the lunch she had brought. Now she was thirsty but had no water; she had drunk from streams by hand and the nearest was farther downhill than she wished to backtrack. Remembering a year at the Welfare Center when water had been available only twice a day, she shrugged.

Lunch finished, she followed a narrow ridge that first dipped and then rose to join the next-higher hill. After a time of strolling, to let blood concentrate for digestion, again she walked fast and hard, swinging arms for balance and flexing her torso as she climbed, pushing herself nearer her current limits.

Underbrush hid the stream; had she not kicked a pebble and heard the splash, she would have missed it. The cool water, tasting of moss and mineral, pleased her. She drank sparingly, rose, and continued the climb.

When she stopped she pushed sweat-soaked hair back from her forehead and looked first up to the next summit, then back to the lessening height of the sun. She was disappointed—to reach the Lodge before dark, she would have to turn back now and make speed.

She did so—and even hastening enjoyed the changing view.

INSIDE the Lodge and walking toward the staircase, she met Liesel. "Well, Rissa—you look as if you had a good work-out."

"I did, thank you. Even with healing yet to come, I feel more like myself again."

"Good. Listen, now—I'm having some fat wallets here to dine—Council members. Hawkman and Sparline won't be here—or Bran, of course. What I'm saying is, the company will bore you spitless. So if you want to eat in your room, or the kitchen—" She grinned. "Besides, these are your new peers—as well they don't see you first with an eye like sunset through dust clouds."

"Make up your mind, Liesel—is it my feelings or theirs you wish to spare?" She smiled. "No matter—if necessary, I would concentrate on learning strangers and being agreeable, but I am in no mood for it."

"Well enough. Shall I order dinner sent to your room?"

"No, I will do it—but thank you." She touched Liesel's shoulder in passing and went to the kitchen; inside she saw no one she knew by name. She approached the cook in charge and asked for a light meal to be brought to her room. "On a tray that will fasten to the side of the bathtub, please."

The man smiled and nodded. "Yes, that's a pleasant way to eat. You've been hiking, I see—the grass stains, I mean. I don't get out enough anymore."

He turned back to his work. She went upstairs and ran the tub full, waiting in a robe until her food arrived. Then in the steaming water she sat munching slowly on the tidbits and staples, then sipping wine, while she thought.

Thought became daydream, then almost trance; she came alert to find her hand rubbing her for pleasure's sake. She stopped, then thought—why not continue?—and did so. Afterward she dried herself and drained the tub and got into bed. She lay there, thinking how she had told Tregare he must free himself from his past—and that if ever she hoped to love fully, even so must she free herself from hers.

Using the methods she had learned at Erika's, she breathed deeply and set her mind to remember, from the beginning. First the girl who tried to satisfy her as she satisfied herself—Rissa could not recall name or face, only her voice and touch. Then Gerard's impersonal usage—she could recapture her discomfort and indifference, the disgust she sometimes felt—none of it seemed important enough to cripple her responses. She moved ahead to Erika's, and those who had taught her many fashions of sexual performance but little of how to involve her own feelings. Here her impressions were pleasurable but lacked intensity. Then Tregare, on *Inconnu*, where sex had been most often a joyless contest. And Ernol —she felt a brief glow, but she remembered her failure, and it died. A future with Bran Tregare? The thought brought only fleeting sensations; she could not hold them.

Stalemated, she shook her head and put attention to the present moment—she was panting, and sour perspiration soaked the bedclothing. All right—she knew that was a good sign, but she was exhausted and frustrated. No point in bathing again this night—she dried herself on an already-used towel and got back into bed on Bran's side, where the sheets were dry. Before sleep came, she thought—well, if she had not found the answer, at least she had cleared a space that might hold it.

Her first doze ended with a start, as something in her mind said that for her there was no answer. She pushed that something, vague and unseen, into a compartment and closed it.

Then she slept.

THE next days she divided between exercise and rest, and studying the business papers Liesel selected for her—deeds and contracts, development plans, articles of establishment—the lot. Liesel did not report on the meeting with Council members, and Rissa did not ask. Occasionally Tregare called and twice she called him, but the talk was of how-are-you, I'm-fine and I'll-call you-tomorrow—as though, she felt, two recordings conversed. Most meals she ate alone, for she knew she was not good company.

Bruises faded, cuts healed; her teeth solidified their roots again. And one day she pulled the tape from her ribs and could breathe freely.

That afternoon brought a cloudless sky. Satiated with details of business on Number One, she set the papers aside and put on walking shoes. Outside, she found the sun hotter than she had expected, and chose to stroll rather than hike.

She passed the gate to the clearing where she and Ernol had

practiced combat. It was ajar; turning back on whim, she entered and followed the winding path. Ahead she heard a brief cry. She emerged to see two naked persons thrashing on the ground. For a moment her mind insisted she saw combat. Then the man rolled to one side and the woman rose to straddle him, and she realized they were coupling. Quickly she dodged through the bushes and back onto the path—reaching the gate, she paused and closed it. She walked farther up the hill until she found a dry, sunlit place to sit. There she thought of what she had seen.

She hoped she had not been seen in return. For in this place she did not know the implications of it—the man had been Ernol, and the woman Sparline.

AFTER a time she resumed her walk. As nearly as she could, she kept a level course along the hillside, seeking a pond she had glimpsed from her window but had not seen at close range. But she did not find it; her route led her into an area of thicker underbrush. Eventually she gave up fighting it and turned back toward the Lodge, taking an alternate path that avoided the gate she had found open and left closed.

She went to her room by way of a side entrance and the rear stairway. She opened her door and stopped; Sparline sat waiting, upright in a straight chair, hands folded in her lap. The tall woman said, "Why not come in and close the door?" Rissa did so and sat facing her, within touching range. "I guess Ernol forgot to shut the gate."

"Apparently. I hoped you had not seen me."

"Rissa! It's all right—nothing shaken."

"Then why are you here?"

Sparline laughed. "Partly I'm just happy and need to talk about it. And partly to be sure you know how things are."

"And how are they?"

"*Will* you get that grim look off your face? Well, I've taken Ernol to me as lover, obviously. He's not the first, I should hope—there's no problem about that. I mean, what he does in bed doesn't affect his career." Her lips moved as if to spit. "One man, once, thought differently—but we can't afford that sort of intrigue. It's no fun, having to rid yourself of someone . . ."

"What happened to him?"

A shrug. "He had trouble finding work at first—everyone's leery of a reject. But he found a place—he *is* capable. Last I heard, he was doing well enough."

"Then what else is it that I should know?"

"Something you mustn't tell Liesel. Rissa—I think I want to marry Ernol!"

Rissa thought. "Is there, here, some reason you should not?"

"Only if Liesel says not. But at this point, she well might. Ernol hasn't proven himself yet—except to me, of course. Oh, he *is* a lovely romp!. Well, more than that, of course—or I wouldn't consider marriage."

"He proved enough to me—twice—against Blaise Tendal. I have looked for him, to give him my thanks, but—"

"Oh, Hawkman's been giving him a quick tour of the properties. Liesel did say she was promoting him—remember?"

"Yes. And—his hand is healed?"

"Good as new, nearly." Sparline paused. "You understand why marriage is so deadly serious with us? It's inheritance—in some ways we're feudal as hell."

She leaned forward. "It'd be safe enough, far as genes are concerned, if I had a Hulzein one-parent child. But we have the techniques without the technicians, so Liesel said we'd better do it the regular way this generation. And she's dead set on choosing for me, or at least having veto power."

"I see." Rissa nodded. "You need time for Ernol to build stature with Liesel before giving hint of your intentions."

"That's right—but I had to talk with *someone!* You understand?"

Rissa did not—she was experienced in keeping her own counsel—but she said, "Of course. And in any way I can, I will help."

"I was sure you would—well, almost sure." Sparline stood, gripped Rissa's shoulder a moment, then went to the door. Opening it, she paused and said, "I bet we looked pretty funny, didn't we?" Grinning, she closed the door before Rissa could find answer.

IT was time, Rissa decided, to come out of her uncommunicative shell. She joined Liesel and Sparline for dinner; at the end of it, Hawkman entered. "I've eaten," he said, but sat for coffee and a liqueur. No one commented on Rissa's bout of seclusion; the conversation touched many subjects, some personal and some business. More than not, Rissa enjoyed it, and afterward found pleasure in the card game, though after an initial spurt of winning she barely broke even.

"Out of practice," said Hawkman.

"Perhaps." She did not feel up to joking and left it at that.

His long arm reached; he touched her wrist. "Are you all right?"

Feeling wonder at what she did, she took his hand in both of hers and held it to her face. Against her will, sobs broke forth and would not stop. When the first paroxysm ebbed, she raised her head and shook it, tears streaming, then pressed her face again to his hand as the sobbing racked her. Finally she was done with it and looked up, blinking.

"Rissa, girl—what's wrong?" It was Liesel who spoke.

"It's—all right now," said Rissa. "I did not know what was weighing on me these past days. But now I do, and it is finished."

Hawkman broke in. "What was it, then?"

"You will not laugh?"

"*Laugh?* Of course not!"

"All right, then—it was that I had not yet grieved for dal Nardo."

"You *what?*"

"Dal Nardo?"

"*Grieved* for him?"

"My father once said that those who kill and do not grieve for killing will rot and die of it. I was very young; although the words stayed in my mind, I did not know what he meant. Now I do."

"But—" Sparline sounded incredulous. "Dal Nardo? I mean, he—"

As though not hearing, Rissa said, "Once before, only, I killed—the policebitch, the Committee's bloodhound at Hokkaido. But there I had no warning and no choice; she would have taken me back to Welfare. So I did what I did—and never saw her face behind the mask. But still, briefly, I felt a pang."

She looked at each of them; none spoke. "But dal Nardo—I did see him—good or bad, he was *real*. And I did have a choice—I *could* have changed identities, or run off-planet. But instead I chose to challenge and to kill."

She saw raised eyebrows and shook her head. "It has nothing to do with what he was or his intent toward me. I *chose* his death, so I must bear its weight. Perhaps of Blaise Tendal's also, to some extent. And until now I had not done so." She tried to laugh, but failed. "None of you understand? Then I suppose you think me deranged."

Liesel said, "No, child, you're sane enough—maybe too sane for your own good. No—my thought is, damned few people can be trusted with power. I think you may be one of them."

Sparline: "I've always avoided killing; maybe now I see why."

And Hawkman, his hand still gripped between Rissa's, said, "I wish I'd known your father. He sounds like a man who knew a lot of truth."

For a moment, Rissa had to clench her teeth—she would *not* cry again. She squeezed Hawkman's hand and released it; involuntarily she sighed. "Well, then, thank you for hearing me out. I had not intended to parade my feelings—for that I apologize. I—"

Lips pursed, Liesel made a rude sound. "Stop it! You don't have to put your armor back together *this* late at night. Either let me pour you a nightcap—*I'm* having one—or trundle off."

Rissa stared. "I—I will have the nightcap, thank you."

"That's better. All around?" Liesel poured for each and raised her glass. "Here's to people who try to know what they're doing!"

The four touched glasses; Rissa drained hers in one gulp. Setting it down, she said, "I know what *I* am doing, this minute—I am going to bed."

Upstairs she lay awake awhile, thinking, testing her feelings. Yes, now she was free of it. Her thoughts turned to her problem with Tregare, but before she could form it clearly, fatigue struck. She sighed and relaxed and let sleep come.

NEXT morning, seeking Ernol, she snacked in the kitchen. He

did not appear, but she learned where he was working—a room on the Lodge's main corridor. She found the door slightly ajar but rapped on it anyway.

"Come in!" She entered; Ernol rose behind his desk. "Good morning. How do you like my office?" He moved another chair near the desk; both sat. "I'm learning so much so fast—I just hope I don't forget half of it."

"You will manage, and I am glad for you. Ernol, I have had no chance to thank you for—for catching the knife. But I do thank you—though not now in the way I had intended."

"You had?" He grinned, then sobered. "Yes—as things are—well, I'll take word for deed and glad to have it."

He paused, watching her. She said, "Yesterday—I am sorry I interrupted you, but the gate was not closed."

He laughed. "Oh, you didn't interrupt—just startled us. If you'd stayed, we'd have stopped, of course, out of courtesy."

"I hoped you had not seen me, either of you. But Sparline reassured me that I did not offend."

"What else—if it's all right to say—did she tell you?"

He is putting me in the middle—I must not allow that. "We talked of . . . several things. Perhaps you should ask more specifically."

His hands clenched together. "It's the business of marriage. Being lovers—maybe she told you—doesn't affect my work, with the others here. But if we marry—she wants to and peace knows I'll do whatever she wants—it'll be said I did it for status. I'd be caught up in house-politics. Well, I wouldn't like that but I could put up with it—for me. But—you see—it's insult to *her*, too." He freed his hands from each other and spread them wide.

"Yes, Ernol—I see that."

"The truth is, if she weren't the *woman* she is, I wouldn't marry her for all the status on this world." Hands now flat on the desk, he leaned forward. "You believe that?"

"I believe it." She decided, and spoke. "What Sparline told me is that while she does wish marriage, Liesel must not know of that wish until you have had time to prove your worth to Hulzein Lodge more fully. Does this satisfy your concern?"

His breath came out in a huge sigh. "Then she does understand—I hadn't been sure, quite. Thank you, Ms. Obrigo."

"I am sure you call Sparline by her first name, in private. Why not me, also?"

"All right, then—thanks, Tari." The name startled her; then she realized Ernol had heard no other. The correction could wait.

"No need—I am still in your debt—but welcome." She rose. "And I must not keep you longer from your work." She left him and walked a few minutes outdoors, before returning to her room and the never-ending mass of business papers waiting there.

As usual, she became absorbed in the facts the dry figures conveyed, and would have read through lunchtime had Liesel not called by intercom.

DOWNSTAIRS she found Liesel picking at a large snack tray. "Not much appetite, today. You want to order something more solid?"

"Thank you, no. This will do for me, also." She ate slowly and said little.

Once Liesel said, "What do you think—" and stopped.

"Of what?"

"No—that one I have to figure out for myself, I guess."

"If you do not share it, then I suppose you do."

"Later, maybe I will." The words were unclear, but Rissa thought she understood. Then Liesel said, "You're going with Bran soon—to his base across the Hills?"

"Yes, but I do not know *how* soon."

"Or how long you'll stay?" Rissa shook her head. "Then most likely you'll miss the next Board meeting of Bleeker, Ltd. Will you give me your proxy, good for a month?"

"Of course—but why only a month? If I go to space with Bran—no, make it indefinite, valid until revoked. And a general power of attorney, as Erika holds for me on earth."

"You think you'll go on *Inconnu*?"

"Bran thinks not. But I do not fancy being a manless wife for years at a time, so for me the matter is not settled until the fact."

"Can't blame you. On the other hand, you can't establish yourself here very well if you go off sky-hooting within the year. Well, we won't solve it all this minute. Let's sign those papers and have that much out of the way, at least."

They did so, and Rissa went to her room. On her viewscreen a light blinked; she turned a switch and Tregare's face appeared, a bandage over part of his left cheek. He smiled briefly, then said, "I was hoping to catch you in person—never mind, though. The message is, I'm finished up, here. I'll be back there sometime tonight. Late, probably; don't wait up. Might start packing, if you want—we can leave for the scoutship tomorrow."

He touched the bandage. "Don't worry about this; I'm not hurt or anything." He paused, then said, "You know something? I've missed you a lot." The screen went blank.

Rissa called Maison Renalle. A recorded voice answered. "Occupant has vacated. No relay code was given." She shrugged, cut the circuit and called Liesel, telling her of Tregare's call.

"Good thing he lets *somebody* know—I haven't heard from him in—oh, the past four days, I suppose. He said nothing more? Just that he's coming tonight and you two leaving tomorrow?"

"That we *can* leave—not that we must."

"Nothing wrong with tomorrow—after all, you're not going off-planet yet, are you?"

"I would think not."

"Well, I want to see him before you leave. You'll tell him?"

"Of course."

SHE thought of packing and decided the chore was too slight to merit doing in advance. She went outside and walked uptrail an hour, then back, enjoying the pull of muscles and the complete lack, now, of pain. As she neared the Lodge, a flash of light caught her attention; at a table on a roof-deck now facing the sun, Hawkman sat, apparently nude. He motioned toward an outside stair, narrow and steep; she climbed it and joined him.

He was shorts-clad, not nude, and what he had waved to catch her eye was a wine flagon, now half-full. He laughed and said, "I'm enjoying the pleasure of good wine in sunlight.

Sit and have some? Your walk probably gut-dried you well enough."

"Thank you." She drained half the glass to quench thirst, then sipped. "It is pleasant here—I had not noticed this place before." She told him of Tregare's call. "I am glad he returns."

"I'm glad he's here at all, after so long. My thanks, Rissa."

She shook her head. "It was largely luck, my part. And perhaps bad luck that he did not come sooner, in earlier times."

"I'll settle for now, and the way it *did* happen." He laughed again. " 'Perhaps' never won stakes, Rissa—it applies only to the future, never to the past."

They talked of other things—her study of the politics and economics of Number One. The "private money," such as Bleeker's certificates, was new to her—he explained how it worked as a handy credit device, and how, if used carelessly, it could ruin the user. "The Hulzeins issue it sparingly," he said. "We prefer to deal in others' paper; it's safer."

They discussed trends and situations on the planet. Finally he said, "You've got most of it, and rapidly. But one thing you're missing. Just because the landowners' power lessens as industry develops, don't sell land short. Industry needs it as much as farms and herds do—in the end, here the same as on Earth, it gains the value of what's built on it. Remember that, for you'll be here to see it happen—especially if I've guessed right and you're not done stretching your years by star travel." His brows slanted as he raised them. "Well? Am I right?"

"In all respects, I think—except that I do not know *when* I will next travel."

"Well, at your age that's no matter. Here—a last glass before we lose the sun?" Emptying the flagon, he poured their glasses full.

Reddening as it sank, Number One's sun neared the horizon. The light breeze grew chill; the sipped wine warmed Rissa's stomach. She saw Hawkman's gaze intent on her. "Is there something?"

"My womenfolks, and their games about the boy Ernol." She began to speak but he waved her silent. "Rissa, don't let them involve you in their web of interlocking confidences —this to be kept from one and that from the other. They're Hulzeins, that's all—it's in the genes, and no malice to it. I learned that before I was twenty."

Now the sun touched the horizon; he held his glass toward it; refracted light purpled his cheeks and forehead. "Sunset seen through wine," he said. "Beautiful." Then; "Their games needn't worry you. The reason is that Liesel can—always could—read Sparline like an open book. Almost as if *all* their genes, not just half, were the same. Don't tell Sparline that, of course."

Rissa drained her glass; she rose abruptly. "Damn! Now *you* are doing it! Hawkman, do you suppose the Hulzein genes are venereally contagious?" The jest drained her momentary anger; when he laughed, she did also. Then she said, "And can she read her son as well as her daughter?"

"Not likely. If anyone can read Bran Tregare, Rissa, it's yourself." He stood. "Come on—let's go to our ablutions and meet at dinner. Wine and sun give me a fine appetite."

RISSA, Liesel, Hawkman, and Sparline—with an empty place for Tregare. Remembering Hawkman's words, Rissa observed the game—Liesel circling in on the subject of Ernol while pretending interest in something quite different, Sparline answering the pretenses and ignoring the real thrusts. Fascinated, Rissa followed the several levels of meaning with real enjoyment.

Then Liesel, balked on one line, tried another. "I need someone to handle liaison with the outland holdings—but I can't think who. Hawkman—Sparline—whose work has impressed you lately?"

Hawkman shrugged. Rissa thought, *That is a weak move; she is running low on ideas.*

Sparline said, "Right now, the cook's; this meat's delicious." Rissa could not hold back her laugh; it rang.

"Well," said Liesel. "I didn't think it was *that* funny."

"By itself, no—but all of it—you and Sparline, like two cats playing, each pretending the other is a mouse."

Red-faced, Liesel scowled. "And of course you know what it's all about—don't you?"

"I would never claim to know all—about *anything*. If I have offended you, I did not mean to. I am sorry."

"Don't think to beg off with apologies! Tell me what you know!"

Rissa stood. "I beg for nothing, and I tell only what I wish to tell. Perhaps it is as well that Tregare and I leave here tomorrow." She turned away.

"Wait!" Hawkman's voice, almost a shout. "Liesel—Rissa—this is partly my fault, I think—but *only* partly. Rissa, don't be so quick to take hurt from a strong woman's lapse into habits of authority. And Liesel! You know better, if you think, than to try such methods on this young woman." He paused, waiting.

Rissa turned back again. "Since you scorn apologies, Liesel, I will make no more. But I had no wish to anger you. And—no, that is all, I think."

Liesel's face slowly regained normal color. "All right." She nodded. "I pushed too hard; I do that sometimes. These games—maybe I take them too seriously."

"Perhaps," said Rissa. "But that is your judgment, not mine."

"For a minute there it looked like a power play, and you in the middle of it. So I—"

"I am only in the middle—not by my choice—of *your* game. And I regret that there must be sides to it, for I wish the best to each of you. Do you see?"

After a moment, Liesel nodded. "Yes—and I'll bet you don't know *why* I believe you." She waited, but Rissa did not answer. "Well, when you got up to flounce out of here, you didn't say a word about all the proxies and such you signed to-day—to revoke them, or anything—so I knew that with you at least, power was no part of it."

Laughter seemed incongruous, but Rissa could not suppress it. "Liesel! I am glad I do not have to explain, for I am not sure I could have done so. And now will you release me from your game?"

"Oh, sit the hell down and finish your dinner before it gets cold, will you?"

"It has already cooled—but still I have appetite." She sat again, ate, and drank. Slowly and hesitantly the talk resumed, but now more straightforward, devoid of hints and traps.

When Rissa had enough of food and drink, she said, "Do we wish to play at cards? If not, I will go and pack for tomorrow after all, as Bran Tregare suggested."

Sparline said, "Cards? Too artifical a game for me tonight."

"Then a goodnight to all of you," and Rissa left the group. Upstairs she packed all but what she would need to use in the morning, before departure.

She supposed there would be no luxurious hot tub on the scoutship; certainly there had been none on *Inconnu*. So she ran her bath full and for a long time lay in it, relaxed. Afterward she brushed her wet hair back and down, inspected it in a mirror, and decided it did not need trimming so soon again. Then she dried it and went to bed.

She was nearly asleep when Tregare entered; the lights came on and she sat up, blinking. He moved slowly and carefully as he came and bent to kiss her; on his breath she smelled raw spirits.

"I'm all waste and half-jettisoned, Rissa." He put a brown envelope on a dresser near the bed. "Been drinking with an old acquaintance, off a ship just in today." He began to undress. "News—not sure what it means, yet—lots to think about." He visited the bathroom, returned and got into bed. "Lots to talk about, too—but tomorrow, if I don't sleep clear through the day." He kissed her again and lay back, breathing deeply.

"I will wake you—you can get up or go back to sleep." She smoothed his hair. "At any rate, I am glad you are here." With the bedside switch she darkened the room, and lay wondering what had happened. When Tregare's breathing took on the pattern of sleep, she shook her head and cleared her thoughts. After a time, she slept also.

WAKING, Rissa washed, dressed, and ordered up a pot of coffee and a pitcher of juice. When the tray arrived, she woke Bran.

"Do you wish to get up or to sleep longer?"

"Neither." He stretched, and gathered the pillows behind him to prop up against. Rissa placed the tray handy to him and brought a chair for herself. He poured for them. "I'm not hungry yet," he said, "so this is just right."

"Do you suffer from last night's drink?"

"Me? No, we stuck to good booze all the way. I wasn't all that far off course, anyway—mostly just tired. Or I wouldn't have tried to bring the aircar home at night." He scratched at the bandage on his cheek. "You got my call, did you?"

"Yes. I tried to return it, but you left no relay code."

"Couldn't—wasn't sure where I was going to be."

"My luggage is packed, as you said. When do we depart?"

"I want to make a family report first, and see what everybody thinks. Maybe right here, if nobody objects." He got out of bed. "You want to call Liesel while I see to the plumbing?" He went into the bathroom.

Rissa reached Liesel in her office and relayed Tregare's suggestion. "It's all right with me," Liesel said. "Now?"

"If that is convenient for you."

"It's fine. I'll be right up."

Tregare returned and got into bed again, shifting the pillows to sit more upright. Liesel's knock came soon; Rissa admitted her and arranged another chair.

"Hawkman's in the city and Sparline's meeting with the section chiefs this morning, so let me pipe the intercom to my office recorder." That done and coffee at hand, she said, "All right, Bran—let's have it."

"The brown envelope on the dresser." Rissa reached to hand it to him. "No—you two look. They're a little fuzzy—copies of copies, at best, but—"

The women looked at the first color print. Rissa said, "This ship, Bran—what kind of insigne is that? And the markings—"

He shook his head. "Keep looking." They did—at the ship from several views, at the body of a woman whose abdomen lay open and empty, and finally . . .

"I do not understand. Is this a mask, a costume?"

Liesel shook her head. "Bran Tregare wouldn't make such fuss over a masquerade. No—somebody's found more of the aliens, the ones UET stole star travel from."

"Not quite," said Tregare. "They've found *us*."

"Then for peace' sake, drop the dramatics and tell us about it!"

"I got these from Raoul Vanois on *Carcharodon*—used to be UET's *General Leamington*. What it was, I want him to join me—he's in low orbit for money, so I offered for a controlling interest, him to stay on as ship's commander. We didn't quite meet terms but I think he'll take it.

"He couldn't seem to keep his mind on the business so I asked him, 'Something you ate?' Then he showed me what I'm showing you. Look down the pile two-three more; you'll see there's no question—the two humans are about average size."

It was the third-next picture. The man and woman on each side were unmemorable, but the creature between them . . .

"Vanois thinks the colors are a little off, but not badly."

"They are quite close," said Rissa.

Tregare gripped her wrist. "What—?"

Her eyes went wide. "I had forgotten! Pictures—my father kept them hidden, except to show us once. Contraband? But now I remember—the thing so tall beside a man, and much thinner."

She looked more closely. "This one wears a cap, but they are bald. And yes—" She pointed out the all-black eyes, triangles pointing downward, with a pair of spurs or tendrils above each. Ears like half-cups opening forward, no sign of nose or nostrils. Below the shallow-angled mouth, an inverted V, no line of chin or jaw; the face tapered smoothly to the long neck. "A brighter ocher color than this, I think, and the brown markings that accent the features—almost like clown makeup—are not so discrete. On my father's pictures the colors shaded more gradually. The hands are hidden, but—"

"In other pictures, they look a lot like ours," said Tregare, "only longer and thinner. Not the feet, though—they're toe-walkers, like a dog or horse; the heel's a hock. That's where most of the extra height comes from."

"All right," Liesel said, "I'm sold on the exhibit. But what's the story?"

"There's a fairly new Hidden World called 'Charleyhorse' because of the high gravity—hard work really gives you a beating. Vanois—*Carcharodon*—landed at their main settlement, only a few hundred people, and found the locals running around in circles, half hysterical. These aliens—the

Shrakken, if he pronounced it halfway right—had been there nearly half a year and just left. Vanois missed them by less than a week."

"But, Bran—why were the people so disturbed? After so long, had they not adjusted to the existence of these—Shrakken?"

"It wasn't that. After the first shock, the folks found the Shrakken friendly enough. Some of them learned our language; apparently nobody could learn theirs. So everyone thought what you might expect—that here's a whole new culture to trade ideas with. But—" He thumbed through the pictures and held one up. "But then this happened." It was the dead woman.

"The Shrakken did that? But why, Bran?"

"That's the worst of it, Rissa—Vanois doesn't know. What he was told—now believe *this* if you can—is that it was an accident."

"Accident?" Liesel sniffed loudly. "Gutted like a bushstomper hung up in the market? What kind of accident is that?"

"She was found like this beside a stream, clothes piled neatly on the bank. Swimming in the raw, I expect. And Charleyhorse has such a nudity taboo, likely the Shrakken had never seen anyone naked. The idea seems to be that they didn't know her for human."

"But still—" Liesel beat a fist against her other palm. "Why, and how, did they do *that?*"

"Vanois couldn't find out. Whether the people there knew or not—he thinks they did—they wouldn't tell it. What they did say, though—well, thinking they were on friendly terms, they'd been free with directions to other Hidden Worlds. And the best they know, the Shrakken are headed *this* way."

Liesel gasped. Rissa took the pictures again. "I do not know whether you noticed," she said, "but this ship is unarmed."

"You mean," said Tregare, "it carries no weapons *we* recognize."

PLEADING hunger, Tregare called a recess for breakfast. When he and Rissa had eaten, he said, "All right, let's tape the rest of what Vanois told me, before I forget it. Raoul's chief medic got it from a fellow named Storrin—only semiscientist he found in the settlement—so bear in mind you're getting it thirdhand.

"The Shrakken don't fit our biological categories. Their arm and leg bones are inside like ours but their bodies are hard-shelled—intricate segments held together with cartilage and ligaments—pretty flexible. They're not warm-blooded *or* cold-blooded, by our standards. Body temperature—to the touch—varies a lot, and against the ambient as often as with it. Voluntary? Nobody knows.

"They don't have jaws. Those shark-mouths hold two toothed sphincter muscles—well, *something* like teeth—that rotate in opposition to each other. Take your arm off in two grinds.

"Storrin guessed we can't learn their language because part of it's not in our hearing range. Some ultrasonic, he thought —and something they do with the little horns over the eyes. Those twitch and change color—maybe radiate something, too.

"How they reproduce—if the Charleyhorsers knew, they weren't telling. Storrin thinks they have two sexes because he saw a couple with what looked like big hard-ons—but segmented, telescoping. The others had no such thing, and neither kind had anything resembling breasts. Maybe they feed their young like birds do, by throwing up." He paused, then shook his head. "No—that's all I remember, for now."

Liesel turned off her recorder feed. "All right—now what does this mean, to us?"

Rissa spoke. "The Shrakken were on Charleyhorse for some time. We know of one death, but not the reason for it. If they are enemies, why did they not kill the entire settlement and leave us no clue at all?"

Tregare turned and slammed his fist into the pillows. "I don't *know*—that's why I can't decide what to do. I had my own plans, but if Number One needs *Inconnu*'s protection . . ." He got out of bed and began dressing. "Well, there's no deciding for now, so let's get on with our own doings. Rissa, are you ready to go to the scoutship?"

She turned to Liesel. "You will say my temporary good-byes for me? Yes. Then I will be ready, Bran, when you are."

And a few minutes later, outside, they loaded their luggage into the aircar.

AIRBORNE, Tregare turned north, away from One Point One and parallel to the Hills. Rissa said, "I thought your scoutship was on the other side."

"It is. Maybe you don't realize how high the Big Hills are; these aircars don't have the altitude to go over the middle ranges. There's a pass, up ahead a way, a winding cut—unless you saw it from topside, as I did, you'd never know it went all the way through. Even so, we'll need oxygen at the highest parts."

From under his seat he pulled the tube and nosepiece. Hampered by the safety harness she fumbled below, found the equipment, and brought it up. He said, "You know how to use it?"

"Yes."

"All right. Start when I do—or earlier, if you feel the need."

They hit turbulence. The car bucked; Tregare fought it level again. "Getting close," he said. "You can't see the entrance yet, but it's always bumpy here, until we get into the cut." They neared the first major rise. Rissa looked, still fascinated by the huge masses, wooded in blue-green forest, that persisted in looking like the smaller rolling hills of Earth.

Then she saw the cut; it was as though a giant ax had struck. Now unseen gusts buffeted the car—it rose and fell abruptly, tipped almost sidewise and back again, yawed, and was flung toward one side of the looming pass. Teeth clenched, Tregare cursed, wrestled the controls and applied full power. The car swooped violently, then steadied and shot straight into the center of the cut. Abruptly they were in smooth air, though Rissa knew they rode a swift current.

Grinning now, Tregare said, "Quite a ride, isn't it?"

"And dangerous, I would think, if the pilot did not know what to expect."

"Too right—first time I tried it was nearly my last."

She was silent, and he asked, "What are you thinking?"

"That sometime I would like to do it myself."

He laughed. "Funny how that doesn't surprise me. Now look—ahead, here, there's a dogleg turn—an old fault-slippage, probably. It's on you before you know it, and if you don't watch closely—*there!*" She saw a cliff before them—a dead end rushing at her—a splash of white at the right side and a shadow to the left. Tregare threw the controls hard over; bucking in brief turbulence, the car plunged into that shadow, into a narrower passage.

"Yes," she said, "that was—"

"Not now! Here comes the rest of it." Here the angle of light was better—in time that she could have done it herself, she saw where he must turn. Then they were in a wider part, climbing as the bottom of the cut rose beneath them. "Time for oxygen," he said, and they adjusted the nosepieces securely.

He turned to her. "You still want to fly this route?"

"Oh, yes. The first turn is hard to see, but directly across from it I saw a marker, a tumble of white boulders. A second time I would not be caught unknowing."

"You spotted that? Good. To be honest, Rissa, I came through in the afternoon, my first time—the light was on *my* side, not against me as it was today. And of course I'd seen it from above, too, or I might not have made it."

"I am glad you did." Then; "Look—we are at the summit." The pass had narrowed again; on either side, sheer cliffs rose high. For a time the aircar passed not far above the treetops. Then the ground below dropped away rapidly, the cliffs receded, and they flew in open air. Now, ahead, Rissa had a clear view of sunlit hills, miles of them, sloping down to greenyellow plains.

She frowned a moment, then said, "On this side the land is higher, is it not? That is a long way, down there, but I think we climbed much farther."

"That's right—and we don't go all the way down. My place is on a sort of shelf—a plateau—a little past halfway."

She craned to see. "Where?"

"Can't spot it from here. Past that next ridge; look off to your right a little." He pinched his oxygen tube and took a few breaths through his mouth. "We can take these things off now."

Unable to see her hands fumbling under the seat, Rissa needed several tries to tuck the equipment into the clips that held it; eventually she managed. "Well! Next time I will look at that stowage first."

They passed the ridge. The next two were lower; beyond them, small in the distance, she saw a flat brown patch. A glint of metal shone. "Is that the scoutship?"

"That's her. We'll be there soon."

"I am glad. I drank too much coffee."

THEY landed beside another aircar, between the scoutship and a large cabin—roughly cut wood on a high foundation. At the rear of the plateau, among trees that began the up-sloping forest, stood other buildings, of the prefabricated type used for storage. "I'll unload us," Tregare said. "You go ahead. We're primitive here—there's an outhouse behind the cabin."

When she returned he still stood near the aircar, luggage beside him, talking to two men. One, she recognized. "Come on and say hello." She walked to join him. "My wife, gentlemen!"

She thought, *He trusts these men*, and said, "Rissa Kerguelen."

The shorter, dark-haired man offered his hand; she shook it. "Hain Deverel, Third Hat." He looked more closely. "Haven't I seen you somewhere?" He nodded. "Sure—on the ship! But you were different—and the name—"

"Yes, somewhat different. It is good to see you again." His recognition startled her—then she realized she was wearing Tari Obrigo's hairstyle and speaking in the voice that matched it.

The bigger man's remaining hair was red. His long face made a grin as he gave a half-salute. "Anse Kenekke. We wouldn't have seen each other much, I guess. I'm Second Engineer and don't get up topside a lot."

"It is good to meet you, also."

They nodded. Deverel said, "Glad to have you here. Captain—you want us to take your things inside? And Anse and I move back into the scout, I guess."

"Afraid so, Hain."

"That's all right; you're the new-marrieds, not us."

Tregare led the way into the cabin; Rissa followed, and behind her, the two others. Inside, staying out of the two men's way while they gathered their belongings, she explored the place.

The overall effect was rustic. Inside, the wood was smoothed somewhat, but unpainted. Windows, irregular in size and spacing but all set high in the walls, were double sheets of thick plastic. A few, in wooden frames, were hinged to open.

The kitchen seemed adequate—a sink with faucets—storage tank in the attic?—a combustion stove with the pressure tank on one side, and a compact dishcleaner. She found a fair supply of foodstuffs and utensils in the cupboards. And in one corner sat a laundering machine.

The bathroom—she was agreeably surprised—held a folding tub that sat under a shower head, plus a washbasin and covered chamber pot. For cold nights, she thought . . .

There was no bedroom; returning to the main room she now noted the large bed in a front corner. The two men had gone; Tregare was unpacking his baggage and putting things away in drawers built into one wall.

"How do you like it?"

"Rather well—it is sturdy and adequate. Did you build it yourself?"

"With some help. I'm not the greatest architect you ever saw, but it's stood up to the storms of a lot of winters."

"One thing puzzles me. You have running water—some source of supply. What is the need for the outhouse?"

"*Because* of the source. The water's near the surface—can't risk fouling it. The hole under the outhouse is heat-fused; it can't leak. Sooner or later, if we were here long enough, we'd have to move the operation."

"I see. But there would seem to be other solutions . . ."

"There would be, if I'd built near the edge of the plateau. Just as well I didn't, though. There've been a couple of slides out there since I was here last—I'd hate to lose the cabin. But it'd take maybe fifty aircar loads to bring in enough pipe to drain from this site."

"It is not important." She looked around. "Where did the men sleep? There is only one bed."

"Which suited Hain and Anse just fine."

"Oh? Oh, yes—what Deverel said—that we are the *new* marrieds." .

"That's right." Finished with his task, he closed an empty suitcase and pushed it under the bed. "You hungry? I'll fix something while you unpack."

"I will do that later. Now I will watch you and see where everything is kept. I shall enjoy seeing Captain Tregare's skills as cook, but I do not expect you to do it all the time, surely."

He laughed and came to her, and kissed her, but in a moment she said, "We are hungry—remember?"

DABBING a last bit of gravy with a scrap of bread, she decided he was not an unskillful cook at all—whatever he did, he did well. Perhaps . . .

"Filled up, Rissa?"

"Yes. It was good, Bran." She stood. "Now I will unpack."

"All right. I'm going over to the scout for a while—make a few calls and check on whatever's come in since I was here last." He left; leisurely, more intent on thought than on action, she stowed her things away.

Finished, she found the stuffy air oppressive and tried to open a window. The latch—dusty, obviously long-unused—was too stiff for her fingers. She shrugged and went to open the door instead. The feel of it surprised her; it swung smoothly, but was much more massive than she expected. Now she saw its thickness, and that the wall was considerably thicker than normal.

Puzzled, she stepped outside and walked around the cabin. At no window could she look in—their placement and the foundation put the lowest a foot beyond her reach, let alone seeing inside. Back to the door—*only one?—that does not fit the rest of it*—she climbed the steps, paused in the doorway and considered what she saw.

Placed two feet from the right corner of the cabin, the door opened inward and to her left. She pulled it nearly shut, then slowly opened it. Straight ahead was the kitchen entrance; on the right the end of the table could be seen—but not the seating, nor the sink and cupboards to the left.

To see the bed—in the left front corner, its head against the far wall—she had to come all the way inside. The left rear of the cabin was bathroom, and its door also opened inward and left.

She nodded. No one could come through the door without giving an alert occupant both warning and time to take cover.

Now she prowled the place. Only one kitchen window faced the hill behind. She moved around, looking out; the part of that slope that commanded a view into the kitchen was sheer stone cliff. Again she nodded and went back into the main room. There had to be more—she was going to find it for herself.

The two men had changed the bed—a fair job but not excessively neat. She stood at the foot of it. Which side? Oh, yes—away from the wall, toward the bathroom. Tregare would want to move quickly. So . . .

Yes—barely hidden inside the bed frame, near the head, she found the holder—and the gun, butt turned toward the foot for right-handed convenience. She pulled it out—a projectile weapon such as Ernol had carried, with an oversized magazine and a tiny bore in the thick barrel. She put it back.

At lunch Tregare had sat facing the cabin's front. She was not surprised to find, in a holder under that side of the table, the first gun's twin. Consistently, the butt pointed to the right.

She went again to the door; now she knew what to look for. The three large embossed leather ornaments hung in a pattern slanting down from the door's upper right corner. The lowest was near her right hand as she took the doorknob in her left; she reached behind it and brought out the weapon.

No needle-spitter, this; it was an energy gun, and heavy. Rissa knew her strength, but she could not hold this piece steady, one-handed. Automatically, before replacing it, she checked the charge indicator and found it near maximum.

There might be more weapons and there might not—but one thing there *had* to be. She scanned the floor carefully, lifting and replacing the small rugs here and there—in the main room, then kitchen, and finally bathroom. She paused to confirm another needle-gun beside the tub, hidden by a hanging towel, then stood, baffled. Finally she laughed and pulled sidewise at the tub. It pivoted around the mounting that held its plastic water-connections. And there she found what she sought.

There was no pull-ring to the trapdoor; only a button in the floor near one end. She pressed it; the spring-loaded segment swung upright with a crash, vibrating for a moment. She looked down; the hole dropped at least twice her height; on one of its glazed sides were metal rungs for climbing. At the bottom she could make out the shadow of a tunnel mouth.

This, she thought, explained the need for an outhouse much better than Tregare had done. She closed the trapdoor and would have replaced the tub, but it swung back automatically. *Yes—of course—that would be necessary.*

She had no reason to doubt Tregare's thoroughness, but she checked anyway. Outside and around to the back, looking at the outhouse, she considered its position—largely sheltered in front by the cabin, and from behind by one of the storage buildings. Entering it, this time she observed the heavy construction. She was not at all surprised to find, hidden in convenient reach of a right-handed sitter, the now-familiar needle-gun.

THE hills brought sunset early. Expecting Tregare's return, Rissa looked through the assortment of kitchen supplies and chose foods for the evening meal. When she heard him at the door, she had an improvised stew simmering. She went to meet him and they embraced.

"Well! Keep yourself busy this afternoon, Rissa? Or maybe take a nap?"

"I found much of interest. Your defenses here are . . . impressive. At first, when we arrived, I noticed nothing—but when I began to be curious . . ."

He grinned. "What all did you find? Now *I'm* curious."

In proper order, she told him what she had found, and how. "I did not go into the tunnel—nor, since I had no idea where to look, search outside for the other end. It is simpler to ask."

"Yes. Well, the tunnel—it's about a hundred meters—brings you back up behind a storage building, in a gully that gives cover if you have to run for it. About halfway—a little less—is a side shaft up to a camouflaged pillbox—looks like just any other hummock, but its guns cover the front approach to the cabin."

"Most thorough. And now—what did I miss?"

Tregare laughed. "Less than I expected—even if I'd set you looking."

"There is more, though?"

"Nothing much—except maybe the real reason this cabin is exactly where it is. From the ridge up there, we're at the precise minimum angle so that if anyone wants to swoop in and drop a bomb and not overshoot—he has to slow down enough to be vulnerable himself, to some little fleabite missiles I've got planted down a little farther out. From the front or sides of course, they'd have no chance—over the ridge was the tricky part."

Rissa nodded. "I am *most* impressed. But, Bran—are we then in such danger, that your precautions must be so thorough?"

He gripped both her shoulders. "Rissa, I take a *lot* of precautions I may not need to—if you mean, do I expect to have to use them. I learned that at UET—give them credit for a few good ideas—and maybe improved on the principle a little. When I built this place—had it built—helped build it—I was playing in local politics just a bit, and the situation was considerably stickier than it is now. But I don't regret any of the work, wasted effort or not."

He released her. "For one thing, word got out—and probably improved in the telling—about what I was doing. It's always good to give the opposition the worries."

"Opposition? Is it anyone I should know about?"

"Not now. One got wiped out as an oligarch, and the rest are running hard as they can to stay in the same place." He sniffed the air. "You started dinner? Good—I wouldn't mind fixing it, but I'm hungry enough that I'm glad I don't have to wait while I do it."

"Yes. So am I. Hungry, I mean. Shall we?"

From a cupboard Rissa had not yet inspected, Tregare brought a bottle of wine. "Let's be a little festive; all right?"

Over the meal, he told her of his own afternoon. "It's the delay that makes it rough," he said. "From *Inconnu*'s orbit the message lag is about eight hours. Doesn't sound too bad, right? But the only times either of us can send is when the sender's pointing the right way when the *receiver* will be, eight hours later.''

Her brows came together, then she nodded. "Yes—I see it.''

"Gonnelsen—my First Hat, remember?—he tried to get a better sync on his orbit, out of the computer. But with the length of Number One's day, it didn't fit—he'd be inside the planet he's orbiting!''

"So your communications are irregular.''

"Damn near nonexistent. It'll improve, oddly enough, as that planet gets *farther* away.'' He pushed his empty plate to one side. "One piece of good news, though. *Inconnu* got a clear copy of a message that came in here garbled a few days ago—too weak a signal to punch through atmosphere.''

He leaned forward. "You won't appreciate this yet—but it was from *Lefthand Thread*, two months out, and homing! Which means it's a lot closer than that now.''

"Left hand? That is good?'' She played up to his baiting.

"The Escaped ship you heard about, that I practically took by force. I had reason—Marrigan was going to take it out in unsafe condition. We can't afford to lose *any* Escaped ship—so I sort of strongarmed him into selling. I was younger then—crude methods were all I knew.''

"At any rate, you took *Lefthand Thread*.''

"Not exactly. I took *Spiral Nebula*—which had been UET's *Wellington*, to start with—and renamed it. Damned near called it *Hogan's Goat*, it was so fucked up—but we fixed it.''

"And this ship is coming here?''

"Or to rendezvous with *Inconnu*—depends on the ships's situation. But it's moving now, Rissa—it all starts to move!''

She looked at him—his face flushed, eyes widened—and said, "The plans you have mentioned, Bran—this is part of them?''

His eyebrows lowered. "I'll tell you all of it, Rissa—soon as I know if there's a hell's chance it might work. All right?''

"Could I not help you decide?''

His palm slapped the table; wineglasses jiggled. "Sure—when I know enough to ask the right questions. Right now, too many loose ends. Even *before* those damned aliens showed up."

"I could guess your plan, I think—but until you wish it, I will not." She rose and put her dishes into the cleaner; when she turned to fetch his, he was bringing them.

He had left the glasses. He said, "Let's finish this in the other room," and took bottle and glasses to a small table there. He arranged two chairs and they sat. After he poured, he looked first at the window before him, then over his shoulder at another. "Those things should be curtained, for night. We can't see out, but somebody could see in." He looked at her. "Can you sew? There's some material in one of those bottom drawers."

"You have needles? Thread? What of hanging rods?"

"Hell, I don't know. Welding rod, off the scout—I could bend the ends and drive them in the wood. But the sewing—"

"If necessary I will staple the cloth together, as you fasten your papers. I do not mind having to improvise."

"Yeah, I've noticed." Looking down at his wine, he sipped it. "New subject. Rissa—you're here because you want to be?"

"You did not carry me to the aircar. In fact, I carried part of my own luggage and climbed inside quite without help."

His hand moved, swirling wine in the glass. "You're not making this easy, are you?"

"I mean to make no difficulties. What would you ask?"

"Do you want to go to bed with me?"

"I do not expect either of us to sleep on the floor, Bran."

"Why won't you give me a direct answer?"

"I will, when you ask a direct question."

"All right! You want to fuck with me, or don't you?"

"I do—of course I do, or I would not be here."

"Then why didn't you say so?"

"I thought the matter was clear enough."

He came around the table, and raised her to stand upright. She accepted and returned his kiss—then his clothes and hers fell to the floor unheeded and she was on the bed, looking up at his taut, unsure smile.

He began gently—that much he had learned on *Inconnu*—but gentleness was only prelude. Their coupling was not unduly brief but, for her, was done too soon. She felt her body move to respond—but then they lay quiet, her response stopped short of fulfillment.

He sighed. "You didn't make it, did you?"

"Not this time. But I began to, Bran. So do not be in too great a hurry—nor will I—and one day it will be as we both wish."

He was off her and across the room, then back with bottle and glasses. He placed them on the bedside stand next to the intercom unit and sat on the bed beside her. His fingers stroked her belly; they reached a ticklish spot; she laughed and wriggled. Then she saw that he touched the scarred area.

"That was done at the Welfare Center. Does it disturb you?"

"Would it disturb *you* if I fathered heirs elsewhere and brought them home for you to raise?"

"I am not ready for such a task. Someday, perhaps—" She sat up. "Bran! Needing heirs as you do, why did you marry me?" *And why have I not told him?*

He lunged toward her, pushing both hands into her hair and gripping it. His face pressed against her, his lips between her breasts. His shoulders shook—and only when he raised his head did she realize he was laughing.

"Several reasons," he said. "More than you know. But the one you're asking about—well, one time on *Inconnu* when you were studying the control room and pretending not to, I took your hair dryer apart. I *thought* it was pretty bulky to travel with, but I didn't expect what I found."

"Then—you knew?"

"I'd seen a reverser before, yes. So—"

"Bran—I said, I am not *ready*—"

"You don't have to be—yet. I don't know how to work the thing, anyway; sure as peace I hope *you* do. No—the only problem is, will you be ready before I leave? Or will I have to leave sperm in the freezers that came with the zoom-wombs?"

Unbelieving, she looked at him. "You would father a child you could not see for—perhaps—decades?"

"It wouldn't be that long for me, of course. But what kind of choice do I have?"

"If I go with you—"

"Where I'm going, that's not possible."

"I can go anywhere you can! If you say I cannot, we shall not remain married."

"As you are *now*, you could—sure. But, Rissa—combat's no place for a woman at the heavy end of pregnancy, or with a young baby. Look—be reasonable—you—"

She lay back. "If you ever tell me your plans, perhaps I will know which of us is correct. Now—may I have some more wine?"

AFTER a silent time, she said, "Bran? What were the other reasons? Why you wanted this marriage, I mean."

He looked at her. "On the ship—you got to me. Two things I like are guts and honesty."

"I was not so honest with you."

"Tari Obrigo, you mean? That's not important; you were in hiding. And you'd hardly trust a pirate with anything as valuable as the reverser." He shook his head. "The only thing that didn't fit was why you let me bluff you into bed in the first place."

"I could not chance it that you were *not* bluffing—I needed to reach Number One. To oblige you in that way seemed a small matter. The body's acts count for little when there is no feeling."

"Yes—I had your body but not you. Except maybe the last night . . ."

"That night, Bran, I *did* feel. I am glad you knew it."

"Yes. Well, then—when Liesel wanted the marriage as a political move, I thought, all right, here's a chance to see if there's anything to it. Then she told me about the duel, and then I saw it—you scared hell out of me, you know that? When dal Nardo almost had you, I swore he wouldn't outlive you five minutes!"

"As, of course, he did not. But then?"

"You know the rest. I said I wouldn't touch you until you agreed, and you told me who you really are, and—you suit me, that's all."

"And as I had hoped, I find that you suit me also, Bran Tregare."

She watched him; he was picking at the edge of the bandage. "Bran, are you ever going to tell me what has happened to your face?"

"Huh? Oh?—I'd forgotten I still had this on." He got an edge of tape between thumb and forefinger and pulled the bandage free. A few fragments of scab still clung to his cheek; he brushed them away. Where the tattoo had been, Rissa saw a patch of new pink skin.

"So that was it—you have had the markings removed."

"Yeah—about time I quit wearing UET's brand. Especially as the unofficial promotions weren't done too well." He grinned. "You know why I had those added? Well, we were on a course that happened to point at Stronghold when I overstretched my Drive. Chasing a UET ship—caught it and took it, by the way. But the Drive was in trouble—even the best grade of tuning couldn't stop the deterioration. We might have reached a Hidden World and might not—but here's Stronghold; why not try it? We faked some papers and the ship's insigne, and the needle to my cheek made me a captain. But the colors weren't right—you saw. So I logged a mutiny attempt by men long dead—and Gonnelsen had to bash me a bruise to hide the difference, along with a fat lip to make it look better." He laughed. "I told him, 'here's your only chance to hit a captain and get away with it, so enjoy yourself!' "

She shook her head. "From anyone else, that story would amaze me."

"Surprises me a little, too, looking back, Rissa. The wine's all gone. Do you—"

"I have had enough for tonight."

"Of everything?"

"No, Bran. Only of the wine."

So he went to her. Again her response began and built, but fell short. Afterward he said, "Still no luck."

"No—but closer, this time. Do not *fret*, Bran—the fault is not in you but in my past. With your help I must overcome it."

"I don't know much about your past; maybe you should tell me."

"Yes. But not tonight—if nothing more, we have prepared me well for sleep."

•   •   •

THE intercom buzzed; she woke to see sunlight slanting in through the window above her. Bran's voice said, "Yes, what is it?"

"Direct word from *Lefthand Thread*. They've got what we've been waiting for."

Tregare sat up. "Good! How far out were they, Hain, when they made that transmission?"

"Not sure, Captain. Two weeks, maybe."

"So, less now. Let's see—standard decel—ten days, maybe."

"Right. Do you want to send an answer?"

"Yes. Tell Limmer—I assume he's still in command—to land at One Point One and refuel, sell off any surplus cargo. He's to deal with Alsen Bleeker as first choice."

"Bleeker? But he's the one, gave us all the trouble!"

"Not any more, Hain. We—you might say we own him now."

Deverel laughed. "If you say so. Any more for Limmer?"

"Just that we'll be talking with him later—and to advise, soon as he knows when he'll be landing."

"Right. I'll get on it." The intercom went silent; Tregare stood and stretched.

"This is good news, Bran?"

"I've had days start a lot worse." He turned to her. "Whoever showers first, the other starts breakfast. Your choice?"

She moved across and clambered out of bed. "I do not yet belong in the kitchen. I smell like a goat."

"All right. Don't take too long or the food'll be overdone."

In the bathroom she made a fast job of it, postponing a shampoo for later, and entered the kitchen still drying herself.

"Am I in time?"

"Sure. I put the eggs on last but the meat's close to done. Just serve mine up with a lid over it." She took the spatula and he moved quickly away. She heard splashing and what might have been called singing—then he was back, body dried but damp hair dripping. She had already begun eating; he sat, uncovered his plate, and cut himself a bite.

"Not bad. If the spaceship business goes bust, we can start a restaurant." She smiled but, mouth filled, did not answer.

Finished, she checked the coffeepot; it was not ready. She walked to the front of the cabin and looked out. The sky was clear. She said, "There are fewer clouds here."

"Yeah. The Big Hills wring most of them out. All year round it's drier on this side."

Now she smelled the coffee, went to pour it, and sat again. "Bran? I would like to take an aircar and cruise about—explore this side of the hills a bit, perhaps take a closer look at the plains below us."

He shook his head. "Not today—sorry. I'm taking a little trip myself. Business. And the other machine's acting up lately —Kenekke tinkers with it when he has the time, but it's still not dependable. Tomorrow all right?"

She hid her irritation. "You do not invite me to join you today?"

"Well, sure—if you want to."

"How soon do you intend to leave?"

"An hour, maybe. Why?"

"That is enough time—I will be ready." Cheerful again, she left the kitchen and washed her hair. He was gone when she came out, and she had time to groom herself leisurely. She was dressed and ready when he returned.

Outside by the aircar, Deverel waited. "Do you want one of us to come with you, skipper, or both stay here?"

"Both stay, I think. Anse hasn't been to Base Two yet, but he doesn't fly aircars—so no use showing him the way until there's something for him to do there."

"All right. Anything comes in, we'll call on Channel D."

"Good enough." As Deverel walked toward the scout, Rissa and Tregare entered the aircar. He energized propulsion, waited a moment for the indicators to show ready, and took off at a high slant.

"You have not told me where it is we go. Base Two, you said?"

"Yeah. We just left Base One. Two is where ships can land."

"Your personal spaceport, Bran?" She looked out over the falling ridges as the aircar crossed them.

"It's primitive, Rissa. Only the basic repair facilities, and less fuel storage than I'd like. But I needed a place away from One Point One, where ships could gather."

"And they are gathered?"

He laughed. "Just one—*Carcharodon*. This morning, on the squawkbox, Vanois accepted my terms and moved across the Hills. Rissa—I have another ship!"

She looked at him until her silence drew his gaze. "I was right long ago—back on *Inconnu*—was I not? You build yourself a fleet and—I am certain—intend to arm it. Two questions remain."

They dipped low over a ridge; he turned right, to parallel the formation. "Only two?" he said. "I thought there'd be more."

"In detail, perhaps—but basically only two. How many ships? And where will you take them?"

"You're right." His voice was low. "The rest depends on those two things. Well, then—how many? I don't know yet—and I wish I did, for the matter of where to go depends on how many I can gather."

"Tregare." His look was puzzled; she laughed. "You have your own roles, as I have mine. In whatever home we may have, you are Bran. But as a ship captain, I can know you only as Tregare."

At his nod, she said, "I cannot imagine you building a fleet to attack Far Corner or Terranova or the Twin Worlds. So—is it Stronghold? Or—Earth itself?"

"How the hell did you figure *that* out?" He shook his head. "No, you needn't answer. It's because we think alike, you and I."

"At some times we do. And—"

"Hold it a minute—we're getting close, and I want you to catch the landmarks." He pointed. "The peak we're passing—there to the right, with the slant-cut top. Now just past it—the half-circle, almost, that ridge makes? We go up and over it—and *there*—the flat-bottomed crater, where once a mountain threw its insides up!"

As they descended, she saw that the crater floor's natural flatness had been improved, in places, by artificial grading. At one side near the rim a group of buildings, blank-walled, formed a short arc.

Near them stood a ship. At the nose, several plates had been removed and now hung from scaffolding.

"Yes," she said, "the insigne reads *Carcharodon*."

Tregare landed near the ship, Unbuckling his safety harness, he removed a gun from his jacket and tucked it into a recess beside his seat. "I don't need this, and Vanois is touchy about being trusted, so why annoy him?" Disembarking, Tregare carried only a briefcase.

They were halfway to the ship when a man walked down its ramp to meet them. "That's Vanois," Tregare said.

The man's appearance surprised her—squat and heavy, with mud-colored skin and hair. The hair and beard were untrimmed and uncombed. In contrast his clothing appeared clean, was brightly colored and tailored snugly.

"He talks an odd jargon sometimes," Tregare whispered, "but don't let it fool you. He's smart enough, Vanois is."

"You are the negotiator here. I will follow your lead."

He chuckled. "Sure. Don't forget—I've seen you improvise." Now they neared the ramp; Vanois stepped off it. Tregare said, "Hello, Raoul. Ready to sign? But hey—first, meet my wife—Tari Obrigo."

"You does me honor." The man's voice was clear and sweet, like a child's. He shook Tregare's hand, then Rissa's. "It's pleasured, Ms. Obrigo."

"And I, Captain Vanois."

The man turned again to Tregare. "It's to sign, now? Yes. But first you says again the terms."

"For a half share and control, you get the amount we agreed—half in Weltmarks, the other half in equipment, installation, and training. Under my direction you keep ship command and full discretion concerning your own people. I think that's the gist, isn't it?"

Vanois nodded. "You says it same as before. Y'knows—I hates it some, you needing control. But I hasn't the money only to keep going as I has—and maybe not that, the way things is gone. With the guns and all—and when does I get 'em? How long is we got to wait here?" As he talked, Vanois briefly scanned the contracts Tregare had brought, and in large, bold handwriting he signed them. He kept one copy and returned the other two.

"In—oh, about twelve days—the ship should be here with the stuff. Has to refuel at the port first, as you did. But the wait's not all waste. I see you've got some plates skinned off the nose already—that's good. I've brought blueprints for all the auxiliary work—bulkhead changes, turret mountings and gunners' positions, conduit and power cables—so you can turn your people loose on some of the preliminary changes ahead of time."

"I likes that. Now—does I get you or someones to oversee, and for if I has questions?"

Tregare frowned. "I can't be here myself much, until later —too much else to do. But we have duplicate prints at Base One, and can confer over the viewscreen. If you run into real trouble, which I don't expect, Deverel and Kenekke can look in and help."

"Shoulds be enough. So—blueprints, you says?"

"In here." Tregare held out the briefcase; Vanois took it and began to pull out the thick sheaf of drawings. "No—keep the case, too. It's handier."

"I thanks you." Abruptly he put out his hand, again first to Tregare and then to Rissa. "Now it's work I needs to do."

He turned away. Rissa said, "Captain Vanois! I—I'd like to ask you about the Shrakken, the aliens at Charleyhorse."

The man's brows lowered until she could hardly see his eyes. He nodded toward Tregare. When he spoke, his voice was lower and quiet. "All I know, I told *him*—when we were drinking. I'm not drunk now and don't have time for it—and to talk of those creatures, I need to be." He turned and walked up *Carcharodon*'s ramp.

RISSA looked after him; Tregare took her arm. "Ready to go? Unless you want to look around here some, we might as well."

"I am ready." They entered the aircar, Rissa leading. "Bran? May I take the controls?"

"Sure, if you want. Certain you can find your way back?"

"I believe so—if not, you can instruct me. Is there time to swing down and see a little of the plains, the edge of them?"

He looked at his watch. "Well—I'm expecting a call back at One. We'd be cutting it a little fine, and there'd barely be time to reach the plains and return. If you want, though—"

"No. As you said earlier, I can take the car myself, a longer time, when you do not need it." She took them up, looked for landmarks, and turned upslope at an angle. To see farther ahead she went high; after a time, she recognized the plateau and steered toward it.

"What did you think of Vanois?"

"He surprised me. At the end, when he was shaken, he dropped the strange speech patterns he had used previously. Why—?"

"Vanois grew up on a colony planet—pretty rustic, I gather. When UET took him into space training he was ridiculed and punished for talking like a backwoodser. So since he Escaped he's made a point of using his childhood argot—and people can like it or not."

"A strange form of pride—and not without its costs."

"What do you mean?"

"It makes his dealings more difficult—if the affectation irritates others as much as it irritated me."

Tregare nodded. "I hadn't thought of it before because I've known him so long it doesn't bother me any more—but maybe that's why a smart man like Raoul is on such a tight money string. I mean, annoying people for no good tactical reason."

"Will he be a handicap to your operation?"

"No. He knows better than to play games in a tight spot."

"Good." They came over the plateau, still high above it because Rissa wanted to see around it in full panorama. Then she dropped the car, fast and swooping from side to side, halting the headlong fall close to the ground. She landed gently; they got out and walked into the cabin.

Rissa was thirsty; she poured cold fruit juice for herself, and at Tregare's nod, for him also. Standing across the table from her he said, "That was a real blue streak landing you made there."

"Was it not satisfactory? I like to try my skills occasionally."

"No, it was fine. I thought you might cut it too close, but you didn't. I just wondered why all the flash. Well, keeping in practice is a good enough reason."

"And perhaps I wished to remind myself that I can do *some* things well."

"What—" The intercom's buzz cut him off; he went to answer. From where she sat, Rissa could not make out the words. Then he crossed to the door and opened it. "Viewscreen call; I'll take it on the scout—like to see who I'm talking to when I can. I wish I'd thought to bring a portable to use in here." He smiled. "This shouldn't take long."

The door closed behind him; Rissa poured his juice back into the pitcher and put it away to stay cool. She waited, and finally Tregare called her. "I'm stuck here for longer than I thought. You may as well go ahead and have some lunch; I'll snack here from ship's stores. If you want the aircar this afternoon I won't be needing it after all. All right?"

"Yes. Perhaps I will." She cut the circuit, thinking that the only way to hold this man to her was to make herself more of a part to his great project. And the doing, she decided, would not be as easy as the thinking.

SHE made a light meal. Afterward she took the aircar downslope, cruising at medium speed, skimming crests and dipping into valleys. An hour later, she crossed the last ridge—at its foot, the plains began. She flew straight out across their beginnings.

She saw few trees, mostly grouped around occasional ponds. A tall grasslike growth covered the gently rolling ground; now it waved in a light breeze. At first she sighted no animals, but after a few minutes a herd—thirty or forty, she guessed—sprang up from concealment among the grasshummocks. About the size of goats, the creatures leaped and scattered, then grouped and ran steadily off to her right.

She swerved and dipped for a closer look—they were tan, like the grass, and slightly dappled. Some had three horns; the rest had none. Satisfied, she returned to her previous course. She looked back once; the herd had stopped running.

The sight of two half-eaten carcasses told her of carnivores, but she saw none. Something dark brown, looking like a small rhinoceros but without a horn, waddled self-importantly across her course and did not deign to look up or hurry as she passed. She knew of no birds on Number One—when she thought she saw a flock, a closer look showed her a cloud of large, brightly colored insects.

She looked at her watch. It was nearly time to turn back, but she went a little farther—for on the horizon she saw a shimmer. She lifted for better view and kept course for several minutes, until she saw it was a vast lake—or ocean, perhaps? No—above ground level of the far side of the Hills it could not be an ocean. Yet she could see no farther shore.

Still curious—but resigned to remaining so, this day—she turned back, holding altitude and pushing the car near to top speed. As she neared the Hills she climbed farther, until in the distance she discerned Tregare's plateau; then she leveled off, as near its height as she could determine. She held steady—course, speed, and altitude—until she approached Base One. She had guessed a bit low—she had to lift a few feet to clear the edge, then touched ground almost immediately and taxied to a stop near the cabin. The door was a few inches ajar; as she climbed the steps, Tregare opened it. His right hand held the big energy gun.

"What—?"

"The way you came in, Rissa—from below and then straight at me—it could have been anybody, and not wanting to give warning."

"I had not thought—I am sorry, Bran, if I alarmed you."

He grinned. "That's all right; it does me good to pull the string tight once in a while. I was only explaining why this hand cannon." He put it back in its place and bent to meet her kiss. Then, "Well, did you get a good look at the plains?"

"Not long enough—far enough, I mean—but good, yes." She reported what she had seen. "That body of water, Bran—do you know what it is?"

"Sure. That's Big Sink—sort of an inland sea, and mostly a dead one. Think of Great Salt Lake on Earth—only twice as salty and maybe the size of Australia."

She thought back, recalling. "Yes. I would not be able to swim in it, would I? The water so much heavier—I would float too high."

"That's right. I tried once; you can almost crawl on it." He looked thoughtful. "Those grassrunners—that herd you saw. If we have time we should go out and bag a couple, while they're in this close. Good eating, the few times I've tasted that meat."

"I am not sure whether I have had any. Except for bushstomper I do not know what animals I have eaten from, on this world.''

He paused. ''*We* haven't had grassrunner—of course I don't know what all you've eaten, other times. But Deverel has a couple in freeze, and—I forgot to mention, we're invited to eat with Hain and Anse on the scout, a little later. All right?''

''Yes. Of course.''

''I'll call, then—and if the menu's not already planned . . .''

''Yes. But, Bran—how much later, do we go there?''

''What? Oh—well, enough, I'd say. If I'm reading you right.''

''I think you are. I will be back in a few moments.''

She was, and in the bed felt herself closer to completion than before—but still not enough to strive. To his look of inquiry, she answered, ''It will happen, Bran—and this waiting, now, is not unpleasant.''

''If you say so. Well, let's go to dinner.''

IF Tregare had not told her, she thought, she could not have guessed the relationship of Deverel and Kenekke. Yet obviously they were a team of long standing; in preparing and serving the meal they worked together without getting in each other's way, cramped though the space was, and with hardly a word about the operation. Instead the talk concerned ships and their people—*Inconnu, Carcharodon, Lefthand Thread*, and others.

''How do you like grassrunner steak?'' Tregare asked.

She was chewing a bite and could only nod. Then she swallowed and took a sip of wine. ''I like it—it has a gamy tang that bushstomper lacks. I see why it must be cooked well-done; a rare cut, I think, might be rather tough.''

''That's right,'' said Deverel. ''Oh, you can age it, but to my mind it loses something that way.''

''At any rate, it's very good. Thank you for sharing it.''

''Any time,'' said Kenekke. ''Lots more where this came from.'' He poured more wine for the other three; his own glass held water.

''I wish we'd hear from Gonnelsen,'' Tregare said. ''He

should be picking up more signals by now if the others are on time—or coming at all."

Deverel spoke. "What do you figure for the minimum?"

"Eight's best, but I'll try with six if I have to. Less than that, we're forced to give it up this time."

"This time?" It was Kenekke. "Look, skipper—when will we be lucky enough to get another advance schedule? And be able to meet the timing?"

Tregare shrugged and drained his glass. "We could always go back to the first plan—though I admit I like this one a lot better."

Well, he was *not* going to tell her—there was no point in asking. She stood. "Suddenly I am very tired. Will you excuse me, please? And thank you again, gentlemen." They said their goodnights, and she returned to the cabin.

AN hour later, when Tregare entered, she was soaking in the tub. "Rissa? You feeling all right?"

"Yes, I feel well. Would you hand me a towel, please?" She stood and began drying herself.

"Then why leave so early?"

"I did not like it, Bran—that you talked over my head, of things you all knew and I did not, as though I were a schoolgirl."

"Oh, hell—I'm sorry. It's just that it would have taken too long, there, to fill you in—repeating, as you say, things they *do* already know."

Wrapping the towel around her, she moved to sit in the kitchen and poured coffee for herself. "And is there time for it now, Bran? For instance, what is this advance schedule, and why is it so important?"

He sat facing her. "All right. You guessed that I plan to take Stronghold. My first idea was simply to scout the place, wait for a time when few ships were in port, and go in by force. But then Bernardez took the *Hoover*."

"It will be one of your ships?"

"If he makes rendezvous on time, it will. But the big thing —that advance schedule, that Bernardez gave me—it's for the next batch of ships UET was building, to send to Stronghold.

Number, names, equipment—and *timing*. Stronghold has that information by now, you see.''

He paced back and forth across the kitchen once, then sat again. ''There's eight ships planned; that's why eight's my favorite number. Because *we* get there first—names and insignia painted to match what Stronghold's expecting—they welcome us with open arms—for just long *enough!*'' He grinned.

''But the *men's* names—surely they will not fit?''

''How could UET put out a roster, years ahead? Half the crews were runny-nosed kids when they sent that schedule.''

Her eyes widened. ''Yes, I see it—the long view, again. But what if you have fewer ships?''

He shrugged. ''So we say the schedule went sour this time; it's happened before. If I have fewer ships they'll run jammed, with all the combat people I can crowd aboard. But I don't think I could get enough—equipped and supplied—into less than six. And I'm still worried about maybe having to leave a ship here, in case the Shrakken come.''

''But I thought you did not expect a battle.''

''I don't, but it pays to be ready.'' His face flushed; he thumped a fist against his knee. ''That time I was at Stronghold—I scouted it, best I could. And it won't have changed much—they'd done a major expansion, not long before. And Rissa—it's not as hard a nut to crack as you might think.''

He paused, so she nodded and said, ''Tell me.''

''The ships in port, the defense and communication centers —those we have to wrap up fast, so no word gets out. The rest we can mop out at leisure, with as little fighting as possible. Offer amnesty, the rank and file aren't apt to make a fight of it.''

''And then?''

''Come on now. Think a moment—you'll see it.''

She scowled a moment; then her forehead smoothed. ''Of course! You sit—the spider in Stronghold's web—as more UET ships come and are taken and no word goes back to Earth. Until—''

''Until we have enough to challenge UET on Earth itself!'' Now he talked faster. ''The crews we capture—both at first and later—enough will come over to us that we can send ships

UET still thinks it owns, anywhere we wish. To Earth, even, and get a toehold on UET's home grounds. So when we go there in force, maybe UET's defenses won't work quite the way they expect, the way they'd work right now. You see?'' He paused. "How do you like it?"

She smiled. "I think UET will come to regret training you in the way they did. It is a fine plan! And—I suppose you have already thought of this, for it is a consequence of the long view—your newer recruits will help compensate for any advancements UET has developed during the years you foreshortened in space."

"An analogy from the edge you had in personal combat, here?" She nodded. "But UET's not that progressive. Except for the weapons they added—and those have stayed pretty standardized—the main differences between the first ships they built and the latest I've seen are matters of interior design—convenience. *So* far, that is—I've got my fingers crossed, there."

"And I, Bran. But what is the timing factor you mentioned?"

"We have to reach Stronghold ahead—but not too far ahead—of the UET ships they expect. To be *sure* of that, my ships have to leave here, armed and supplied, in less than two hundred days. If they're not ready—at least six—the whole kite comes down, and we have to start over, or forget it."

"I see. No wonder you become impatient, waiting for word."

"Too true, Rissa. And eight ships is my *top* hope—unless one just happens to come here, that I can persuade to join up or let me buy control. And damned soon, now."

"Eight? I know of three—oh, yes, the *Hoover!*"

"All right—there's *No Return*. I was landed—fake insigne —on The Islands, a UET world that's mostly water. It's where I bought up that load of women, in fact. Not long after, the *Bonaparte* landed, and Peralta—he was First Hat—recognized me. We made a deal: he wouldn't expose me, and I wouldn't kill him. I'd help him take the ship and—come time to put a fleet together—he'd take my orders. So far, it's worked out.

"Malloy's *Pig in the Parlor* I bought into, same as with Vanois. And Jargy Hoad—he's the one helped me design this cabin—Jargy was riding Second Hat on *Inconnu* when we took the *Peron* in space and renamed it *Deuces Wild*."

"So it is your ship, and Hoad your man?"

"Correct. And Ilse Krueger on *Graf Spee*—she's a voluntary ally, like Bernardez. Just plain likes the idea.

"Now, if only enough of them show up on time . . ."

"All have been informed?"

"Should have been. I sent word to enough drops, right after I got the schedule from Bernardez. There's quite a network, Rissa—for long-haul word between Escaped ships. And figuring those messages by effective time gets pretty tricky."

"I can see, it would be. But otherwise, all is settled? Six or more ships, you will go—fewer, and you will not?"

"That's right."

"There is one thing more, Bran. Will we go on *Inconnu* together—or you alone, again unmarried?"

He stared. "Now look, Rissa—I *told* you—"

"But I have another thought. The—the zoom-wombs are still operable, are they not? And the techniques available, to extract sperm and ova and combine them?"

"I suppose so. But, you mean you want—?"

"I wish to go either with you, or my own way, alone. If you need to ensure an heir, this is how it can be done."

"But you said—how could I leave a child I wouldn't see for years? So, how can *you*?"

"Gestation can be delayed—until either we return or it is decided here that we likely will not." He was silent. She said, "Well, Bran? You have no reason now for leaving me behind —except that you do not want me with you."

Slowly his scowl cleared; he nodded. "All right. I'll figure some job you can do on *Inconnu*, to make it look good."

"An excuse? No—I think I will excel at weaponry and navigation."

"Weapons, maybe—and turret operators are pretty well protected. But you don't have time to learn navigation."

"I think you are wrong. On *Inconnu*, as you have mentioned, I observed. And at turnover I learned this." She recited Number One's coordinates with respect to Far Corner, then transposed them. "So, you see, I could guide us there again. I do not think the rest of it would be too difficult to learn."

He shook his head. "What I can't figure is why—when I know better—I keep underestimating you."

She reached and squeezed his hand. "Perhaps Erika Hulzein taught me too well—always to keep something back, in case of need—so that no possible enemy could prepare for me fully."

"I didn't think I was your enemy, Rissa."

"And of course you are not. But it may be, Bran, that in a part of my mind *every* person is considered a potential enemy." She released his hand and clamped both of hers together. "Bran—I had not thought of that before."

He stared at her. "You think maybe that's why—?"

"Perhaps, yes. It has become late—shall we try again and see?"

But later, panting and sweat-drenched, she was forced to accept the fact that her body was not yet ready to yield its defenses.

NEXT morning, Tregare took an early call from Vanois and left for Base Two. Rissa stayed behind. "In time I will become used to Vanois, but not today, I think." After breakfasting, she went to the scout and asked Deverel whether he could give her some instruction in navigating.

"Our computer here doesn't have full simulation," he said. "Just the records of *Inconnu*'s own travels. I don't know—"

"If Tregare has not said I should have full access, then let us start from the beginning, from Earth. Even UET has *those* records."

"You're right. And—pardon me, Ms. Kerguelen, but the skipper *didn't* say."

"He will." She smiled. "Meanwhile your caution is quite proper. Now, shall we proceed?" She ran the first four trip records, calculating ahead as the data unrolled before her and checking at the end of each run; she caught herself in error once and realized she had hurried too much. She turned to Deverel. "Now, if there is a tape I may see, in which destination was changed in mid-voyage, I would like to try it. If not, we can turn the machine off."

He hesitated. "There's the Escape itself, of course, but—"

Then he shrugged. "I can't think of any reason you *shouldn't* see it—"

"Only if you feel sure, Hain Deverel."

"I'm sure enough. Here—I'll punch up the start for you."

She watched the record, stopping the tape to work out her own figures and then running it to see how well she had done.

In a quick side-glance she saw Deverel smiling, and soon found the reason for his amusement—not merely one change of goal on this trip, but three—and now she remembered Tregare's story. "The second," she said, "was when Farnsworth retook the ship, briefly. And then Tregare . . ." She punched in the final course-figures and waited, and found she was correct.

"The skipper—he told you about that, did he?"

"On *Inconnu*, the first evening out of Far Corner. I mentioned hearing that after Escape he mutinied against his own people. Like any person, he resents being maligned."

"Saved our heads, the captain did." It was Kenekke's voice; Rissa had not seen or heard his entrance. "Not for the first time, nor likely the last."

"True," said Deverel. "But don't be so modest, Anse. You saved a few heads yourself, on that trip."

Kenekke waved a hand. "Who didn't?" He looked at the figures from Rissa's last simulation run. "That's how it went, all right. You studying to navigate, Ms. Kerguelen?"

"Yes. But I thought you were an engineer, not a navigator."

"We work with the same numbers; it's simpler that way."

"I see I have more to learn than I had thought. May I ask you questions when I know what to ask?"

"Any time. Say—sounds like you're coming along, on *Inconnu*."

"I hope to do so."

"Good. A man keeps a steadier head, with his love close to hand." The big man smiled, turned, and left the control room.

Unsure what to say, Rissa looked at Deverel. He said, "Anse is right. He doesn't talk much, but when he does, it pays to listen."

Before she could stop herself she said, "How long—?"

"Anse and I? From before space—in UET training, when they'd have killed us for it. Nobody was more eager than us for Escape."

"UET would have killed you? I do not understand. In North America, among freepersons many ways are accepted."

"But not in UET. What they want is robots, zombies—and they manage to build themselves a lot of those. They caught a couple of boys in the cadre next to ours—and we saw what happened to them."

She shook her head. "Do not tell me, please. Though perhaps I imagine worse than the reality."

"I doubt it." With obvious effort, he laughed. "But that's light-years gone and here we are on a fine world, waiting our chance to set teeth into—well, to teach UET a lesson, maybe."

"I hope so. Thank you, Hain, for helping me. I will leave you now."

SHE decided to explore Tregare's escape tunnel. Carrying a handlight, she swung the tub, opened the trapdoor and descended the vertical shaft. Above her the door closed; she pointed the light up to find the latch that would release it from below. She walked through the featureless tube, past the shaft slanting upward on the left, to the gully exit. Yes—it did give good cover.

She returned to the side shaft and clambered up to the small pillbox. Vision slits looked out toward the cabin—she could see the left side and the front—and the area between it and the scout. The emplaced weapons were two energy projectors, similar to those on *Inconnu*—but she knew they must be powered by a lesser source than the ship's. They were mounted so they could be locked together for elevation and traverse or disengaged for separate targets. Aiming, she moved the locked pair back and forth to get the feel of it.

She returned to the shaft under the cabin, operated the latch and waited while the tub pivoted and the trapdoor raised, and climbed up into the bathroom. Her hands were dusty; she washed them.

She spent the rest of the afternoon hiking upslope behind the plateau, circling above the cliff that overlooked the cabin's kitchen window, and then returning by way of a narrow ravine that debouched into a talus slope. Picking her way down, the rough rocks cost her a bruised ankle.

She found that Tregare had not returned; she ate and spent the evening alone.

THE next day he was back briefly, but took the aircar across the Hills and was gone the night again. The following morning he returned and woke her early, for breakfast and for love-making too brief—surprisingly so—for any chance of satisfaction, before disappearing into the scoutship. That day he joined her for dinner and stayed the night, and for the next few days they were together more than not. He showed pleasure at her navigational progress and one day announced that Peralta's *No Return* was homing for rendezvous. But for the most part he was busy, even though present in body, and could give her little of his attention.

Her days and nights repeated themselves, so much alike that they blended in her mind and she lost count of them. She walked a lot, for exercise. Bran installed the promised curtain rods and provided material, and she curtained the windows. Kenekke pronounced the second aircar fit for service; in it, she explored the surrounding terrain. But finally, after a trip to Big Sink, where she had to laugh at her attempts to swim in—on, nearly—the heavy liquid, she could find nothing new to learn here.

She decided to return to Hulzein Lodge—and perhaps to One Point One—and concern herself with her business affairs on the planet. But before she brought herself to tell Tregare of these plans, one night when her thought was not strongly upon pleasure, her body answered to his and she lay gasping, shaking her head.

"You did it!" he said. "This time, peace save us, you did it!"

"Yes—yes, Bran! And I do not know how, or why. For I was not even trying . . ."

"Maybe that's it—maybe before we tried too hard."

"Yes. Or—perhaps it merely took time, and a number of small acceptances between us, to make possible this greater one." Then she said, "Bran—I had thought, these past few days, to go to the Lodge and the city, to consult with Liesel and others about my holdings and their management. This is necessary if I am to go with you soon. But now I do not want to leave you."

His fingers smoothed her hair back from her face. "Well, why don't we both go? I've got business there myself, and best to handle it before I'm needed again here and at Base Two. I think Vanois is straightened out for now, and Deverel can help him if need be."

"Then it is settled." She touched his body, then shook her head. "No—it is too late now, this evening."

"We'll wake up early." He turned off the light and she snuggled against him for sleep.

CHEERFUL the next mid-morning, Rissa accepted Bran's offer and took the aircar's controls. She looked under the seat and checked placement of the oxygen equipment, then fastened her safety harness and energized propulsion. She lifted parallel to the ridge above them and climbed in an arc to bring them in line with the pass and rising toward it. She looked to Bran and laughed. "I am quite excited—the pass . . ."

"You know what to expect?"

"I think so. We go against the current, so I must not stint on power. At the dogleg I am prepared for turbulence. For the first turn I do not have a specific landmark, but the sun favors me—and I will pick one, for times when it does not."

"Good. Look—I'm sorry I had to keep you waiting, but there was word from *Inconnu*; I had to reply, and advise Gonnelson. And Vanois had some questions."

"It is all right. We kept *them* waiting, did we not?"

He laughed and squeezed her shoulder. Then they rode in silence to the pass.

Entering from this side they found little turbulence, only a strong headwind; Rissa increased power and fitted her oxygen nosepiece into place. As she had recalled, the entrance was much wider than on the far side. When the cut narrowed, she was somewhat above summit altitude, moving at an angle that showed her the turn well before she reached it. "This time, Bran, I make it easy for myself. Another time I will take it low, as you did."

"Coming back, you'll have to—the current doesn't give you time to get much higher."

"Oh, yes—of course. I am just as pleased to do it this way first."

Then she was into the turn—at this height the turbulence was less—through the dogleg and second turn. She held most of her altitude until she was out of the cut and past the "bumpy stretch," then turned toward the Lodge and set a constant rate of descent. After testing the air, she stowed her oxygen gear. For a few seconds she glimpsed One Point One, a smudge in the distance—then a ridge crest cut off her view.

As she passed a hilltop and sighted the Lodge, thunder boomed in a clear sky; peripherally she saw a flash of light. "Bran—a ship landing?"

"Nothing less. If it's Limmer—and I hope it is—he's nearly a day early. Must have come in fast and used top decel. I hope it doesn't mean something's wrong." He shrugged. "Well, we won't be long finding out. Soon as we land, I'll call the port."

"Yes. Bran—did you notice? Back there I tried to see how close I could set our rate of descent. And I do not think I missed by more than twenty feet, vertical."

He laughed. "That's good guessing *and* good luck—the wind stayed constant."

"Luck is a fine thing to have—without it, I would still be in Total Welfare." Making a small correction, she brought the car to ground near the Lodge.

A young woman answered the door. Inside, needing no help with the single suitcase each had brought, they went to their room. Bran went to the viewscreen terminal as Rissa walked into the bathroom. When she came out he was saying, "—this afternoon, then. If anything comes up and I can't make it, I'll call you back. Open a bottle." He cut the circuit and turned to Rissa; his face showed tension. "That was Limmer."

"There is bad news?"

He shook his head. "Don't know yet. But the reason he's here so fast, and took a beating from high-gees to do it—*he's met the Shrakken*. In space."

TREGARE reached Liesel by intercom. She joined them, followed by a servitor bearing a lunch tray. As they ate, Bran talked.

"Limmer didn't know what they were, of course. When the ship came in screen range it wasn't converging, but passing on a skew, in close to his same direction. Nearer, he could make out its insigne—placed funny, like in the pictures Vanois had, and no known language or lettering. He called it—the answer came garbled, but he recognized a word or two of English. Then his comm-tech fiddled frequencies and scan rates, and got a picture—of sorts—from inside the other ship. The description's vague, but it fits the Shrakken, all right."

Rissa said, "And then what happened?"

"Nothing. That was the closest approach. The skew diverged until Limmer lost signal."

Liesel said, "The big question is, where were they headed?"

Tregare beat a fist against his thigh. "That's the trouble—Limmer doesn't *know!* His computer's gone unreliable—he had hell's own time getting here at all—so until it's fixed or we run the tapes on someone else's, we won't know. That's why I'm going to town this afternoon."

Liesel nodded. "We have interface terminals at Maison Renalle. Not programmed for that kind of problem, but—"

"Nothing shaken," said Tregare. "By tonight, you will be. And we'll know."

ENTERING the aircar, Tregare took the passenger's seat, Rissa the pilot's. She flew fast and low; at the spaceport she landed at the safety perimeter around *Lefthand Thread*. Climbing out, Tregare said, "He's kept him in good shape."

At the ship's ramp, an armed guard met them. "You're Tregare? And who else?"

"And Tregare's wife." The woman nodded and let them pass. Unsure of this ship's interior design, Rissa fell behind so that Tregare could lead. He climbed past the level she expected; they entered the control room.

At first look, Limmer repelled her. Hulking and stoop-shouldered, he loomed; scars gave his swarthy face a permanent sneer. But his voice, when he spoke, was low and resonant. Shaking hands, he said, "Tregare! It's good to see you again!"

"You too, Limmer. And this is my wife—Tari Obrigo."

Taking her hand, the man half-bowed over it. "My pleasure, Ms. Obrigo. I suppose you already know you've married a nova in full explosion, and you seem pleased enough about it. So, my congratulations to both of you."

She had to laugh. "Thank you, Captain Limmer. And—my pleasure, also."

"She manages," said Tregare. "Now, then—you have your people working on the computer, naturally. Is it fixed yet?" Limmer shook his head. "Then let's have a quick look at the viewscreen tapes, first thing. After that we can go over to town and use a terminal there to analyze the rest of it, once I program a little."

Limmer turned to his control console; the screen lit. Among unfamiliar stars a glint appeared; magnification drew it closer, until Rissa recognized a ship—and on it, the insigne patterns Vanois' pictures had shown.

Sound came—garbled—only a few isolated words were clear, but those words were in English. Then the outside view vanished, the screen streaked and wavered, showing a picture, barely recognizable, of two Shrakken. For a moment, both sound and picture cleared—"Shrakken. And you are—" Then the noise level rose and obscured all meaning, and the picture vanished into flickering chaos.

Limmer turned it off. "That's all we got, before they were out of range. Do you know what those things are? I think *I* do."

"What is it," said Rissa, "that you think?"

"Underground rumor says UET never invented star drive— that they stole it. Except for weapons, that ship's damned near a duplicate of yours, Tregare. I think I met some more of the creatures UET robbed."

Rissa nodded. "You are right, but there is more. Tregare—?"

Quickly, Tregare summarized the news from Charleyhorse. "So that's why we need to analyze your course-data—and fast. Want to come along?"

"Like I want to wake up alive tomorrow. Give me a minute first, though." Limmer gave a few brief orders on his intercom, acknowledged the response, and turned back to Tregare. "All right; my First's briefed to handle things while I'm off-ship." He opened the control console and brought out a tape module. "It's all on here. I'm ready to go if you are."

Outside, at the aircar, Tregare said, "Tari? Do you know the air traffic rules in the city?" She shook her head. "Then I'd better drive it this time. You watch; see if you can figure the system." With Rissa beside him and Limmer in a seat behind, he raised the car to perhaps fifty meters and took a circuitous path—Rissa saw no clear pattern—to Maison Renalle.

Inside, Tregare spoke briefly at the admission desk and they went to a room Rissa recognized as security accommodations. The computer terminal sat in a corner; Tregare worked at its controls for some time before inserting the tape module. "First we'll see if this is the same ship that was at Charleyhorse—at least, if it came directly, we will."

"Charleyhorse?" Limmer frowned. "You mentioned that one, earlier—it's not on my charts, Tregare."

Tregare nodded. "None of us have all the new ones—ever. If there's blank at the end of your tape, I'll add it. If not, I can fill it in for you later. All right, here we go."

Lacking detailed knowledge of Tregare's programming, Rissa did not try to interpret the readout. She waited; finally Tregare said, "The angle's off a little—enough to indicate a slight course change. But ten to one, this is the ship that hit Charleyhorse."

"And can you see where it is bound?" said Rissa.

"Hold on—I'm punching for extrapolation." He looked at the result and shook his head. "They were slowing—maybe to take a group of sightings and locate themselves better. Or who knows what?"

He turned away from the terminal. "Considering that Charleyhorse probably isn't exactly loaded with navigational talent, my best guess is that the Shrakken found their directions were a little off—and were correcting course for *here*."

Rissa said, "Then let us hope they arrive well before your deadline for leaving."

He stared at her. Then he laughed, and Limmer said, "You married well, Tregare."

RETURNING to the port, Tregare took a different routing. This time he showed Rissa the indicators—arrows painted on roofs and paved streets—that guided him. "Those tell you which way to go, and the way they're drawn—solid, dotted round or square, or double line—all in different colors, you'll notice—the four altitude lanes they apply to. Above those, you needn't follow any pattern, but for local hops it wastes time to go that high." He gave her the altitude figures; she repeated them and nodded.

"Yes, I can remember that easily enough."

At the port Limmer shook hands with both. "I'll refuel and sell off cargo I don't need, as soon as I can. Should I buy any-thing—for the sake of appearances—so nobody thinks some-thing's funny?"

"Let 'em think what they like." Then; "Or say you intend to load up at an outer-planet mine. You're stocking food any-way, so that'd fit." Limmer's perpetual sneer came close to imitating a smile; he threw a half-salute and turned away. Tregare lifted off and headed north, toward the Lodge.

After a time, Rissa spoke. "Limmer—was he one of your men on *Inconnu*?"

"Not at first. A lot of our people Escape by jumping ship on a colony planet and hiding out until one of *us* comes along. It's a big help—otherwise we'd always be short of trained people for newly Escaped ships. I found Limmer on UET's iceworld colony Hardnose; for a few years they had a regular Underground Railroad there. I was short a Second Hat, then, and he filled the bill until we got him a ship of his own."

"At first he gives a poor impression—but he improves with acquaintance."

"Too right. His face, Rissa—he got those scars at UET's Academy when he was fourteen years old."

Between her teeth, breath hissed. "UET! Always UET—and the Presiding Committee, its puppet. Tregare, I *must* go with you—to Stronghold and then, peace willing, to Earth."

He looked at her; low-voiced she added, "Some there—it will be hard to grieve for their deaths."

He did not answer; during the flight neither spoke again.

IN their room at the Lodge, viewscreen and intercom set to record incoming calls but not to interrupt, they proved again that Rissa's climax the night before had been no fluke. Then for a while they shared the tub. Out of it and dried, while Tregare still steeped himself, Rissa checked the intercom and found a recorded call from Liesel. She dressed, told Tregare where she was going, and joined Liesel in her office. She reported Tregare's conclusions about the Shrakken; then the talk turned to Rissa's business affairs.

The board meeting of Bleeker, Ltd., had gone as expected. Rissa now owned the warehouse complex; her recommended changes were under way. Fennerabilis would sell the North Point area but wished to speak with Rissa directly—by screen, at least. Arni Gustafson could help her in hiring a patrol boat for the fishing season to control poachers. Rissa was not invested into Hulzein holdings, as such, so as not to waste the control value of her moneys. And when Rissa and Tregare left on *Inconnu*, Hulzein Lodge would handle her affairs on commission as Erika did on Earth.

"And we've covered all the small stuff," said Liesel. "Now, then—has Bran told you his plans yet?"

"Some of them. Has he told you?"

"Not enough for my liking, but I won't ask *you* for them."

Rissa laughed. "Good—then I will not have to refuse you *or* risk breaking confidence." After a moment she said, "And while we were gone, how has it been with—with all of you here?"

"Us?" Liesel grinned. "Same as always, except that in a few days Hawkman's leaving—be gone a month—for Big Icecube's moon."

"The sixth planet, yes. But on what ship? At the port I saw none but *Lefthand Thread*, and—"

Liesel nodded. "And that's Bran's. I guessed it was. Well, Number One has a ship of its own—only colony I know of, UET *or* Hidden, ever to build one. Just short haul, for insystem work, but it makes a difference in what we can manage. And the last I counted, *we* own better than a third of it."

"I see. But why does Hawkman go?"

"A ship's out there—Norden's *Valkyrie*—loading towing-pods with frozen methane and ammonia."

"To speed organic development on a marginal planet?"

"Right! But *after* delivering that load, *Valkyrie*'s headed for a drop point. So Hawkman's taking our latest messages and moneys—yours, as well—for forwarding to Earth."

"That is good news—though we shall all miss Hawkman. And what else occurs?"

Liesel grinned. "You won't ask straight out, will you? All right—Sparline pretends to think I don't know what she's after with young Ernol. She got her nerve up to move him into her room openly, and she's been waiting to see what I'd do."

"What *will* you do?"

"Nothing, of course. His work was improving, and still is."

"Then what is your attitude—your intentions?"

"Sit back, make no decisions until I have to. How I feel—oh, no! You're too involved; you couldn't keep it from Sparline, and that'd spoil the game."

"Such games are not mine. Enemies are too plentiful to waste the joys of friendship in deceptions and stratagems."

"I like to keep in practice—and keep Sparline on her toes, too."

"As you like. For me, I do not think I need practice."

"Just so you don't find out the hard way, that you're wrong." Liesel shrugged. "Now, then—how is it with you and Bran?"

"As couples will, we have differences. Now that he has agreed that I go with him, I think we will solve them. If you mean, am I glad in the marriage, the answer is yes. For no political reason, but from coming to know the man better."

"I'm relieved—do you know why? Neither of you could stay with a weak person. But I was afraid you couldn't put up with each other's strengths. Does that make sense?"

Rissa thought. "Yes—very much. It gives me an insight I had lacked."

"That's good. I—" The intercom's buzz interrupted. "Yes?"

"Bran here. You done pouring figures in my wife's ear with a funnel?"

"Sure. Matter of fact, we've been swapping stories on *you.* How you can face either of us after this—"

"Bran! She—"

He laughed. "I know. Look—Rissa, could you come up here?"

"Of course." Liesel waved her away; as she left, they were still talking.

As she entered the room upstairs, Tregare was saying, "Yes

—you would, at that!" He cut the circuit and turned to Rissa. "Sometimes the Hulzein genes scare me."

"Then you must half-frighten yourself. Now—what is it?"

"Not urgent—but we have to arrange the zoom-womb thing, and we might as well do it early. So—when's a good time, and how many do we want to set up?"

"My time is not planned. And how many do *you* want?"

They decided on three, seniority to be by order of deposit. Tregare turned to make an investigative call, but the intercom sounded again. "Bran Tregare here."

Sparline answered. She wanted to see both of them but since Tregare had calls to make, settled for inviting Rissa to her room. When Rissa arrived there, she entered to hear Bran's voice ending the talk. It was certainly her day, she thought, for being on both ends of the same conversations.

Sparline rose to greet her. "You're looking fine. How's married life in the wilds?" She sat again, and Rissa also.

"I am—happy, with Bran. I believe that tells all of it."

Sparline looked at her more closely and smiled. "I think you're right. Well, I'm glad. But what about when he leaves?"

Rissa explained—not Tregare's plans, but the compromise they had reached. "So I can go with him and provide him heirs, also. That is one call he is making—to arrange it."

"*Three times* you'll be cut open for those ova?"

"Cut open?"

"Rissa—I've *seen* the scar they gave you in Welfare."

"Oh—I forgot I had not told you," and she explained.

Sparline showed relief. "But even with this reversible, it's no picnic, what I've heard. Well, they can tell you more at the Hatchery."

"Hatchery?"

"Delayed Reproduction Center—Hatchery's what we call it."

"Yes. Well, in any case," said Rissa, "the method must be less strenuous than normal gestation culminating in childbirth. Though if circumstances permitted, I would expect to do it that way. So I will not allow you to frighten me." But she smiled to show the rebuke was only jest.

"Point taken," said Sparline. "Well, you seem to have things in hand. Have you talked with Liesel about your new holdings?"

Rissa nodded. "She reminds me of Erika—and holding a greater proportion of wealth here than any group could hold on Earth, she is perhaps even more effective."

"Don't sell Erika's gang short—they may own South America by now."

"It would not surprise me. And now, Sparline—have things gone well with you, also?"

"Well enough. Rissa—did Liesel say anything about—?"

"You and Ernol?" Sparline nodded. "No, not really. And since she did not, I am free to air my guesses. Though they *are* only guesses, and I would not bet on outguessing Liesel."

"Well?" Sparline's hands clenched together.

"She loads Ernol with responsibility—it is her method of forcing growth, and I think she is pleased with the results." *No—I need not say that Liesel considers it a game.* "When Ernol achieves some particular degree of status—you can guess better than I what it might be—I feel Liesel will agree to the marriage. Though not without making a show of resistance."

Sparline laughed. "Oh, she'll make me fight for it—she always has; that's all right." Now her hands freed themselves of each other, flexed and relaxed. "Thanks, Rissa. I *thought* that was the story, but I'm too involved—too *wanting*—to trust my own judgment."

"And, as I said, you must not rely too heavily on mine."

"Don't worry—I won't push until the signs are right—when she gets impatient for the fun and starts to nudge. I'll know . . ."

Rissa stared. "*You* enjoy it, also! I am lucky to be a Hulzein only by marriage." Then; "No—I did not mean—"

"It's all right—I know what you meant. By most folks' standards, I suppose we *are* strange. But that works both ways. Rissa—the mere idea of being *you*—it scares me spitless!"

Which of them laughed first? Rissa was not certain. They stood and clung together for a moment; then Rissa left the room and returned to her own.

Tregare greeted her. "I got hold of the DRC—Delayed Reproduction Center—all right. But you know what? We can't do it all at once—at least *you* can't—you can leave one ovum every fertile period, and—"

"I know. Well, the question of seniority is settled."

"Sure." Then Tregare shook his head. "But at that rate, how in the name of peace did UET ever raise a cargo of sperm and ova?"

She thought. "When did UET ever care what it did to its slaves? The available techniques—remove the ovaries, keep them alive *in vitro* and hasten the ovulation cycle by chemical means. It has been done with pigs and cattle—and to UET, people are no different."

"Well—maybe they took out only one per person." Then he shook his head. "No. It would cost more, that way. So—"

"For the time being, Bran, forget UET. Until you are ready to move on Stronghold."

FIVE met at dinner. Hawkman had returned. He had trimmed his beard quite short, outlining clearly the shape of jaw and cheekbones; Rissa complimented him on the effect. "I am pleased to have a better look at you, at last."

"That's your disadvantage, Rissa—you women can't grow anything to hide behind. Of course, in the case of present company—" He raised his glass. "—that's a blessing to us men. Right, Bran?" Laughter was general; then the talk took other paths.

Later, for the first time since the duel, Rissa partook of drugsticks. Relaxed, in a lull between past conflicts and those to come, she let the smoke enhance her senses, let her mind float in introverted euphoria, enjoyed the total freedom from tension.

When Hawkman brought out cards, Bran would have stayed—but Rissa pinched his arm lightly and he said, "No—it's been one long day. Tomorrow night, maybe."

Upstairs in their bed, her senses tuned to peak, she climaxed almost at once—then soon again, and then—she lost count and did not care.

FOR three days, waiting for her body's clock to signal release of an ovum, Rissa marked time. She kept busy. By viewscreen she completed purchase of Fennerabilis' peninsula, and contracted to outfit and crew a patrol boat to guard her interests there. She inspected her warehouse complex; changes were progressing well, and she found another to make and ordered it.

One afternoon when Ernol was free, he and Rissa practiced combat again—each wore a minimum of protective clothing and for the most part Rissa taught him newer techniques. Sparline watched; afterward she consented to practice with Rissa, but the moves were only demonstrated, not carried through with full force. Compared to Rissa or Ernol, she tired quickly—yet it was obvious to Rissa that with regular practice Sparline could have been expert.

Rissa's thermometer, on the fourth morning of waiting, told her she was near to ovulation. And the viewscreen told Tregare that Limmer was ready to move ship to Base Two.

IN their room they breakfasted quickly, and called word of their day's plans to Liesel's office recorder. Dismantling the hair dryer, Rissa put the magnetic reverser in her shoulder bag. Bran drove the aircar and left Rissa off at the DRC—the Hatchery—before going to the port.

"Call me when you're done here?" She nodded; he closed the aircar and took off again.

The Delayed Reproduction Center occupied an old building —concrete and stone with exposed wood beams. Entering, Rissa saw "Director" on a door at the main corridor's far end. She passed other doors; some stood ajar and showed her empty rooms.

The "Director" door opened into a smallish room; behind a desk sat a young woman, reading from a microfilm projector. She looked up and said, "May I help you?"

"I hope so. My husband and I wish to leave cells on deposit for three zygotes, to be gestated at a later time."

The girl brushed fingers back through curly brown hair; her blue eyes opened wider. "That's unusual, these days—but we do have the equipment and a skeleton staff. I'd better let you talk to Dr. Marco." She rose and led Rissa into the next room, through a door behind her desk.

This one was larger—its walls lined with books, file cabinets, a mirror, and equipment unfamiliar to Rissa. Behind the central desk Rissa saw an old woman—small and thin, with faded brown eyes in a yellow face. But the white hair, cut very short, was still thick. Filipina, Rissa guessed—or from somewhere near those islands.

The woman said, "I'm Estelle Marco—Dr. Marco, more or less. You have business for us?"

"I am Tari Obrigo. My husband, Bran Tregare, arranged for me to come here. Our request is—"

"Yes, I recall—I'm the one who talked with him. Well, we can accommodate you. I'll do the work myself; I've instructed a couple of my assistants but I'm the only one that's actually done it, on humans."

The old face grimaced. "Back on Earth, that was—in the early days of the project, before UET got impatient and switched to butchery to speed things up. Best luck I ever had was when mutiny took the ship I was on and we escaped to here."

"Butchery?" Rissa repeated the guess she'd made to Tregare.

Estelle Marco shook her head. "No. Oh, they tried that, but the equipment cost too much in quantity. So they spayed only a few before some bright sadist got an idea UET liked even better. They *could* speed up the cycle, you see—so why bother with the fancy machinery?"

"But what—I can't imagine—"

"If you had their kind of mind, you could. All those Welfare women, you see—wasting their ova into tied-off tubes. So this doctor—so called—cut them open again a little higher on the belly, and brought the tubes outside to empty into little containers he taped on. *Then* he used hormones to speed the cycle about ten to one—until the supply ran out and they quit producing." The woman's face moved as though to spit.

"Dr. Marco—what did it do to them?"

"You can increase production of ripe ova, but you can't turn the uterus on and off like a faucet. They went into constant menstruation—terribly heavy flow, from the cockeyed hormone balance. A number of them simply bled to death."

Rissa gasped. Dr. Marco said, "But he had a simple answer to that one—hysterectomies—so they wouldn't die of it. Not right away, at least. The incidence of cancer was frightful. The worst of it, though—you've never seen what it does to a girl to be accelerated through menopause before she's twenty."

Rissa could not control her shudder; sidelong in the wall mirror she saw she had gone pale. "And, of course, if it worked, they are still doing it—they would have done it to me!"

"I suppose they are, the sons of jackals! Although it *didn't* work all that well, to anyone with a gram of medical conscience. Forced ripening made for a high proportion of defective zygotes, including nonviables. Most of the mistakes died young, but you've noticed the high incidence of albinos among the younger people here? That was one side effect."

"Yes, I had noticed—and wondered."

"Well, now you know." The Director clenched a fist, all bone and tendons. "I wonder—the male-oriented hierarchy of UET—would they have done it if it cost the men what it cost the women? But for sperm—just tell an unsterilized male employee to jerk off in a bottle—and don't tell him it's slaves he's siring for the mining colonies."

The old woman paused. "Wait—you said—they had *you* in Welfare? Then I can do nothing for you without surgery. Are you sure you want—?"

Rissa opened her shoulder bag, displayed the stolen reverser and explained.

"Oh, yes—I'd heard rumors. Never saw it done, though. Do you know how to operate that thing?" Rissa nodded. "All right—let's go to my lab and get to it. Reversible or not, the tubes closed off for so long—at the least, they'll need blowing out, so we'll see if they're open or not."

Rissa followed the old woman to another room, stripped and sat on a high, padded table. She placed the device against her belly—the cold metal made her flinch—and in the sequence she had learned, activated the controls. She found herself holding her breath and realized she had expected to *feel* a change within her body; her brief, uncertain laugh held no tone of amusement. "Well—that should have done it."

"So. Lie down, put your feet—yes—a routine exam, while we're at it." The old hands moved gently; Rissa felt herself relax. "Now—a little inert gas, not much pressure. When the gauge drops, we know you're open." Expected hurt did not come; only a quick discomfort that vanished before she could name it. "Good—some slight clogging, but it's gone now."

She felt the intruding apparatus leave her body; the doctor turned and set it on her work counter. "You can sit up now."

Rissa did so. "And what is the next step, Dr. Marco?"

"Depends. Do you know when you can expect to ovulate next?"

"Tomorrow, I am almost certain. My cycle is most regular, and this morning's temperature was tending—"

"Good." Marco nodded. "Well, then—if it's tomorrow, come in the next day. We want the ovum as near to one day along as possible."

"And then how—?"

"Nothing to worry about. A little plastic tubing, that's all. *Very* thin—just big enough to take the ovum without bruising it. Not flexible enough to curl over by itself, but it won't scratch tissues, either. Tiny bulb at the end helps there, too." Marco's forefinger thrust upward and slightly to one side. "Slant it to one corner firmly into the little funnel where your tube empties—apply a little suction. *Thwop!*" She grinned. "Then pull back, rotate, and go to the other one—we won't know which fired, but we don't care, either."

Although Rissa had asked nothing, the doctor added, "It won't hurt, not enough to bother. There's one thing, though."

"And what is that?"

The old woman smiled broadly; her remaining teeth were yellowed but showed no decay. "Until we have the ovum, you sleep alone. Because if you were to conceive, and the zygote had time to start dividing, passage through the tube might harm it."

Rissa shrugged. "It comes at an inconvenient time, but of course two days of abstinence is much less than with the natural way." She put her feet down and stood. "For today, then, this is all?"

"Yes. As I said, day after tomorrow if you're right about that, we'll see what we've got. Will your husband be coming with you, then, for his part of it?"

Rissa paused. "I doubt that he will be free to do so. But perhaps—may I call him from your office?"

"Of course. When you're dressed, come along."

RELAY reached Limmer's ship; the one who answered nodded her head and fetched Tregare. "Bran? For today, I am finished here."

"All right. I can pick you up there in a few minutes."

She waited longer than she expected, before Tregare arrived. Dr. Marco greeted him. "Do you want to make your own deposit today, captain?" He followed her out; soon they were back. The doctor said, "When it's time, then, Ms. Obrigo," and Rissa agreed.

She took Tregare's hand; they walked out to the aircar. Before turning on power, he said, "Everything all right? What all happened?"

She explained the procedures. "But meanwhile, Bran, we are barred from one another. For if I were to conceive, the zygote might be jeopardized."

He frowned, then grinned. "What the hell, I already had to service myself once today. Know something? It felt silly—the old lady waiting outside the door for me to load her little bottle."

She laughed. "Poor Bran! At least you are done with it—I must return for three extractions."

"Maybe I'm not done. Marco'll make do with one sample if she has to, but she'd like one more in reserve. All depends on whether I have time to go back again." Now he applied power and raised the aircar, turning toward the port.

She was silent; he waited, then said, "Something wrong?"

"Not with me, Bran—but—*Oh*—!" She repeated Estelle Marco's description of UET's methods. "It is *worse* than what I had guessed!"

He reached and gripped her knee. "Now I *know* I have to go to Earth. Or somebody has to—and who else is there in shape to try it?"

She was blinking back tears; with the back of her hand; she wiped them away. "They will not be the same men—after all the years, those will be dead."

"Same kind, though. UET doesn't change—except for the worse."

Now he dropped, and landed beside *Lefthand Thread*. "Rissa—we need to settle what we do right *now*. I have to ride to Base Two with Limmer—I know just where I want his ship sitting, and it's easier to show, or land it myself. Once landed, moving a ship across a field is damned wasteful."

"I will miss you, Bran. Perhaps in two days I can join you."

"Yes. I hoped you could go pack us up at the Lodge, bring our stuff here with someone to take the aircar back, and come along on the ship. But two days—it won't work."

"Also, Bran, it would leave the car on the wrong side of the Hills."

"I figured we could make a trip for it later, in the other one. Well—" He turned and kissed her. "Come when you can, then. Call first to see if I'm at One or at Two; all right?"

"And you call me if there is any reason—or none at all."

He got out; as she flew back to the Lodge, her thoughts ranged much farther.

SHE did not wish to talk, so she entered the Lodge from the rear and went to her room. Both screen and intercom terminals showed calls waiting her attention; she left them to wait longer. She stripped to bathe but then sat, chin in palm and mind stalled at dead center. She felt hunger—both she and Tregare had forgotten lunch. She shook her head; she could wait until dinner. The action broke her trance; she filled the tub and wallowed in it, splashing, for a few moments, like a child. She rose and gave herself a sketchy toweling, wringing most of the water from her hair but leaving the rest to dry of itself. Then she attended to the recorded calls.

Item: Fennerabilis wanted a minor contract change. She thought briefly and shook her head; the request was after the fact, and she begrudged the time it would take to analyze it. Also he had not mentioned a monetary adjustment—until he did, the answer was no. And since it was his proposal, any follow-up would be his, also.

Items: Sparline, Liesel, and Hawkman, in that order, wished to talk with her when she returned. She told each—Hawkman personally and the other two in recording mode—that she would meet with all of them at dinner.

Item: Deverel had word from *Inconnu* but declined to record it. Of course—he had no assurance of the terminal's privacy.

She put on a robe and called Deverel. "Hain? Tregare is with Limmer, at the port. Later today they move ship to Base Two. If it is urgent, I can punch *Lefthand Thread* up for you on relay."

The picture was unsteady, but she saw he smiled. "Not that urgent, Ms. Kerguelen—just that another ship's coming. I'm not sure which—at that point the tape got noisy. But it's good news."

"Yes, and thank you for telling me." There was something more—oh, yes— "When I return to Base One, Tregare and I wish to return your hospitality, and Anse's. Belatedly, I know . . ."

His hand waved away her apology. "Well, thanks. Anse and I, we'll be looking forward to that. Any time it's convenient." He turned aside and said, "Okay, Anse—I'll help you with that stuff in a minute." Facing back to her; "We're loading a few things to take down to Base Two—a few local delicacies for the incoming ships that they probably won't find in One Point One. So I guess I'd better get back to work."

She smiled. "And so should I, here. It is good to see you again." He waved a hand as the picture faded. Rissa breathed deeply; the talk of real here-and-now events had cleared her mind.

It was a good time, she thought, for small chores. She took the reverser from her shoulder bag and concealed it once more in the hair dryer. She packed Bran's suitcase. Hand and foot she trimmed her nails, with special attention to the fighting talons—the broken one was growing back, but slowly. She brushed her drying hair, grasped the hank of it behind her, and brought it forward to inspect the ends. A bit ragged—she trimmed the offending wisps, then coiled the mass and pinned it at the crown of her head.

No new calls showed on either communicator; she turned both switches from "Record" to "Receive."

She went to the bathroom. Returning, she chose clothing and dressed. She touched the intercom switch, then shook her head. She rummaged for another pair of earrings and exchanged them for those she wore. She poured a flask-cap of brandy and sat, looking out at changing light and shadow on the slope of hills and, from time to time, sipping.

The trouble was that now she *did* want to talk. But she waited.

When the intercom sounded, Sparline answered her greeting. "Dinner's early tonight. Ready in a few minutes?"

"I am near starvation. Bran and I forgot to eat at midday." To Sparline's giggle she answered, "No, not that—unfortunately. Our preoccupation was less pleasant."

"Anything wrong?"

"Not here, not now—not with us. We can speak of it later —but *not* while dining."

"All right—last one to the table gets short rations!" The intercom clicked silent. Leaving the room, Rissa was smiling.

SHE found Liesel and Hawkman at table. As she sat, Sparline entered, accompanied by Ernol. Keeping all reaction from her face, Rissa glanced quickly from the pair to Liesel.

The older woman chuckled. "Don't hold your breath, Rissa. Ernol's here to celebrate his promotion to chief of Liaison. Custom of the house."

"Yes. I recall you mentioned need for such a position."

Servers brought food and wine; as usual, during the meal there was little talk. When only wine and coffee remained, Sparline brought out drugsticks. Rissa abstained—and so, she noticed, did Ernol. The other three smoked briefly, and Liesel waved away Sparline's offer of another round. "Later, maybe. First let's talk from sharp minds, not mellow ones. Now—Rissa, how'd it go with you today? And with Bran?"

"With Bran, as intended; tonight he guides Limmer to Base Two. With me—I cannot join him for two days—it was thus—" She related first the procedure at the Hatchery. Then, hesitantly, she repeated what Estelle Marco had told her. "Bran was as angry as I. He—" She stopped.

Unsmiling, Hawkman laughed. "I think I know. Liesel?"

"Peace, yes!" She slapped a palm on the table. "You're not giving anything away, Rissa. My son, little as I've seen of him, can't fool me much more than my daughter can. He keeps his plans secret, so far—and that's his right. I can't guess the details, of course. I wish I could—*anyone* can benefit from consultation. But in the long run, I know what he's up to."

Rissa shook her head. "How can you know? What is it you suspect?"

"*Suspect?* Pull in your kite, girl—I *know!* He'll go to Earth—when and by what route I can't yet guess—and do his damnedest to pull UET out by the roots like a rotten tooth! What *else* could I expect from Bran Tregare?"

She glared, red-faced; then the corners of her mouth

twitched into a half-smile. "If I'm wrong, Rissa—I'll give you my half of the Bleeker bet, free and clear."

Again Rissa's headshake—*these people!* "Liesel, you have out-gamed me. But you must realize—Tregare's is a long-term plan."

"Well, I should hope so. I wouldn't want to think my only son believes real life is like the entertainment channels."

"He does not. His plans are—impressive."

"That's good. I—"

"Liesel." Hawkman spoke. "Let's get down to business."

"What business?"

"The business of how we can *help*."

"When he doesn't tell us anything, how can we?"

"Let's find out." He turned to Rissa. "What does he need most? Money? Men? Probably not. Weapons?"

"I am not certain."

"But ships—*ships*, that's what. Of course. Liesel, what do you say we ask Bran if we can invest in this enterprise?"

"Hawkman, in the name of peace, how can we get *ships*? They come and go—the only one here is already his. What do you mean?"

Instead of answering, he said, "Rissa, when does he plan to leave?"

"I do not know." She hesitated. "And before I say more, I must consult with Bran—for already, even to you, his own family, I may have said too much." She gestured. "If only you did not play games with secrets from each other! I am accustomed to it with *enemies*, but here—"

Hawkman clasped her hand, then released it. "Excuse me a minute, all." He left, and returned with the screen terminal from Rissa's room. "You want to call him now?"

She tried the port; *Lefthand Thread* had gone. She switched channels and called Deverel; he reached Limmer at Base Two and then Tregare was on the screen, barely recognizable as the picture wavered. "Rissa? Everything all right? We're fine here."

"Tregare—yes, and here, also. But I am at dinner with your family; Ernol is with us, also. And—I did not mean to break confidence, but Liesel guessed your plan—the goal of it—and I could not deny her guess." She could see that he scowled; she said quickly, "I have called now because—they want to help."

"Help? How?"

Hawkman turned the screen partway toward him; at an angle Rissa could still see it. "Son? We'd like to buy into your venture a little, if we may. My thought—and Rissa neither confirmed nor denied it—is that whatever else you may need, you'd like more ships. Am I right?"

"I could use more ships, no matter what I intended. But only under my complete personal control."

"That's understood. Bran—do we have the start of an agreement?"

"Sure, Hawkman. But in the time I have—"

"Bran!" Rissa leaned toward the screen. "Later reinforcements could help, also. If you left installation teams at Base Two—?"

"Yeah—maybe. All right—you can buy in all you want; I accept, and gladly. Too bad it couldn't have been earlier, but that's *my* stubborn fault, so don't try to apologize and make it worse." He turned to one side. "Just a minute, Vanois." Then, facing the screen again, "Hot skull-session going here; I should get back to it. Tell you what—can I call you tomorrow, or come over in a few days and talk at length?"

"I leave tomorrow," said Hawkman. "Riding the local packet out to Big Icecube. So let's settle one thing—if I can get you Sten Norden's *Valkyrie*, do you want her? And with or without Norden?"

"Holy peace! You need a lot of deciding in a hurry! Yeah, I know—circumstance won't wait." He paused, running a hand up his forehead and through his hair. "All right. I want the ship. I'll buy into it—arming *Valkyrie* in return for its use on my mission—or I'll buy Norden out fairly, at his own option to stay on or not, long as he's willing to take orders. He's a good man; I'd like to have him along." Bran shook his head. "Just make it all clear, in the dickering." A pause, and then, "Look—Hawkman—how long you figure to be gone?"

"A month—maybe less. Why?"

"Then that's all right; I'll see you when you get back."

Hawkman smiled. "I'm glad of that. Well, I won't keep you longer, now."

"Yeah. I haven't said thanks yet. Well, I do. To all of you."

The screen went gray. Hawkman looked around, face to

face, at all of them. "Well, Liesel? Do you approve of our new venture?"

Her brow wrinkled. "I'm not sure. Oh, it's all right, Hawkman—I'm just thinking of some of the consequences."

"Consequences?" said Rissa.

Hawkman answered. "I know what she means. Why do you suppose we—or *any* groundhogs, except UET, of course—never bought into ships before?"

She thought. "Most people, no matter how much money—yes, I see it. But the Hulzeins take the long view, so—"

"And what good," said Liesel, "does the long view do you, if your ship's people decide to keep going and not come back? A second generation of Escapes at our expense? No, thanks!"

"But now," said Rissa, "with Tregare—"

"With Tregare, yes." Liesel nodded. "And no matter he's out for war, and peace take commerce!—he'll turn us a profit, too, before he's done." She sighed. "I hope I'm alive to know it."

"Wait a minute," Sparline said. "The *Valkyrie* was our next relay to Erika's faction. And what about the cargo commitment?"

"Frozen gases are in no hurry," said Liesel. "We buy the rights and sell them to the next ship that turns up free-lancing."

"And I wasn't happy," said Hawkman, "Using *Valkyrie* for our relay to Earth. Towing those pods, that first leg would be a slow haul. Odds are we get a faster chance before the year's out." He shrugged, then grinned. "Or maybe *buy* ourselves one, now we're into the habit."

"Hawkman!" Liesel's voice came near to anger. "On only one drugstick you say that? A ship we can't control, once it's up?"

He laughed. "Drug or no drug, we can control any ship *we* ride. Liesel—haven't *you* ever wanted to see Earth again? And now—with Bran Tregare going there?"

After a moment, Liesel said, "A new thought, Hawkman—it'll bear nursing a while. To change *all* our plans?" She touched his hand. "But that's you talking, not the drugstick!"

Even seated, Hawkman managed the hint of a courtly bow. "I do like being appreciated—especially by you. And—"

"Just a minute." Sparline's voice held an edge. "You'd leave me holding the baby—your plans for this whole *planet*?"

"You've never had half the responsibility you could handle," said her mother, "and that's my fault. Now reef it in, Sparline—this is all kite designs, so far, not firm planning. But truly—if Hawkman and I were to do such a crazy thing, I'd have full confidence in your management."

Her gaze on Ernol, she grinned. "And besides—wouldn't that simplify your own plans?"

Sparline's knuckles rapped the table. "Liesel—you're impossible!"

Hawkman laughed. "No, my dear—only highly unlikely."

After a pause, Ernol spoke. "Some of this I don't know enough about, to make sense of it. Yet. But one thing—Madame Liesel—"

"No, Ernol!" Sparline pulled at his arm. "Not now."

Eyes narrowed, Liesel waved a hand. "Let the boy talk."

Rissa leaned forward. "No—it's not fair, Liesel. He has no way to know your games."

"He won't learn any younger."

Ernol shook his head. "I never thought I was stupid, so I guess I just don't know the language. All I wanted to say, Madame Hulzein, is that while you're here, what you say goes." Liesel's mouth tightened. "Now wait a minute—let me finish, please. If you leave, what you say *still* goes—in a way. I mean, if Sparline still wants to and you leave me in proper status for it, we'll marry. If you don't—well, I couldn't accept the status from her if you didn't give it to me. It wouldn't look right."

He stood. "I guess that's all. Should I go now?"

"You try it," said Liesel, "and I'll kick you. Sit back down and listen." She sighed; Rissa heard breath catch in her throat. "Ernol, you've damned near convinced me. There's just one thing. You were lying a *little*, weren't you?"

"No. Not any. I only lie when I'm joking."

"Well, I guess we can't have everything. And you're young yet."

"I don't understand."

"Sparline, you can *teach* him, can't you?"

Sparline gasped, spread her arms wide and whooped, then reached to smother Ernol in arms and kisses. After a time she sat back and said, "But Liesel—why did you give me the game so *easily*?"

Liesel could not suppress her smile. "I never like to waste intelligent innocence—it has such great possibilities. I trust you to develop them."

Before Sparline could answer, Rissa said, "Now I understand. Yes, Liesel—this is one way to do it, and a good one."

An hour or so later, carefully keeping her euphoric mind in step with her gravity-bound feet, Rissa made her way upstairs. Once she was in bed, sleep came soon.

THE next day Hawkman left; Rissa saw him briefly at breakfast. Liesel was busy, Sparline away to One Point One. Deprived of company, Rissa came close to sulking. She called Bran, but he had time for only a few words. The day seemed like ten. When she woke next morning, thinking, *Now I can get this done with*, she came alive again.

SPARLINE had more business in the city; Rissa rode with her. "Shall I drop you at the Hatchery? I go within half a mile of it, anyway."

"Let me off where you are going. We are early for my appointment, and I will enjoy the walk."

"All right." Sparline landed at the end of a row of aircars, beside a domed building labeled "Fennerabilis & Associates." "If you want to meet me here I'll be in the Offworld Trade section—if I go anywhere else I'll leave a note in the car."

"That is fine. Thank you." From the air Rissa had noted the DRC building; she set off toward it. About halfway she recognized the building to her left; she was passing Bleeker's headquarters. She looked at her watch—still early—well, why not? She went inside and proceeded to Room 522.

The receptionist—the same she had met twice before—looked up. After a pause, he smiled. "Ms. Obrigo—I'm sure Mr. Bleeker will see you immediately." He rose and led the way.

Bleeker stood to greet her, one hand pulling at his goatee as he reached the other to shake Rissa's. "Ms. Obrigo. What business brings you here?"

She accepted his motioned offer to sit. "Nothing in particular. I was passing and thought to say hello. How are you?"

He sat also and clasped his hands on the desk. "You mean that, don't you? I know gloating when I see it, and you're not. Well, I'll tell you—it was a real shock when Liesel Hulzein played her sleeping dummies and took control. Hard to swallow."

He smiled. She thought his smile would never be attractive, but now it was more relaxed. "But I did swallow it—had to— no choice. And you want to know something?"

"Of course, if you wish to tell me."

"It's a relief, that's what! I'm as good as most, I think— kept my holdings when a lot went under. But once I knew the Hulzeins had the crunch going on me, I ran scared—anybody would. And now it's over. I'm just a figurehead, and it's no secret."

"Yet you do not seem depressed, Mr. Bleeker."

"And I'm not." He leaned forward. "There's a time coming here—some won't believe it, but it's true—when the big ones will shake all the rest off the tree and then have it out among themselves."

He smiled again. "All right—Liesel ate me alive, you might say, but she didn't skin me. I still have my holdings, just not the control—and it's to her own advantage to run things well. And when the showdown comes, I'd bet you anything I'm on the winning side!"

"You have discussed it with others—this showdown?"

"Used to, some—over drinks and such. No more, though— now I *know* it's real, it's too dangerous to gab about. Am I right?"

"If about the one thing, then about the other also, I would say."

He nodded. "You belong with the Hulzeins, all right; you keep a tight string."

She looked at her watch. "Oh—my appointment is soon. I—"

"Sure." Bleeker stood; again he offered his hand and she took it. "Well, I'm pleased you came by. Wanted to tell you—

nothing shaken, your part in all that happened. And Weltmarks or no Weltmarks, I'm *glad* you finished Stagon dal Nardo."

"I am never glad of killing. But dal Nardo—it was difficult to grieve for him."

His face lost all expression; before he could speak, she turned to leave. "Good-bye, Mr. Bleeker. Another time, perhaps."

She walked out and left the building. Walking briskly, she reached the DRC building with minutes to spare. Inside, she met Estelle Marco in the corridor and was directed to the laboratory. She removed her clothing and climbed onto the high table. Soon the doctor entered.

"You're ready, I see. All right, feet up there—yes. Now—" The old woman's hands moved surely; within her Rissa felt the fingers probing, then a slight pain—then, for a time, nothing. She tried to follow what the doctor had told her would happen —the plastic tube searching for her own, partially withdrawing and rotating and again advancing—but could localize no sensation. Finally she did feel it, being drawn out of her.

"A moment, let me look—yes, you're all right. Put your clothes on, if you like—or maybe you'd rather see this."

Rissa stood and followed as the doctor took the collector to a workbench and examined its tiny transparent receptacle under a microscope. A pause. "Well, we caught it all right." She turned to face Rissa. "Now, then—do you want the cells stored separately, or conceived first?"

"Is there advantage one way or the other?"

Marco shrugged. "Some say so—that only the stronger sperm stay potent in the freeze. If that's so, you're betting for a more hardy zygote, but with less chance of getting one at all."

"Conception now, I would say—and the zygote itself frozen at the proper stage. Which is—?"

"After the habit of cell division has been reinforced a time or two. I prefer to freeze while a division is in process; an action halted midway has momentum to restart when the zygote is thawed."

"Very well. Do it so, please." Now Rissa dressed herself. "And are we finished, then, for this time?"

"Yes. Call me a day or two ahead, if you can, when you're ready for the next try."

"I will. And thank you, doctor."

Already moving apparatus into place for the next step, the old woman smiled and waved her good-bye. Rissa smiled in return, nodded, and left.

OUTSIDE, she broke into a jog, laughing in exhilaration. At the aircar she saw Sparline's note:

> Plans changed. Little trip with F's people, their transport.
> They'll return me to the Lodge so this car's yours for the day.
> —S.M.

It was not yet noon but Rissa felt hunger. Debating with herself, she decided she could wait. Flying low and fast she returned to Hulzein Lodge.

Entering, she met Liesel in the main corridor. "Back for lunch, are you? But where's Sparline?" Rissa explained, and a few minutes later joined Liesel in the dining room.

They chose luncheon from what was most quickly available and soon were served. Liesel said, "Bran called. The incoming ship—he finally got a clear message—it's Peralta, on *No Return*. Be here in less than a week, now, and the routine's the same as Limmer's was—refuel, sell cargo, stock supplies and move to Base Two."

"Then he has four ships—only two more are needed! Unless —you know he does not wish to leave Number One unguarded against the Shrakken." She paused. "Did he leave word for me?"

Liesel chuckled. "He put me on hold while he recorded something to your extension. It's short, is all I know—probably just saying join him when you can if not sooner."

"That would be both welcome and sufficient. And—is there any reason not to do so at once?"

"I'd like a little of your time first. Not much—just a few decisions you should make in the line of business. But you haven't said—how did it go today in town?"

Telling the morning's events, Rissa ended with, "Bleeker has adjusted well; he no longer minds that you decide for him."

"Hah! I don't, really. At first, yes—then I began asking his opinions, and with the pressure off, he's making good choices again. I set policy—after that, he has a fairly free hand. If he doesn't know it, though, I'll wait awhile before I tell him."

"Yes. Well, I am finished, and I see you have been waiting for me. I would like to hear Bran's message, and then we can confer."

"Sure. I'll be in my office."

Upstairs, Rissa played the screen's tape. First, a request for information from the warehouse construction superintendent —he was not available, so she, also, recorded her answers, along with questions of her own. Bran's call came next; the picture hardly existed, but his voice came clear.

"Rissa? I'm at Two, staying on *Lefthand Thread*. Call me here when you're ready to come through the Hills. I miss you."

She called the scout; Anse Kenekke relayed her to Limmer's ship, and soon Tregare spoke to her. "Everything go all right? You ready to come here?"

"Yes, and yes. Where shall I meet you?"

"The cabin's best. I may be late, so eat when you get hungry. You're not nervous about running the pass?"

"No, Bran. The angle of light will favor me."

"All right. Be braced for the rough spots—remember?"

"Surely. And I hope you will not be kept *too* late."

He laughed. "No chance. All right—I'll see you then."

"Good-bye, Bran." She checked the tape again; it held nothing more, so she joined Liesel downstairs. The conference was brief; Rissa found most of the decisions obvious, and Liesel did not disagree with any.

"That does it, then. And now you're off across the Hills?"

"Yes. Two minutes to pack and I can be on my way."

"You and Bran come back when you get the chance. And going through that damned pass of his, be careful."

"There is no way to be careful there. One can only be cor-rect—and I intend to be."

"Then I won't worry." They said good-byes. In not much

longer than the two minutes she had predicted, Rissa had the aircar rising along the line of the ridges above.

SHE had the oxygen equipment out early; the pass was no place to have to scrabble under the seat. Ahead she saw clouds—*if the sun is obscured in the pass itself*—then she saw another way. Tregare had followed rising ground levels to the mouth of the cut. She began to climb, gaining altitude far ahead of her turning point. She wondered—if the approach could be made so easily, why had he not done the same? Expecting the unexpected, she concentrated her alertness and veered away from the Hills to make her direct approach, when she would reach the cut from greater distance as well as greater height.

Ahead she saw it, then came abreast and turned. Still climbing at full power, she pointed toward its center. First there was calm—*this cannot be all of it*—then an invisible current shook the car and thrust it downward at a rate that shocked her. Dropping, the car lost forward speed; she saw only one choice and took it—deliberately she went into a dive.

Adrenaline hit her; time slowed. Would it be enough? When her speed satisfied her, she pulled the nose up sharply and shot —pitching wildly—through the entrance turbulence into the narrow cut, higher and faster than Tregare had done.

Into grayness! She went through a brief bright patch; then the sun was lost again. Her eyes readjusted soon enough to glimpse the white tumble of boulders. She cut sharply into the turn she could not see and narrowly missed crags at her left. *Too soon!* Only her higher altitude, giving more width for maneuver, had saved her.

The second turn! The light was against her now but she knew it had to be soon—saw a shadow and swung into it—the cut widened again and she was safe. Well above summit height, she stayed there until the ground below came its closest and began to drop away.

She spoke aloud. "Next time, peace knows—I'll *ask* first!" But she thought, all things considered, she had not done so badly!

She made a slow, curving descent, barely topping the last

ridge before her direct approach to the plateau. She saw the scoutship but not the second aircar; Tregare, then, was still at Two. She landed, saw no one about, and went into the cabin.

Its door was locked. She turned her key in the pattern that opened without setting off alarms. Inside, she opened their suitcases and stowed the contents into drawers.

She had a shower, long and hot. She called the scoutship and found herself automatically relayed through to *Lefthand Thread*. Tregare was not aboard, and the man who answered did not know how to connect her with *Carcharadon*, so she said, "Then please tell Tregare that his wife arrived safely at Base One." He acknowledged and she cut the circuit.

SHE went outside and met Kenekke guiding a sort of motorized wheelbarrow, piled high with boxes. "Hello, Anse. Now I see why I got automatic relay when I called the scout."

"Hi, Ms. Kerguelen. Yes, I set it that way when I go out."

"Have you been here all along? Since we left, I mean?"

"No, I've spent some time down at Two. Hain's there now."

"Do you take turns between here and there?"

"More than we'd like, but it's only for a little while."

"Good. Well, I will not interrupt your work further." They smiled and she went back into the cabin.

Restless, she paced the main room. Then, in the kitchen she poured fruit juice and sat. *I cannot be inactive like this—I must learn the work they do at Base Two and help with it.* Decision made, she went to the scout; Kenekke admitted her. "If I might trouble you a moment?" He nodded. "Are there reading-tapes here, and a projector?"

"Yes, sure. What kind of tapes do you want?"

"Technical material. If possible, on the installation of weapons. That is what Tregare is doing, and I wish to help—if only because, if I stay in that cabin much longer, I shall begin chewing it into small pieces!"

He laughed. "I could gnaw a few chunks off this scout, myself. Well, let's see—there's not much on weapons as such, but it's jury-rigging for installation that concerns us now."

"Yes—that is what I would like to see."

"It won't be on tapes, though—the captain worked all that out on paper. He made copies. I think I can find you a complete set, or nearly."

"I will certainly appreciate it, if you can." The man looked through a chest of large, flat drawers, removing drawings and sheets of notes, and piling these on the cart-table. Finally, "I think this is most of it, Ms. Kerguelen." He frowned for a moment. "I'll have to remember; the captain said that around other folks, we're to call you Ms. Obrigo." He shook his head. "I guess I don't have to understand it."

She touched his hand briefly. "You and Hain heard my true name because I could tell Bran Tregare trusts you. I am not certain whether it is so important here to hide my identity. But on Earth thirty years ago, it was a matter of death. And, as we know, UET has long fingers."

"*UET!*" Kenekke's face and voice made a snarl. Then he hunched his shoulders, rolled his head from side to side; she could sense the crackling tensions leaving him. "If it's against *them*—don't worry; I won't make any slips. And neither will Hain." He smiled tentatively. "They wanted you bad, eh? I hope you stuck 'em a good one!"

"They thought so, apparently." She hesitated. "Enough so, that to get off Earth safely I had to kill a Committee policebitch. And another of their hounds, I am told, was sent to follow me to Terranova—but he did not expect me to get off at a halfway point when I had paid to go so much farther."

"Their greed—they can't believe we're not all as greedy." Kenekke laughed. "You go spacing for them—they keep everything you own tied up, and think that ties *you*. I walked off from the whole lot—and they're welcome to it, for I have freedom, and—"

"And you would not trade! Of course not. Neither would I." She started to pick up the large, awkward papers, trying not to lose the pile of smaller sheets. Kenekke took the oversized drawings and fashioned them into a long roll. Then he slid the smaller notesheets into a plastic folder.

"Here—easier handling, this way." She thanked him and returned to the cabin.

She had had her fill of fruit juice; she made a pot of coffee.

She put the papers in the best order she could determine —Tregare's numbering system was helpful, but she found it somewhat cryptic—and began studying drawings along with the correlated notes. At first it was like learning a new language, but she persisted and soon was understanding more than not of what she read.

Dark approached. She turned lights on and closed the curtains, and suddenly realized she had forgotten to eat dinner. She was hungry but—let's see now—she turned a sheet, looked back to the previous one, saw the discrepancy she had missed, and nodded.

PART of her mind heard the aircar land, but she paid no conscious heed until the knock resounded at the front door. Then she sprang up and ran to open it.

"Bran!" She hugged him and raised her face; his kiss was quick and light, and he did not return her embrace. Puzzled, she stepped back—then saw his hands held out from his sides, black with grime, and the smears on face and clothes.

He laughed. "Let me clean up; then I'll greet you properly." He gestured. "See? You got a smudge on your front, there."

She brushed at it and shook her head. "I do not care. But, all right—get your clothes off; I will run the tub for you."

With the water running at the proper heat, she went to the kitchen for her coffee, and brought a chair to set beside the tub. Tregare slid down into the hot water. "Aah—this is good!"

"Since when do captains get their hands so dirty? And how does the work progress?"

"Captains do what they know best, like anybody else. Progress? Not bad, except someone misread a drawing and welded a turret mount in, the wrong way around. That's how I got so pretty—cutting the thing free and helping manhandle it into place, then welding it in right. Simpler to do it than tell it."

She nodded. "Some things are—I have also found that true. But I meant—what proportion of work is done, on Vanois' ship? And have you begun on Limmer's?"

"Limmer's? *Lefthand Thread*'s already equipped." He

paused to rinse lather from his hair, then said, "I guess I haven't filled you in on that part of the operation. All right —you guessed it back on *Inconnu*—my arsenal's on a place called New Hope. I ran onto a group of Escaped UET technicians trying to make a living there. Pioneer world—not much market for their talents—making farm machinery was about the size of it. But some of them were weapons experts, so we made a deal."

She smiled. "Tregare, the Good Samaritan at a profit."

"Right again. I provided the equipment they needed, and drawings, and samples of a few pieces of hardware. Yes—that missing projector you noticed, for one. So they build weapons for me. And when Limmer picked up the first load, he had them equip *Lefthand Thread*, just to be sure everything worked."

"First load?"

"Enough to arm six more ships, to make up the eight I want. Only three on UET's schedule are armed, so five of mine—if I have eight—get rigged with dummy hull plates to hide the weapons. Limmer's is fixed that way—that's why you can't see it's armed. For combat, the plates are jettisoned." Trying to reach behind him, he winced. "Hey—scrub my back, will you? Bruised my shoulder—not much of a thing, but right now it hurts to reach back that way."

"All right." She rubbed lather onto him, then rinsed it, splashing water up as he bent forward. "Now—tell me something of the weapons themselves, since I am to train in operating them."

"Sure. Well, there's two kinds, plus a defense—of sorts— against one of them. Three separate jobs, there; take your pick."

He leaned back again. "The energy projectors—*Inconnu* mounts eight—are the trickiest to handle. Each one is a pair of lasers—above visual range—that have to converge on target *and* heterodyne for peak heat in the infrared. You can blow a hull to vapor—*if* you're tuned right and your convergence is on. Tuning's tricky because frequencies drift as the thing heats up when you fire. UET never bothered; they just set it to creep through the hot part of the spectrum in the first five-six shots."

"But on your ships it is different?"

"Yes. You've got a tuning lever—for one component only, because it's the difference that counts—and a monitor display. When you're on-peak, your scope shows a circle; if it tilts, you move your right-hand lever the other way to push it back."

"That does not sound too difficult."

"Except that with your left hand you're controlling convergence. If the light on either side of your scope starts blinking, you move the range lever in that direction until it goes out. So you're watching and doing two things at once, and it takes practice to get your coordination down to a reflex."

He grinned. "Now, then—you've got both hands busy. How do you aim and fire?"

"A foot pedal, I suppose?"

"Partly right. You don't have to aim. Control picks your target and sets the computer to stay with it or change to another. And the projector fires whenever both range lights are out *and* your circle's within five degrees of optimum.

"You do have a foot pedal, though—it's an override— doubles your combined range-and-tuning tolerance to let you take poorer shots. But that's only for when you're losing and can't get a shot off, otherwise."

"So I have one entire foot free—I can play chess, or scratch my other ankle!"

He laughed and reached for a towel; standing in the draining tub, he dried himself. "Rissa, I suppose you've eaten?"

"No. Kenekke let me borrow your drawings of how the weapons are to be installed. Studying them, I forgot dinner."

He put a robe on and they moved to the kitchen. He looked at the sheets on top of each stack of papers. "You've got pretty well into it, for one day. But why? You won't need to know these things."

"I will, Bran, if I am to help you at Base Two. I cannot spend my days here, idle. I become—lonesome."

Now he gave her the overdue embrace and a longer, intense kiss. Then he ran his hand through her hair to the back of her neck, and squeezed gently. "Well—if you want to get your hands dirty, why not?"

"Good. Now I will clear the table of these papers. Then, shall I prepare food, or will you?"

"My imagination's more into weapons than food—but so's yours, I expect."

"I will do it; you have worked harder."

"All right. Here—I'll take care of the notes and drawings." He evened each stack neatly and put them on the main room's small desk. Then he set the table, poured two glasses of wine, and sat while she set food to cook.

"What are the other two weapons jobs, Bran? You have missiles, I know."

"Yes—fusion and neutron heads, two of each. Short-haul drives souped up to fifty gee, while they last. Missiles and missile defense, you understand, are control-room jobs. You feed your target to the computer by holding it on-screen—if the missile's fired, it'll follow and seek. Computer control activates your launch button only if range and relative velocities are right for a hit—but again, there's an override to widen tolerances so you can take a desperation shot if it's that or go under."

Standing, she sipped her wine and nodded. "The combination of human and computer control—its design impressed me." She stirred a pot of steaming vegetables a moment, then said, "And the defenses, Bran?"

"Partly automatic—if the computer, the detectors, sense anything incoming at missile-grade acceleration, projectors facing the right way lock on it and fire continuously. Tuning and convergence have to take their chances—there isn't *time* for adjustments—the damned things are coming too fast!

"The rest of it—well, far as I know, it's untested. Sort of a countermissile—two kinds, really—one with a warhead and the other blows a cloud of powdered metal to make like a ship and fool the attacking missile. We mount two of each—could use more, but where's the space for it?

"These can't be steered; you point 'em and that's that. I can't guess how many gees the drive pulls, but I looked at the drawings and if it lasts more than three seconds I'll eat it for dessert. Either kind blows when the drive does, or by proximity." He shook his head. "Frankly, I'm not counting on those gadgets much—either option—in a tight passage."

"Then I do not wish to work in missile defense." She sniffed the air and decided dinner was ready. "Just a moment.'' She brought the food to the table; they served themselves. ''I think—the projectors, Bran.''

''That puts you out in a turret by yourself. I'd rather have you in Control with me. There's still the missiles themselves.''

''I will learn and practice both, and then decide.''

He shrugged. ''Fair enough, I guess.''

THEY ate in silence for a time; then he said, ''What happened since I left the Lodge?''

She told him of her latest visit to the Hatchery and her meeting with Bleeker. ''And Liesel has as good as approved Sparline's marriage to Ernol. Oh—and Hawkman suggests that perhaps he and Liesel may consider going to Earth—buying a ship of their own!'' She reached and touched his hand. ''It is because you are going there, Bran—and it was first Hawkman's idea.'' She laughed. ''Initially, Liesel was quite shocked.''

''Yeah.'' Tregare grinned. ''And then she saw the chances to be had there, if I can shake UET up enough. Well, it's fine with me if she winds up owning the whole damned planet! It's in a lot worse hands, peace knows . . .''

''The idea is only tentative, Bran—they must talk with you.''

''Sure—timing and all—well, I'm willing. The more I think about it, the better I like it. There's a problem, though.''

''I am sure there are many. Which do you mean?''

''Erika's group. I'd hoped to work with them—sent messages with feelers, guarantees of cooperation. As Tregare, of course—no hint of the relationship. But if Liesel is there, too . . .''

She pushed her empty plate aside and refilled her glass. Swirling the wine gently and watching the light refracted through its ruby tinge, she said, ''You do not think the two groups could work as allies?''

''For a while, maybe. After that, I'd worry about Hulzein-eat-Hulzein.''

''Yes.'' She nodded. ''And, Bran—I am a protégée of *each* faction. I would not wish to see either hurt.''

''No, you wouldn't. Me, though—and Erika—you can't expect me to have tender feelings toward the heirs of that skinny old harpy.'' He grinned. ''Yes, I saw her once. Liesel dressed me as a serving-boy and said if I kept my mouth shut, I could see my dreaded Aunt Erika. I have to admit she impressed the hell out of me; even in memory, she still does.'' He tapped fingers against the table top. ''I wish, just once I could have faced up to her. We might have got along, at that—if I'd lived through it.''

Rissa was shaking her head. ''It is too bad, yes, that you could not have met as equals. But, Bran—'skinny old harpy' —*Erika*? Slim, yes—but wiry, not skinny. Do you know— when she was seventy she gave me my final testing in unarmed combat? And came close to beating me, overall.''

''I'm not surprised. Liesel was hell on wheels when I was a kid; I guess she hasn't kept in practice, here. Come to that, I don't keep it up too well myself—in space, especially.''

She looked at him. ''Bran, are you in need of exercise?''

''Combat practice so soon after dinner? Peace, no!''

''I was not thinking of combat.''

Smiling, he stood and laid his robe over the back of the chair. ''I was wondering when we'd get to that.'' He came around the table to hold her. ''Let's exercise.''

Two days without him had affected her more than she had realized. Her body moved without conscious intent—fiercely, violently. Then, in almost a scream, she cried triumph.

Later they went through Tregare's drawings together, she explaining what she understood of them and he adding or correcting when necessary. When they were done, they talked for a time. Finally Rissa stood and moved to hold his head against her.

''Bran? It is not so late—is it?''

He laughed. ''I'd've asked if you hadn't.''

This time was more quiet for her, and gentle; climax brought fulfillment and peace. In a very few minutes, then, she slept.

AT breakfast next morning, Tregare said, ''How'd you like the pass, eastbound? Forgot to ask, yesterday, since obviously you got here all right.''

"I—I hate to tell you," but she began.

Almost immediately he interrupted. "Clouds? You went in with an overcast? You should have turned back."

"Perhaps. But I thought—" She continued. This time he heard her out. Then he shook his head.

"I tried that trick once—going in high. Damned downdraft caught me off guard—time I got straightened up, I was too low and too slow to make it. All I could do was turn downhill to get speed. You reacted faster, to get away with that dive and still climb the pass."

"Or—from time to time the downdraft may vary in strength."

"Maybe. Anyway, your luck was in. But I hope you won't try it again under those conditions!"

"Unless it is necessary, I will not, certainly."

"All right." He pushed back his chair and stood. "Time we got dressed." He stacked the dishes to soak and joined her in the front room. "We'll take Anse along today; Hain can do the watch here."

"You brought Deverel up with you last night?"

"Sure. He gets lonesome down at Two—same as I do."

"Yes. Well, I am nearly ready, except—what do I need to take with me? I mean—will we return here tonight?" She twisted her hair into a knot atop her head and secured it with a clasp.

"And every night—unless something comes up and we have to work straight through. I don't expect that, but it could happen."

He called the scoutship; Kenekke was ready and met them at the aircar. Tregare took the controls. They rode in silence until close to landing; then Tregare said, "Remember, both of you—it's Tari Obrigo joining our work force today. I'm sure of the people I *know* on these ships, but there's some new to me."

"Yes."

"Sure, captain."

"All right." He landed midway and to one side of the path between the two ships, where crates were being moved from *Lefthand Thread* to *Carcharodon*. "Tari, you come with me. We're starting the fourth turret; I want you to mark the cuts for the torch men—in the existing structure and on the girders to be installed. Then spot the holes for the new bulkheads and the projector mounting itself. I'll check you first time 'round —after that, *you'll* be checking the work.''

She nodded. "Yes, I can do those things. I will need the drawings, though—I do not remember all of it yet."

"Hell, yes, you'll use drawings! I wouldn't try it from memory myself, and I *drew* the damn things!"

She touched his hand. "Bran—perhaps I do not joke enough . . ."

He looked at her, then grinned. "All right—you got me. Well, let's get to it." They entered *Carcharodon* and climbed upship. Kenekke left them to join three men sorting out piles of components in a storage area. As they passed the control room, Vanois and Limmer stopped arguing over a circuit diagram long enough to give them brief greetings.

Then they neared the top of the ship and Rissa could see the magnitude of the work—some nearly completed and some only begun. She saw that structural members had been cut away and replaced to fit around turret and missile positions without weakening the ship. "Tregare—seeing this in three dimensions—it gives me a *feel* for the work, that the drawings could not."

"I know; it's the same with me. Well, this is where we start on Turret Four, and here's your chalk and measuring tape. This end sticks where you put it—" He demonstrated. "—unless you twist it or flick it, like this. So one person can do all of it."

"Yes. I knew of these, but had not used one before." She stood, looking at the sections to be removed. "Lacking a place to anchor a power hoist, we must move everything by hand?" He nodded. "Then there must be more cuts—no need to measure them precisely—to divide the girders into manageable weights."

"Almost right. More cuts, yes. But we reuse as much as we can, so you cut the right sizes to fit the new structure."

"Of course. Well—in that case—" She looked at a drawing, then to Tregare, catching him in a half-smile. "Your design uses that junction of four girders, unchanged—merely cut free and inverted, then rotated a quarter turn?" He nodded, and she climbed onto a protruding beam to take a measurement. "Then I shall begin here, mark to remove the junction, then work from there toward the perimeter cuts. Do you agree?"

"That's about the way I've been doing it."

"All right." She began work—measuring, marking, climbing from point to point. As the morning progressed, the air grew hotter; when she paused to check a drawing, she was sweating freely. "No," she said, "that is wrong. I can lessen the waste by taking the longer segment *here* and using *this* for three shorter ones." Taking Tregare's silence for assent, she rubbed away a few chalk marks and measured anew.

She had lost track of time when Tregare said, "Everybody else is stopping for coffee and what all. You want to?"

With the back of her hand she wiped her forehead. "Yes, I would enjoy that." As she followed him downship she noticed her muscles had grown tense; she shrugged and moved her neck, relaxing. "That is harder work than I would have thought."

Half-turning as they entered the galley, he said, "It is when someone concentrates on it as hard as you do."

Side by side at the end of a long table they found two seats. Rissa sat and Tregare brought coffee. She did not know the man and woman who sat facing them. The woman—dark, scar-cheeked, hair hidden under a bandanna, spoke harsh-toned. "You're Tregare's new wife?"

"I did not know he had an old one. But yes, we are married."

The woman laughed. "Didn't mean it that way, but that's all right—you caught me out. I'm Corane Flerot, Second Hat here on *Carcharodon*. I don't marry anymore, but I wish you luck. You look like you've been working. What at?"

Rissa explained and Corane Flerot nodded. "That's a help. I'm no good at that kind of thing, myself. Navigation, yes—but not building from drawings." She paused, then said, "You going to space with him?"

Tregare answered. "Yes. Probably as a turret operator."

Fingers clawed, the woman's hand darted at Rissa's face. By reflex, Rissa caught the wrist and thrust it aside; she stopped her countermove when she realized the other made no further effort. Puzzled, she saw Flerot smile, as she said,

"Good—you've got the reflexes for it, all right."

Rissa released her grip. "That was not, perhaps, the safest way to find out."

"Maybe not—quick, though." Flerot touched her scarred cheek. "Does this look as though I always do things the safe way?"

Tregare showed the small knife his right hand held. "Usually not as dangerous as this was, Corane. You're alive this instant because I knew my wife is faster than you are." He put the knife away. "Well, nothing shaken. More coffee, Tari?"

"Yes—a little, please." Tregare rose, but now the man across from him—tall, thin, with a lined face—stood also.

"You don't know me, Tregare, except a name on a roster—Bartol Hannaway. But Corane and I are freemated. If you killed her, then captain or no captain, it's your death or mine."

Tregare's hand on Rissa's shoulder kept her from speech. He said, "You making some kind of challenge, Hannaway?"

"No. Just stating a fact, so you'll know."

"All right, I've heard it. Now here's one for you—you'll live longer—both of you—if you don't play stupid games with people who have work to do."

"Tregare!" said Rissa. "All of you—this goes too far—I am not angry, nor was I hurt. Once I saw it was a test, only, the danger was past."

Corane shrugged. "My fault—I'm sorry. Now calm it, Bartol."

The man muttered an apology and left the table; the woman followed. Rissa stood and said, "I do not want more coffee after all. Shall we return to our work?"

"All right. Let's go." They climbed again to the turret site, and she continued measuring and marking, occasionally changing her mind and revising the way the cuts would be made. When she finished, she turned to him and waited.

"Is it satisfactory?"

"Yes. A little different, in places, from how I've done it—but looks like a standoff for minimizing waste. You want to mark your intermediate cuts on the drawing now, and compare?" She had scribbled figures on the girders themselves, so she did not have to remeasure to mark the print. Then they looked at it alongside a copy he had marked.

"It's about even, all right. Some places you save more material or muscle, some places I do. Might's well do it your way, for the other four turrets."

"All right. And now, with the measurements determined, it will go faster."

"Yes. Don't forget, though—the odd numbers are left-handed with respect to this one, so one accessway can serve a pair. That's what somebody forgot on the one yesterday."

"I will remember. After lunch I will begin on Turret Five."

"Why not do Six and Eight first? They're the same as this one. Then you can transcribe your figures onto the inverted drawing for Five and Seven."

She nodded. "Yes, that is reasonable—for I shall have to change my orientation only once."

"Good. Hey, it's nearly lunch time—let's knock off and go to the galley."

Rissa shook her head. "Let us eat alone, you and I. Here, or in the aircar."

He looked at her. "Flerot and Hannaway—they bothered you?"

"She did not. Nor you—but then you and he—Bran, will you be able to trust that man?"

"*I* don't have to deal with him—he's Vanois' problem, and Raoul wouldn't have him around if he made any real trouble. Unless he insists on it, he has none with me." He shrugged. "But all right—let's go downship. You go ahead to the aircar and I'll bring our lunches there."

They descended; he stopped at the galley level and she continued down and out of the ship. Outside the sun's heat felt pleasant, and the air was clear. She climbed into the aircar and waited; soon Tregare brought their trays and they ate.

In the afternoon Rissa set to work on the other two even-numbered turrets. Tregare checked her markings on Six, then left for other duties; on Eight she worked alone. When she was done she returned to her morning's location and found the torch crew cutting to her markings. Removals were complete and reconstruction had begun. For a while she watched, but did not interrupt the work. After a time a tall man pushed back his welding mask and said to her, "You marked this one for us, didn't you?"

"Yes, I did."

"Good job—everything fits. A little different from Tregare's layout, but works just as well." He rubbed his thumb knuckles into his eyes. "Gets to you, watching a weld too long. A break helps." Then, "Tregare really married you, did he? That's what we heard."

"Yes. Nearly a month ago, in a dueling arena near One Point One. Had you heard that, also?"

His harsh bark, she realized, was meant to be a laugh. "No, they didn't tell us that. It's true?"

"Yes. I had just fought a man, unarmed and naked, and killed him. I was bloody and I stank. My face looked as though it had been stepped on—which it very nearly *had* been. That is how we were married."

After a moment, the man nodded. "I believe it." With one finger he touched her arm. "Back on Earth, in the Slaughterhouse, I knew Tregare. When he was little—too young to take the hell UET put us through. Used to hear him cry at night, the first weeks. Daytimes, though, you'd never know it—cross him then, he'd spit in your eye just for starters." He nodded. "I knew then—if he lived—he'd be a man to lead something. And now I guess he's ready for it."

His look was expectant; she said, "And when he is ready to tell of it, he will do that, also."

His hand made a vague salute. "Sure—I know. Well, tell him John Kragen's with him, no matter what or where."

She smiled. "I will, surely." He pushed the mask down and turned back to his work; his torch flared and she had to look away. A quick glance showed her the rest of the work was going well, so she left and went downship to the control room.

There she found Corane Flerot on duty alone. Rissa paused, in doubt whether she should enter, but the woman said, "I talked to Bartol. He didn't mean anything, except standing up for me the same as Tregare for you. He had to—you see? But he's not the man to hold grudges. Will Tregare see that?"

Rissa looked at her. Her head was uncovered now; grizzled

hair, short and uncombed, stood out in crinkled masses. Her scarred face was totally serious. Rissa said, "To Tregare, the matter is done."

"I'm glad. Bartol's courage shouldn't be wasted against his own leader."

Rissa thought, then said, "And what of your own part? To threaten—not me of myself, but Bran Tregare's wife? If Bartol had died . . ."

"Yes. My fault, it would've been. Ms. Tregare—"

"Ms. Obrigo."

"All right. Maybe I get more reckless as I get older and uglier—which takes some doing—I got most of these scars from UET. But I'll watch it from now on. Is that what you meant?"

Rissa nodded. "But I am not angry with you, Corane—only concerned for you."

The woman smiled. "Want to try a little unarmed combat sometime? Practice rules, I mean—nothing lethal or maiming."

"If you wish. But why?"

"Maybe to show Tregare you're not all *that* much faster."

"She's fast enough." It was Tregare; Rissa turned to face him.

"We are speaking in friendship. It is all right."

He smiled. "That's good. Corane, I'm not knifing for Bartol; tell him that."

"I will. He didn't really want trouble either, you know."

"Sure. We're all on a tight string these days. Once we finish this ship, we can take a rest before Peralta gets here." He put a hand on Rissa's shoulder. "If we're done for today, let's go home. Kenekke's ready."

"Yes. Corane, I am glad we talked, and that all is well between us."

WHEN the aircar was up and Tregare's course set, Rissa relayed the welder's greetings. Tregare nodded. "Kragen, eh? I thought he looked familiar, but I couldn't place him and he didn't say anything. He was finishing at the Academy when I was first sent there—didn't make officer rank, I guess. Quiet fellow—never threw his weight around like some did."

"He remembers you also. Even as a child you impressed him as one who would someday lead."

"Lead?" He shrugged. "We all do what comes to us, I think."

"Of course, Bran. I have noticed how very passive you are."

He laughed and patted her knee. "One for you." Then they did not talk until he landed by the cabin. "I'll check with Hain for messages and be right back."

"All right. By that time I shall be steaming and sodden in the tub."

Inside the cabin she saw in a mirror that her face was soot-streaked. Her hair was dusted with it also; the welding and cutting left a deposit on every uncovered surface. She undressed while the tub filled, removed the clasp from her hair and shook it free, and slid gratefully into the hot water.

She was kneading lather into hair and scalp, eyes shut against the stinging liquid that trickled down her forehead, when she heard the door open and close. Tregare's voice rose. "News, Rissa! Peralta's *No Return*—it's a lot closer than we thought—practically here, in fact. His signals are weak because his transmitter's output stage blew, and no spares. But he'll land at One Point One tomorrow or the next day, then move here as soon as he can."

She was fumbling for a towel and not finding it. He laughed and handed one to her, and she wiped her eyes free of soap. "Will we go to the port again, as with Limmer?"

"I don't see the need; Peralta's dealt here before, and I gave him instructions." He started to turn away. "I'll put something on the stove. Any preference?"

She laughed. "Hot and plentiful will suffice." She stood, and rinsed hair and body under the shower while the tub drained. She dried herself quickly, wrapped her damp hair in a towel, put on a robe, and joined Tregare in the kitchen.

"Coffee's ready," he said, "or wine. Take your choice."

"Both," she said, and served herself before she sat. "Bran?"

He looked up from the stew he was stirring. "Yeah?"

"Tonight I will mark the lefthanded drawing, for turrets

Five and Seven. But tomorrow I will finish that work by noon. Aside from checking the crews' progress, what is there for me to do?''

"Well, let's see—I'll be giving the missile and antimissile berths a last lookover, before the sheet-metal work seals off the structural members. You might hang in with me, check the drawings against the finished job, so you can mark cuts for those on other ships. Which reminds me—''

He went to the main room and rummaged in his desk. "No —they're not here.'' He came back and served up the stew —along with bread, cheese, and some fruit—and sat to eat.

She tasted a bite and found it too hot, blew on it and sampled it again. "This is very good. But—*what* isn't here?''

"Drawings for ships of *No Return*'s class—the nose section's all different. I may have prints on the scoutship—if I didn't forget, and leave 'em on *Inconnu*. If I did, we'll wait until Peralta gets here and draw our own.''

"Or we could join him earlier, at the port.''

He shook his head. "No use to that. You can't see what you need to until we pull some plates off—and we won't do that until the ship's at Base Two.''

"I see.'' She ate in silence; when she was done, she poured more wine and coffee for both. She cleared her side of the table and spread the two complementary drawings across it. "I will mark this now, and you can check it for me.''

"All right.'' Glancing up, she saw that he watched her.

After the first few markings, she caught the knack of transposing from one drawing to its mirror image, and the chore was done sooner than she had expected. She stood. "There, Bran. Is it correct?''

He turned the sheets to face him and she saw how he compared them—one index finger to each, moving simultaneously as he glanced from one to the other. Her forty minutes of work were inspected in hardly more than five. He nodded. "No mistakes.'' Then; "I need a shower.''

"Very well. I will finish drying my hair now.'' When she had done so and brushed it, she took off her robe and got into bed. When Tregare came out of the bathroom she threw the covers back, and waited.

"That's where I was hoping you'd be,'' he said, and went to her. He was in no hurry, nor was she; laughter and dalliance persisted for some time before they joined. Afterward he said, "Every time's different, isn't it?"

"Yes." Her fingers moved along his back, brushing a welted scar. "Sometimes it is difficult to wait until the next."

He laughed. "This particular wait doesn't have to be so long. About like last night. All right?"

"Oh, yes—I can manage that quite nicely."

NEXT morning on *Carcharodon*, Rissa laid out the two remaining turret sites. For part of the afternoon she stayed with Tregare, studying missile berth arrangements—then inspected the work in progress on the turrets she had marked the day before. She found two minor errors, but none of consequence; the corrections took only a short time.

Back at Base One, Tregare searched the scoutship and found drawings applicable to *No Return*. After dinner they spread these on the table and began planning modifications.

"The main difference in the *No Return* class," Tregare said, "is that instead of sixteen main longitudinal beams they used twelve heavier ones for the same size hull. The gaps are wider, but not *quite* wide enough to put two turrets in one of them. So instead of eight projectors, four missiles, and four countermissiles, it'll have to be six, three, and three. You see it?"

She checked a measurement, then said, "The missiles, yes. But our projectors—Bran, I am not a structural engineer—but see here? At the nose, where all twelve beams join. Must it be that way?"

"It's overdesigned, sure. But what—?"

"*Here*, just below the turret sites—why did they not add another girder ring and omit every second beam from there to the tip? In that case we *could* squeeze in extra turrets."

He looked more closely. "Hey! I'll have to run the stress factors through the computer, to be sure of it—but I think you've given Peralta some extra firepower!"

He took the drawing to the scoutship; a half hour later he returned. "Well, it works! Want to start figuring the changes?"

"I have already begun." She continued, calculating how best to convert the removed beam segments into a ring-shaped member—and at what point—with least wastage. Then she began adding and rearranging the necessary runs of power and control cables. She was not concerned with the circuitry itself, but only with physical access. When she finished the proposal, Tregare looked through her notes and sketches. He suggested two minor changes and approved the rest.

The work had taken longer than she realized; it was past time to be asleep.

Now on *Carcharodon* she had little to do. She finished next morning's inspections in an hour, then accompanied Tregare on the remainder of his own rounds. A little ahead of the usual morning's break, they went to the galley. Over coffee she said, "Except for making a last inspection this afternoon before we leave, I have no more work today. Might it be a good time to learn the projector controls, if Captain Limmer would allow me to use a turret on *Lefthand Thread*?"

Tregare swallowed coffee, then spoke. "Sure. I'm free for a while, long enough to set up a good run of simulations and turn you loose with them."

As they left, others began to come in; Rissa greeted Corane Flerot and saw that Tregare had stepped aside to shake hands with Bartol Hannaway. That residue of worry left her mind.

Downship, across the field to Limmer's ship and then up to its control room, she walked beside Tregare. Holding a sheaf of papers, Limmer met them. "Just going below to look for some spare equipment the men can't find. Nothing critical, but it says here we're supposed to have them." His warped smile came briefly; Rissa no longer saw it as a sneer. "But what can I do for you?"

Tregare explained. "Do you have simulations already programmed, or could I set up a few for her?"

Limmer moved to a control panel, touched switches and observed a digital readout. "There's a few on here, set up to pipe into Turret Eight—mostly straightforward, chase or be chased. You might want to add some trickier stuff—skew approaches, hit-and-run, multiple targets and the computer being indecisive—you know?" Tregare nodded; Limmer turned to leave.

"Thank you for letting me use your turret, captain."

"Any time." He paused. "Like to see you both for lunch, if you're free."

"Be glad to," said Tregare. "Something on your mind?"

Limmer shook his head. "Nothing special—just to boot ideas around a little, see how things are firming up."

"Sure." Tregare nodded. "See you then." Limmer waved a hand and left. Tregare turned to the control panel and punched a sequence into the computer, paused, did another, and repeated the process a number of times. "That should hold you for an hour or so, anyway. If you run out and want more, the Repeat button will rerun the programs in different sequence, with parameters changed enough to make it a new problem."

"Thank you. Shall I go to Turret Eight now?"

"I'll go with you." They climbed and entered the turret; for two, the fit was cramped. He pointed out the auxiliary practice controls. "Here's Start and Stop; there's Repeat. And your range and tuning indicators and controls—remember; right hand controls the circle, and left your range lights. Foot pedal for tolerance override—the less you have to use it, the better. Got it?"

"Yes." On a readout tape at one side of the console she saw a column of two-digit numbers, mostly between 40 and 50. The last number, 44, was starred. She pointed. "What is that?"

"Scorekeeper. On each problem it prints the percentage of time you had destructive energy level on target, compared to what was possible. Shooting with the override pedal down counts only half points. Last number, with the star, is the overall score for the series."

"And is this a good score?"

"It's fair—somebody's learning. At least he's pretty consistent. But a good journeyman gunner beats fifty, more than not."

"And an expert?"

He laughed. "Might have known you'd ask that. Well, there was an old-timer when I was in UET, a one-eyed old hellion with hooks for a right hand. In competition—simulated, like here—I saw him hit eighty once, and average seventy-two, with controls he modified himself. On *Inconnu*, now—anyone who can average sixty is first string."

"I see." She squirmed past and sat at the controls. "Shall I begin?"

"Go ahead. I'll call off your first scores—unless you want me to set for delay between sequences, you won't have time to look."

She shook her head and punched Start. The scope lit with an ellipse slanting left; she pushed at it with her righthand lever, overcontrolled, moved it back. Her left range light was blinking; she moved the other lever to extinguish it, then back as the other light blinked—and the circle was leaning again. Back and forth, learning the patterns of coordination, she moved. A dot appeared within the circle. "That's a hit," said Tregare. The dot vanished.

She concentrated, eyes slightly out of focus to see all indicators without glancing back and forth. The dot came again; this time she held it several seconds, then regained it momentarily before scope and lights darkened and a bell rang. "Twenty-two," said Tregare.

Again it began. Now she perceived a pattern—the circle tended increasingly to slant left. Circuit components heating, she recalled, and began to compensate automatically. Range drift was reversed from the first exercise, but also relatively steady. This time when the bell rang, Tregare announced, "Forty-one."

She nodded; she was learning. "Forty-seven." "Thirty-eight"—range drift had reversed halfway through. "That was a side pass." Then "fifty-three" and Tregare squeezed her shoulder once and released it. "All right; you're getting it. I'll go take care of some things and see you at lunch."

Already busy with the next simulation, she nodded. When the bell rang she risked a glance at the readout—49—and looked back to see a range light blinking rapidly; her side-glance had given the computer a head start, and she finished with 39. But after that run she made her glance more quickly and was ready for the next move.

Now as she learned to gauge situations faster, her scores—the average of them—improved. She was sweating, and her hair—worn loose today—fell forward on one side and blocked peripheral vision. She shook it back—the circle tipped and lost its central dot but she recovered it—and ignored the sudden frantic itching of her nose.

Her arms and wrists tired—the levers moved only side-to-side and were so placed that she could not rest her forearms on the console's edge. She lost track of time and of the number of simulations she had run.

Her score began dropping—not only from fatigue, but because the runs were becoming more complicated. The first time her range took a discontinuous jump, she was caught by surprise; then she realized the computer had changed targets in mid-exercise. After that, she was on guard and recovered faster.

Finally the bell rang for several seconds; when it stopped, the panel remained dark. She let go the levers—she had not touched the override—and flexed her stiffened wrists and fingers. Only then did she think to look at the final readout.

The starred number was 44.

SHE took a string from her bag and tied her hair to hang from the back of her head, letting air cool her neck. She looked at her watch—she had been in the turret almost two hours; the time was close to noon. She started downship, paused at a latrine cubicle to relieve herself and wash, and went to the galley. Tregare sat with Limmer at a corner table; she joined them and poured herself coffee.

Tregare greeted her. "Well, how'd you do?"

"Forty-four, overall. As you said—somebody's learning."

Limmer whistled. "On a *first* series, that's damned good!"

"True words," said Tregare. "And I put in some pretty fancy stuff, too, after the basic runs." He sipped from his cup. "Well, how'd you like the job? Mind you—in real action you'd never be at it so long at a time, or without pauses between targets. On the other hand, you might *start* bushed, so it evens out."

"With practice, it is a job I can do. And I like the challenge of it. But you make it more difficult than it need be."

"What?" Tregare shook his head. "I *know* you're not saying you want all easy ones. So what do you mean?"

"The controls, the physical design." She reached out over the table, pantomiming. "Side-to-side—the motion becomes tiring. Hands and forearms in midair with no resting place.

Now—'' She moved her hands differently. "If the levers moved on a *slant*—out and *back*, in and *toward* one—there would be less fatigue, better performance. And they should be shorter, placed somewhat closer, and the console's edge padded so the arms could rest there.''

She looked at him. "Would it be difficult to arrange it so?''

He shook his head. "Not very. Hey—you know? I'd forgotten—I wasn't on weapons much, myself—but the old buzzard I told you about, back with UET? That's pretty nearly the way he modified *his* controls. The top brass didn't approve, of course, but the captain did—he *liked* having the top gunner in the fleet!''

"Then—would you mind, Captain Limmer, if we experiment in Turret Eight?''

"Not a bit. What do you need?''

"Someone of average size and reach, to serve as a model. If I designed for myself, it would not suit the larger personnel comfortably. Given the measurements I will make you a layout drawing this afternoon and we can see if the modification is feasible.''

"No problem,'' said Tregare. "*Pivot* the lever mountings, is all—then shorten the levers a little and pad the console edge. No need to move anything; the seat's adjustable—which I should have showed you.'' He looked up. "Well, now—here comes lunch.''

Rissa had no more to say; the men also ate in silence. Afterward Limmer asked of Tregare's prospects for additional ships, and the status of tentative deadlines.

Tregare answered slowly, pausing to consider his replies. He concluded, ". . . so I have to decide pretty soon. *Inconnu*'s wasting her time and substance, out there on signal watch—I know that better than anyone. So I've set a day, in my own mind, when I call her in to top off fuel and supplies.''

"What is—I mean, what determines that date, Tregare?''

"The day that if *Inconnu* got signal from an incoming ship, it'd be too late to outfit her to join us. Then, if I don't have six ships, we'd have to give it up.'' He rubbed the back of his neck. "Even *with* six, I could use another to guard here in case the Shrakken come.'' Now his fist clenched. "If only they'd get here now and have done with it!''

"And if they do not?'' said Rissa. "What will you do?''

Tregare shook his head. "I've tried to ignore that decision but I have to make it. Give it all up, if I have what's needed? I *couldn't!* But to leave this world without protection—"

"At the port, you mentioned defense missiles."

"Sure, Tari—but the port's *all* they can defend. The outlying settlements . . ."

Rissa snapped her fingers. "The packet—the locally built ship that took Hawkman to Big Icecube. Could you arm it?"

His eyes narrowed. "Hey! It's big enough—two turrets, maybe three—we've got the spares. And range is where it's limited, not power or maneuvering." He slapped his hand on the table; coffee splashed from his cup. "All right! That settles it. Shrakken or no Shrakken, six ships and we *go!*"

Limmer nodded. "I'll drink for that." This time, Rissa thought, his grin needed no scars to make it sinister. And the fact that his toast was in coffee dregs did not lessen its impact.

LIMMER sent a man with her to Turret Eight; he sat and put his hands over the table, moving until he found his most comfortable reach. Tregare had been right; there was no need to relocate the lever mountings, but merely to pivot them. She marked the angle on the console with chalk, excused and thanked the crewman, and made her sketches.

She went to *Carcharodon* and checked construction progress; she found no errors and was pleased to see three projector mountings in place. Tregare joined her as she inspected the third one; then they went downship, met Kenekke at the ramp, and flew back to Base One.

As Rissa landed the aircar she saw Deverel coming out of the scoutship. He met them as they climbed down, and said, "News, Tregare—Peralta's landed! He says give him two days and he'll be here. At Base Two, I mean."

"Good." Tregare nodded. "Tomorrow I'll mark a landing circle for him, to place him for quickest transshipment of weapons. He say anything else?"

"Yes. If anybody's shorthanded, he's got supernumeraries. He made a quick stop at Tweedle of the Twin Worlds, since it was on his way—and found some Escaped UET officers—stranded when the old Underground Railroad got too hot to service."

"He have any trouble getting away from there?"

"Peralta?" Deverel laughed. "He used fake papers, of course, and filed for a two-week stay but refueled the first night. He turned almost the whole crew loose on shore leave—to paint the town all colors but be back aboard before most of the hell they raised could simmer down. Then while UET was still deciding how to start investigating him, he took off without clearance."

Tregare grinned. "That's Peralta, all right. Did they chase him any?"

"Not to show on his screens, anyway. Classic misdirection —he headed for Twaddle, fast enough to make a sling turn and go back past Tweedle—just short of plowing air—about four times as fast as anything local could manage on short notice. Anything that went after him was too slow, too late, and going the wrong way."

"He's good, all right—one of the best. I'll be glad to have him along—mostly—"

Rissa looked at him. "You do not trust this man?"

"He's always kept his promises. But he can't seem to forget he was senior to me in UET." Tregare shrugged. "Never mind. It's good news, Hain, and—"

"And let us celebrate it," said Rissa. "Hain—Anse—we owe you two a dinner. Tregare, is this a good time to pay our debt? In perhaps an hour?"

Tregare touched her shoulder. "Make it two."

FOUR filled the cabin's dining area nearly to capacity. Laughter and pleasantries accompanied the meal. When Deverel complimented her on the meat dish, Rissa said, "I am glad you like it, for it was an experiment. I had not seen stomper prepared in this way, but I recall that it worked well with Argentine beef."

"It's top," said Deverel. "Share the directions with me?"

"No, with me!" said Kenekke. "Hain wouldn't follow them, anyway—he's an improviser."

Rissa laughed. "Then I shall have to write it down twice."

Now, when the talk turned to business, Rissa felt herself a part of it and listened carefully, speaking only to add or ask a fact. When the talk slowed, wine combining with fatigue, the two men excused themselves and left. She closed the door behind them and turned to hug Tregare. "It was a fine evening, Bran."

"Was?" She laughed and shook her head. "Well—that's better."

NEXT morning, after inspecting error-free work on *Carcharodon*, Rissa went to *Lefthand Thread* for an hour's gunnery practice. Then, over coffee with Limmer—Tregare called to say he was too busy for the usual morning break—she arranged for a technician to modify Turret Eight's controls. Jury-rigged but workable, the job was done by noon. She lunched early and quickly, seeing no one she knew, and returned to test the results. Her morning average had been 52, including a fair share of complex situations.

Now, seat adjusted to best comfort, she began a series. On the first run, learning the new feel of the controls, she scored 48. Next came a straightforward approach; her readout was a surprising 70. She smiled—surely it was not to be so easy—and ran the rest of the series without looking at individual scores; she knew she was doing well and did not want to give the computer the quarter-second advantage of a glance aside.

At the end—she ran the full two hours—the starred figure was 63. Her watch read close to break time, she went to the galley and waited. People entered; the place began to fill. She watched for Tregare. If he did not come soon, she would go and look for him—but there he came and crossed the room to join her.

"How did it go? You get the turret modified?" She nodded. "How does it work?"

Speaking quietly, forcing herself not to smile, she told him her scores of morning and afternoon.

His response did not disappoint her. "Sixty-three? *Average?* On your third series?" He had leaned forward; now he sat back. "Well, I guess you can quit practicing—you're an instant expert."

"I shall do no such thing. Until I have scored eighty and averaged seventy-two, I will practice daily. Then, if I achieve that, perhaps less often."

He laughed. "What if I told you I made those figures up?"

She looked at him. "I do not think I would believe you."

"All right—so I didn't. Well, obviously I'm impressed as all hell. Pleased, too, if that needs saying. Uh—does this mean you won't want to bother learning missiles?"

She considered. "I should know that task, I think—for possible emergencies—but not immediately." She paused. "Bran, I think the changed controls would improve *any* gunner's efficiency. Why has no one suggested it before?"

He shrugged. "I don't know. The controls are adapted from UET's and most of us are UET-trained. Nobody said anything to me—and I've only practiced gunnery enough that I could man a turret in a pinch—so I never thought of it."

She took his hand. "I do not mean to show myself off—"

"Little Ms. Deadpan, announcing your scores with downcast eyes? The hell you didn't!" But he was smiling. "Sure, I know what you mean. You're not putting yourself up, and you *do* have a right to be proud."

Now she smiled also. "Thank you. I do not wish to be falsely modest. But not braggart-proud, either."

"Whatever you say, gunner." He stood. "Well, back to work."

"Yes." He left, and she returned to the turret for another hour's practice. She averaged 68.

FIRST, next morning, the intercom woke her; then came Bran's voice. "He *what*? Did he land on that goddamned circle I drew for him, or not?"

"He hit it allright." She recognized Kenekke's tones. "Damned near got a missile up his tail, though, when the watch rousted Vanois to scan a ship coming down without clearance."

She blinked her eyes into focus and saw Tregare, nude, standing by the intercom. Frowning, he shook his head. "Has he talked to you? To anybody?"

"To Vanois. Just said he wants to see you—nothing more."

"That makes us a matched pair. All right—thanks, Anse. Tell Hain there's no special hurry; we'll leave at the usual time, regardless." He cut the circuit and turned toward Rissa, but she saw that he looked beyond her, at something not present.

She analyzed what she had heard. "It is Peralta? He moved to Base Two without notification?"

Now he looked at her. "Middle of the night, the damned fool! And that scares me." Morning air was chilly; he shivered and reached for his robe. "It's a little early, but would you like to get up and have breakfast? I—"

"Of course—you need to think aloud." She put on her own robe, went to the kitchen and started breakfast. When he came from the bathroom she took her turn there and rejoined him. Coffee was not ready, but he had poured fruit juice. He was pacing; seeing he was not yet ready to sit, she seated herself.

"Bran?—what Peralta has done—how bad is it?"

At the far end of the room, he wheeled and stopped, facing her. "That's it, you see. He hasn't done any one thing too far off course. But it's the pattern—he's telling me he's his own man, not mine. Well—peace be blown, he isn't! Oh, hell—Timar's *ambition* . . ."

"Have you a plan to deal with him?"

He shook his head. "No—only to keep my string loose, make him commit himself first, if he's going to." He looked at the stove. "Hey—everything's ready. No, sit still—I'll get it."

As he served them, she said, "I do not see what he feels he can gain at this time. His ship is not yet armed, and—"

"Ship's weapons are no use when you're on the ground side by side. But you heard Hain last night. Peralta has supernumeraries—extra manpower. For all I know, he's made himself a private army to try a takeover at Base Two." He began to eat, and Rissa thought, *The talk is helping*.

"If you were to call Limmer or Vanois, could Peralta intercept?"

"Not if we scrambled. I've set different codes for point-to-point with each ship. But—"

"Before we go there, it might be well to confer."

"We? Oh, all right—" He waved a hand. "If I left you here, you'd probably follow in the other car, anyway. But—wait a minute—I see it."

"Yes, Bran?" Yes—now he was himself again. She waited.

"Check me on this. If the status is quo, I tell Vanois and Limmer to seal ship until I say open. If he's already taken over—"

"He has not. There would be time for warning, and there has been none."

"True words. All right, then—my ships buttoned, everybody waiting. We go down there—coming in low, of course, out of Peralta's reach if he's got hold of something and juryrigged it. Now, then—what do I do?"

He was not asking advice, she knew—only for a response. "You said it yourself, Bran."

"What?" He washed food down with a swallow of coffee. "Oh, yes—make him commit himself. So—we land with *Lefthand Thread* between us and *No Return*, and go aboard fast. And then—"

"And then, Tregare, you know exactly what to do—do you not?"

"Peace knows I do! We go about our business, exactly as though Peralta still sat at One Point One. Until he makes *his* move."

THERE was more to it. Tregare called Limmer and Vanois, learned that all was quiet so far, and gave instructions. He told Deverel and Kenekke, "You both stay here today, one of you at the board at all times. If the string gets tight and I yell for help, come in the scout. Wasteful, I know, but this has to be decisive."

Deverel nodded and Tregare continued. "If you have to come, circle Base Two below the traverse angle of *any* ship's projectors, because you won't know for sure whose hands they're in. Interdict the ground completely—kill anything that moves—because unless somebody gets stupid and disobeys orders, none of them will be ours. You got it?"

"Sure have, captain," said Hain Deverel. "But I hope we don't have to do it."

"So do I—and I *think* you won't. But just-in-case is what wins arguments."

TREGARE drove the aircar south, away from his usual route. He hopped a ridge and circled back, low, hugging treetopped hills. He dropped into the crater with Limmer's ship shielding him from Peralta's, grounded quickly and taxied close to *Lefthand Thread*. As he and Rissa left the aircar, the ramp came down; it began to rise again while they still traversed it.

Inside, they climbed rapidly and found Limmer in the control room.

"Everything quiet so far?" said Tregare.

"Yes, and with Vanois, too. Your man Kenekke has us relayed through. Tandem scramble plays hell with the picture, but voice is clear enough."

"Good. Will you pipe a feed down to the galley squawk-box? I didn't have all my coffee at breakfast."

Limmer looked startled. "Sure, Tregare. But what are we going to do now?"

Tregare laughed. "Wrong question. The right one is, what's Peralta going to do—and when?" He turned to leave. "Let's let *him* make the mistakes."

THE wait lengthened. Coffee became a mere excuse; taking only occasional sips, they sat while it cooled. Once, cursing in barely audible tones, Tregare stood and paced. Rissa started to speak but he waved a hand, slammed a fist on the table, and sat again. "I know—and I will! Standing on my *head* I can outwait Jimar Peralta!" But in his face she saw strain grow.

When the intercom sounded they had waited nearly three hours. A voice said, "Tregare? Do you hear me?"

Limmer whispered, "Peralta." Tregare nodded and motioned to Limmer to answer. "Limmer speaking. Do you have a message for Captain Tregare?"

"Tregare! What the hell do you think you're doing?"

Limmer raised eyebrows in query. Tregare whispered, "Tell him I'm busy. Ask him again if he wants to leave a message." Limmer did so; Peralta merely repeated himself.

Tregare smiled; Rissa saw him relax. Speaking now in normal tones he said, "Tell Peralta that Tregare requests his company—his alone, from *No Return*—at lunch. Here, on *Lefthand Thread*. At noon, sharp." Audibly, he yawned. "I believe that's all."

As though Peralta had not heard the message, Limmer repeated it. There was silence, then Peralta's voice. "Tell him—tell Tregare—oh, all right! I'll be there."

Tregare's hand chopped air; Limmer cut the circuit, and said, "What do you think he'll do now? Should we—?"

"We do nothing. He'll come."

"Yes," said Rissa. "He is on a tight string, and you have tightened it further." She smiled. "But I expected no less of you, Bran Tregare."

PRECISELY at noon, Rissa sat at a table set for four, screened temporarily from the rest of the galley. Across from her sat Limmer, and to her right, Tregare.

Limmer looked at his watch. "He intends to make us wait."

"He won't," said Tregare. "Would you have the food served, please?"

"His, too?"

"Sure. If he eats it cold, it's his own fault."

They were well into their meal when the slim uniformed man approached; his walk gave Rissa the impression of boundless energy barely held in control. The escorting crewman said, "Here you are, Captain Peralta," and walked away.

Rissa studied the man, seeing a thin, dark face with eyes that moved constantly; his glance caught her gaze for a moment, then slid aside. *Tension drives this man—tension, and what else?*

Limmer looked up at him with his scar-drawn sneer, Tregare with no emotion at all; neither spoke. Peralta gestured. "Your courtesy lacks something. You eat before your guest arrives."

Tregare said, "My invitation was for noon; my watch reads twelve past. Was it that long a walk?"

Scowling, Peralta sat at Rissa's left. He took a bite of food. "Pah! It's cold."

"At the time specified," said Rissa, "it was served hot."

Tregare looked at her and gave his head a minute shake. "When you weren't here on time, we thought maybe you'd changed your plans. And we were hungry."

Peralta pushed his plate away "Well, I'm not—not for *this*. So eat, then." When they did, he scowled once more. "Tregare—what's this all about?"

Tregare moved his own plate, empty now, aside. "I think that's *my* question."

"What—"

"You brought your ship here at night—without permission, let alone instructions—and landed without identifying yourself. And the only word you sent *me*—by the way of Vanois—was a summons." He smiled. "I'm sure you can explain why. So start now."

"Tregare—you don't own me—"

"I own certain rights to your loyalty and the use of the ship I helped you take. It's a long time you've profited by that ship, free and clear—now I'm collecting what's due me."

Peralta leaned forward. "What you're admitting is, you need me. Well, all right—but the terms want changing."

Tregare shook his head. "What I earned and what I need may not be the same. I need the ship, yes. You? Maybe not, the way it begins to look."

"*My* ship, you're talking about, Tregare!"

Limmer chuckled; Peralta glared at him. "Tregare, this is between *us*. We don't need the gargoyle—or the woman."

Limmer's expression did not change. He stood. "I like my face better than your manners." He turned to Tregare. "Don't worry—I know how to take orders. While we're both under your command, he's safe." he walked away.

Peralta gestured toward Rissa. "I said—the woman, too."

Before Tregare could speak, she said, "I did not think to be under your command, Peralta. If you think differently, perhaps you would like to prove it."

Snorting, Peralta batted a thumb across his nose. "Everybody's brave—everybody's a hero. All right, then—stay. But keep your mouth shut so it doesn't catch anything."

Interpreting Tregare's brow-lowered glance, she did not say what she intended. Breathing deeply, she waited.

Very quietly, Tregare spoke. "If you're done bulldozing my people, Peralta, maybe we can get to what's clawing you."

"All right!" The man pointed a finger. "Command, that's what! Rightly, I'm senior between us. I realize you have a head start here, but I want a share of command and I'm going to have it!"

"No shares, Peralta—committees don't win wars. And who was senior, and what did it matter, when we got your ship for you?"

"It matters now!" Half-crouched, Peralta stood. "Tregare! Maybe you haven't noticed, but we're just the way I wanted it—you and me, one on one—and I think I can take you!''

Rissa laughed. Peralta, his concentration broken, jerked sidewise to look at her. ''You are wrong,'' she said. ''We are two to your one—not that Tregare would need my help.''

Now it was Tregare who laughed. ''Come to that, she probably wouldn't need mine, either. Didn't you hear the gossip at One Point One? About my wedding?''

Still crouching—balanced and bobbing slightly, ready to move—Peralta said, ''Something—yes—a woman beat some fat slob, both unarmed? That won't matter here. You think I'm fool enough to come without—?'' His hand brought the knife up; he half-lunged toward Tregare, then pulled back. ''You see—?''

Through the time-shock Rissa watched herself; very slowly, it seemed, her hand swung the tall coffee mug. Liquid splattered Peralta's face and chest; she caught the blade in the mug as she swept it down. She felt the jar as the heavy rim caught Peralta's hand and wrist. Then the knife clattered away and she recovered her balance. Her backhand swing—full-muscled, unrestrained—brushed his other hand aside; the base of the mug glanced off his jaw.

She fell across the table; as she pushed herself upright, the mug rolled away. She saw Peralta reel, pawing the air for balance; he stumbled against a chair and fell backward. She took the chair and raised it, a leg aimed to lunge at his throat.

Tregare caught her arm. ''Don't! It's my job, if anybody's. And we have to *try* to talk, first!''

''No!'' She saw Peralta raise a gun; she pulled free. The chair was off aim now; she twisted down with it. The legs went to either side of his head and neck, but one knocked the weapon loose, spinning away, and then the rung between them pinned Peralta's throat.

Calmer now, but still moving in slowed time, she jumped to stand on the chair—steadying herself with one hand to its back, prepared to leap in any direction. Tregare stared as Peralta bucked and kicked, gripping a chair leg in either hand but lacking leverage to free himself.

Now the man kicked both feet into the air—and again, higher. She felt the chair wobble; she reached out, ready to catch a foot and twist it if she had to jump. But Tregare moved forward; as Peralta's legs came up again, he caught each at the ankle and held them nearly vertical. "Now, then—" Rissa was surprised to see that he laughed. "—can we stop this foolishness and sit down and talk?"

Peralta cursed. Then; "Let me go! I can't breathe!"

Tregare nodded to Rissa; she stepped down. "All right—get up and behave yourself." He moved the chair away and pulled Peralta up. The man felt his neck and jaw, brushed at his clothes. He replaced his chair and sat.

For Rissa, time began to approach its normal pace.

"Damn it, woman—you didn't have to do that! I wasn't—"

"You thrust a knife at Bran Tregare. I had no choice."

"But I only *flourished* the damned thing and pulled it back."

"And the gun?"

"Just to hold you off me, was all. You had me *down*, and—"

She shook her head. "No matter, it was too late. You had triggered the—the—" She looked to Tregare. "Time slowed, you see, and my body acted."

Peralta's eyes narrowed. "Berserker! If I'd known that—"

"Not quite the same," said Tregare. "Her mind still works—but when danger triggers the reaction, she's a fighting machine that doesn't stop till it's settled. I have a little of that myself, but not trained to the peak hers is."

Peralta turned to Rissa. "I'm lucky you didn't kill me—right?"

"Thank Tregare for that—I *would* have."

"Do you still want to?"

"No, the effect is over now. Though I wonder—can Tregare afford to trust you alive?"

The man rubbed palms over cheeks and eyes. "I—I can see how you feel. I did it all wrong, didn't I? Got pressured up—you and your waiting game, Tregare—and pushed too hard, too fast." He looked at each of them. "Can we start over now, and talk?"

"Just a minute." Tregare left; when he returned with fresh coffee and mugs, Limmer accompanied him. The two sat.

"I think," said Tregare, "you two have something to settle first."

Limmer's sneer-mask hid whatever he might have felt. Peralta shook his head. "I owe you satisfaction, Limmer—if you want, you can have it. I was half-curdled with tension, but that's no excuse. Would an apology do? Either way, I owe you that."

They all waited—until Limmer said slowly, "Depends on you."

"How's that?"

"The apology suits, for now. But you buck Tregare's authority again—*any* way—I'll have you for it, then or later."

"You'd go to kill me, you mean?"

"Or let you live, maybe—but with a face like mine, or worse."

For a moment Peralta went rigid; then he breathed deeply. "All right. I apologize, Limmer. And I guess you're being fair enough, considering . . ."

"Accepted." Limmer stood. "Well, I've got work to do."

Looking after him as he walked away, Rissa said, "*I* would not wish to insult that man."

Peralta shook his head, then said, "Well, Tregare, how do we stand? If you want me off the ship, it's going to cost you. Local rumor says you're into Hulzein money, so you could buy me out fairly, shaking nothing."

Tregare paused a moment. "If that's what you want, Jimar, I think we can dicker it. But I have an offer you might like better; stop to think about it."

"Is command in it?"

"No. Forget that. Here it is—you and *No Return* follow my orders until the job's done or I free you of it—and I think you know the job I mean. Afterward you and the other shareholders have the ship to yourselves, free and clear of me." His hand forestalled Peralta's answer. "Except that if we win it all, you'll end up with a few *more* ships to your string, likely. Now—what do you say?"

Peralta chewed his lower lip. "Do I have to decide it now?"

"I'd feel better if you did." Tregare waited, then said, "But the idea's new to you—I'll give you time to think on it. Is three days enough?"

"I—yes. It'll do."

"Then—" Tregare frowned. "You started pulling hull plates yet, for the installations?"

"Waiting until we had things settled."

"Either way it needs doing; our time's limited." Now he watched Peralta closely. "One thing, though—you've got only the two choices—there's no third. You understand me?"

Head lowered, Peralta looked aside. "I—I'm not sure."

"You're not stupid, Jimar—you can't help but think, cut your losses and lift off. Well, don't try it—that's all. Or Limmer wastes a missile blowing you to dust before you leave atmosphere. I've got too much invested in that ship."

Peralta snickered. "So you'd blow it up?"

"Before I'd be robbed of it, I would."

"If you don't trust me, Tregare, maybe you *had* better buy me out."

"Trust?" Tregare shrugged. "After today, you've got to prove that. I'm just making it simpler for you."

"I see." The man rose to leave. "If I get off, you'll want my First Hat briefed. I'll tell her to expect word." He nodded once to each of them and left.

"What do you think, Rissa?"

"Buy him out, of course. He may be all right, but why risk it?"

"Why? Because he's so *damned* good in a tight passage. If I could be sure of him—"

"Well, then—*you* will decide, Bran. He only thinks the decision is his."

UPSHIP they met Limmer in Control; Tregare reported the happenings the other had missed. When he came to Rissa's part, Limmer chuckled. "I wish I'd seen that—Peralta always fancied himself a fighter."

When Tregare spoke of precaution against Peralta's absconding, Limmer turned to his controls and punched a sequence. "There. Until further notice, Number Two missile has *No Return*'s name on it. Neutron head, so we could chase ship and salvage it, though of course most of the instruments would be burned out."

At the end of his narrative, Tregare asked, "Who's Peralta's First Hat?"

"Hilaire Gowdy. I've seen her onscreen once or twice—big woman—not young, but quick-minded. I could like her, I think—*and* depend on her."

Tregare gave a lopsided grin. "You think, too, I should buy him out."

Limmer shrugged. "You said it yourself—command can't

be split. Can he keep from trying? Buy him out or kill him while you still can—that's what I'd do."

"He gets his three days." Tregare spoke flatly. "Given time to think, I doubt he's fool enough to make promises he won't keep." He shrugged. "I'd better call the scoutship. I haven't relieved my men there, from alert status."

FLYING upslope from Base Two to the cabin, Rissa said, "Bran, you say command cannot be divided—but you *do* confer with your people."

"Oh, sure—when I have time for it I ask advice and I listen—any man does who isn't a fool. But then *I* decide. And it's that last part Peralta wants a bite of."

"I see. Others may have their chance to persuade you, but if they do not—"

"You've got it."

"Yes." She thought, then nodded. "It was the same with Erika—and now with Liesel."

Back to the cabin and inside, Tregare sat brooding. Finally Rissa said, "Bran? Does this problem worry you so much?"

He shook his head. "It's not that. Oh, some, sure. But what's got me down is the way Jimar has *changed*. I'd heard rumors—which is why I took the precautions—but I hadn't really credited the stories." Looking up at her, he said, "He's always had ambition to burn, but back at the Slaughterhouse, Peralta was one of the fairest cadet officers we had. I never thought the day would come, when I couldn't trust that man behind my back."

"He was your friend, then?"

"Not quite that, maybe. But sure's hell he had my respect—and deserved it."

She put her hand on his. "Then let us hope he still does."

"Hope, yeah." But Tregare brightened up a little, and could talk of other matters.

IN the morning, Rissa proposed a schedule for her work on *No Return*. Tregare answered her. "Until I've settled with Peralta, you and I stay together at all times on that ship. I know it'll slow things down but—" He waved away her protest. "This is as much for my safety as for yours."

And when they met with Limmer, before going to *No Return*, Tregare told him, "We do *all* the preparatory work first, before any weapons go aboard. Get them unpacked, but keep them groundside. Until I'm sure of Peralta one way or the other, that ship stays unarmed."

Rissa spoke. "But you said—in this situation, all landed side by side—that ships' weapons are of no use."

Tregare grinned. "Yes. But you see, I've thought of a way —given a couple of working turrets and maybe a missile—I could lift that ship with a good chance of getting free. And if *I* see it—maybe Jimar does, too. I wouldn't bet against it."

Peralta, when they boarded *No Return*, was cool and polite. Inspecting the drawings, he demurred at Rissa's plan to remove half the forward beams and brace the remainder with a ring of girders. "Or at least," he said, "hold off until we know for sure that there'll be time for such extensive work and still meet deadline—whenever *that* is."

Rissa frowned—Peralta's objection was not logical and would make the work more difficult—but seeing Tregare's gaze on her, she did not speak. When the two went upship alone, she marked to her plan anyway. Tregare raised his eyebrows but did not object. And later, walking from Peralta's ship to Limmer's, he said to her, "Notice the bulkhead seals just below the open-hull area? Not standard, and all new. Sure as peace, he's thought of the same trick I did!"

Peralta joined them and Limmer for lunch. He protested the delay in initial weapons installations. Tregare said, "It looks slower, but we get fewer mistakes with all crews working at the same stage of the job. We learned that on *Carcharodon*." Rissa thought, *When he wants to be, Tregare is a good liar.*

THE next day, work proceeded smoothly. "Too *damned* smooth, in fact," Tregare said at dinner one evening. "I've got Limmer accidentally mislaying some parts and supplies, to stall the job until Peralta has to make up his mind." But Jimar Peralta showed no signs of doing so.

The day before Tregare's ultimatum was to expire, he and Rissa stayed away from Base Two. He sent Deverel and

Kenekke instead, and spent most of the day in the scoutship.
At mid-morning Rissa joined him there; he sat at the control
console, drumming one hand's fingers against its edge.

He grinned up at her. "The only good thing is, I already
know I can outwait him. But it's no fun."

"Why do you think it best that we are not there today?"

"Peralta's boiling with alternatives. If he could reach me
directly—I've deactivated his scramble channel here—he
couldn't help but try them on me. But he can't talk without
Limmer's hearing what he says, so he can say only yes or no.
For me, Rissa, that insult was a lucky thing."

"You know the man better than I." They sat together,
speaking occasionally but not often. At noon Rissa brought
food from the cabin and they lunched; then she left him to his
vigil and walked for a time to ease her own tensions. In late
afternoon, as she approached the cabin again, she saw him
emerge from the scoutship.

He waved and shouted, "It's over." When she was in
speaking range he said, "Peralta leaves the ship tomorrow;
Hain and Anse are bringing his signed agreement. He didn't
even ask much more than his share was worth—just enough so
we could dicker a little and both save face."

She ran to him; his arms tightened around her and lifted her
off the ground as they kissed. He set her back on her feet, and
she said, "Now—tomorrow—we can do the work as it should
be done!"

"Sure, but right now let's celebrate!" They started toward
the cabin; from above came thunder.

"BRAN?" But he was running for the scout; she followed. Inside she found him at the comm panel, grinning and talking
rapidly.

"Jargy, you old goat! Why didn't you call in sooner?"

The picture wavered; the voice came quiet and deliberate.
"Not sure who ran the place these days, Tregare—three ships
at Two and none of them *Inconnu*. Thought I'd wait for a hail
before putting down."

Tregare nodded. "Sure. But shouldn't you go to the port
first, and refuel?"

"No need. I hijacked a fuel pod in space not long ago. Just

topped off from it—emptied and jettisoned it a few hours ago.''

"Good enough. Hold a minute? And listen in." Leaving the circuit open he called *Lefthand Thread* and told Limmer where to place a landing marker.

"All clear, Jargy?" The streaked image nodded. "Fine; set her down, then. I don't think you and Limmer know each other, but a bottle or two will take care of that."

"I'm sure." Then; "You're not at Two, Tregare?"

"No. At the cabin—remember? But we'll be down in the morning."

"Good. Then—" Hoad paused, looking to one side before facing the screen again. "Hold it a minute. Got a passenger who wants to talk with you."

"Passenger?" Another person moved into view. Almost, looking over Tregare's shoulder, Rissa could recognize the wavering face.

The man spoke. "Tregare? In case you can't see me any better than I can see you, I'm Osallin, from Far Corner. And I'd like to ask how it's fared with Tari Obrigo who shipped with you from that planet."

Before Tregare could answer, Rissa pushed beside him to the screen. "Osallin! We *do* meet again! But how—?"

He laughed, and now she knew him. "If you're still with the alleged brigand, my concern was probably needless. Unless . . .''

"Bran Tregare is now my husband, and his dark deeds have been somewhat exaggerated. Though for a time . . ." She gasped, then laughed at Tregare's gentle pinch below her ribs. "But you, Osallin—how is it that *you* are here?"

She could see the shrug he made. "UET was nosing too close to me; time was short. So when *Deuces Wild* landed, I pulled the chain."

"I do not understand."

"Standard practice, Tari. For UET's benefit, my chief business rival—Kirchessel, his name is—pulled a coup and wiped me out, possibly killing me in the process. Did a lovely job of bombing my office to destroy the evidence—after my own boodle was safely out and packed for boarding, of course."

"This Kirchessel is, then, your friend?"

"*And* successor as Hulzein agent on Far Corner. As I said, Tari—standard practice, though of course with misleading variations. Now the codes you've been using to me are valid until you change to the new ones I've brought you. And—"

Rissa leaned forward. "Is there word from Earth, from Erika?"

Now he laughed again. "Ah, *is* there, though? You won't believe what she's been up to—no, I can't tell *that* over a circuit. But I have it all here. It's true I shouldn't know about it myself, but I'm a code expert with incorrigible curiosity, so I do know. But you'll see—tomorrow you'll see."

"I shall look forward to that. And to seeing *you*, Osallin."

They ended their talk; Tregare and Jargy Hoad exchanged a few more remarks and signed off. Leaving the scout, Tregare said, "Five ships, Rissa! Only one to go, and Hawkman's dickering for *Valkyrie*! Let's *really* celebrate—dinner with Hain and Anse when they get here, but wine and love beforehand!" She laughed and they went into the cabin.

THEY were still in bed, he reaching across her to refill his wineglass, when they heard the aircar. He sat up. "They're late. I'd forgotten the time—it's almost dark." Then; "Something's wrong with that car—it shouldn't be so noisy."

He crawled over her, out of bed, and went to the door. As he opened it a few inches, she saw him reach under the leather flap and bring out the energy gun; then he dove flat to the floor. A hissing, tearing sound came—the door jounced partly open to slam against his head and shoulder, and smoke boiled from its center.

From outside came more smoke; Tregare got to his knees and leaned his weight against the door, closing it. He threw the locking lever, then scuttled toward her on hands and knees. One hand still held the gun; the other tugged at her arm.

"Down out of there! Here—behind the bed—for now."

She rolled out and joined him on the floor. "What *is* it?"

"Peralta! Peace knows what he's done with my men, but he's got the aircar!" The sound came again; wood charred and fell away from the door, exposing red-hot metal.

"But, Tregare—what does *that*?"

"Ship's projector—it's got to be! Lucky he doesn't have

ship's power—this whole place would be vapor and us with it. How he ever got the car off the ground—that's what sounded wrong—he's overloaded past all safe limits.''

Once more the ear-rending noise. The door's center blazed white; molten metal erupted, and for seconds a blinding beam charred wood beside the kitchen entrance. Tregare leaped to the door and gave a piercing scream; over his shoulder he said, ''Let him think he hit somebody!''

Then; ''Rissa! The pillbox—get there fast—and get Peralta!'' He ducked and moved to the side window. ''I can see him here, at an angle.'' He fired, blowing the double panes out. ''Now maybe I can keep him in the car until you get there. Then I'll try to lure him out. But if I can't, the car's expendable.'' He moved toward the rear of the window, aimed, and fired. ''Get back in there, Jimar! Wait until you're invited!'' And to Rissa; ''Move! If I give three quick shots or he gets out of the car, hit him with both barrels.''

She was already moving, time-sense slowed to agonizing pace. Swing the tub, push the release—she ignored the ladder and dropped to land with knees bent, catching balance with hands to ground. The jar hurt her feet but she ran—blinded by darkness, one hand brushing the wall for guidance. When the hand lost contact, she stopped and felt for the access shaft and climbed to the dimly lit pillbox.

She swung the twin projectors, still locked together, to cover the aircar, then looked to see her target better. The car's front was torn away; the projector jutted from a ragged opening. It shot a flare of ionization—Peralta was still inside. Melted plastic splashed from the car—Tregare held stalemate. The cabin wall smoldered in several places—Peralta looking for a weak point?

Cabin and aircar exchanged shots. Peralta's flare seemed slightly weaker—power running low? Still the man did not leave the aircar, nor did Tregare give her the signal.

The firing ceased. She held her aim on the shadow, dimly seen through blackened plastic, that was Peralta. Nothing moved.

Then the aircar inched forward; she tracked the motion. It turned slightly toward her, then away again, approaching the cabin from a changed angle. As it turned, Peralta fired.

He has Tregare pinned against the wall!

Only when the smoking corpse, haloed with blobs of molten plastic, toppled from the aircar, did she realize she had fired.

WITHOUT conscious thought she jumped—slid—down the ladder. Which way to turn? Yes. She ran along the tunnel and climbed, breathless, up the shaft. Memory found the latch for her; the trapdoor lifted and she pulled herself up.

She saw Tregare—*he is alive!*—rubbing something onto his right side. She ran to him but he turned sidewise, his left hand half holding her and half fending her off. They kissed; she pulled back to look at him, but had to wipe tears away to see him clearly.

"Oh, Bran! I was afraid I was not in time!"

He handed her an open jar of orange salve. "Here—you can reach it better," and she saw the angry burns on his right arm and side. He smiled at her grimace of concern. "It's not serious—just painful as hell until we get the gloop on it. Hey—gently, now!"

She smoothed the odd-smelling stuff over and around the burns. He said, "This is just from side flash—the beam dissipates in air and I caught the losses." His left hand touched her cheek. "You caught on that he was swinging to pin me, didn't you? I fired the three shots, all right, but his heavier beam drowned them so you couldn't see. Anyway, you got him in time—and I was moving up to the corner, beside the door, so he couldn't have got a direct hit without backing and turning some more."

She stood holding the jar; he took it and gave her a towel for her hands. "Come on—let's get to the scout and find out what happened at Base Two."

THE smoking projector effectively blocked the doorway; they could not pass without burning themselves. Tregare went to the blasted window and dropped to the ground; Rissa followed. She said, "I am afraid I ruined your aircar."

Tregare barely glanced at the smoldering remains. "We can get another. And except for the wiring, maybe salvage the projector." He led the way into the scoutship and called Limmer on scramble. On the screen, the man's scarred face appeared.

"Tregare? Thank peace, you're all right! Peralta—?"

"Medium well done, I'd guess." He motioned toward Rissa. "*She* got him for me. Now what in hell's name happened down there?"

"Peralta signed the agreements right here before me—your men were here, too. Then he and they went offship. Not long after, you called. I went out and marked site for Hoad's landing and came back aboard. The next I knew, a lot of Peralta's people poured off *No Return*, armed—killing or capturing anyone they could find of mine and Vanois's. I sealed ship and so did Raoul—I saw his ramp go up—but all I know of *Carcharodon* is that it hasn't been taken. We don't have scramble except through you, and I couldn't raise you—so we haven't said much in *No Return*'s hearing.

"I did warn Hoad, in clear, but Peralta's men had already boarded him. There was a hell of an explosion over that way, a little later—"

Rissa gasped. *Osallin?* "—and then Peralta loaded the projector on your aircar and took off with it."

"What about my men—do you know? And what's the situation *now*?"

"Deverel and Kenekke?" Limmer shook his head. "I'm sorry, Tregare—I don't know. And the setup here is that Peralta's soldiers hold groundside against us; we're bottled up. Do you want us to try a sortie?"

Tregare did not hesitate. "Anything but that—stay sealed. Wait a minute—" He paused. "Is groundside lit up? Who controls the area lighting?"

"Vanois. Remember—he ran circuits so he could move supplies at night without having to go to your powerhouse every time. You want me to—?"

"I'll call him. Now—you have people armed and ready—right? But don't move until I give the word."

Limmer agreed; Tregare cut the circuit and called Vanois. The story was roughly the same. Tregare spoke briefly, concluding, "I'll be calling in the clear, so when I want groundside lit I'll just say, '*Hit it*.' Between now and then, cut it all dark." Vanois acknowledged; Tregare tried to call *Deuces Wild*, but received no answer. He shook his head and turned to the flight controls.

Putting concern for Osallin out of her mind, Rissa said,

"Bran? What do you intend?"

"Same as I told Hain and Anse a few days ago—take this scout down there and kill everyone that's outside a ship. It's not a thing I like, but they've left me no other way."

"Might you not better wait for daylight?"

"Can't afford to give them that much time to hit Limmer and Vanois."

"Yes, I see—but I have a thought."

He looked at her. "Go ahead—I'm listening."

"They must not know whether you are alive—but what if *I* call, and see who speaks for *No Return* and what is said to me?"

After a moment he grinned. "Here—I'll set up the call."

Rissa waited, then recognized Hilaire Gowdy, *No Return*'s First Hat. The woman's face and voice showed tension. "Well, I see *you're* alive, Ms. Tregare. What's happened?"

Rissa shook her head. "No—we speak of what has happened where you are."

Gowdy's throat moved, swallowing. "If Peralta wins, you ask me to speak my own death." Rissa wanted to reassure her, but did not need Tregare's headshake to advise against it. She waited.

Gowdy shrugged. "This much, then. Jimar took his armed force offship and controls groundside. There's been killing—I don't know how much. I've sealed ship; I now control *No Return*. When I open it again, and to whom—that depends on what's said to me—by you, by Peralta, or others."

Tregare stood out of screen's view; Rissa looked to him, but he gave no sign. To Gowdy she said, "I tell you only this—keep sealed until you yourself are convinced it is right to open."

"There's no choice for me, is there?" Hilaire Gowdy nodded. "All right—agreed."

Rissa cut the circuit and looked to Tregare. He said, "That was well done. Now buckle in—we're hitting Base Two."

THE scoutship, Rissa learned, was not a vehicle for comfort. Takeoff was harsh—accelerations, turning or otherwise, stretched her body's tolerance. Tregare took the scout high, then coasted downward and slanting toward the crater. Rissa said, "What if Hain and Anse are caught outside with Peralta's gunmen?"

He shook his head. "I have to go with the odds—they could be dead, or captive and under cover. If I don't assume that, I can't act at all."

Before she could speak he said, "Hold it!" and lit the screen.

"Vanois?" The bearded face appeared, the head nodded. "Get ready! In two minutes—*hit it!*" The screen went dark.

Looking ahead, Rissa could see nothing except shadows of hills below. "Tregare! When the lights come on suddenly, we will be blinded."

"No. Five seconds ahead I put on dark goggles and coast blind. Here's a pair for you." She fumbled and found his hand.

"But how could you have thought ahead, for *this*?"

"I didn't. They have other uses—that's what I thought of. Now get ready—and brace yourself—this kite hasn't even *started* to ride rough, yet."

First tensed, then deliberately relaxing, she waited. The scout coasted smoothly. Then, as the ground ahead sprang into brilliant illumination, it swung to one side and all orientation was lost. Four ships grew in her view, rotated, and shot off to one side as forces crushed her first in one direction, then another. Ground rushed to strike her—four towers ahead—ground washed in flame as the towers, the ships, passed on either side within grazing range and the surface again fell away. Sidewise pressure as Tregare turned the scout; he said, "Good pass—I got their main group. The rest'll be disorganized; I can take my time now."

Diving again, slower and with less gyration, he raked the ground once more with flame. And again, and again—each time, she realized, less wary of retaliation. Then after two passes when he held his fire, Tregare circled high to inspect the area.

"Time to land, I think," and the scout dropped.

He came near to hitting *Lefthand Thread* as he landed, in line with *Carcharodon* on the other side. He picked up the energy gun—Rissa had not noticed he had brought it—and said, "Now let's see who's on the reception committee."

The ship's ramp came down; at the top, holding a gun,

stood Limmer. Rissa saw no movement elsewhere. "Bran—shall we go?"

After a moment he nodded. "Anybody that's left, sure as peace isn't organized. Let's *move*."

As they reached groundside a man, coming from behind *Carcharodon*, ran toward them. Tregare's gun swung toward him—so did Limmer's. Then Rissa shouted. *"No!"* and pulled at Bran's weapon. "It's Osallin!"

Limmer had fired once, but the steep downward angle sent his shot high. Now he raised the gun and waved it. "Sorry! I didn't know . . ."

Now Rissa ran to meet her friend; she saw blood on his face, but even with a slight limp he moved briskly. They met, embraced.

"Osallin, it's so *good*— I was afraid—are you all right?"

"Yes, Tari—a half dozen of us fought our way groundside, got clear just before the blowup. The others—" He shook his head. "I don't know. We got separated."

His one hand held an envelope. "Here—I told you—Erika . . ." Then he looked past her. *"Sniper!"* He pushed her headlong to the ground. Above her she heard the hissing crash of an energy gun—then, nearer to hand, another one, and the bark of Limmer's projectile weapon. Dazed for a moment, she listened to the ringing silence that followed. Slowly she rolled and came to her feet.

Heat rose from Tregare's gun. "Got the bastard," he said, "or Limmer did—maybe both of us. But your friend . . ."

Osallin lay on his side, face turned upward, one leg twitching rhythmically. Rissa knelt beside him. "Osallin—are you . . .?"

His smile was quiet; he could have been resting. But then she saw the cords standing out in his neck, and looked closer to see the charred smoking circle low on the right side of his abdomen. She gasped—energy guns!—there would be a matching circle on his back, and between them . . .

"No pain yet," he said. "But soon—can you free my arm? It's pinned under me, and there's something—"

Gently she worked the arm loose for him; his hand still held the envelope, now charred at one corner. "Here," and she took it. "Now, then—" While he talked, his fingers worked at the flap of his shirt collar. "I'm afraid the ship—*Deuces*

Wild—is a dead loss. Rather than let the attackers have it, Hoad blew the drive."

"No," said Tregare. "If he'd done that, every ship here would be knocked flat."

Osallin worked a small pellet free of the collar flap and waved his hand. "All right—not blown in a spacer's meaning, but melted to slag. The exciter, when it runs wild—"

"Yes, I know! Peralta—that peacefouler's cost me a *ship*!" Then Tregare, too, looked closely at Osallin. "But I'll worry about that later." He stepped back.

Rissa looked at him as Osallin said, "Aren't you going to look at Erika's report?"

"I—I will do that later, also. There will be time."

Osallin nodded. "Then you know. Ah, I wish . . ." He brandished the pellet. "When the pain—you won't stop me?"

"Osallin! Is there *no* chance?" She did not cry with lungs or body, but tears ran down her cheeks.

"With *this*?" He gestured toward his mutilated side. "I know some anatomy, Tari."

"In—in this place, Osallin, my true name is safe."

He smiled again. "I'm glad . . . Rissa. Did you ever know my first name? It's Bret."

"Bret." She moved to take his hand—then, seeing fear in his face, clasped the shoulder instead. She shook her head. "No, Bret Osallin—I would not interfere. I only—"

"Of course. I should have known. Hold my hand, then, until . . ."

She did; for a while they spoke. Then he said, "It's time. I don't care to scream." Squatting on her heels, she leaned to kiss him, and kept her hand to his cheek as he put the pellet in his mouth and bit through it. For a moment his smile stretched to grimace; then the features slacked into repose. He gasped once and did not breathe again.

TASTING salt tears, Rissa sat until Tregare's hand on her shoulder recalled her to present needs. "Rissa—there could be other snipers. Limmer and I have been eyeballing the perimeter, but that's no guarantee. We'd better—"

"Yes, of course." She stood; they walked toward *Lefthand Thread*.

"You going to read your report from Erika?"

She opened the envelope. In the glare of lights she looked at the enclosure and shook her head.

"What's the matter?"

"The corner that's burned away, Bran—that was the introductory code group, the key. Without it there is no way I can decode this report."

"But—peace take us! It could be *important!*"

She shrugged. "There will be other reports, Bran—but never another Osallin."

"No—nor another Jargy Hoad. He was . . ."

"But you do not yet know that he is dead."

"If he killed his ship—and he did—he went with it."

For the rest of the way they were silent. Then, up the ramp and inside—Limmer sealed ship, the two in turn shook hands with him—Rissa turned to Tregare. "Bran? We forgot to clothe ourselves."

He laughed—shuddering, a release of tension. "I could've used bandages—the damned harness rubbed me raw." He turned to Limmer. "Can you fix me up? I guess we could use robes, too."

"Sure, captain. Follow me, you both?"

TREGARE robed and bandaged, Rissa wearing a coverall, they sat with Limmer to a belated evening meal. For a few minutes he left them. Returning, he said, "*Deuces Wild* is dead, all right—and Hoad with it, and all his officers. Some crew survived—a couple of dozen, about—after they wiped out Peralta's contingent."

Limmer sat, and continued. "Groundside's buttoned up pretty well—enough that my crew and Raoul's have started piling the dead ones far enough away to burn tomorrow without stinking us out, here."

Rissa half-stood. "No—not Osallin!"

Limmer's brows raised; then he shook his head. "I wish I'd thought. I should have, I suppose—but so many of our own, too, and all we can *do* is get rid of them. I'm sorry."

Before Rissa could answer, Tregare said, "What about the wounded?"

"Our medics are doing what they can. Now then—there's still a few stragglers skulking around the outskirts, but no sniping. What's your pleasure there, captain?''

Tregare said, "Put somebody on the squawkbox—announce amnesty for any that surrender." He took a last bite of food, chewed and swallowed it before asking, "Any word of my men?"

"A squad of Peralta's—holed up in the south warehouse—claim to have them and some others as hostages. They're demanding terms you won't like."

Tregare's hand chopped air. "Then don't tell me. Can you put me through to them?"

Limmer nodded, and punched buttons on the intercom. "Can't guarantee a good connection, but try it."

"All right." Tregare moved to the unit. "You in the warehouse—this is Tregare. Do you hear me?" Faintly, barely audible over shouts of insult and defiance, they heard a "yes."

Tregare's mouth formed a snarl. He said, "You can listen to me and maybe live, or keep yelling from empty heads until I find time to kill you. It's your choice." After a few scattered cries, silence answered him. "All right—that's a start. Peralta's dead—and, if you haven't noticed, so are most of your groundside gunmen. Now—here are my terms—

"Put all weapons outside and let my people come in. I hear you have hostages. You'll be permitted to live in the proportion that *they're* alive. Unless you try resistance—in that case you all die!"

He beat his fist against the table. "Make no mistake—I've had enough of this! Now—what do you say?"

There was sound of confusion—hubbub—then a voice spoke. "There was a dozen of us got cut off in here. And ten hostages—two died, but not by us—they were wounded and we've got no medics. We lost three of our own that way, too. Where does that leave us?" A pause, then the voice added, "Peralta didn't give us much choice, you know."

Before Tregare could answer, Rissa stepped forward. "May I speak with Hain Deverel or Anse Kenekke?"

"Who? Just a minute—oh, you mean Tregare's men. Yeah, they're here." Less distinctly, as though turned away from the intercom, the voice said, "You, there—the one that's not hurt—come answer the woman."

Then; "Kenekke here. Hain's not walking so good but he'll be all right. Instructions, captain?"

Tregare said, "You're in charge, Anse. Get all weapons jettisoned outdoors, then line up Peralta's troops—to our right, as we come in. Our people to the left. You stay at the box; if there's any loose-stringing tried, give a yell. But if that man told the truth about the casualties, I'm killing no one. Got it?"

"Right, skipper." Tregare set the intercom to receive-only.

"Limmer—how soon can you have a team over there?"

"Right away. I held one landing party in reserve. Back in a minute." When he had left, Tregare turned to Rissa.

"Shakes well, do you think?"

"Yes, Bran—I see no mistakes."

"Good. Now let me check with Vanois." Using the channel through Limmer's control room relay he reached *Carcharodon*; questions and answers were brief. "All right, Raoul," Tregare concluded, "stay buttoned a little longer and keep *No Return's* ramp covered until you hear from me."

He turned to Rissa. "Now comes the big one." Throwing two switches, he spoke into the unit. There was a pause; then a voice answered.

"Gowdy speaking. This is a savage night, Tregare."

"Not by my choosing."

"I suppose not. Well, what do you want of me?"

"What do you offer?"

"Peralta's dead, isn't he? For you to be alive, he has to be. All right—I'll open my ship to you and meet you groundside, with as many or few of us as you decide—none armed, of course."

"And aboard—how many are armed?"

"All were. But we had a skirmish here—a nasty one—and all Peralta's side are dead or locked up. I'll empty the ship totally, if you like. And hostages—me included—can precede you when you board."

"Gowdy—why do you offer so much?"

"We've both had our fill of treachery. I offer only what *I'd* ask, in your place."

As though she could see him, he nodded. "I accept. Wait while I clear it with Vanois—he's covering your ramp. When he puts a spotlight on it, it's safe to come out."

Quickly he called *Carcharodon* and confirmed the arrangement. When Limmer returned, Tregare borrowed trousers and shoes. Then, to Rissa, he said, "Do you want to come along?"

"Do you think I would stay behind?"

• • •

RISSA had seen Hilaire Gowdy occasionally but had exchanged only a few words with her. Now she watched the tall, heavily built woman walk down the ramp and approach. Her crew—what was left of it—lined up alongside the ship, hands held in plain view. Limmer's men moved down the line, searching them.

Not merely heavy, the woman was badly overweight. Beside the large, hooked nose her cheeks bulged. Her graying red hair—curly, an untamed mop—she pushed back with one hand; she reached the other out to shake Tregare's. "Captain, I'd better explain my position—then you can decide."

"All right. Where do you want to start?"

"With Escape, when you helped us take the ship. Then and after, my loyalty was Peralta's. Not yours—only *he* swore that. So although I knew some of his plans, I couldn't tell you."

"Some of them?"

With no indication of humor, the woman grinned. "He planned every way he could think of—and kept changing his mind. First—to get a couple of working turrets and take off with men in suits manning them, to disable Limmer's weapons before he could get us. Then you held the projectors back—spotted the bulkhead seals, I expect. I told him you probably would."

Rissa looked to Tregare. "That was the trick you thought of?" He nodded.

Gowdy continued. "A couple of other ideas, he'd have needed help with—he sure wouldn't have got it from Limmer or Vanois, so he dropped those. Until today, I really thought he was going to play it fair—and I think maybe *he* did, too."

She frowned. "But this morning he got with the bunch we picked up on Tweedle. I knew something was up but he wouldn't say what. Then all hell popped, groundside, and he tore up your aircar to load the projector and power pack. He barely made it off the ground with that load—damned near crashed on the first ridge."

She clasped her hands together, moving one over the other. "I didn't know what to do. I locked myself in the control room to think. Then I decided my oath wasn't binding—not to a man who was breaking his own. So I tried to call you—not to say exactly what he was doing, but just to get away from there, and that here wasn't safe either. But it didn't matter—scrambled *or* clear, I couldn't reach you."

"Not your fault—your scramble was turned off, my end. And—hell, I forgot to switch the clear channels into the cabin!"

"I see." She turned to Rissa. "When *you* called, I figured Jimar for dead, but I couldn't be sure. If he'd killed Tregare, you see, there could be a catfight—him and Limmer and Vanois. Or the whole thing just break up, everybody going separate ways. And there I sat—ship unarmed and its nose torn open—and Limmer ready to put a missile in me if I tried to lift. So I *couldn't* commit myself to anything—not then."

"And now?" said Rissa.

"If he—Tregare, if you'll have me in your command, I'm your person, and *No Return* is your ship."

"One thing first," said Tregare. "I killed Jimar." Rissa turned to him; he grasped her shoulder. "I gave the order—I'm responsible. I want to know how you feel about that, Hilaire."

She shook her head. "He was out to kill you; there's no blame. If you mean my personal feelings, it's a long time since Jimar and I were lovers. He turned to younger women when we were still with UET and I wasn't fat. We stayed friends, but that's all. He didn't give me First Hat as any favor—I *earned* it."

"All right." Tregare nodded and reached to her. "Shake hands on it, then—Captain Gowdy."

Before speaking, the woman wiped her eyes. "Thanks, Tregare. If you want to come upship, we can scan the roster and I'll tell you who's safe to trust. Except for these here and six locked up inside, I don't know who's still alive, but—"

"Yes," Tregare said, "Let's do that." The new captain turned and started up the ramp; Tregare and Rissa followed.

Low-voiced, she said, "Have you thought, what if the ones aboard are *not* locked up?"

He shook his head. "Gowdy's not Peralta, and you heard her estimate of his earlier chances. Besides, I trust her."

"And I, too—but I like to make sure of such things."

He squeezed her hand but said nothing more. Looking up, she was surprised that Hilaire Gowdy, fat and all, was climbing at good speed. And when they reached Control, the big woman's breathing was slow and even. She sat at a desk and began to spread out the roster sheet.

"One thing, Tregare—none of my say-so, but I'm curious— what happens to those you can't trust? There's been a lot of killing."

"I agree. No—I'll just leave them here—on the planet, I mean, not Base Two. The local economy's always short of common labor, Hilaire."

The woman nodded. "Good. I wouldn't have liked it, having to point my finger and know I was making death. Well, let's get to it."

When the list—with the known dead marked off—had been divided into "yes" and "no," Tregare called Limmer for a casualty report. He copied the figures, said his thanks, and cut the circuit. He looked up from the paper. "I'm surprised—except for a handful of Peralta's ground force, he's accounted for the lot. Well, not the losses on *Deuces Wild*—all we know there is who survived. Let's see those lists again."

He crossed off more names, then counted. "Limmer and Vanois aren't so bad off. But what with the dead and the unreliables—your six and the warehouse nine are all I know of those, that still live—*No Return*'s shorthanded as hell, even if you get all that's left of Jargy Hoad's crew. We're in trouble."

Hilaire Gowdy rubbed her forehead. "The worst is, Tregare—several of those fifteen could be all right; Peralta stampeded some, I know. But we can't tell which—we'd have to take chances."

He shook his head. "No more chances, Gowdy. I—"

Rissa interrupted. "Tregare! There is a way. We should have done it sooner—oh, I am stupid! So many lives—"

Brows raised, he looked at her. "What are you talking about?"

"I have not told you? No. Well—before I challenged dal Nardo—that morning I spoke with his supervisor, Arni Gustafson. And she questioned me under a truth field, though she did not know I recognized it."

He nodded. "I've heard of those. If UET had them when I was a kid, I'd never have lived to get off Earth. But the trouble is, *we* don't have one."

"I will call her—ask if the equipment can be moved—if we may borrow it. Or if not, we might use it where it is."

"How in the name of peace do I transport that many people across the Big Hills in aircars? I'd be all month at it."

"For you to be *certain* of your people, might it not be worth it to lift a ship across and back, once?"

While he considered, Gowdy spoke. "She's right, Tregare. And I'd feel better if you put me through it, too."

Sidelong he looked at her. "More for your peace of mind than mine, I'll do that—if we get the use of the thing." Yawning, he stretched, then winced. "The burns are acting up. Too much work to unwrap and salve again. I need a pill and some sleep."

"Take Peralta's quarters—the woman who shared them is one of the six locked up. Knowing Jimar, you can be sure of full security."

"All right; thanks. A few chores first." He called the other ships and verified that Deverel and Kenekke were informed and well quartered. Then he and Rissa followed Gowdy to Peralta's stateroom. When she had gone, he inspected the console of monitors and control overrides, more than twice the size of his similar installation on *Inconnu*. He shook his head.

"He could fly the ship from here, or near to it. Rissa—if I'd only seen this before—I'd have *known* he couldn't possibly give up command." He yawned again. "Help me off with this robe?"

As she did so, she said, "Bran? Will you have to grieve for the man who was once your friend, or close to that?"

"Grieve? I don't know. I can't let it out, the way you do —yes, Sparline told me. But in spite of everything that happened, for a long time I'll feel—sad, I guess." His mouth twitched, then tightened. "Such a waste, such a damned waste! And Jimar was a man who always *hated* waste."

A few minutes later, with the room darkened, Rissa heard his breathing deepen into sleep. It was some time before she could free her mind of all that had happened—*and Osallin is dead!*—and relax enough to follow his lead.

NEXT morning Limmer brought the lockbox from Osallin's cabin on *Deuces Wild*. The combination had not been set; the box opened at her touch. While Tregare still slept, Rissa scanned Erika's formal reports; she found the amount of forwarded profits to be greater than she had expected. Osallin's commission, she decided, must be forwarded to his successor. She looked for the new codes he had mentioned and found them. She made an entry in Osallin's notebook so that when next she visited Hulzein Lodge, she would handle the matter in routine fashion.

Now she came to the packets containing Osallin's own portable assets, and frowned. Who did these now belong to? She leafed through them and pursed her lips—the total was nearly 20,000,000 Weltmarks; she had not thought Osallin to operate on such a scale. Then she saw the note—a bold, hasty scribble—on the back of one envelope.

> Tari Obrigo: There's fighting aboard—some kind of attack—I have to go help. People can get killed that way, so—if I do, what's in here is yours. I have no one else—relatives on Earth are sixty years ago, I'd guess. And I know you'll use the boodle, if it comes to you, the same as I would. To fight UET!

The signature was a huge scrawl, underlined.

Rissa nodded; on this basis she could accept the money without qualms. Another 20,000,000 in UET stock—why not? And now she sat and thought of Osallin the man, her first friend off Earth. She waited for crippling pangs of grief to strike, for in a way his death was her doing—and he had saved her own life. But all she felt was a deep, gentle sadness—a longing wish that he could be alive. Again she nodded. "I will miss him; that is all."

When Tregare woke, Rissa could see that he was irritable from pain, but for the most part he concealed it well. They breakfasted with Gowdy; Limmer and Vanois attended also, and Tregare set out his new work plan for arming *No Return*.

Kenekke and Deverel—the latter aiding his bandaged right leg with a crutch—met them at the scoutship. "Good to see you both up and around," said Tregare. "Sorry I can't say the same for the aircar at Base One. Peralta shot the cabin up pretty well, too—but stopgap repairs shouldn't take too long."

Deverel grinned. "Same for me, captain—I heal fast." Tregare and Kenekke helped him into the scout, seated and harness fastened. He looked up at Rissa. "Ms. Kerguelen—I hear it was you that got Peralta. Is that right?"

"Tregare stayed and kept Peralta pinned in the aircar. He gave me the safer task—manning the projectors at the pill-box."

Deverel gripped her hand. "Sure—just to keep you out of trouble. Not because he could depend on you—nothing like that."

Surprisingly, she felt embarrassment. "Stop it, Hain—or I will kick you, and you will have *two* sore legs." He laughed; she seated herself and strapped in.

"If you clowns are done performing, I'll lift this thing." Tregare's words were light, but his voice showed strain. Well above the burned area, Rissa touched his shoulder.

"Only a little longer, Bran, and I can dress your arm and side again."

"Sure. But right now I wish somebody else here was checked out to fly this beast." He applied power and the scout lifted; he winced at the pressure of acceleration and made the climbing turn gradually, to clear the next higher ridge. Seeing his jaws clench, Rissa did not speak.

When finally he topped the edge of Base One's plateau, Tregare tilted the scout into a drifting, sidewise descent. Suddenly his hand shook and the scoutship bucked and faltered. Cursing, he lifted it and tried again. Now he attempted no finesse, but slewed the vehicle across to its landing spot and brought it down in jarring, irregular bursts of deceleration. It touched at an angle and wobbled, but came to rest upright.

"Horses' leavings!" He shook his head. "When I was fifteen I'd have been flogged for that landing!"

"Bran—" She touched his forehead; he was feverish. "Let us go inside and tend your burns. Anse—make Hain comfortable? Then—in half an hour, perhaps—let us confer as to how we can clear the aircar away from the cabin."

Kenekke stood, looking at the car's remains. "Peace at the gates! You sure did a job on it!"

"There was no choice—I will tell you later. Come, Bran." She helped him to rise and leave the scout. At the cabin doorway they looked at the debris. "Now that it has cooled, we can squeeze past. But carefully . . ."

Inside, she sat him on the bed and gingerly pulled away the dressings. The injuries were worse than she had realized; on arm and side both, tissue had sloughed away. The wounds oozed blood and serum.

"Bran! Will the salve—the things you have here—be enough? Why did you not have these tended at Base Two, by those who know more of treatment?"

His head had dropped forward; he raised and shook it, face taut in an attempt to smile. "Get the salve, but spread it on the new bandage, not on me. And the pills—in the metal container —I'll need two, for now." Now his smile was more convincing. "I've been hurt worse, Rissa—and probably will be again —it's cumulative shock, is all. Patch me the way I said, leave me a quart of water at bedside, and call me for dinner."

When she brought the things he had asked for, he was lying down—right side up, exposed for her ministrations. She did as he had told her; he swallowed the pills and lay back again. She arranged his covers, kissed him gently, and went outside.

KENEKKE awaited her. "The captain all right?"

She told what she knew; he nodded. "He's not for doctors, much. The burns sound bad, but not *big* enough to be really dangerous, if you follow me. No, it's strain and shock—he's right about what's needed. Forget about calling him for dinner, though—wait until he wakes up and asks for it."

"You are certain he is in no danger?"

"Sure I am. Why, I've seen him—no, this is no time for you to hear of it. Now, then—" He pointed to the wrecked aircar.

Looking, Rissa did not see Peralta's corpse. "But where is—?"

"That? I wrapped it, so as not to have to touch it, and dumped it over the edge, out there. A thousand feet to the first bounce, I'd bet. Waste of time, digging and covering for that one."

Abruptly she felt a qualm, an ache that doubled her over and brought tears. Kenekke caught her arm to support her, but she shook her head. A spasm racked her, then several more before a final lesser one. Finally she straightened and wiped her eyes. *I have done my grieving for Peralta.*

"What—?"

She shook her head. "I am all right now. It is over." Now she looked at the aircar. "Anse, how can we move that thing?"

"Tried to drive it right inside, didn't he? And came close. Well, most of the controls are burned away, and the rest fused solid.'' He pushed at it, downhill away from the cabin—but although the lower part of the car was undamaged, the wheels would not turn. ''Wheel brakes must have set—and no releasing them, that I can see.''

''How are they controlled? From the body to the wheels, I mean?''

''It's a fluid mechanism, with hoses. An old principle, and simple.''

''Then let us cut them.'' He brought cutters from his belt toolkit. ''No—not that one yet. The rear one first.'' He bent and cut it; fluid spurted. Under the car's weight the wheel pivoted a few degrees and rotated slightly.

Rissa studied the ground beside the car. ''Now the left of the front pair, and we can push the rear sidewise, pivoting on the other one.'' He made his cut; they pushed and the aircar turned. Its nose, the projector forming a grotesque snout, scraped and came clear of the cabin's doorway.

''A little more. It must be facing down, or we cannot control the pivoting rear wheel.'' They moved in farther. Then she motioned toward the remaining wheel, and he cut again. ''Now!'' she said. ''From behind we can move the tail uphill and turn it enough.''

The car's mass resisted; with one more to help, it would have been easier, but the two had hard going. Grunting and shoving, a little at a time, they turned the nose toward downhill. ''A rest, now!'' she cried, and wiped sweat from her forehead, catching her breath.

Kenekke, panting also, nodded and laughed. ''I see what you're up to—down and out and over, to follow the man who brought it.''

''Oh, no—Tregare thinks we can salvage the projector. Downhill first, yes—but then swing the rear to pass above the scoutship and into the rocky ground below the first hummock. Ready?''

They pushed again—slowly, then faster, the wreck moved. As it suddenly accelerated, Rissa tripped and fell. She saw Kenekke pulled into a run, laughing as he swung his weight to the side and held on, dragging for a moment behind the runaway. Then he let go. The gutted aircar plunged into the boulder field, jounced a few times and came to a halt. She sprang up and clapped her hands. ''Bravo, Anse!''

He came trotting toward her, first with a slight limp and then none at all, and shook her hand. "You thought it right —but you missed a good run!"

Now he looked at the cabin—charred wall and ravaged door—and shrugged. "No time to do a right job here, but you'll want stout metal over that hole—well, we've got it. And I see there's a window gone. I'll be able to cover it only from outside, but it'll seal the draft, and you can look out."

Rissa brushed her hair back from her forehead. "Those repairs will be most helpful—I had not thought that far. Now, though—are you not hungry? I am. Come in and I will fix something for us."

He shook his head. "With those pills I don't *think* we'd wake the captain, but let's not chance it. Besides—Hain's in need of company by now, and food as well. So join us, instead."

"Yes. Thank you. I had not thought."

"Nobody thinks of everything—but you come close, you and Tregare." He led the way into the scout; they found Deverel on a cot beside the communications position. He smiled and waved a hand. "Any messages?" said Kenekke.

"Limmer wanted to know if we got here all right. I said yes, except that halfway you got nervous, and jumped out and walked."

Laughing, Kenekke reached and mussed his partner's hair. "That's your lie for today, Hain—now you're stuck with the truth."

"Wish I could say as much for you. What's *your* story?" As Kenekke in the small galley began preparing the meal, he and Rissa related their morning's work and afternoon's plans.

"Aircar's a dead loss?" said Deverel. "But not the projector?"

"Yes, that is Tregare's estimate," said Rissa. "You understand—he hoped to lure Peralta from that shelter, but instead the man moved to ram the cabin, and—"

Deveral waved a hand. "Sure—I know—just getting a fix on what we'll have now, to work with."

"Yes." Rissa excused herself for a wash-up, but made it brief.

Kenekke brought the food—the meat's aroma sharpened Rissa's appetite—and they ate. When they were done,

Kenekke said, "I'll see to that door and window now. No help needed at the first, anyway, so sit and relax, Ms. Kerguelen." He waved a hand and left.

Rissa turned to Deverel. "I must call someone in One Point One. From here, how is it done?"

"Me, I'd go through the port—but maybe your business is none of theirs. Channel C is direct to Hulzein Lodge, and they can route you in on relay."

"Yes. Thank you, Hain." She reached for the switching panel.

"Private conversation? Should I go someplace?"

"No, no—it is on Tregare's business. And if it were on mine, I would trust you as he does."

The screen lit, wavered and produced a faint picture; she recognized Ernol. "Hello," she said, "It is good to see you again. And how are—things—with you?"

More than seeing his smile, she deduced it. "All's fine here. Liesel grumps sometimes, but the way she'd scold a kitten. And what's been happening out there with you?"

"Too much to tell now—there was trouble, but it is over—Tregare or I will give more detail when there is time. Now, though—before I ask you to relay me through to the city, is there news Tregare should know?"

"Let me think. Norden hasn't said yes or no on the *Valkyrie*; Hawkman's still working on him. Keep the time-lag in mind—things may have changed. And—your investment plans are going well, Liesel said to tell you. I guess that's all. Now, who do you want to talk with, in One Point One?"

"Arni Gustafson—dal Nardo's superior, while he lived."

"Oh—yes. Just a moment; I'll see if I can reach her." The picture shattered into shifting streaks of light; sound crashes came from the speaker. Then the screen cleared partially; the wavering silhouette Rissa saw was something like what she recalled of Arni Gustafson.

The voice was clear. "Gustafson speaking. Who's calling?"

Briefly, Rissa had to sort her identities. "Tari Obrigo, Ms. Gustafson. And I am afraid I call to ask you a great favor."

"Good thing I can recognize your voice—from the picture, you could be a bushstomper. I won't ask where you are. Now—what's the favor?"

"The first day we met, you questioned me. When—"

"Of course I did—how does that work into any kind of favor?"

"If your truth field equipment is portable, might Tregare and I borrow it for a time? Or if not, use it in your office? In either case, we would inconvenience you as little as possible."

The woman gasped. "Truth field? You *knew?*"

"I had encountered them on Earth. And my hearing range includes the characteristic sound they make."

Rissa saw a shadowy fist clench and shake, but heard a chuckle. "And you *beat* the field, didn't you? I smelled something at the time, but couldn't be sure. You knew, so you talked *around* my questions."

Briefly, silence. Then, "All right—even if I wanted to, there's no point my trying to buck Tregare *and* the Hulzeins. I'll make a deal. I don't know if the gear is feasible to move—I'll have to ask—but you can use it. *If* you tell me what you hid from me."

Rissa thought, then laughed. "It no longer matters; I will tell you. It was only that—I was new on Number One, and alone. Dal Nardo threatened me. Lacking a counterthreat, I invented one."

"The zombie gas?" On the screen, the shadowy head nodded. "Of course—that would be it. I'm going to replay the tape of that interview—to have a good laugh at myself and maybe to learn something." A short pause, then; "I hope *you* learned, too—that humiliating an egotist can be damned dangerous."

"I knew that—but I could see no other course. Looking back, I still cannot. Can you tell me what I might better have done?"

"With dal Nardo, probably not. Just don't make it a habit."

"I intend not to. But Blaise Tendal was much the same, and—"

"Wasn't you, killed Tendal. But—are you into any more scrapes?"

"Not of my choice, nor centered on me."

"Something, though. No—it's none of my business—"

"I do not mind telling you," Rissa said. "A man thought he should have Bran Tregare's place, and tried to kill him to get it. He is dead by my hand, instead."

The silhouette shook its head. "You married trouble, girl. But if you're not unhappy, why should I fret for you? All right, I told you—you can use the truth field. When I find out *how* you can use it, where can I reach you?"

"Through Hulzein Lodge. And thank you, Arni Gustafson."

"Better save your thanks—the field doesn't always tell you what you'd like."

"In this case, only truth itself is important. It is a matter of loyalties—those who fail the test will merely be left to earn livelihoods on this world. If I had thought earlier to use this method, many dead might still live."

"You had a shootout, did you? Across the Big Hills, where everyone knows something's doing, but no one knows what. Never mind—I don't need details. But when will all of us—groundhogs and spacers alike—learn to work together, instead of living on each others' blood?"

"It was not like that. Only the one man was jealous of command, but he had the loyalty of others. Sane or not—and I am not certain of that—he was so audacious that he nearly deserved to win. But he underestimated Bran Tregare."

"Thought you said *you* killed him?"

"I did—while Tregare played bait for his attacker and came close to dying for it."

"And you think that's admirable—well, maybe it is. I don't understand you, Tari Obrigo—or your man Tregare, either. I'm a peaceful sort—stodgy, even, you might say. I'll defend myself, but otherwise I want no part of fighting."

"Nor, ordinarily, do Bran or I. But there may be a difference—Arni, have you ever been a slave?"

"Hell, no! What kind of talk is that?"

"*I* was, under Total Welfare—and Bran in UET's Space Academy. Slavery leaves marks, and only some can be seen. The scars that do not show—perhaps they are why you and I do not understand each other fully."

"Maybe. We can talk later. About the field—I'll let you know."

The screen went dark. Deverel said, "You told her a lot."

"Too much, do you think?"

"I don't judge you any more than I judge the captain. You play bigger games."

"Hain! It is not a game. Unless—the game of trust."

He raised himself on the cot, half-sitting. "Look—I didn't mean anything. If it's trust you're playing, you sure have mine. All you've done—"

"And you have mine. Now rest—you need to do so." She smiled and left the scoutship.

SHE found Kenekke at the cabin door. He had cleared charred wood away in a rough rectangle. Now he tried to hold a sheet of metal in place with a knee and one hand, and manipulate a welding torch with the other. As she approached, the sheet slipped down and he cursed.

"Can I help?"

He looked around. "Sure. Can you use the torch or hold this thing while I spot the corners?"

"Either."

"Take the torch, then. Now, then, let me—all right, it's centered well enough." Careful to keep the flame well clear of him she spotwelded the two upper corners to the damaged panel. "Fine," he said. "Thanks—that'll hold it for me." She returned the torch; he spotted the lower corners and ran a bead solidly around the perimeter. When he finished, he wiped sweat from his forehead. "Not much for pretty, but good as new for stout! How's Hain doing?"

"Comfortably. And now, if the door latch is cool enough to touch, I must go in and see to Tregare."

He touched it. "Just warm now." She nodded and went inside.

Lying on his unhurt side and breathing heavily, Tregare slept. He had pushed the covers down to his waist; even so, sweat stood out on his face. The water jug was half-empty, but the chamber pot beside the bed had not been used. *I should have brought that for him—he has been up, and he should not be.*

She refilled the water jug and gently pulled the first cover up to his shoulder, in case the fever should settle. She sat beside him for a time, but he did not wake or move. She looked around the kitchen but found nothing that needed doing, so she went outside again.

At first she saw no one, then heard a shout and turned to see Kenekke emerging from a storage building, tools slung from his belt and carrying a large sheet of heavy transparent plastic.

She ran to meet him. "Shall I help you with that?"

He bent to rest one edge of the sheet on the ground. "Sure —this thing isn't so heavy, but it's awkward. Want to take the back corner, and we'll carry it vertical?" She nodded; they picked up the sheet and proceeded, past the outhouse and around the cabin's corner, to the gaping window hole. They laid the plastic flat on the ground.

"We'll need a ladder," he said, "but first I'll get this ready." He adjusted the torch's flame to its narrowest and quickly, precisely melted a small hole near a corner of the sheet, then others at intervals around the perimeter. "This is too big to go in the frame, and that's a day's job even if I had the right tools for it. So we'll nail it to the outside." He unsnapped a hand tool from his belt. "Nail gun—works by compressed gas. Just put the nozzle against a hole and pull the trigger. Now I'll get that ladder."

While she waited, she walked across the plateau a little way, until she could see, below a notch in the flattish surface, the downward sweep of hills. The sun's rays slanted; the pattern of light and shadow among the trees caught her interest. She watched until Kenekke hailed her, then rejoined him. The ladder leaned against the wall, to one side of the window.

"Pretty down there, isn't it, this time of day?" he said.

"It is. I will never get used to the size of these Hills." She looked at the window. "What do we do first?"

He tipped the plastic up on one edge. "I'll hold this so one corner's where it belongs; you go up the ladder and pin it. Then we put the ladder t'other side; you go up again; I pivot the sheet into position. You'll have to brace it on so it doesn't lean out—lucky there's no wind—and when I have it right, pin it again. Two holes is best. I can take it from there."

Yes, she thought—it would work. The first part went easily, but on the other side she stood on the ladder with both hands occupied, balancing with no real handholds, until the first nail was driven. Then she grabbed quickly for a ladder rung, drove the other nail, and descended.

Kenekke grinned. "Perfect. But it's funny—all the things you've done—and on the ladder, not high enough to hurt if you did fall, I could see you were nervous."

She thought. "I was—yes. But not from the height. It was that I could not use my hands or eyes, or even very much of my attention, for balance. Only my feet and legs—and the rung hurt my shins. It made me feel anxious, yes."

"Well, it's done. I can do the rest. And thanks."

"I should thank you, Anse. It is my comfort, and Tregare's, that we are restoring."

"If it wasn't for you two, Hain and I, we'd be dead meat. I tell you—yesterday I didn't have much hope for seeing this day." He laughed. "But here we are!"

"Yes." She smiled at him. "Well, I will look in on Hain, and also see if any messages have come."

IN the scoutship, Deverel was much as before. He said, "The Gustafson woman called. Once I convinced her I knew the situation, she said her gear's portable but lots more than an aircar load. I thanked her and said you or the captain would be in touch."

"Good. Did she give any idea of the size of the equipment? Could this scout handle it, for instance? Because I would not like to load an aircar much, for the pass—and the more trips, the more time wasted."

"The scout? Sure—the stuff's not one big hunk. But—"

"Is there a fuel problem?"

"No. But who—? I mean, the captain's not able, yet."

"I studied the controls on *Inconnu*. Except for complexity —and orientation, landing vertically and not horizontally— they are quite like an aircar's. Surely the scout's are not so different."

He stared at her. "Look—if I let you take this thing up and anything happened, I'd be better off *with* you than facing Tregare."

She laughed. "I would not try it without his permission, surely—this is his property, not mine. No—I will ask—but not until his fever ebbs and his head is clear."

Deverel grinned. "*That's* a relief—you had me worried." He nodded toward the comm-panel. "You want to call Gustafson back?"

She looked at her watch. "I do not know her working hours; she may have left her office." She shrugged and punched for Channel C. "I may as well try."

At Hulzein Lodge, a girl relayed her call; Arni Gustafson answered. "From the lousy picture, it has to be Tari Obrigo. I was just leaving, but go ahead—did you get my message?"

"Yes, and thank you. Now, may I ask—how many normal aircar loadings would your equipment make?"

"Oh—three, I'd say."

"Then—to here, perhaps nine."

"What—?"

"It is not an easy route. But there may be a quicker way; I will not know for a day or two. I called only to thank you, ask my question, and let you know that action will not be immediate."

"That's considerate; I appreciate it. All right—call me when you decide. And if it's urgent, this terminal relays through to my home at night."

"I see—and I will not disturb you there with any matter that can wait."

They said good-byes. Rissa cut the circuit and sat quietly, thinking. Then she shrugged. "For the moment there is nothing I can do; I will put the matter aside."

"It's good you can do that," said Deverel. "Some can't." Then; "How's the repairs going?"

"Temporary measures are complete. Anse is quite efficient."

"From the looks of you, you've been working some, yourself."

"Yes—for one person alone, some of it would have been quite awkward."

"Given to understatement, as always!" She had not heard Kenekke enter. "She did a share. What I came to say, though—the captain's awake; I looked in on him."

Rissa stood. "Is he all right?"

"Improving, is my guess. Wants to see you."

"Then I will go. Thank you."

SHE hurried to the cabin and found Tregare sitting up, propped against a wadded mass of pillows, one cover pulled up over his chest, but leaving arms and shoulders free. He was still sweating, but much less, and his face was more relaxed.

"Bran? You look better—but should you be up, this way?"

He smiled. "I'm past the hump of it—weak, though." He gestured toward the empty jug. "Thought I'd get myself some water, and nearly fell out of bed on my face."

"I'll get it." She filled the jug in the kitchen, returned and poured his glass full. He reached for it, hand somewhat shaky, and drank it dry. She poured another; he sipped a little and set it down.

"I should not have left you so long, Bran."

"Most of the time, until a few minutes ago, I was dead to the world. Heard you and Anse a few times, working outside—and I see things are fixed as well as we need, for now. You're here soon enough—just right. Because I'm hungry, and too washed out to fix anything myself."

"What would you like?"

"There's some stew left, frozen. I think I'm in shape to tackle it."

"All right." She put the container to thaw and heat, and returned. As she sat beside the bed, an odor reached her; she carried the chamber pot to the outhouse and emptied it, rinsing it at an outdoor spigot before taking it back inside.

She said, "While the stew heats, I have time for a shower." He nodded, and soon she stood under the stream of water, grateful for the relaxing heat.

At dinner his appetite surprised her; she had expected him to be more eyes than stomach. He took two helpings, and finally said, "That feels more like it. Now—you suppose you could change the dressings again? And after we've digested dinner a little, help me take a bath? That pot wasn't the only thing that's stinking."

For the most part, the bandages came away cleanly; only at a few spots did they stick and tear the crusts forming over the burns. Tregare raised his arm and sniffed at it. "Looks like the last lost hope of peace, doesn't it? But it's not as sore now, and smells of clean healing."

With a soft cloth she patted away cakings of old salve; with a damp one she sponged clean the skin around the wounds. "We will leave you unbandaged until after your bath, so as not to wet the dressings."

"Sure. Won't hurt to let a little air at the burns, either, long as I'm awake and can keep them from rubbing anything."

They sat for a time. Then she helped him up and into the bathtub, filling it only to a level that did not reach the lowest burn. He sat with the injured arm resting on the side of the tub, leaning to keep the burned side higher than the other.

"I can't do much of it," he said. "Just pretend I'm a baby." She laughed and set to work. To wash his head she

leaned him forward—and to the left, away from the burns.
For the rest she worked gently but quickly, careful not to
tickle after one such accidental transgression caused him to
start, and make an alarming splash. "I'll remember that," he
said. "Tregare never forgets a tickle!"

Rising, he needed less help, and stood while she dried him.
He sat again as she spread salve thickly on fresh dressings and
applied them. Then she brought him a robe.

"What's this for? I'm going back to bed now."

"Not until I change much of the bedding. You sweat so
heavily, you have soaked it." So he waited while she stripped
the bed and put on fresh covers, retaining only the top spread
which was dry and odorless. Then she removed the robe and
helped him into bed.

"I'll need to be by the wall," he said, "so if we bump, it's
on my good side."

"Yes, of course."

"And we can't—but maybe tomorrow, Rissa."

"When you are healed enough, Bran—not before."

"We'll see, then." He raised his face to her kiss; she turned
the lights off and got in beside him. Her thoughts were busy;
some time passed before she slept.

IN the morning Tregare's fever had gone; during the night he
had not sweated noticeably. From the waist down, he dressed
in his normal clothing—and without help, except that he could
not straighten the bandaged arm enough to manage his boot
snaps. He added a light, loose jacket that did not bind on the
burned areas.

He ate with evident enjoyment. Rissa waited until after-
breakfast coffee to report her dealings with Arni Gustafson
and her ideas about moving the equipment. "And so, Bran, if
you think—"

He waved his good hand. "Wait now—you want to fly the
scout—just like that, without being checked out in her?" He
tapped a finger on the table. "First place, the scout's been a
hole card—nobody outside Base Two, except Hulzeins, knows
it exists. But maybe that's not important now—let me think
about it."

Rissa thought a moment, then nodded. "I have not given it
away, Bran."

"Good. But *if* we use it, I'll have to fly it."

"But why?" She repeated the arguments she'd given Deverel.

Tregare paused, then said, "You're good with an aircar. But, you ever fly a racer?" She shook her head. "They do everything twice as fast and twice as hard. *You* might climb into one cold and learn it before it killed you—the average aircar pilot wouldn't. And the scout—it's kitier, compared to racing aircars, than they are to the ones you're used to." He shook his head. "You're capable, peace knows—but all at once, it's too much to try."

Chin resting on clasped hands, Rissa leaned forward. "Then a step at a time, Tregare. You think I could not lift it safely?"

"Sure you could—just apply power until it raises, and more if it starts to wobble."

"And then, going high for safety, would there not be leeway to experiment and learn the scout's responses?"

"Yes, but—"

"The landing, you will say—that I must get it right the first time. But that is not true. I can practice against the altimeter —high enough to come to momentary stop in midair, with plenty of height in which to drop and regain thrust."

Brows lowered, he looked at her. "Peace on a planet—of course you could!"

"Then I have your permission?"

He laughed. "Not so fast! It's a good idea—a *damned* good one—and sooner or later we'll do it. But for now—taking the scout to One Point One—let's wait and see. Maybe I'll be healthy in time to do it myself."

She thought, then nodded. "Very well, Bran—I agree to that."

Later, Tregare walking slowly and carefully, they went to the scout. Once he turned to her and said, "I'm just taking it easy, not to jar anything. I could move fast if I had to." She smiled then, and they climbed the ramp.

Inside, Deverel was clearing the breakfast table, limping but no longer using the crutch. "Up and around—eh, Hain?"

"Right, skipper—the bruise was worse than the gouge. It's not too sore if I keep it loosened up. Anse changed the bandage—I'm healing cleanly. But how's yourself? We've worried."

"Coming fine, now. Thing was—at first there—when by rights I should have rested, I had to act fast. So yesterday I paid for it—shock and fever. Taking it easy now, but on the mend."

At the comm-panel, he punched a conference call on scramble. Soon Limmer, Vanois, and Gowdy—each on a screen segment—faced him. He said, "Casualty reports first—right? Up here it's just Hain and I, and we're both mending."

Limmer said, "Here, add five dead—we found two more, and three wounded didn't make it." He gave the total figures, by ships. "There's less than half a dozen in sick bay—energy guns mostly kill you or they don't."

"Walking wounded?"

Limmer shook his head. "I don't even have a count on that. People on the job, they stop by for treatment; the medics haven't bothered keeping records."

Tregare laughed. "If it doesn't worry them, it doesn't worry me." Then he sobered. "But it's hell we had to lose so many." He shook his head. "No choice, though, that I can see.

"Well, then—with all the cleaning up to do, I expect the regular work's been stalled. But are you ready to start again now?"

"Pretty much so," said Limmer. "Except—I wish there was some way to move *Deuces Wild*. When *Inconnu* gets here— and others—the hulk will be in the way, slow things down. And the blowup put it on a tilt. Anyone landing or taking off, you see—the blast could knock it over, maybe wreck another ship."

Squinting, Tregare frowned. "Which way's it leaning, and how much?" Limmer told him; after a moment, Tregare nodded. "I think I see it, but check me. If you put the winch-tractor over by the crater wall—azimuth one-fifty, say—dug in so it can't move—"

"You talks foolish, Tregare! Tractor won'ts move it a ship—can'ts even to pull it over."

Tregare grinned. "Hear the rest, Raoul, will you? Now— run the cable to *Deuces Wild*. Take at least a half turn around the ship—a full one, if possible—before you attach it, high as you can manage. There's extra cable in supplies, if you need it."

"I still says—"

Limmer's voice growled. "Like Tregare said, let's hear *all* of it."

"All right—guess me the azimuth of the westernmost landing leg."

Vanois answered. "Close to two hundreds ten, it is."

"Perfect!" Tregare gestured. "Run your winch tension up until the safety clutch smokes; then blow that leg out with thermite and hit the override! You see?"

"I sees! Ship starts to fall, you puts a *twist* on it."

"Yes," said Limmer. "If it lands rolling, even a little, there's barely enough slope that maybe the winch can *keep* it rolling."

Tregare nodded. "Just be sure you blow the cable free before *Deuces Wild* starts to wrap up in it—or that tractor comes out like a cork, out of *any* hole we could dig."

Limmer chuckled. "And slack tension first. Sure, Tregare. And we'll salvage what's worth it, starting now, *before* it gets jarred up."

"Fine. Now, then—after that, assuming it works, you can start cutting *No Return* for the extra turrets; it's all marked. And whenever the mountings are in place and inspected, the hardware can go in. We'll be down to help on that."

He continued. There were questions, and he answered them. Then; "Hilaire—if you haven't told those other six of Peralta's that their lives are safe, do it. And tell the whole fifteen they won't be locked up much longer—that I'll decide who can rejoin the ship, that wants to, and the rest go free in the city."

He turned to Rissa. "Can you think of anything else for now?"

She leaned over to face the screen. "Only—my greetings, also."

"That's it, then. I'll be down there as soon as I'm feeling friskier—which shouldn't be too long from now."

But when the screen darkened and he rose to leave, she saw that he moved more slowly than before. "It is time you rested again, Bran. Do not try to do too much, yet."

"All right. See you later, Hain." Several times, on the way to the cabin, she wanted to help him, but she knew better than to try.

• • •

TREGARE'S impatience grew, but not until the fourth morning, after the evening when they first again made love, did Rissa agree he was fit for real work. Scabs were beginning to flake off the lesser burns; only a few deeper ones still needed covering. He flexed the arm, wincing slightly but not able to extend it fully.

With the two men from the scout, they attacked the problem of Peralta's stolen projector. Kenekke had cleared debris away; all four could get handholds on the surface-burned shell. With Tregare favoring his arm and Deverel his stiff leg, they rolled it onto an improvised skid and hauled it to the scout. There they rigged a winch to pull it up the ramp, swing and place it, half-protruding, in a supply hold emptied for the purpose. Deverel wound a length of cable around the nozzle to tie it down. Tregare said, "Time for a breather. You got any coffee?"

"Fresh is better," said Kenekke. "Only take a minute or two." As he prepared it, the others sat.

When the coffee was poured, Rissa said, "What is next, Bran? Do we go soon to Base Two? Or across the Hills for Ms. Gustafson's apparatus?"

"Both—in that order. But not until tomorrow."

"Good. If I inform her today, she will have time to prepare. But today, what do we do?"

"I thought we could clear away a little more slag and see if the aircar might be worth fixing. Then—let's all take the rest of the day off. Though peace knows *I've* been loafing enough!"

AFTER a half hour's work, Tregare looked at the gutted aircar and shook his head. "At One Point One or the Lodge, even, I'd say we fix it. But here—no way to move it that wouldn't cost more than it's worth—well, when somebody has time we can salvage motors and landing gear, maybe a little more. Meanwhile—Anse, you want to spray it for mothballing?"

"I'll do that." They separated—Kenekke to a warehouse, Deverel to the scout, Rissa and Tregare to the cabin. Inside, he took off his boots and lay down.

"No getting around it," he said. "I'm still not up to much."

"Are you sure you wish to do what you said, tomorrow?"

"Have a start, anyway. I won't take the scout up unless I'm certain of myself. If I start to poop out—at Base Two, say, or in town—that's where we stay. All right?"

"Very well. I will tell Arni Gustafson that we may be there tomorrow, or perhaps not until the next day. Then I will come back and we can have lunch."

Aboard the scout she made her call. Arni Gustafson agreed to have the equipment ready for moving the next day, and to arrange for a vehicle and loading crew either then or the day after, as needed. "At the port, then?" she said.

"Yes, I believe that is best," said Rissa. "And thank you."

She returned to find Tregare cooking lunch. They ate without talk. Afterward he said, "Not much company, am I? I need to rest a bit more; then I have to go through some schedules. So feel free to go walking, take the aircar out—whatever you want."

"Yes. I will walk—the car gives me no exercise." She kissed him and left. But once outside she ran, not walked, the length of the plateau and back. Then she began climbing the uphill trail—an animal track, barely discernible. She lost all sense of time. When she saw the sun near the horizon ahead, she had almost reached the top of the great ridge. Regretfully, she decided the remaining daylight was not enough for her to top the crest and return safely. She turned and stood a few moments, savoring the fall of hillside, the plateau tiny below her, the next ridge and the sweep of plain beyond—then she ran downhill.

Pell-mell, she ran—too fast for caution, leaping boulders and ditches—until dimming light forced her to slow her pace. The rest of her descent was anticlimax, but she had exerted her body's strength more than in a long time, and the effort relaxed and calmed her. She found Tregare asleep in the cabin; she showered and changed clothes before waking him.

During dinner she confirmed her guess that the scout should land at the port rather than in the city. "Oh, it'd be safe enough," Tregare said, "to set her down in Gustafson's side lot. But there's rules, so no point in shaking anything when it's not needful."

"And can I begin learning to handle the scout?"

"Not between here and Two—it's a short, low haul, and the

projector makes an unbalanced load. But crossing the Big Hills I'll take her high, and you can try your hand. Whether we go there tomorrow, or next day."

"I look forward to that learning."

"I'll bet you do."

WHEN the scout lifted next morning, Rissa saw the effect the projector made; Tregare kept the small ship tilted at an angle, to compensate. All four were aboard; he had left the cabin locked, its alarms set, but unguarded. Remembering the previous flights, she watched him closely; now his control was deft and sure, and he landed alongside *Lefthand Thread* almost gently. His scheme, she saw, had worked. Near the southeast crater wall, clear of the other ships, lay *Deuces Wild*.

Limmer had a crane ready. With much signaling and a few clangs, the heavy projector swung against the rim of the cargo hold, the entrance, and then the ramp. But no damage was done; as the load swung free and was grounded, Tregare waved the operator a salute of congratulation.

Leaving Deverel and Kenekke aboard, Rissa and Tregare followed Limmer to his galley. Vanois and Gowdy joined them. Over coffee, Tregare stated his plans. "I'll have the equipment here today or tomorrow. Then we check out the ones that fought for Peralta and see if we can trust any."

Limmer spoke. "I say test everyone—and I'll go first, if you like."

Hilaire Gowdy nodded. "I've already said I *want* my loyalty proved out."

"No!" Vanois shook his head. "I lets no machine see my mind. Is my word not enough, Tregare, then you buys me out. Not like Peralta—I wants no part of command except how we's already agreed. But I doesn't do that thing you say."

Tregare looked at him, then smiled. "Raoul? You have any objection if we all *say* you took the test and passed?"

"I—it's not—I'm not understanding you, Tregare."

"Clear enough to me," said Limmer. "He trusts you, same as I do, but he doesn't want you setting a bad example for people who maybe *need* checking out."

"Tregare—you means what he says?"

"That's right, Raoul."

The man shook his head again, frowning. "Then I changes my mind. I does what you asks." He laughed. "Tregare—sometime you drives someone crazy!"

WITH its lopsided burden removed, the scout lifted straight and true. Tregare took it high—into black sky, stars shining—then gave Rissa the controls.

At first she overcontrolled badly, but less each time, as she adjusted to the machine's speed and power. Turning the scout, changing speed and altitude, she recognized the truth of Tregare's cautions to her and realized how little the aircar had tested her abilities.

Hardest, she found, was changing thrust gently enough to avoid hard, jarring lurches. Finally she tried two "landings," dropping the scout to a halt at arbitrary heights. After the second, Tregare laughed. "You might have walked away from that one, but maybe two inches shorter from the impact!" He resumed control. "You're doing damned well, really. Couple more sessions like this, with the same grade of improvement, and I'd turn you loose with her."

"You were right, Bran—it requires practice. But must the power control be *quite* so sensitive? It is like a gun with a hair-trigger—I do not see the necessity."

"Yeah—well, this one's jury-rigged. Couple of circuits burned out, and we had to make do with nonstandard parts. Before that, it wasn't quite this touchy. Maybe Limmer's got spares."

Now they descended; Rissa watched One Point One expand and slide away to one side. Tregare touched ground at a corner of the port, near the administrative offices. Leaving Deverel and Kenekke in charge of the scout, he and Rissa walked to the building, where she called Arni Gustafson. After exchanging greetings and confirming their agreement, she reported their location.

"Nearest corner, eh? Fine. Expect the stuff in about an hour." Rissa thanked her and terminated the call.

She turned to Tregare. "There will be time for us to have

lunch. It is past noon and I am hungry."

"Me, too. We could eat with Hain and Anse on the scout, but there's a cafeteria in the building. Then, again—about half a mile down the line, alongside the aircar rentals, there's a restaurant that knows what food's all about."

"Bran, are you sure you feel like so much walking, yet?"

"Sure—I haven't even started to get tired today. Don't worry—I won't strain anything."

She let him set the pace, somewhat more slowly than usual but without the obvious caution of recent days. Clouds passed overhead; for a time they walked in shade, then once again the sun shone bright around them.

The restaurant pleased Rissa; simple and somewhat rustic inside and out, it reminded her of the cabin's design. Service was prompt and the food well prepared; she ate quickly. "I am glad you chose this place, Bran. Cafeterias—serving office workers—I have eaten in some of those."

He grinned. "So have I. Well—shall we go?"

THEY strolled lazily, except for the last of it when a brief shower caught them; as they reached the scout, it ended. Rissa pointed toward the city. "The groundcar coming—towing the cargo flat—it must be what we wait for." The flat carried a stack of crates, and three men rode it also.

"Could be," said Tregare. "I'll go up and make sure things are cleared away for loading in the scout."

Rissa stayed; she sat on the ramp and watched the vehicle approach. The driver brought it near, then turned to back the cargo flat toward the ramp. Rissa stood and beckoned until it almost touched, then raised her palm to signal stop.

The driver, face shadowed by a floppy leather cap, jumped out. "Tari! I *thought* it was you. Haven't seen you since— well, you look every bit snooky again. But—different."

"Yes?" Then the cap came off, and with the eyes unshaded and the short fair hair revealed, Rissa recognized Felcie Parager.

"Felcie! Yes—I am fully recovered." She decided not to mention the disguise components she no longer wore. "It is good to see you again."

The girl looked at the scoutship. "I've never ridden one of those before. What is it? Not a real starship, is it? Of course, I've never ridden *that* kind either. Do they make little ones, too?" She turned back to Rissa. "You've been having it more peaceful lately? But Arni said—"

Laughing, Rissa grasped the girl's shoulders and shook them gently. "One thing at a time, Felcie—or perhaps two. I would not say I have had a peaceful time, but the trouble is past. Now, though—this scoutship—armed starships carry them. But what do you mean, that you expect to ride in it?"

"Arni wants someone to go along with the equipment, and I'm elected. She showed me how to plug the stuff together and adjust it, and I brought the operating manual in case I forget. All right?"

"I—"

From behind Rissa, Tregare spoke. "Sure—Gustafson's quite right, wanting one of her own people to keep an eye on the gear. You prepared to stay with us a few days, though?"

"Yes—naturally. You're Tregare, aren't you? I remember."

"We've met, have we?" He snapped his fingers. "Of course! At the duel—you were the medic's aide. And you two knew each other before—right?"

"My first day aground here, Bran. Felcie—Felcie Parager —when I left dal Nardo's office, she drove the aircar that took me to Hulzein Lodge."

He reached and shook Felcie's hand. "And now you're our technician? Versatile—I like that. Well, let's start loading."

Deverel and Kenekke joined Felcie's crew, getting the crates aboard and stowed. Tregare moved to help, but Rissa touched his shoulder and shook her head; he smiled and stood where he was. She turned to Felcie. "Only a few days ago, Tregare was injured. He improves rapidly but is not yet recovered."

"Sorry to hear it," the girl said. "Arni hinted you'd had trouble. What happened? UET raid you? Wild animals stampede? I hear there's some big ones in the Hills. Or—"

"Felcie!" Rissa turned at Tregare's word, but he was smiling. "Nonstop questions, eh? Trouble is, that way you bury some of the answers." He paused. "I'll say this much—we had a local problem. Nothing to do with UET—or the wildlife hereabouts."

When Felcie spoke, her voice was low. "I got too nosy. Sorry."

"Don't be," said Tregare. "If I don't like a question, I don't have to answer it—nobody does. And I know you don't mean harm, Ms. Parager."

Her frown cleared. Before she could answer, one of her loading crew approached and said, "We're done here."

"Oh, yes—let me get my things out of the car, and you can take it back and turn the job voucher in to Ms. Gustafson." She brought back a briefcase and one suitcase, and the groundcar left. "Well," she said, "I'm ready."

They boarded the scout and Tregare lifted it. He went only high enough to clear the Hills comfortably. Noting, after her own experience, his smooth touch at the controls, Rissa thought, *When we came down on Peralta's force, his hurt was worse than I knew.*

Felcie said, "I've never seen the Big Hills like this before —all of them at once, from above. They're—I don't have words for it!"

"Nobody does," said Tregare. "This world is one of a kind."

HE angled down toward Base Two, the same deceptive sidewise drift he had tried at the plateau. This time he managed it almost perfectly, needing only two brief spurts of power to correct his course. As they grounded, Rissa said, "Now I see I have *much* to learn before piloting this craft."

"You'll learn it." Deverel stayed at the comm-panel; the rest left the scout. Limmer came down *Lefthand Thread's* ramp to meet them.

"You're back soon," he said. "Good. I've set up a shack— prefab, plastic panels—for the equipment. Behind the ship, and powered from it."

"That's fine," said Tregare. "Five men loaded the gear in quick time; you might assign the same number to unload and unpack." He motioned toward Felcie. "She's our technician; she can tell them how to arrange it all."

Limmer pointed a thumb. "She's one of yours, Tregare?"

Felcie spoke. "I'm here for Arni Gustafson—it's her equipment. All right?"

Limmer nodded. "Right as can be, young woman. All it is, I like to know who I'm dealing with." For a moment he stared at her, then turned away. "I'll round up a crew for you."

Looking after him, Felcie whispered, "He's—*frightening*."

"Only at first," said Rissa. "He did not choose his scars. Tregare trusts him, and so do I. Do not fear a man merely because he has been hurt."

Felcie's voice was indecisive. "If you say so—nothing shaken."

Limmer's men arrived; they carried the crates into the new brown plastic building, opened them and arranged the contents as Felcie directed, then left. With Rissa's help, Felcie uncoiled and attached the connecting cables. Kenekke piled the empty crates outside. When Felcie consulted her operating manual and connected to Limmer's power outlet, Tregare said, "Is it ready now?"

Felcie made an adjustment of a dialed knob, then another, and nodded. "Yes, Tregare. Should I show you how to read the indicators? Mostly it's simple—anything in the red, something's wrong. Then you—"

"That'll do for now. Sit down there; we'll give it a trial run."

The girl's eyes widened, but she sat, waiting.

"All right. Are you here to spy on me, for anyone?" She shook her head. He watched the indicators and smiled. "You have anything in mind besides tending the equipment and getting it home safe?" She nodded. "What is it?"

She leaned forward. "You're going to space—I want to go, too!"

Tregare laughed. He turned a switch and leaned back from the panel. "You're solid green on the board, Felcie. And the field's off now. Tell me about it."

"Just—*tell* you?"

"That's right."

"The whole city's talking—what's Tregare up to? Arni says leave it alone, you're trouble." She shook her head, her hair so short it barely quivered with the motion. "Well, maybe she's right, but whatever—you're getting ready to *do* something. And I want to be part of it."

Tregare looked at her. "You think you do—I guess you're old enough to know. But—you leave here, for where and when

I'm going, you leave forever. Oh, you can come back to the *place*—but everyone you knew, you'll find dead or near it. *Time*, Felcie—we can't any of us beat it.''

Her return gaze held steady. ''I know. But I don't have that much here—no parents or family, being a zoom-womber—nobody I *need*. Friends, sure. But I make friends easy, always have—I can out *there*, too.'' She leaned forward. ''Tari—Tregare—I want to go.''

Tregare looked to Rissa; she gave him no sign. He said, ''All right if I don't give you an answer just now? I'm not saying no, I just want to think on it.''

Felcie breathed deeply. ''That'll do, Tregare—and thanks. Now what do you want me to do here?''

''Come eat, so you don't starve. That's what I'm going to do.''

DINING on *Lefthand Thread*, Rissa watched Felcie's reactions —the girl could not hide her obvious interest in her companions. Except for occasional sidelong glances, scarred Limmer ignored her, or pretended to. Shaggy Vanois returned her stares until Felcie looked away. Catching Felcie's gaze on her several times, Hilaire Gowdy finally said, ''What the hell are you gawking at?''

Felcie reddened; she looked down and then up again. ''All right, since you asked—heart failure pretty soon if you don't knock some of that lard off!''

Gowdy inhaled a gasp, then let it out in a laugh. ''Well, you're right, peace knows. Funny—you're the first that's had the gall to say it. Even—''

''Like she said, you asked.'' Tregare was grinning as he spoke. ''Now, then—Felcie's got the truth field working. No sense in wasting the evening. Hilaire? Can you bring those fifteen of Peralta's down to the new building, under guard? In about an hour?''

''You want them first, do you?''

''That's right.''

''They'll be there.''

• • •

RISSA sat beside Tregare as Felcie, on his other side, explained the finer points of operating the field. "Yes, I see it," he said. "All right—here comes the first batch."

Unhandcuffed and unhobbled, the fifteen filed in. Only Gowdy followed; she was armed, but the gun rested in its holster. Rissa thought, *Certainly, she is sure of herself.*

"Who's the top ranker?" said Tregare. Gowdy indicated a stocky man whose head was bandaged. "All right—sit down there and name yourself."

The man sat. "Elrain Hardekamp, onetime First on the *Attila*. And you're Tregare—all primed to kill me because I wasn't on *your* side, when I'd never seen you before."

"Easy, Hardekamp—no matter what you say here, your life's safe. Now tell it—why you mutinied with Peralta, and how you stand now."

The man half-stood, then dropped back to his chair. "Mutiny? No such thing." He shook his head. "Two years, nearly, I hid on Tweedle, UET looking for us all. Then Peralta came and got us out. He wanted my oath and I gave it."

Hardekamp gestured. "What he said was, we were joining an Escaped fleet—that he wasn't in command, but he should be. Our first job was to take care of that for him—well, it didn't work. I don't know who's right and who's wrong, but I went with the man who saved my butt on Tweedle. I guess I'm stuck with that."

"Maybe." Tregare waited, then said, "Peralta's dead by my doing. Would that stop you from joining me, if I offered?"

Hardekamp rubbed his hand across his face. "That's a straight offer?" Tregare nodded. "I don't know what was between you and Peralta—no way I could, you see. But I'm trained for space, not groundhogging. So if *you* don't mind, we being on the wrong sides from each other lately, then neither do I. I'll sign it or swear it, whatever."

Tregare looked at his instruments and nodded. "You're a truthful man. Forget the oaths; I'll settle for a handshake."

When that was done, he said, "All there was with me and Peralta—I might as well tell all of you—I helped him take his ship from UET, and he owed me service for it. But he couldn't forget he'd been senior in the old days—he wanted command

and tried to kill me to get it. He lost." He shook his head. "I would have bought him out fair. I offered that, and I'd rather he'd accepted."

"So would I," said Hardekamp. "Or that he'd stayed. He was a fox, that one—the way he got us up free from Tweedle. But you must be a better one, Tregare."

"Maybe, maybe not. I'm here—let's get on with it."

The next few questionings were brief; the men and women followed Hardekamp's lead, and the indicators stayed green. Then a tall man, one eye bandaged and right arm in a sling, sat.

He said, "I won't bother lying, Tregare. You killed my brother when you flamed groundside. I wouldn't ship with you if the world was burning away under my feet! So kill me and be damned to you. But if you were any kind of man, you'd give me a fighting chance."

Tregare stood; his hands shook. "I'm sorry about your brother. But Peralta gave *me* no chance. I had to make my own. I give you better than that; you go free to make your way on this world." He gestured to Gowdy. "Get him out of here!"

The rest of the interviews took little time. Tregare shook his head at one man. "You're out." To Rissa he said, "The indicators flickered; I'm too tired to find out why."

When it was done, they slept again in Peralta's former quarters. The next day all personnel were questioned under the field, and Tregare designated three more to be grounded; he did not state his reasons. Limmer, with Kenekke riding "shotgun," delivered the five to One Point One and brought the scout back barely before dark.

NEXT morning Tregare and Rissa inspected new installations on *No Return*, found few errors and decided to return to Base One. Over lunch, Rissa said, "Felcie, would you like to come with us, or must you stay to guard the equipment?"

"Oh, I'm sure it's safe here. I'd like to go with you."

So five rode the scout to the plateau. Nothing had changed; there had been no intrusion. Once aground, Felcie was shocked at the effects of Peralta's foray—the damaged cabin and wrecked aircar. "What a snick! Looks like somebody used *ship's* weapons!"

"We did," said Rissa. Felcie's mouth opened, but closed without replying. "Come, Felcie, I will show you a little of the place. All right, Bran?"

"Sure. I've got some calls to make."

Rissa gave Felcie a conducted tour. First the cabin—but no mention of its defenses. Then outside—to the plateau's edge with its sweeping view of lower Hills and plain, then back past cabin and outhouse for a short climb, far enough to see the plateau as a whole.

"It's well planned," the girl said finally. "And I love the location! I've never been far into the Big Hills on the other side—a little higher than Hulzein Lodge, but not much. How'd you ever get an aircar over here—special model, or did Tregare bring it in his ship?"

Rissa laughed. "I will not tell you just yet. I may have the chance to show you, instead—and I would not want to spoil the surprise."

The sun neared the high-flung horizon. They returned to the cabin, found it empty, and went to the scout. Deverel and Kenekke were absent; Tregare worked at a sheet of scribbled calculations. He looked up. "You see all the sights, Felcie?"

"Yes, and I'm really impressed." She paused. "I almost forgot—could you give me a circuit to Arni? I haven't reported in yet today."

"And how about yesterday?" said Rissa.

"Oh, I called her in the afternoon. You were busy; the tall man—Kenekke—arranged the circuit for me."

"All right," said Tregare. He punched for Hulzein Lodge and asked for the relay; an unfamiliar face appeared briefly and then Arni Gustafson came to the screen. "Hello," he said. "Ms. Parager's here to talk with you."

Felcie moved to the screen. "Everything's fine, Arni. The equipment behaved a hundred percent snooky, and now I'm up at a different place. Wow—was there ever a fight here! Oh, not now—before I came, I mean. You should see—"

Tregare cleared his throat. She looked at him. He neither smiled nor frowned, but she turned back and said, "I think I wasn't supposed to say anything about that. Pretend I didn't, will you, Arni?"

Over her shoulder, Tregare said, "Let's say, Ms. Gustafson, that I'd appreciate it if you—and anyone there with you—doesn't repeat it."

Gustafson nodded. "Don't worry. I neither meddle nor tattle. And Felcie—put it firmly in your mind that anything you see on that side of the Hills—except the scenery—isn't to be talked about when you come back."

"Yes, Arni, I will. But—maybe I'm not *coming* back!"

The woman half stood. "They won't let you? But—"

"No, it's nothing like that. I—I want to go to space, and maybe they *will* let me!"

Arni shook her head. "Well, I like you—like having you work for me, too—but peace knows I don't own you. You're young to make such a choice but old enough to have the legal right, if you want. Think it over, though—carefully."

Felcie nodded; the woman said, "Now, then—when do I get my gear back?"

Felcie looked to Tregare. He said, "If you need it, I'll have it to you tomorrow. But if you can spare it for a while—"

"The need's not urgent. But how long do you mean?"

"Is a month too long?"

"What have you got over there—a full-sized army?"

"No. Sometimes I wish I did. But—not all I do hope to have, are here yet."

"Oh? Well, it's your business. I won't ask further. Let me see—all right, you have the month. But if I *should* need to use it, will you provide me transport?"

"Sure. This scout carries a dozen or better in reasonable comfort—more than that if you don't mind riding cramped."

"Agreed, then. Felcie—any more to add?"

"No. That's all."

"All right—report acknowledged. Thanks, and out."

The screen darkened; Tregare said, "Anyone getting hungry besides me?"

"I'll call you when it's ready," said Rissa. "Come on, Felcie." Then she paused. "Where are Hain and Anse?"

"Down at Two, in the other aircar. Now we need it, Anse has it working solidly again. They'll stay the night, I think."

"Oh. I only thought, if they were here, we would all eat together again." She shrugged and led Felcie off the scout and into the cabin.

• • •

THE girl insisted on helping in the kitchen. At first, ignorant of the arrangements, she was less help than hindrance. But eventually the dinner was ready. Rissa called Tregare and they sat and dined. Afterward they had wine and coffee; Felcie accepted only the latter. The conversation became awkward—Felcie would begin a question, then stop and withdraw it. Finally she excused herself and went outside. "I'll be back in a few minutes."

Tregare gestured after her. "Real question box, isn't she? Likable youngster, though."

Rissa smiled. "She has lived in a friendly world, apart from the power struggles of the oligarchs. She has not had to learn, as we did, to guard what she says. And—"

He held up a hand. "The aircar—they came back after all." He stood and went to the door.

"What is it?"

"I'm remembering last time an aircar came and we thought it was them." As he opened the door a crack, he had the big energy gun in one hand, but after a minute or so he replaced it and closed the door. "This time it's all right." He came and sat again.

Rissa frowned. "I had hoped—but in fairness to Hain and Anse, we cannot have her sleep on the scout."

"What are you talking about? The bed's big enough. On *Inconnu*—"

"That was different. It was—mechanical—except, somehow, for the last night. But only you have seen me in full response."

Felcie's entrance cut off his reply. For a moment, Rissa thought the girl had eavesdropped, for she said, "My—that's a good big bed. Looks comfortable."

"Yes," said Rissa, "but we—"

Felcie laughed. "Tari, I slept in mixed beds all my life, until I got a job and could afford a room to myself. All us zoom-wombers did—things were *crowded*. And when we got old enough, some would be having sex and some not—nobody paid any mind. So don't worry—you won't embarrass me any."

No one answered; she looked hard at Rissa and then said,

"Oh, I see—it's *you* who needs privacy." She laughed. "Well, I've never understood that problem—but just say when and I'll go take a bath and won't come out 'til you call me."

Solemn-faced, Tregare said, "That'll be fine—won't it, Tari?"

"I—I suppose so." Then; "Yes, of course it will. Thank you, Felcie."

But later she could not, at first, escape the feeling of being watched. She had almost despaired when her body's habit dissolved her inhibition overwhelmingly. When Felcie rejoined them, she said, "If that was as good as it sounded, I envy you two."

Neither answered, but Rissa smiled and squeezed the girl's hand.

NEXT morning, Rissa flew the aircar; Kenekke stayed with the scout while the rest went to Base Two. On inspection they found *No Return*'s installations nearing completion—ready, in a few more days, for the hull plates to be replaced. These would need to be cut and divided into permanent and disposable sections, for the weapons had to be camouflaged—no UET ship carried the turret pattern Rissa had designed.

After a pause for coffee with Hilaire Gowdy, Rissa took Felcie with her to the practice turret on *Lefthand Thread*, where she ran a full simulation sequence. She no longer checked her individual scores—only the average, an encouraging 65.

"Could I try that?" said Felcie. "Just a few runs?" Rissa agreed and explained the controls. As the simulations began, she saw that Felcie's reflexes and coordination were good, but that she was overeager—overcontrolling in her haste and slamming down the override in frustration when she could not get her shot. Finally Rissa stopped the sequence.

"You push too hard. You do not do so in driving an aircar, do you? Well, then—this is even more delicate. Try again, but moving more gently. And I suggest you do not use the override at all, at this stage of learning."

The advice helped; Felcie's scores improved. But Rissa decided that gunnery would never be the girl's best skill.

• • •

THE time was near to noon; they went to the galley and found Tregare already seated. As they joined him, Limmer entered and also sat. His mouth bent into his sneer-smile. "It's going well." He looked to Rissa. "What have you two been doing? I didn't see you around anywhere."

Felcie was silent; Rissa said, "First, finishing inspections for today on *No Return*. Then I ran an hour of simulations in the practice turret, and Felcie tried it also."

"And how did you like it, Felcie?"

"I—I didn't do very well." Almost in a whisper she spoke.

Limmer frowned, then shook his head. Felcie said, "I'm sorry, captain."

"No, no—I don't mean *that*! What it is—but you can't help it, I suppose—I wish you weren't afraid of me. And you are, aren't you?"

"I—"

"This face—I can't blame you. But it's too bad, because you—you could almost be my daughter, if I'd had one. A few years too old, you are, but not much." He leaned forward; Rissa saw Felcie trying not to flinch. "You look almost like her, some younger than when we met—"

"Who—?"

"The woman who was with me ten years and more—from long before we escaped until—" He shook his head. "UET caught us at Franklin's Jump. I got the ship away, barely, but they holed us—and that's where *she* was."

The man had tears in his eyes. "You remember her, Tregare?"

"Vanessa Largane? Of course. And you're right. I only saw her—oh, about biological thirty, I'd guess, and her hair was longer. But take off a few years, and with a UET regulation haircut—yes, Felcie's practically her image."

Felcie's eyes brimmed. She reached forward, hesitated, then put her hand to Limmer's scarred cheek. "I *am* sorry, captain. And I promise—I won't be afraid of you any more. It was just that—"

"I know." Rissa said it quickly. "I did not, myself, immediately appreciate Captain Limmer as he has shown he deserves."

Limmer rose. "I can't imagine what's holding up the food here. I'll go see." He walked away.

Tregare began to speak, but Felcie interrupted. "Oh—I'm so *ashamed!*"

Tregare gripped her hand. "Don't be. You reacted the way everybody does. Then you made it up to him. Not everybody does that."

"But he's your friend—I should've realized!"

"Peace on a pedestal!" Tregare's hand slapped the table. "Quit flipping your string, Felcie—I tell you, you've nothing to regret." He smiled. "That's the first time I know of that he's been able to talk of Vanessa since—it happened. Now—" He looked around. "Here he comes—and likely wanting no more said about it."

Felcie nodded. Limmer sat and said, "There was a mixup. We'll be served now." His prophecy was a good one; they ate without conversation until food was gone and coffee into its second pouring. Then Limmer said, "What's on the afternoon schedule, Tregare? I'm free if you need me."

"Sure. Come along if you like but I'll only be checking the cutmarks on *No Return*'s hull plates. Not the most interesting job of the lot." He turned to Rissa. "You have anything special you want to do?"

"I had thought, since Felcie is here, to take the aircar and let her see something of the plains below."

Felcie said, "Thanks, Tari, but how about another day?" She turned. "Captain Limmer?" Rissa frowned, but Felcie ignored her. "Do you have—pictures—of Vanessa Largane?"

"Why, yes—I guess so. In my quarters someplace. I haven't looked—for so long. But—" He did not ask the question that showed in his face.

"Could I see them? I mean—if it's all right?"

After a pause, Limmer nodded. "Sure." He stood. "Come with me. Maybe it's time I looked again, too." He took her arm as she rose and led her out. At the doorway he turned and said, "Long as you don't need me on those hull plates, Tregare—"

Rissa shook her head. "I fear she pushes him too fast, Bran —as she did the controls in the practice turret."

Tregare smiled. "People are more flexible than computers.

If he couldn't face up to it, he wouldn't have agreed." He drank the last of his coffee. "You want to come see how we cut hull plates?"

"Not especially. But if that is what you must do, I will join you."

TREGARE erased a marking and redrew it. "It's not as simple as it looks," he said. "The hole has to match the trumpet-shaped funnel that seals to the projector's pivot mount. The funnel's not symmetrical—you've seen one?" She nodded. "So we set it for lefthand or right—simpler than making two models—and I have to compensate."

He grinned. "The missiles, now—that's simpler. But for all of it we'll need duplicate covers—in case we have to use the camouflage trick more than once."

"And my idea, for extra turrets on *No Return*, makes it no easier."

"Worth it, though—if they surprise the hell out of somebody at the right time."

She touched his arm. "Time, Bran—will there be enough?"

He shrugged. "Who knows? We'll keep pushing, as if we did know. Two more ships, though—I wish we had them already. That costs me sleep, some nights."

"I know—I wake to hear you breathing as no sleeper does."

His arm hugged her shoulders. "Next time, say hello."

Before she could answer, two men brought a drawing, arguing over its interpretation. Looking, Tregare found the flaw. "That circle's from somebody's coffee cup. Don't try to work on your break time—not with a sepia print."

When the men had left, he said, "More likely they were sneaking breaks into work time—but the way I said it, they'll listen better."

She nodded. "Yes. You have a good touch, Bran, with such matters."

"Maybe; I hope so. Hey—I'm done here! Let's *us* take the aircar down the hills."

•   •   •

TREGARE flew it; Rissa pointed and said, "There—toward the water, the Big Sink!"

"All right, if you want—but we can't get all the way there and back before dark. How about the hummocks off there to the south? Want to see those?" She agreed.

The pattern of hummocks covered miles—each mound roughly fifty feet high and three hundred across, spaced irregularly and densely covered with short grasslike growth.

"Bran? Shall we land on one?"

"No. There's some odd stories from the early days—I don't know how true, and I don't want to find out the hard way. I'll set us down in that gap—looks like a river used to run there."

Aground, they walked along the dry canyon and looked up at the hummocks to either side. The sun's heat warmed them. They came to the edge of a cliff, where the canyon floor dropped, looked down into the shadows for a time, then turned back. Rissa's foot caught against a rock; she stumbled. Tregare caught her arm; momentum swung her to face him squarely.

She broke the kiss. "Here? The ground is rough." A moment later she laughed and said, "With our clothes on, Bran?"

"Why not?"

"All right—but wait! There is a rock under me!

"Now—that is better."

SHE lay, his face against her shoulder, and looked into distance; she felt joy that they shared peace. Then she saw it.

"Bran!"

"What?"

"Look!" She pointed; he lifted his head and turned to see. From the nearest hummock something had raised—long and thin, shockingly swift. It lashed the air, then swept the ground around the hummock. Rissa smelled a stench like stagnant swamp. The thing raised itself again, emitted a harsh, clacking sound, then retracted and was gone. Rissa said, "I am glad you knew not to land us there."

He whistled, a short, tuneless burst. "I never saw that before. Don't know anyone who has—it was just Backhills talk. Well, now we know."

As they got up, she said, "But we do not, Bran. We know it is big and *looks* dangerous. We have not seen it do any harm."

Now they walked; he reached to stroke her hair. "Let someone else find out about that. You and I—we'll just leave it alone."

"Yes, Bran." And a few steps further; "I would like to fly the car now."

"Sure." When they got in, she lifted it and flew over a few hummocks, not high. Twice the ground split and something reached for them, but each time she sped away.

"What do you think?" she said. "Is the reaction defensive or predatory? And in either case, what possible natural target could there be?"

He shook his head. "I've got no idea, and I'm not inclined to investigate."

"Yes—we face enough dangers without seeking new ones."

Now she flew faster, rising to clear the ridge above, and the next. Her angle of approach was unfamiliar, but soon she located the peak with the slanted tip, then the half-circle ridge, and finally the crater.

She landed near *Lefthand Thread*. As they stepped outside, Felcie came down the ship's ramp to greet them. Rissa said, "Are you ready to go upslope with us? Or are there things yet to be discussed here, first?"

"Well—I—"

Tregare said, "If we're invited to stay for dinner, I accept."

"That's not—well, maybe so—" said Felcie. "But let *me* say something." She took a deep breath. "I'm staying here— with Derek."

Rissa looked at her, then at Tregare. "Derek?"

"Limmer," said Tregare. "I hadn't heard his first name in years."

Rissa said, "Felcie! What has happened?"

The girl laughed. "Well—I'm married, I think. Not that it matters—but is it valid, a ship's captain and all, you're in bed with him and he stops in the middle and says the ceremony —and *then* you finish?"

Rissa stepped forward and cupped the girl's face between both hands, looking up into her eyes. "And is it—yes, of course—I *see* it is right for you. But I am surprised—that all has moved so quickly."

Felcie grinned. "I guess I'm shameless. When I cut him out from you after lunch, I knew what I wanted. Sure didn't expect to get *married*, though—or not so soon, anyway."

Tregare moved and clasped her to him. "Somebody should kiss the bride."

When he was done, Rissa said, "I think you have done the job completely."

"And who better?" It was Limmer, descending the ramp. "Tregare—Tari—stay and help us celebrate, will you?"

Tregare gripped his shoulder tightly. "I'll celebrate you under the table, you old war dog. You may be prettier, but I'm the better drinker."

THEY went to Limmer's quarters. Dinner was late, sketchy, and fragmented, but drink and drugsticks abounded. Rissa enjoyed the euphoria and heightened sensations, but realized she paid for them in a shortened, fragile attention span. Once she found herself hugging Felcie, both of them laughing and crying at the same time.

Then they sat side by side, solemnly listening as Limmer and Tregare sang. The song began, "When I was a boy at U.E.T., twice a week they maybe let you pee—" Then the two men's versions differed, and Rissa could make out none of the worlds until the chorus line, twice repeated.

> *Yes, THAT is the reason, you can plainly see,*
> *Why there's only one latrine in all of U! E! T!*

Laughing and breathless, the men pummeled each other's shoulders. Tregare said, "You got the middle wrong, Limmer! It goes 'Some time later, when we were men, they told us we could hold it twice as long again.' Now let's try it once more."

Rissa shook her head and missed Limmer's protest as she retreated to the bathroom. For a moment she closed her eyes; when she opened them, she had forgotten where she was.

She heard loud voices and opened the door. Limmer and Felcie, nude, were embracing. Tregare clapped his hands and chanted. "Don't wait—celebrate! Don't wait—*celebrate*!"

She went to him; he kissed and held her, mumbling words she could not understand. He laughed and pointed; she turned and saw the newlyweds coupling. "Us too?" he said.

She shook her head. "Not here. And—Bran, I do not feel well."

"You lie down, then. Next cabin's empty." He led her to it; she sat heavily on the bed, then lay on one side, drawing her knees up. He touched her shoulder. "You all right?"

"I—will be." She closed her eyes, heard the door close, and could not summon purpose to open them, to see if he had gone or stayed. Then another door slammed and she knew he had rejoined the revel. After a time, she slept.

SHE woke to find herself not on but in the bed, and unclothed. Beside her lay Tregare. She yawned, stretched, and decided that except for residual nervous overexcitement, she had recovered fully. Her clothes hung neatly over the back of a chair; she got up and began dressing.

Tregare opened his eyes, sneezed once and sat up. "How are you, Bran?"

"I've been better. Worse, too, though—I'll manage."

"Thank you for putting me to bed. I do not remember it."

"Thank Felcie—she put us *both* to bed, after I helped her with Limmer." He grinned. "I *told* him I could outdrink him." He looked around. "I guess I left my clothes in there. No robe here, either."

"I will get them, if anyone is awake to open the door."

For a moment he looked at her. "You want to know what happened?"

"I did not ask."

"Well—*nothing* did."

"I am sorry if you were disappointed."

"Oh, peace drop off a cliff! It was my own choice."

She went to him. "I would not have minded, Bran, if all were willing. We have said, remember, that outside our bed we each are free. But this time I am glad you did nothing, for it is not well to make such decisions when drugged."

"That's what I thought—with what little brains I had working."

"I will go see about your clothing."

•　•　•

FELCIE, wearing a robe, answered her knock. "Derek's still asleep. I guess you're after Tregare's clothes? I just plain forgot to take them along last night."

"Bran says you got me into bed. Thank you."

Felcie gathered Tregare's things and handed them over. "Tari—"

"Yes, what is it?"

"Oh—nothing." Rissa nodded and returned to the other cabin. Tregare dressed; after they had washed, they went to the galley.

His appetite had not suffered, she noticed, and hers was normally hearty. They were drinking coffee when Limmer and Felcie entered. Neither said anything beyond greetings; Rissa thought they seemed embarrassed. Well, that was *their* problem.

Then Limmer said, "I guess we got a little tipped up last night. And I noticed you left early, Tari—everything all right?"

She looked at the scarred, sneering face, and her resolve melted. "Quite all right. It was only that I had much more drink and drug than usual and reacted poorly—so I went to let my mind clear without disturbing your celebration." She smiled. "As I left, it seemed your wedding night proceeded well."

"She told you, did she now? The ceremony, I mean? Well, I couldn't think of a better time for it."

"It was most fitting." Then, to Tregare; "Should we not go upslope this morning? There are calls to make, and—"

"It wouldn't be," said Limmer, "that you're uncomfortable here, about anything?"

She shook her head. "No—truly not." He did not look convinced, so she rose and went to him. "Men always kiss the bride. I think that is most unfair to the other women—and to the groom." She bent down, and the kiss was long and firm. When she straightened again, she smiled and said, "Now we have had our due also, you and I."

He laughed. "All right—whatever my question was, that answers it." Then; "Tregare—any special instructions today?"

"Just that you could expand weapons training, if you haven't already—set up some simulations so people can practice on their own ships in as many turrets as are handy to rig.''

"*Carcharodon*'s already in the business; I'll get onto *No Return* today. And you've got the hull plates marked?''

"Yes, and numbered. Not duplicates, though. Have somebody take care of that—two spare sets all around.''

"All right.'' They shook hands. "If anything needs it, I'll call on scramble.''

Tregare and Rissa left the ship. At first they did not see the aircar; then it emerged from behind a building and taxied toward them, Deverel driving. He came alongside them, leaned out, and said, "Thought I'd fuel her while I thought of it. We going back to the scout today?''

"Yes,'' said Tregare. "And right now, unless you've something more to do here.'' Deverel shook his head; they entered and he took the car up. His piloting was competent and cautious; Rissa wondered about his inward reaction to some of her and Tregare's maneuvers. Well, he had never complained. . . .

AT the cabin they found that Kenekke had completely repaneled the door and cut away the burned wood from the front wall, exposing blackened metal. The men went to the scout, Rissa into the cabin. She made coffee, bathed, and changed her clothing, putting the discarded garments to launder. As she turned the machine on, Tregare entered.

"Word from Hawkman, Rissa! Sten Norden's agreed to sell —*Valkyrie*'s on her way here. Hawkman stayed and sold the frozen gas contract to—I forget the name—it's a ship I don't know.'' He poured them coffee and sat. "One problem—Norden wants off. Says he's too old to change—to command an armed ship that means business.'' He scratched his cheek where the tattoo had been. "So who do I put in charge? I know Norden personally, but none of his officers.''

"And if you install one of your own, there might be trouble?''

"Using the truth field? Not hardly. And my man—or woman—would have a cadre along, too, for coordination. But—''

"Who are you thinking of? Do I know any?''

"You've met a couple; you may not remember them.

Gonnelsen, my First on *Inconnu*—"

"I remember him, though we did not speak together. A very—*contained*—man."

"That's him. Well, he'd be ideal—but he doesn't *want* command. He had first offer of *Lefthand Thread*—Limmer was new with me then—and turned it down. So—next in line is Zelde M'tana, my Second. She could handle it."

"The tall African woman, yes. I liked her. And she is a striking person."

"True. But more important, she's capable—*and* has the command-type mind."

"Then she is your choice?"

"I think so. The only knot in the string is—it'd be my Second Hat taking over, in charge of Norden's First and the rest."

"Why do you not—no, I must think longer."

"Let's hear it. Then we can both think."

"Two heads—? All right—why do you not name Zelde M'tana acting captain of *Inconnu* until you—both of us—rejoin that ship? If you explain the reason to her and to Gonnelsen—and you say he does not wish command—might not that solve it?"

He squinted, looking past her into air. "Yeah, that'll do it. I had another idea, but this is quicker and more plausible."

"And on *Inconnu*, who replaces the woman?"

"Hain moves up to Second. And for Third—" He paused, then grinned. "You want to see my new Third Hat?" She nodded. "Then go look in a mirror!"

"Tregare—Bran!" She shook her head. "I cannot do it. I am not qualified."

He counted points on his fingers. "One—you're learning navigation and control. Two—you outscore any turret gunner I have; I want you in charge of that department, and to do the job right, you need some rank. Three—when it comes to officer material on *Inconnu*, you're the best I've got. Now—is that enough?"

She argued no further. "All right—there is a paper I have seen but not yet read. It is old; the edges are frayed. The cover says, 'NEW Ship's Regulations,' by order of Bran Tregare, and the date. I wish to study it."

He nodded. "Sure. There's a copy in the scout—maybe

two. I'll find you one. You already know most of it, though —do your job, obey orders, no fighting without captain's permission, no drink or drug on duty. Oh, there's more—but some of it was just me showing off, and isn't to be taken seriously now." He chuckled. "Maybe I should publish a new edition."

The laundering machine buzzed and turned itself on. Rissa said, "Then I will read both versions."

LUNCH came late, as breakfast had; then they went to the scout. Tregare taped a message for *Inconnu*, ordering and explaining Zelde M'tana's promotion. He stopped the tape and said to Deverel, "That makes you Second; all right?"

"Sure, captain—it's the same job, just a little more rank. Now who fills in for *me*?"

"Turn your head a little and you're looking at her."

Deverel blinked, then smiled. "Congratulations, Ms. Kerguelen—the skipper makes good choices. But watch out for him—on his bad days, he's a real tyrant."

"Thank you, Hain—or do I say 'sir,' now that you outrank me? Before, of course, I had no place on that ladder."

Palm forward, Deverel spread a hand. "Even on ship— which we aren't—rank only means precedence of command. It doesn't get in the way much."

"On *Inconnu*, you mean," said Tregare. "Ships differ. All right—let me finish this tape before the next signal window comes up and passes. What's the date?" Deverel told him; he nodded. "Three days left—and they can catch signal on the way in. After all this dull time sitting watch out there, *Inconnu* deserves a little fling in port."

"Three days until what, Bran?"

"Until we could last get a signal from a ship close enough to get here—and still be outfitted in time to join us." He restarted the tape and gave orders for *Inconnu*—return, refueling, crew leave, and the move to Base Two. At the end he said, "We're only five ships; it's not enough and I know it, but we can talk about that when you get here. I hope someone can convince me I'm wrong. Good speed; we await you."

He turned from the machine to Deverel. "Give Limmer the gist of it, to tell the others." Then, "Hain? You think there's any chance we could do it with five?''

Deverel shrugged. "If anyone could, it's us.''

THE day after *Valkyrie* landed, Rissa and Tregare flew the pass to meet with its captain. On board his ship, Norden—white-haired, but younger than Rissa had expected—served brandy to his guests. He introduced a thin, pale man. "Kile Ressider, my First.''

They shook hands. Ressider said, "Pleasure, Tregare. By the way, nobody's told us—will this be my ship, under you, or are you bringing someone in?''

Tregare looked at him. "Except for where you bunk, does it make any big difference in your plans either way?''

"My question was asked first.''

"Like that, is it?'' Tregare shrugged. "All right. I need one of my own commanding, because I don't *know* you yet. If you can't live with that, I'll buy you out—fair shares—you'll have the money to buy into another berth if one comes along.''

"Not so fast!'' Low, close to the table, Ressider waved a hand. "I've heard about you, Tregare—If I'd believed it better, I wouldn't have pushed. Wait a minute—let me *think*.'' He closed his eyes hard, then opened them. "I'd work under Sten indefinitely—but he's leaving—and *sure*, I hoped for command someday. Now I won't be getting it. I don't *know*!''

He shook his head, pale wispy hair flying as Tregare waited. Finally, "Oh, all right. Staying First on *Valkyrie*'s better than buying into an unknown setup.'' He reached to shake hands again. "You can depend on me, Tregare. Ask Sten.''

Norden said, "I trust Kile with my life. I should—twice, he's saved it.''

Rissa thought, *It does not matter—Tregare has the truth field*. But she listened as Tregare said, "You have a better chance than you think, Ressider. If plans work out, we'll have more ships than officers good enough to command them.''

"And if plans don't work out?''

Tregare grinned. "You know better than that. Dead men don't command much of anything.''

Ressider took a quick breath, then laughed. "*Now* you tell me. All right, I'm still in it. Now—who takes over for Sten?''

"Name's Zelde M'tana. Not likely you'd know her—she didn't come up through UET.''

"Then where did she train?"

"Didn't, formally. Was living with a ship's captain—gradually learned and took charge in his name while drugs and sickness killed him. You've heard of Parnell and *Chanticleer*?"

Ressider sucked in his breath. "Yes—of course—but I thought that ship was lost."

"Not so. Zelde changed its name to *Kilimanjaro*. But she'd been pushed uprank so fast—all the way from cargo to captain—that some of the crew wouldn't accept her in permanent command. So a coalition bought her out, and she got off. I found her on Fair Ball; she's been with me ever since."

"I'm convinced—from someone like that, I can learn."

"Anyone can. I did." Tregare rose. "Sten, I want to stand you dinner—and catch up on a lot of talk—before you vanish groundside and look for what to do next. All right?"

"Of course. And I should say, the terms are fair. Your representative, Hawkman Moray—I like the man."

"That's good—so do I. He's my father."

Norden stared. "Tregare—I never knew you were Hulzein-connected."

"Until recently I wasn't, effectively—we left each other alone. But now we work together."

"I almost wish I were staying on. I knew—your aunt, would she be? The one in Argentina. About fifty-five she was then, and one hell of a woman. She's the one who persuaded me Escape was possible, and next time out we *did* it. Her name—?"

"Erika. My aunt, yes. I saw her once—but she didn't know it. Well, then, dinner—when's convenient for you?"

"Tomorrow, the next day. Either. I'll be packing, to get off before you move the ship. So, whenever it suits you."

"Day after tomorrow, then. I'll pick you up, help you move into town." They shook hands and said good-byes; Rissa and Tregare left the ship.

SHE checked the day-count on her watch. "Bran—I forgot—yesterday I should have been at the Hatchery for a pre-ovulation check. It may not be too late. Take me there now?"

"All right if you just take the aircar yourself and come back when you're done? I mean—I'll drive you if you want, but I do have a lot to take care of around here.''

Rissa said, "Yes—I remember the traffic markers well enough. Where will I find you?''

"Hmm—how about over at the corner where we landed the scout?''

"Yes." She kissed him and got into the aircar. She found the DRC building with no difficulty, and Estelle Marco was free to see her almost immediately.

This time Rissa knew what to expect—the slight discomfort of gas moving inside her, after the cold feel on her belly as the "faucet handle" opened passage to her ova. This time no blockage was found, and in a very few minutes, after talking briefly with Dr. Marco, she was outside again. As she got into the aircar she heard slow thunder. Looking toward the port, she saw the ship descend.

She flew a little faster than the city's traffic rules sanctioned, and landed where she had agreed. She did not see Tregare, so she got out and walked toward the new ship, less than a mile away. When she neared it she saw its name: *Graf Spee*. She thought, *Why, it's one of his! Now he has the six he needs!* She tried to remember more of what he had said.

At the ship's ramp she met an armed guard. She said, "Is Tregare aboard?''

The man said, "If he is, who wants him?''

"Tell him Tari Obrigo.''

"I never heard of you.''

"Nor I of you—but be advised that Tregare will want to know I am here.''

"I'll see." He talked into the unit strapped to his wrist, listened, then nodded. "Captain Krueger says you can go up. Sorry—we never know who anyone is at a strange landing.''

"In such case, would not courtesy be the safer course?'' But she added, "Aboard I will say nothing to your disfavor.''

She did not wait for an answer, but climbed the ramp and entered. Inside, the ship was nearly a twin to *Lefthand Thread*. Guessing, she tried the galley first and found Tregare sitting and talking with a slim blonde woman. He looked up and waved a hand as Rissa approached.

The woman stood; she was considerably below average height. Tregare said, "Tari, meet Ilse Krueger. We're six ships now!''

As Rissa shook hands she looked carefully at Ilse Krueger—pale curly hair, blue eyes slightly tilted, strong cheekbones that dominated the thin face. Thirty years, biological? Or thirty-five, perhaps? And for all her look of fragility, the woman's handclasp had strength.

"Let me see if I remember," said Rissa. "You are freely allied, with nothing owed?"

"He told it right, I see." Coming from so small a body, the deep voice surprised Rissa. "Yes. Bernardez and I—if he gets here—we're in it because it needs doing. Like poor Hoad—except that he was obligated and we're not. Of course if Tregare pulls it off, we'll all profit." She motioned. "Here, let's sit down. There's coffee and things. Now—I hear you've married this great beast. Nothing wrong with that, if your tastes run so. He tells me you're a match for anything on two feet." She sniffed. "Can't say you look it, but looks can fool a person. I—"

"Peace, Ilse Krueger! So many quick words—give us a chance to know each other. I am not that difficult to know."

Tregare laughed. "I told you, Ilse. Didn't I?"

"You've told me a lot of things—mostly true, I grant." Then, to Rissa; "All right—*you* talk for a while."

"What is to say? My life, until now? Very well. I am Earth-born, was Welfared as a child, and am Escaped. I am trained in combat and have needed to kill three. Tregare and I have married; when it is time, I go with him on *Inconnu*. What else would you know?"

"You don't like me, do you?"

"I have no dislike. If someone pushes, I push back. Nothing more."

Ilse Krueger paused, then said, "We're different, that's all."

"Lots different," said Tregare. "And both valuable to me, different ways."

The small woman laughed. "All right, Tari—we're both working for the same maniac. I think we can get along." But Rissa found neither words nor tone convincing.

"I hope so," she said, "though I do not entirely understand."

"Don't worry about it," said Tregare. "Time to go, anyway."

He stood. Ilse Krueger said, "Wait a minute. It just struck

me—I've heard the name Tari Obrigo before, earlier today."

Tregare's brows rose. "So? She's known here."

Krueger shook her head. "No. It was one of my passengers, fresh out of freeze but young and strong enough to start moving right away. He was asking for you groundside, Tari—for you and two or three other names."

UET? "What did he look like?" Rissa waited.

"I barely glanced at him. Slim, about Tregare's height— white face, dark hair. That's all I remember."

Rissa frowned. "Do you know his name?" Though if he *were* UET, it hardly mattered. . . .

"Just a minute. The list should be under these papers." Krueger found it, ran a finger down the margin and turned the sheet so Rissa could read it. "This one."

The name meant nothing to Rissa; she repeated it and shook her head. "I do not recognize it, but I thank you for the information. I will be on guard."

"Both of us," said Tregare. "Well, Ilse, you can be at Base Two in three days? We'll have the crews ready to start converting."

"Good enough, Tregare. I have cargo to dicker off—I'm already set for refueling—and that's all."

"Then I'll see you next, probably, across the Hills." He shook hands—Rissa did not—and they went downship and outside.

Krueger's manner still bothered Rissa. "I do *not* dislike her . . . yet. Is there some reason she should resent me?"

"She doesn't. Ilse just has to crowd everybody a little. You got off easier than most; I think she likes you."

"I felt no communication, no rapport. But I suppose that is not necessary, to exchange information over a viewscreen."

"Forget it—I guarantee there's no problem. Now, then— what happened at the Hatchery?" She told him; he said, "Good. They get the ovum from you day after tomorrow— right?" She nodded. "We'll stay at Maison Renalle that night —have Norden to dinner, and maybe Ressider—even Ilse, if you don't mind. And—"

She touched his arm. "Yes, Bran. But we will be there first for a time, before the rest. *Then* you may invite anyone you wish."

Hand in hand, arms swinging together, they walked toward the aircar. Pointing at it, he said, "I've ordered out a couple more of those—newer models but not much different. As things are, we're running too low on mobility."

"Who pilots the third one? I mean—through the pass?"

"No hurry. Two will hold us for a while. Hawkman's due back soon; likely he'll visit us and can bring it then."

"That is feasible. And what are we to do now?"

"Wait. Get the word to some people I know, to be on the lookout for Mr. Nosy Stranger. And catch up on some business in the city. Is Maison Renalle all right with you?"

She nodded. "Although I shall not stay hidden—it is not practical—assured safety in our own quarters will be welcome."

"Sure. Too bad we're stuck, for now, with the need to fill that peace-jangling zoom-womb!"

"I am no fonder of the restriction than you are. But it is necessary."

TREGARE carried their luggage into Maison Renalle—then, after checking them in, up to a room Rissa recognized as security quarters. Relaying through the Lodge and the scout, he called Limmer and gave him the news. "So paint two more landing circles. Expect *Valkyrie*—Kile Ressider's acting captain until Zelde gets here—two days from now. Krueger with *Graf Spee* the day after. I may be one day later, maybe not—either way you can go ahead with the hull plates."

As Limmer cut circuit, Sparline's face appeared on the screen. "So you're in town! Why didn't you stop by?" She smiled and shook her head. "Never mind—I know you're busy, Bran. But, Rissa—I'm coming in tomorrow myself. Can we meet?"

They arranged it for mid-morning at the Maison, and for Tregare to join them for a noontime meal. When the call was done, Rissa said, "Bran—what do they, at the Lodge, know of what has happened with us? I have not spoken of your business to any, even Liesel."

"I've sent in progress reports every day or two—on the work, though, nothing about Peralta's caper and all that."

"Then how much may I tell Sparline?"

"All you want. This is family—social. My reports were business."

"Good." She looked out the window. "The sun is still high,

but it seems much later; I am hungry." Then she laughed. "No wonder—I am used to our early sunsets, behind the Hills!"

They had dinner served in the room. Afterward, Tregare made a few calls, then studied papers at a small desk. For a time Rissa watched an entertainment channel on the viewscreen, sound turned low. Then she switched it off and read for a while. Tired from the previous night's excesses, they went to bed early.

TREGARE was up and gone early the next morning, leaving without breakfast. Rissa woke in time to kiss him good morning, then could not get back to sleep. She ordered breakfast and ate, then showered and washed her hair. She was still drying it when Sparline arrived. The two embraced; Rissa stepped back and said, "I suppose I could have clothed myself before welcoming a guest. Would you like coffee or anything?"

"Coffee's fine." Rissa ordered it, put on a robe, and sat.

Before conversation got far, a boy brought the tray. Rissa poured, and said, "I have not kept in touch well, I know."

"Reading between the lines of Bran's reports, I'm not surprised. Rissa, what in the flaming name of peace has been *happening* over there, across the Hills?"

"Well, so that I do not waste your time, what do you know?"

Sparline summarized. Rissa said, "You have not heard the matter of Jimar Peralta, who commanded *No Return*." She told the story, but could not bring herself to speak of Osallin. "It will not happen again, that sort of thing. We have borrowed Arni Gustafson's truth field equipment and checked everyone at Base Two. And of course Bran will interview the people of the new ships the same way. You know of those two?"

"Yes. I played the tape off the relay last night. But, Rissa —Bran's all right now?"

"It has been—about two weeks, I think. A few spots are still scabbed, but he dispensed with bandages several days ago."

Sparline nodded. "He heals fast—he always did." She touched Rissa's hand. "You're definitely going with him, are you?"

"I—" Rissa laughed. "I am to be Third Hat on *Inconnu*!" Seeing Sparline's puzzled look, she said, "Oh, it is not nepotism—he convinced me the appointment is valid, or I would not have accepted it."

"Sure—I know that—about both of you. Just seemed quick."

"To me, also. And now, Sparline—what occurs at the Lodge?"

"Well, Hawkman's due soon on the packet. Liesel's eager as a bride, but never tell her I said so! Ernol, now—for a while there, trying to learn more than he could in such a short time, he really wore himself out. But now he's on top of the job, and not even Liesel can shake him. He and I, we're all but married—I think Liesel's waiting only until we can all be together, to announce it." She put a hand to Rissa's shoulder. "You and Bran—you *will* visit the Lodge before you leave, won't you?"

"Of course. We would not depart without seeing all of you first. And not only once, with any luck." She smiled.

"I'm glad. Rissa—it's a short time you've been here. But I feel I've known you a lot longer."

Not smiling now, Rissa said, "I know. I feel much the same."

THEY were talking of other things—business matters, the conduct of Rissa's local holdings in her absence—when Tregare entered. He hugged Sparline, then Rissa, and said, "Let me order us lunch. I came in the back way, past the kitchen, and saw something—brought in fresh—I haven't had for a long time." He spoke on the intercom, then said, "Just wait—you'll see."

When the meal came, Rissa ate with enjoyment. "You were right, Bran—this is delicious. A marine creature, is it not? But at what stage of evolution? Not fish—the texture is different —yet not the equivalent of mammal. Reptile? Amphibian?"

He shook his head. "No Earthly analogue—here, evolution's taken some sidetracks. This critter's scaled and cold-blooded, but has a four-chambered heart and births its young alive. The lower front fins look a lot like hands."

Rissa's cutlery clattered against her plate. "Bran—could it be *intelligent*?"

He grinned. "No chance. In another half billion years it might start to be, maybe. Right now it's strictly an eating machine—mostly teeth. Bright for its habitat, but that's not saying much."

She resumed eating. "All right—but for a moment you spoiled my appetite."

After the meal, the three left Maison Renalle and walked toward the major retail district. "If you're after clothes, Rissa," Tregare said, "bear to your right after I leave you."

"Yes—I had not thought before, but my wardrobe will not suffice for our travels." Then; "Whom do you deal with next?"

"Man named Carlingen, in the Open Exchange up ahead here. Struck me, we might run low on sheet metal. *Graf Spee* can take it across the hills."

They parted, and the two women shopped for clothing. Rissa sought utilitarian shipboard garb; Sparline's choices were more ornamental. By mid-afternoon, both were satisfied; they stopped at an outdoor café and shared a small bottle of wine.

"I wish you weren't going!" Sparline said. "Or Bran, either. And now Liesel and Hawkman want to go to Earth. By the time I see any of you again—if I ever do—I'll be an old woman!"

Rissa sighed. "The long view—between stars, the years compress. It works well for dynasties. But for individuals—Sparline, I wish I had answers for you, but I do not."

"Oh well—" Sparline tried to smile. "Ernol and I—we'll breed our heirs and raise them—then maybe *we'll* go to Earth."

"It is a possibility. Now, shall we return to Maison Renalle?"

As they entered the Maison, an attendant called to Rissa. "Ms. Obrigo? A young man was asking for you—and others. He didn't say who he was; I called your room, but you were out. He gave me this."

He handed her a memo sheet, and she read:

Rissa Kerguelen
Lysse Harnain

Tari Obrigo
Cele Metrokin

The man said, "I told him nothing—only that if I saw any of these persons, I'd show them the paper. Then he left—said he'd be back later."

"Yes. Thank you." *No Laura Konig.* She showed the note to Sparline. "From Earth, not Far Corner. But Erika, or UET?" She turned to the attendant. "What did he look like?"

"Nothing out of the way, at first look. Thin, pale, medium tall. Black hair—a little long for here, and tied back. Quiet-speaking man. But he moves like a cat."

Rissa shook her head. "I do not recognize anyone from the description." *Except Ilse Krueger's inquisitive passenger.* "But it is unlikely that I would know him."

"Instructions, Ms. Obrigo?"

"If he returns while I am here, put him through on the viewscreen, but do not tell him the number of my room."

"Right—I'll do that." The two women left and went toward the room. On the way, Rissa told what Krueger had reported.

Sparline said, "What are you going to do? What if he doesn't come back while you're here?"

"I will leave a blind relay set up to the Lodge, then to wherever I expect to be at a given time. For a while, at least."

"Aren't you worried?"

"Not greatly—there is no point to it. As Bran would say, merely exercising normal caution." They were at the door, Rissa opened it and stepped inside. When Sparline had followed and the door was closed, a man stepped out of the bathroom. He fit the attendant's description—as well as Krueger's.

Watching his hands, Rissa dropped her parcels and circled to the man's left. "Who are you? How did you get in here?"

Tight-lipped, he smiled. "It's you, all right. Don't you recognize me? Not a very friendly greeting from my own sister."

"Ivan?" Shocked, thinking rapidly, she paused. "How can I be sure? Tell me—oh—the day our parents were killed—what color dress did I wear?"

He frowned. "I don't remember much from then, clearly—or from before Erika's, for that matter. But—*red*, I think—and your hair was in pigtails and—no, that's all I get." He shook his head. "But who besides Erika knew those four

names?'' He spread his hands wide. "I have papers from her
—will that help?''

Suddenly she knew. *"Ivan!"* She rushed to embrace and
kiss him. Then, "Sparline—my brother, Ivan Marchant. *He* is
the one who has been asking of me. Ivan, this is Sparline
Moray—she's a niece of Erika's.''

Sparline shook the man's hand, but said to Rissa, "You're
sure? How?''

"When he looked puzzled, just now. Ivan studied far ahead
of his age group, as did I. And when he struck something he
could not solve and went to ask our mother or father, his face
had that exact same expression.''

She turned again to her brother. "Oh, Ivan—it is so good to
have you here! Now tell me of yourself.''

"For starters," said Sparline, "how did you get in here?''

He grinned. "I learned a lot about security measures at
Erika's. And compared to Earth's, yours are behind the
times.''

"Yes.'' Rissa nodded. "Always, the time lag plagues the
Hidden Worlds. But you have not said—how did you come to
this place?''

"To the planet, on *Graf Spee*—but I didn't know it until
this morning, because I was transshipped in freeze. At Terranova, by one of Erika's agents—I knew that much in advance, and the name of this world she'd just learned of—we
agreed it sounded good. Then today, getting off the ship, I
heard the name Maison Renalle. I figured it *had* to be a Hulzein connection, so I tried the wild chance that you might be
here.''

Sparline said, "The attendant said he gave you no information. How did you locate this room?''

"He tried to call here. I watched him punch the number.''

"Part of your specialty? What are some of the others?''

Now he did not smile. "What I do best, Ms. Moray, is kill.
I'm very, very good at killing—and there's always a market
for it.''

Rissa touched his arm; he looked at her, then relaxed.
"Ivan? Are you here for that purpose?''

He put a hand on her shoulder. "If that's what you want of
me—or anything else. It's your money that got me out of Welfare and into Erika's for two years, putting me mostly back

together. I owe you service. And I don't have anybody else. So now I've found you—and who did I find, by the way? Which name goes here?''

"Here, and with the Hulzeins, my own. Publicly, Tari Obrigo—though I no longer bother with that name's disguise. But now—sit down, shall we? Have some wine and tell me what has happened.''

They sat. Sipping pale wine, Ivan began. "As I said—two years at Erika's. She's a great old one, isn't she? Taught me, had me taught—broke most of the blocks Welfare'd carved into my mind. Not all, but most.'' His mouth tightened, then made effort to smile.

"You shocked her once, Rissa—you know that? When she heard what happened to the *scheisskopf* that killed our parents, she knew it was your doing. And she said, 'Peace knows what I've turned loose against this world!''

"Peace knows, indeed—but what of yourself, Ivan?''

"I—before I left Earth, I paid a little of our debt myself. Got two members of the Committee—one by poison and one with my hands. It was a hot time for a while, I tell you—but I chose the two I was the size to impersonate, and got away with it. Partly due to help set up by Erika. Why, I shipped out—believe this?—disguised as a UET agent supposed to be sent in a disguise of his own, to get a look at the Hidden Worlds. The Underground caught him and stripped his mind. Erika persuaded them not to waste his perfectly good identity.''

He drained his glass; Rissa refilled it. "Now then, Rissa—and Ms. Moray—do you think I can be of any use to you?''

"You are *welcome* with us,'' said Rissa. "For now, at least, I do not think you need kill for us.''

Sparline gave a faint laugh. "Maybe you're a little behind the times, about Rissa. Nobody has to do her killing for her—or for her husband, my brother.''

"Husband? You're married, Rissa?''

"Yes—and he should be here soon. I have married Bran Tregare Moray.''

"*Tregare?* Tregare the *pirate*?'' He laughed. "Peace be pampered, but you made a great choice! Back when I was still on Earth, that name was giving UET hermorrhoids. What it must be like there, by now—with the Underground playing its deadly pranks—''

"UET expects attack by Tregare?" *This could wreck his entire plan.*

"UET's scared of its own shadow—and the more scared, the more brutal. That kind of power can't keep a clear conscience. The second Committee member I got—Shelda Fainsway, and the disguise was a real chore—begged me to do it fast. She'd supervised enough torture to know what it was like, and—"

"Did you oblige her?" said Sparline.

His lips pulled apart in a snarl. "Not right away. I—" Then his face went blank of all expression, as Rissa had seen it at Erika's.

"Ivan? There is something? Something you need to say?"

His voice was dead monotone. "One thing Erika couldn't fix. I'm not potent with women—and not interested in men, for that matter. In Welfare the worst punishments—the pain-shock reinforcements—were done by women. And the way they did it—well, two years didn't cure me; I think it's permanent. So I gave Shelda Fainsway a little—only a little—of what she'd helped authorize doing to me."

"Ivan—" Rissa shook her head. "I cannot blame you—such beasts—and as you say, my arrangements for Newhausen were hardly gentle. But do not surrender yet to what was done. You are—how old?"

"I don't know—let's see. Forty-seven chrono, I'm told; probably only about twenty-two bio. But what good does that do?"

"Your mind is hardly more than two years out of Welfare. Give it time to heal."

"Well, maybe." He looked at her. "How come you seem *older* than I do? I don't mean looks, but the way you think."

"I have had the chance to do more and learn from it. As you will now, also." She poured more wine. "Now let me tell you of my life since leaving Erika and Earth."

She told it briefly, then said, "Did I omit anything, Sparline?"

The other woman shook her head. "Not that I know of."

Ivan said, "They make mistakes, don't they? You, me, Tregare—they let us live. I suppose they can't kill everyone who might be dangerous."

"I—" Rissa began; then the door opened and Tregare entered. "Bran!" She ran to him. "Here is—"

His kiss sealed her mouth; then he reached a hand to the other man. "Hello, Ivan Marchant. I'm glad you made it to here."

"Bran—you knew? Why did you not tell me?"

The handclasp done, Tregare shook his head, grinning. "I didn't know—I found out when you did." He gestured for everyone to sit. "You fooled Liesel's alarms, Ivan, but you missed one of mine. A gadget in my pocket started buzzing, and I came back here on the run." He turned to Rissa. "You two had already gone up here—if it was trouble I'd be too late to help. So I unlocked a special monitor circuit—when you came in I was watching, with one finger on the sleepy-gas button. Right at first I almost pushed it—but I knew you'd be mad as hell, Rissa, if you didn't get a chance to handle things yourself." She returned his smile.

Ivan said, flat-voiced, "Then you heard it all?"

"No. First, just to where Rissa knew you. Then I had to reassure the clerk so he didn't call for help, and missed some. Then you were saying the Underground uses my name to scare UET with, and I want to hear more about that—so I switched off and locked the monitor again. Now, then—what kind of thing do they say?"

Ivan relaxed. Rissa thought, *If Bran knew his trouble, he would feel shamed—but it is all right now.* Her brother said, "Anything and everything—the wilder the better. Let's see— that you have fifty ships, maybe a hundred, and all armed. That you've begun exterminating UET colonies. That you're force-growing zygotes from extracted sperm and ova and have millions of fanatic troops on a world UET never heard of. That you've allied with aliens that have faster-than-light travel. You name it; it's been said." He paused. "Is that the kind of thing you want to know?"

Tregare grinned. "Exactly—and it helps my purpose. Because the one thing they've missed, apparently, is what I *do* plan." He drank some wine. "And *that* part, if you don't mind, I'll tell you after we've had a little talk—on the other side of the Big Hills."

The truth field, Rissa thought. Well, Tregare could hardly accept, on faith, a man whose mind had been mauled as Ivan's had. Her brother said, "Of course. Not before you're sure. I understand, Tregare."

"Good. Well, then—anybody else ready for dinner? I am."

• • •

AFTER the meal, Sparline left to fly to the Lodge. Ivan arranged for a room of his own. The next day, with Tregare still busy obtaining supplies, Rissa took her brother on a walking tour of the city.

About mid-afternoon, they heard a rumble and turned to see *Graf Spee* lift to cross the Big Hills. *She accomplished her business quickly*, thought Rissa, and reflected that unless Ilse Krueger had stayed behind, she would not be joining them for dinner. Reminded, she told Ivan of the evening plans; they turned back toward the Maison. So when Tregare arrived with Norden and Ressider, all was ready.

They had dinner in a small private room off the Maison's main dining hall. Tregare, Norden, and Ressider dominated the talk, pooling information on colonies and Hidden Worlds each had visited. Rissa paid close heed and occasionally asked a question. Ivan spoke little; she could not guess his feelings. He drank sparingly, as did she; the others ended the evening in jovial, reminiscent mood. But afterward Tregare drove his guests to the port—Ressider to *Valkyrie* and Norden to a nearby hostel—and brought the aircar back safely.

RISSA and Ivan, next morning, rode with Tregare to the port. He landed alongside two new aircars. "These are the ones I said I was ordering," he said. "Quick delivery, and all checked out. Make free with one today, if you want. I'll leave word for Hawkman, when he arrives, to take the other to the Lodge. And I'll use Old Reliable, here, and see you at the Maison."

"Yes," said Rissa, "when all our today's businesses are concluded." She kissed him and he walked away toward *Valkyrie*.

Flying back over the city, Rissa explained the traffic indicators. Ivan nodded. "Yes—with your light traffic here, it's a good system. When you come to need more levels and get into diagonal routes, the transitions get harder to indicate."

Explaining her mission as they flew, she went to the Delayed

Reproduction Center. Estelle Marco drew forth the ovum successfully and assured her that the first zygote was frozen at an optimum stage; the second would be formed and join it shortly.

Rissa introduced the doctor to Ivan but did not mention their relationship. When the older woman was absent for a few minutes, Rissa said, "Ivan? Why do you not deposit sperm here? You can, can you not?" Expressionless, he nodded. "Then you should do so—your genes are worth preserving, and in case—"

Scowling, he said, "What for? Oh, I can—and Erika had my plastic valves opened, thinking there'd be a psychological difference or something. But they'd gotten that from me several times already, back at Welfare. You must know that much."

"But that was to breed slaves—here you would sire free persons."

Estelle Marco returned. Rissa raised eyebrows to her brother, and finally he nodded. She made the request for him. Marco agreed, and a few minutes later they left the building.

In the aircar he said, "You know—it's been a long time since I'd even done *that*."

"You should. It is healthier than nothing at all."

He said nothing; when she looked at him, his face was pale and tense. "If I could kill *all* of them—maybe then—"

"To take away their power is better—and that is what Tregare plans to do."

SHE flew south, along the rise of the Big Hills to their left. Far in the distance they saw the beginning of that gigantic fall of stone monoliths piled like matchsticks—the Slab Jumbles. She said, "I wish there were time to see that place more closely—I have not been there. But now it is time to turn back."

They had flown a long way; noon was past. Expecting disappointment, Rissa opened the compartment in which sealed snacks were usually kept, and was pleasantly surprised to find that Tregare had provided them. They ate in flight.

Halfway to One Point One, they saw *Valkyrie* lift. Rissa took the car higher; they watched the ship cross the Hills and begin to drop again. "Now I see better," she said, "where Tregare's base is, from the city. I have gone usually by a roundabout way—and once so busy with other matters that I did not pay heed."

Ivan did not answer; when she turned to see him, he said, "Let me fly this thing for a while?"

"Of course. When I find the proper switch—the older model does not have this feature—I will change the controls. Yes—it is here—are you ready?" He nodded, and she gave him control.

The car wiggled briefly as he tested its response. Then he dove full out, pulled up short, spun to one side, and climbed steeply, until the propulsion unit labored. She was reaching for the oxygen tube when he laughed and began a steep descent that gradually leveled at breathable height.

"That was good," he said. "At least there's still a few things I'm good at." He shrugged. "I'm done with it; take over?"

She did so. "Ivan?" He said nothing; she spoke again. "Twice while you flew, I thought you meant to kill us both. Is it as bad as that for you?"

"It shouldn't be, I suppose. But you're right—if I'd been alone, I might have taken it all the way straight down."

"Ivan—I say this again—give yourself time to heal."

"Maybe, maybe not—heal, I mean. Two years at Erika's didn't do it."

"But you have *many* years. Do not throw them away."

Finally he said, "All right, Rissa. I won't—that's a promise."

"Good." She looked ahead. "And now we approach the city. See? Beside Maison Renalle—I believe that is Tregare's car."

WHEN they entered the room, Tregare was at the viewscreen. The picture was unrecognizable; Rissa was not surprised to hear Limmer's voice.

". . . and that's the size of it, Tregare. Krueger says the truth field's an insult. No contact with her since she walked out, and all her people with her. She's doing her sulking on

Graf Spee. Naturally, I haven't started work on that ship."

"Good—and don't, until I clear it. I'll call her direct, on scramble. Now, then—how about Ressider and *Valkyrie*? Any trouble there?"

"Not a bit. He was there—just arrived—when Krueger blew up. As soon as she left he said, he and his people were ready for the interviews, so we could get to work. He's all right, Ressider is."

"Yeah, he is. Well—so's Krueger, but she takes some handling. Look—I'll call her now—be back to you as soon as I can." He cut the circuit and turned to Rissa. "Everything go all right at the Hatchery?"

"Yes, Bran—there are no difficulties. And then we flew south, within view of the Jumbles—not near to them, of course, in the time we had. But—here, there is trouble?"

"No—and there won't be. Just a minute—I have to call Krueger." He punched out the call code. First the Lodge, then Kenekke on the scout, and finally a smudged screen speaking with Ilse Krueger's voice.

He cut off her protests. "Ilse! One of two things, and no argument. First—will you do the interviews in Limmer's shed?"

"No! Tregare, this is outrageous. If you don't trust me—"

"No argument, I said! So the second thing—take off, and right now. You're out of it."

He is bluffing! He needs that ship!

"Tregare! You can't—"

"Your hull's intact and you're fueled. So in—let's see— fifty minutes, either you're lined up for questions, or you've left for wherever you want—and no hard feelings—or Limmer has a missile with *Graf Spee*'s name on it so you *can't* take off, and we'll talk about buying you out. There's your choices— make up your mind."

She tried to speak again; he said, "Except to Limmer, I'm done talking. He'll tell me how it came out." And he cut the circuit.

Ivan whistled. "You don't play around, do you?"

Rissa said, "Bran—were you not overly abrupt with her?"

Tregare laughed. "If Ilse Krueger were a foot taller she wouldn't be so ungodly picky about everything. She's been chewing at command—no, not like Peralta, but trying to get a wedge in. Yesterday at the port she wasted more time, that way, than not. So I've been waiting for her to make a real issue. Now we find out once and for all if she takes orders or gets out."

He gestured silence. "Hold it—I have to call Limmer back." When he had the circuit, he repeated what he had told Krueger, then added, "I told you this way because you have to know, if she calls. But one thing, Derek—if you hadn't guessed already, the missile's a bluff. If she calls it, fire a dummy, so she'll think it's a miss. Right?"

"Yes. But for a minute there, Tregare—you had me worried."

"Sure. Now another thing—if she does show up for interviews she'll be spitting mad, so allow for that in reading the indicators. If you're not sure, pass her but say it's routine I do a repeat on all top personnel. Got it?"

Limmer chuckled. "Tregare—it's a good thing nobody else gets to question *us* under that gadget."

"Yeah. All right—I'll get off your channel so you're free to deal there." When the screen darkened, he turned to Rissa. "Now do you like it better?"

She nodded slowly. "Yes—of the four possibilities, two add the ship to your mission; the other two at least let it escape harmlessly. I did not see past what you said to Krueger." She smiled. "But then—with luck, neither will she."

Some minutes later, Limmer's Second called. The crew of *Graf Spee* had reported for questioning, and Ilse Krueger was certified trustworthy. "That calls for a drink," said Tregare. "I *thought* she'd come around, but peace knows she had me sweating."

Several drinks later, he said, "It's been a day; I'm ready for bed." Ivan excused himself and left, and Tregare said to Rissa, "Now that ovum's out of you, I hope you didn't think I meant sleep, right away."

"No, Bran—I did not think that."

THE next morning, the three flew to Hulzein Lodge. Tregare went ahead; Rissa stopped at the spaceport with Ivan, to pick up the rest of his luggage. Castel met them at the Lodge, guided them to the room assigned to Ivan, and said, "Madame Hulzein will be in her office now." They found Tregare there also.

He said, "Liesel, meet Rissa's brother—Ivan Marchant." Ivan stepped forward and shook her hand.

Liesel gestured. "Sit down, sit down." Then; "Ivan—you'll have newer word from Earth. How much newer, since Rissa left? And tell me how things are—were—with my sister Erika."

Ivan cleared his throat. "You look so much like her—only younger—it's a shock. Rissa's told you—and I left only two years after—in that time, Madame Erika hadn't changed much."

"What was the situation there, as you saw it? And call me Liesel, if you please."

"All right—Liesel. Erika wasn't much for formal, either. Well, let's see—she had to be over seventy, but she kept in good shape, active. And she had things well in control. UET tried a putsch in South Western-Hem but Erika's government—and she *owned* it, by then—cut off the main body of Committee troops in the Matto Grasso. Erika collected quite a big ransom for them."

Liesel slapped her desk and laughed. "Always make a profit when you win!"

"Yes—I know." Ivan frowned. "Toward the last, I didn't see much of her. She had some project going—I don't know what. Frieda took charge." He looked at Liesel. "You know Frieda?"

"My sister's daughter? Of course. She was about fourteen when I last saw her. But what's *your* impression of her? And how old was she when you left?"

"How old? Between thirty and thirty-five, I'd guess. But there's something wrong with that one; to tell you the truth I was glad to get out of there."

"For any specific reason?" said Rissa. She remembered the incident of Maria Faldane.

"Well—she was trying to reproduce. When she miscarried, she ordered her doctor killed. Erika intervened, but—" He shook his head. "She just wasn't stable. You never knew—"

Liesel sighed. "The Hulzein genes gone to seed; I was afraid of that. We may as well forget any effective liaison with her group. I wish—"

Tregare said, "Before I was born, Erika closed the door. And if you could be on Earth right now—never mind the objective travel time—she'd be nearly a hundred, or more likely dead a while." He saw Liesel wince, and said, "You know what the long view means; you knew it when you left Earth. Liesel—you can't reshape the past, so face what *is*."

She nodded, the heavy crowning braids bobbed with the motion. "Oh, you're right, Bran. But—if only Erika could have realized! We could have—"

Tregare reached to grip her hand. "*We* still can. She can't; that's all."

Liesel turned to Ivan. "Then Frieda has—or had—no daughter?"

His hand gestured negation. "The rumors—nothing but monsters, mostly born dead. There was talk that one was kept alive for a while until she gave up on it. From what I heard, that was a bad time—I'm glad I wasn't there then."

Rissa said, "This would have been before I was there? But I heard nothing."

Ivan shrugged. "Erika kept good security in her own circle. The story didn't leak until you'd left—and then by someone who wanted to start trouble." He shuddered. "He got it, all right. It was then I knew I had to get out, and fast. It's a good thing we're *all* out of there."

"The Argentine Establishment itself," said Liesel. "Was it in danger when you left?"

"I don't know. A lot of rumors, was all—nothing solid. Power plays I didn't understand, and Frieda in the middle of them. For all I know, the Establishment could be wiped out by now—or it could own the planet. That's Frieda for you."

"I see. Well," Liesel turned to Tregare, "we have to be alert for any word from Earth, don't we?"

He nodded, and Rissa asked Liesel, "Have you no later word through Osallin?" Then she gasped. "But I have not told you! He *came* here—to Base Two, rather—and was killed in the fighting." She shook her head. "I shall miss him. He was a good friend." Then; "But, Liesel—*have* you later information?"

"I'm not sure; I'll have to check the dates. *Graf Spee* brought a dispatch—it's still being decoded—and it's signed by Frieda and initialed by Erika. I figured out that much."

She sighed. "Sorry to hear about Osallin; from his reports that I've seen and from what you tell me, I think I'd have liked the man. Wish I'd met him. As for Earth—I suppose we can only wait and see. And by the way—with Osallin gone, what about Far Corner?"

"His successor is named Kirchessel; Osallin brought the new codes. And there, too, we can only wait."

Tregare stood. "Nothing we can do now; that's certain. Rissa—I haven't had any real exercise since forever—or since I got burned, anyway. Want to hike uphill a way if I get a lunch packed for us? And how about you, Ivan?"

Ivan nodded. Rissa said, "Yes, of course." She went to her room and changed clothes, then met the others downstairs.

AT first, until their muscles loosened, they walked slowly. Then the trail steepened; the three began to exert themselves, becoming short of breath until they gained second wind. Tregare turned left onto a narrow, overgrown trail Rissa had not noticed before. It bent sharply uphill, so steep that they needed to grasp bushes to help keep balance. Panting now, they continued until the slope eased—cresting a ridge to see, ahead through the trees, a small dark-blue lake.

Rissa said, "Bran—did you know this was here?"

Tregare laughed. "I spotted it once, from aloft. I was guessing I had the right trail to it."

"It's beautiful here," said Ivan. "Not just the lake—all of it."

"Yes," said Rissa. "And the climb has given me an appetite." She sat on the ground, Tregare on a stump, Ivan on a mossy boulder. They ate bread and cheese, meats and fruit, with sips from a bottle of tart red wine. They spoke little—mostly of their surroundings, pointing out oddities of plant life and the few small, scuttling animals they saw.

They fell silent. A fish—or something like a fish—jumped and splashed back into the lake. Rissa lay back and dozed.

Tregare's voice woke her. ". . . for sure, then, no counting on the Earthside Hulzeins?"

"I wouldn't think so," said Ivan. "You *are* going to Earth, are you? Or maybe I shouldn't ask."

Tregare laughed. "Oh, I've thought of it—several ways. I always have lots of possibilities in mind, Ivan—so if one goes sour, I scratch it off and don't waste thought on it. But it makes a difference whether there'd be a stable Hulzein connection on Earth, maybe sixty-eighty years after you left."

Rissa opened her eyes and saw Ivan shake his head. "I couldn't guess—not even two years from when I left, let alone the time until *you* could get there."

"No matter," said Tregare. "There'll be news. If not from the Hulzeins, then from someone else. And if not here, maybe the next place I land."

"The long view." Ivan said it a moment before Rissa would have. She sat up.

"Yes," she said. "It is hard to think in such terms, but it is necessary."

"Damned hard," said her brother. "I guess I'll have to work on it."

Tregare stood. "Before we turn back, should we go a little farther?" He led the way; they circled half around the lake and climbed one side of a looming promontory, then came out to its tip and gazed at the scene below. The Lodge looked very small; beside it the aircars were mere dots.

"And this," said Rissa, "is less than halfway to the top."

"Top of the first—and lowest—major ridge, you mean," said Tregare. "Well, I've had my workout climbing. On the way down, I'm willing to take it easy."

In no great hurry, they descended; when they reached the Lodge, the sun was low. In their room Rissa and Tregare shared a hot tub, then bed, before going downstairs to dinner. Liesel was first to the table; shortly Ivan joined them, then Sparline and Ernol.

"Ernol—my brother, Ivan Marchant."

The two shook hands; Ernol said, "If you fight like she does, unarmed, I'd appreciate a practice session sometime."

Ivan grinned. "I worked more with weapons—unarmed, maybe I'd be the one learning. Sure, though—I might have a couple of new moves for you."

Servitors brought food. "Eat now, fight later," said Liesel.

• • •

WHEN coffee and liqueurs were served, Tregare excused himself and returned a half hour later. "Talked with Limmer," he said. "Things are moving well. But we'd better go across tomorrow, Rissa, and check the work before anyone does any cutting. *Spee* and *Valkyrie* are the same class as *Lefthand Thread*, but not the same age. There may have been some modifications."

"Very well. Bran. And Ivan goes, also?" Tregare nodded. "Good—Ivan, you will have a new experience." Then, "And did you speak with Base One?"

"Yes. Hain caught part of a message from the packet. It's pretty close, now, but he missed the landing date—noisy signal."

Liesel smiled. "Hawkman—he'll be here soon—and about time! But, Bran—you and Rissa are leaving again, so soon?"

"Only for two-three days. Why? Something's up?"

"Well—" Liesel looked at her daughter. "This girl's had long enough to try out her man. When Hawkman gets home, I think we'll marry her off and get it over with."

"Mother!" Sparline was up and around the table, hugging and kissing the older woman. "Mother—I'm so glad!" Never before had Rissa heard Sparline call her mother anything but Liesel.

Ernol said, "I am, too," and leaned to kiss Liesel's cheek. "Thank you—and I guess this means I'm doing my job all right?"

"You don't have to ask that—you *know* you are. Now there's one question—only because Hawkman and I may be going to Earth, leaving you and Sparline in charge here."

Ernol's brows raised. "Yes?"

"Names. By custom, you'd each keep your own. But you've come up fast; some of the oligarchs could get snicky. 'Ernol Lombuno? Who's he?'—you know? So if you'd like to add the name Moray—*or* Hulzein—we'll put it in the contract."

"I—hadn't thought of the possibility. I—"

"You don't have to decide now, think it over. Whatever you and Sparline prefer, that's how it'll be."

Ernol nodded. "It's a great compliment, Liesel. My own

name—a Lombuno commanded troops that won victory against terrible odds. But I'd be just as proud of Moray or Hulzein, too.''

Holding Ernol's hand in both of hers, Sparline looked up. "Whatever Ernol decides, that's what I want, too." She smiled at him. "And if you take Moray or Hulzein, I get to add Lombuno."

Her mother laughed. "She's got you there, Ernol. Well, you two figure out what you want. Now, then—anybody for cards?"

Tregare shook his head. "Not me—not tonight." Rissa followed his lead, and one by one the group dispersed.

TREGARE, next morning, lifted the new aircar toward the pass. Rissa, Ivan beside her, followed in the older one. "Watch carefully," she said. "At the crucial points there are landmarks." She showed him the oxygen equipment; they fitted the tubes into place. Ahead, Tregare came abreast of the pass; she saw him turn up and into the buffeting currents. Then she, too, turned.

As they climbed, she did not speak. When the dogleg loomed she said "*Now!*" and swung the car viciously, at full power, into the first turn. She heard Ivan's whoop; when they were through the second and into more open space, she glanced aside to him. He was beating his palms against his knees and laughing.

"Oh, that's beautiful, Rissa—I'm glad you didn't tell me ahead of time!" His next words did not disappoint her. "Let me try it sometime?"

"If you have the landmarks correctly." He reported what he had seen. "Yes—that is right. Of course the reverse trip is somewhat different. You will see."

When they neared Base One, Tregare swooped toward it, then up again. On the car's speakers Rissa heard the sound of his call and an answer but could not make out the words. He swung up and along the ridge above the cabin, and she followed, as he took course for Base Two.

After a time, the crater and its ships came into sight. Ivan whistled. "Five, by God! And he's arming them all, isn't he? What's he—no, I mustn't ask yet; right?"

"Soon," she said. *If the truth field shows him clear of UET's booby traps . . .*

She landed beside Tregare's aircar, where he waited. He said, "Ivan—you mind if I ask a few questions, in that building over there?"

Ivan looked puzzled; then his face cleared. "Truth field? Sure—you'd be crazy if you didn't. I mean—I know where I *want* my loyalties to be, but maybe Erika's people didn't spring all the triggers UET planted in my head, back at Welfare. Maybe some weren't geared to that situation. If that's true, I want to know it—as much as you do, maybe more." He grinned. "Let's go."

TREGARE'S questioning was painfully deliberate, with pauses while he looked from Ivan to the indicators and back again. At one point he said, "We're getting a wiggle I can't pin down. Let's try it from another angle." He frowned and shook his head. "All right—Erika, not UET, trained you for killing. But what if she did exactly what they wanted?" He looked down, and up again.

"No reaction. Well, then—" His voice came harsh. "It's killing time, Marchant! *Who's your target?*"

Ivan leaned forward, tensed. "The enemies!"

"*Whose* enemies?"

He tried to rise; Rissa clutched his shoulder. "UET's! *You!*"

Rissa gasped. *So he* was *the UET plant we feared! But watch—watch and listen . . .*

Ivan sank back in his chair; his eyes widened. "But how could they—?"

Tregare's pointed finger held his gaze. "They knew where Rissa had gone. They knew she meant to get you out. So they planned for it."

Rissa said, "But *you*, Bran—they could not know—"

"Not me personally," said Tregare. "*Anybody* opposing UET. Right, Marchant?"

Ivan nodded; he looked down at his fingers, spread them, then clasped them together. "Do you have to kill me—or maybe just turn me loose somewhere I can't hurt anything?" His clenched hands beat down on his knee. "Oh, *hell*—here I thought—all this way, and I even found *Rissa*—I was hoping, but—"

"No!" said Rissa, and Tregare shook his head.

"Nothing like that," he said. "If you weren't pretty well defused already, you couldn't have got that up top and said it to my face. But a few precautions. You mind working under a hypnotic? Not to plant anything *into* you, but to spring what else is still there?"

Ivan shrugged. "Whatever you say." From a drawer Tregare took an ampoule, and made the injection.

NOW the questions came fast. Twice Ivan crouched and snarled, ready to attack. Each time Tregare fired a repetitive *"Why?"* forcing the man to consider his answers until he saw past their origin to his true feelings. Gradually the responses became less violent; soon Tregare could handle each with only a few questions, nodding as the indicators held a steady green.

Finally he turned to Rissa. "He's safe now; Erika must have got most of it out. I'd bet my life on him—in fact, I'm going to."

Yawning, he stood and stretched. "That was *work*! Well, I'd better get on and see Limmer. Ivan'll be a while coming out of it—you'll stay with him and bring him along later?"

"Yes, Bran. I will seek you first on *Lefthand Thread*."

"Fine. If I go somewhere else, I'll leave word." He left, and she took his seat at the field controls. *Can I do it?*

She had to try. "Ivan—the women at Welfare, who hurt you—remember?" He winced. "What did they do? Show me what they did."

He lay supine, spreadeagled on the floor, reliving what he told. Again and again she shuddered. Tie a boy down, arouse him sexually—then punish that arousal with vicious pain. No wonder normal response was killed!

She thought, then said, "Get up and sit again. Now—Ivan, how old were these women?" Middle-aged, most of them, he told her. She nodded. "Ivan—they are all *dead* now, or near it. Do you realize they are dead? *You* have killed them, Ivan —simply by traveling among the stars, by staying young while they aged and died." She leaned forward. "Dead people cannot hurt you, Ivan. They cannot touch you—you are beyond their dead reach!"

His brow wrinkled; he shook his head. Quickly she said, "Spit on them, Ivan—*spit on them*!" He spat. "Trample their bones to dust!" His feet beat against the floor. "Now they no longer exist. You have destroyed them. You are free of them. Your body can do as you wish it to—and there will be no pain, but only joy."

His face twitched; again he shook his head. "It is true!" *He recovers from the drug—there is little time.* She went to the door and locked it, came back and undid his clothing and her own. "Here is how it will be with you, Ivan, from now on."

She watched his smile begin. "You see, brother? There is no pain. . . ."

CLOTHED again, and he also, she sat with him as he came to full awareness. He looked up at her. "I dreamed. I dreamed that I—was all right again."

She squeezed his hand. "And you *are* all right—forever now, you are. The past has no more power over you."

He sat up. "But—what really happened? It seemed—"

"What does it matter? Your mind and body know they are whole again."

"But you—" He frowned. "No—that was my mind, I guess, and the drug. You wouldn't—"

"Always, I do what is necessary. Believe what you will—I cannot see your dream, to know if it is true or not. Unless you wish to tell me . . ."

"No!" He got to his feet slowly; she stood also. "I'll keep that to myself; sharing it might spoil it. But—whatever—my life's thanks to you!"

"You make me very happy, Ivan. Are you ready to go to the ship now?"

"Yes—a little shaky, but improving fast. And *hungry*!"

She laughed. "And so am I. Shall we go and see if it is lunchtime yet?"

ABOARD *Lefthand Thread* and upship, they found Limmer,

Felcie, and Tregare in the galley. Lunch had begun; Limmer waved for two more servings.

Rissa introduced Ivan. Felcie said, "Tari's brother? You just got here? You're a little older, aren't you? What's it like on Earth, when you left? Not too snooky, I bet. Are you glad to be here?"

Tregare laughed. "Don't worry, Ivan—you get used to it. Answer what you can keep track of and let the rest hang or come later. All right?"

Ivan smiled and slowly nodded. "I'm a little smeared yet, Felcie; it took a hypnotic to pull some bugs out of my head." He turned to Tregare. "Did it all come out right?"

"Sure—there wasn't much—less than I expected. But from the looks of you, it made more difference than I thought."

Ivan shrugged. "Tensions I didn't know I had—now they're gone." He looked to Felcie. "You asked—well, by chrono I'm three years older than Rissa. Not quite that, bio—I rode deepfreeze all the way here. Came in on *Graf Spee*. Peace knows, *yes*, I'm glad to be here. What Earth's like—or was—that's no fit subject for mealtimes."

Counting on his fingers, Limmer chuckled. "You'll do, man—you got *all* of them!"

The talk—light, friendly chatter—progressed. At first Rissa watched Ivan closely, but soon decided his adjustment was stable and complete. Certainly his responses seemed open, unguarded. Apprehension gone, mentally she sighed in relief.

AFTER lunch, while Felcie showed Ivan around *Lefthand Thread*, Tregare and Rissa inspected the preliminary work done on *Valkyrie* and *Graf Spee*. Only a few minor corrections were needed; cutting and reframing could proceed, then the arming itself.

Coming downship in *Graf Spee*, they met Ilse Krueger. The small woman wore a coverall suit; her hair was pulled back into a tight knot. She said, "Welcome aboard, Tregare—Tari. I was down in Drive when you came in, I guess. Everything going all right, above?"

"Fine," said Tregare. "And is everything all right with you, Ilse?"

She shrugged. "*Now* it is. First here, I felt Limmer was

crunching me—and *you* sure as peace were. But then I asked around. When I heard that *everybody* got the truth field treatment—well, after Peralta I couldn't argue with that logic. But you didn't have to give me that garbage about shooting me down if I didn't kowtow the right way!"

"Oh?" Rissa recognized Tregare's best deadpan expression.

"Yes, *oh*! Not much I'd put past you, Tregare—but blowing up an unarmed ship and all aboard it, out of spite for losing an argument? I didn't believe that for a minute, you peace-bedamned pirate, you!"

Tregare laughed. Rissa reached to grip the woman's shoulder, gently. "Ilse Krueger—I find that I *like* you."

Ilse patted Rissa's hand. "That's good—and I'm glad—but I'm a bitch on jets and never forget it. You ought to hear—"

"Then we are much alike—otherwise I would not now be alive."

Tregare said, "You can trade stories some other time. But Tari has a point, Ilse. We married in a dueling arena. She'd just killed a man twice her weight—a *skilled* man—without weapons."

Ilse blinked and stared at Rissa. "I wouldn't have thought it. But I guess I should have—short haul or long, what other kind of woman would Tregare take up with?"

"Could have been you, Ilse—when we first met, on South Forty. You had your own little harem then—the twins—so I left the string loose. But I've always figured I missed something worthwhile."

Ilse Krueger smiled. "Well—someday, maybe, Tregare. Unless your dueling woman would kill me for it."

Rissa shook her head. "Our binding is not exclusive. If you wish to go fulfill yourselves together at this moment—" *But how will Bran react when I tell him—as I must—of Ivan?*

Tregare turned her to face him. "You mean that, don't you? But—" He grinned at Ilse. "—right now I think we're due back on *Thread*."

Bidding Ilse Krueger good-bye, Rissa felt the other was now indeed friendly. Going downship, she said as much to Tregare.

"Sure," he said. "I told you—with Ilse, it's just that the shakedown takes a little time.

• • •

THEY entered *Lefthand Thread*'s galley and found Ivan and Felcie there before them. Ivan said, "We're invited to stay for dinner. I didn't know your plans, Tregare, so—"

"Derek thought," said Felcie, "if you'd like, if you're not busy, we could get all the captains together—Vanois, Gowdy, Ressider, Krueger—you *aren't* busy, are you? I hope—a real party, Derek thought—maybe—"

Tregare waved a hand. "Sure we can stay, and thanks. But not late—I want to reach Base One sober enough to read Deverel's message log and make sense of it." He turned. "I'd better call Hain now and tell him we'll be a while here." He left; Rissa sat and accepted coffee.

"How do you like the ship, Ivan? Did Felcie show you how we install the weapons systems?"

"Yes. She had me running simulations on a projector turret, too, and—"

"He's *good*! First he overcontrolled, the way I still do sometimes—then he got the feel of it and his scores went up like a kite. Give him a week, Tari, and he'll be real competition for you."

Ivan said, "I don't know about *that*—but it's the kind of thing I learn fairly easily, now my coordination's come back."

Tregare rejoined them. To Rissa he said, "The packet should ground late tomorrow. Shall we meet Hawkman at the Lodge tomorrow night?"

"If we are not needed here—surely. And what of *Inconnu*?"

"Another day—maybe two, if Zelde M'tana decides not to land at night. But Limmer's marked her a landing circle."

He turned to Felcie. "Is that spare cabin still free?" Brows raised, she nodded. "We don't have a change of clothes along, but we could freshen up a little before dinner."

HE and Rissa left. In the vacant cabin they showered, lay together for a time, then rested. After some thought, Rissa told him what she had done for Ivan—and why.

Tregare frowned. *Have I made a mistake here?* But he said, "He's not sure it was real?"

"He prefers, I believe, not to know."

"Funny . . ." He shook his head. "Two years with Erika's psych techs couldn't do it. And yet—"

Relieved, she said, "Two factors, Bran. First—on a very deep level, he saw me as the one person he could trust. Second —you had cleared away the residue of UET's mental implants, geared to a Hidden World situation. Then when I convinced him that those who hurt him are dead—and still I saw he was not totally free, so I—Bran? What do *you* feel?"

Smiling, he ran his fingertips up her cheek, into her hair. "You said it right, what you told him—always you do what is necessary. That's good enough for me."

"I am glad, Bran." She rose and began dressing. "But—Ivan must not know that *you* know."

He stood also. "Sure—I see that. Don't worry—far as I'm concerned, he never *had* a problem. All right?"

"Very much so." She kissed him. "Now—shall we try to be on time for dining?"

THEY were nearly the last to join the group. Limmer and Felcie, Ivan, Vanois with hair and beard trimmed to neatness, Hilaire Gowdy—these were there ahead of them. As they sat, Kile Ressider entered; he greeted those he knew and was introduced to Ivan. To Tregare he said, "I've been thinking. I shouldn't have expected command, when you have someone who's worked an armed ship. At first I had reservations. Now I don't."

Tregare grinned and accepted Ressider's handshake. Before he could answer, Ilse Krueger joined them; he shrugged and motioned Ressider to a seat.

Ilse greeted the others; Rissa introduced Ivan. ". . . and he was the one you told me of, who inquired about me!" Nodding, Krueger shook hands and said, "This one's brother, are you? You a duelist, too?"

"No, not especially. I'm trained to kill in the easiest way, not to follow ritual unless I have to. But that's only training, in case it's needed. I mean, don't be—"

"Frightened?" Her blonde curls, worn loose now, swung as she shook her head. "Nothing much scares me. I'm the smallest person ever to survive UET's Space Academy gauntlet—and I've got the scars to prove it." She smiled. "That's not any kind of challenge—just fact."

Ivan smiled also, and moved the chair beside him for her convenience. "Sit here, won't you?" When she did, he said,

"I wish I knew how to fly a ship." Then food was brought, and the woman's answer was lost to Rissa in the noise of general conversation.

Saying little, Rissa looked from one to another, observing. Vanois used his native jargon only a few times, then spoke in more normal patterns. Hilaire Gowdy ate sparingly; already—in less than twenty days, Rissa guessed—the loss of weight was noticeable. Ressider talked with Limmer and Felcie, too far away for Rissa to hear what was said.

She turned to Tregare. "Your group becomes, I think, a viable entity."

"Yeah—since Peralta, it's shaken down pretty good. When *Inconnu* gets here—"

"Then you will firm your schedules, to leave this world."

He gripped her hand. "And that's when it all goes on the line—our next thirty or so chrono-years. And maybe the next thousand, for the whole peace-losing human race!"

THE party after dinner was much as Rissa expected. Liquor and drugsticks abounded, though she and Tregare used both in moderation. The size of the group varied—people suddenly absent for a time and then back again—but Limmer's quarters proved too small; headquarters reverted to the galley. When Tregare said to her, "Time to go, I think," she looked around to see who was present.

"Ivan? He is not here."

"He'll be all right. Hain can come pick him up tomorrow."

They said good-byes to those who listened, and went down-ship. Outside, by the aircar, he said, "Who flies it? I can—but would you rather?"

"You—I am sleepy now and would be rested later."

She dozed on the way and woke at Base One. Tregare went to the scoutship, she to the cabin. She slept for a little while but woke when he joined her.

NEXT morning they rose early. While Rissa made breakfast, Tregare visited the scout. He returned just as Rissa was preparing to call him, and they ate.

"The packet lands sooner than I thought," he said. "I left

word for Hawkman to bring the new aircar; he'll be at the Lodge this afternoon."

"And did you speak with Base Two?"

"Yes. I'm going there for a while—come along if you like." He paused. "Limmer's turning out to be my key man; what do you think of taking him and Felcie along to the Lodge? I'd like him to feel a real part of the Hulzein Establishment."

She nodded. "Of course. And I owe Felcie a ride through the pass; I've hinted of it to her. But you say nothing of Ivan."

"*He's* all right. But we'll be taking Krueger to the Lodge, too. Sometime during the party last night, Ivan moved in with her."

"He—?" Rissa laughed, stood and leaned over to kiss her husband. "I would not have thought—but his instinct was right. He took his strengths to the strongest woman."

"You consider her stronger than Gowdy?"

Rissa shook her head. "Hilaire is older. He may never—it was older women who hurt him so terribly. You remember, I told you—"

"Yes—and you told me to forget it, too, so I am. But—Ilse at the Lodge—you think it'll be all right?"

"If she oversteps herself, Liesel will correct the matter."

"I expect so. All right—you want to come to Base Two?"

Upon consideration, she did not. Tregare and Deverel took the aircars; Rissa went to the scout, talked with Kenekke, and spoke on the screen with Liesel and with Ernol. Later, carrying a snack in her shoulder pouch, she hiked uptrail. She ate beside a stream; from the ledge where she sat, it dropped so far that the breeze whipped it into spray. Her seat gave her a view of the plateau and the hills that fell away below it.

Returning, she was only a few minutes distant when the aircar landed. Deverel had brought Limmer and Felcie; Tregare, she learned, would bring the rest in an hour or so. She showed the two around the plateau and cabin, briefly; then they boarded the car and she set off for the Lodge.

FELCIE'S response to the pass did not disappoint Rissa; when they were through it, she turned to see Limmer's scarred smile.

He said, "She wasn't really shaken, you know." Rissa nodded and he chuckled. "I see why everyone needs to go through that as a passenger first, though. Splash yourself if you didn't."

In a long, smooth swoop, she approached the Lodge. Seeing a new aircar on the ground, she landed beside it and was not surprised when the Lodge door opened and Hawkman came out. She leaped down, ran to him, and hugged him. "Oh—it's so *good* to see you again!" Then she turned to introduce him to the others.

"Limmer," said Hawkman, shaking hands. "Bran Tregare speaks well of you." Then; "Felcie! I hear you've left local bureaucracy for space?" She nodded and he laughed. "Your mind always did run too fast for one colony." He picked up some of the luggage. "Well, let's go in, shall we?"

Inside, Sparline met them. Limmer and Felcie were shown to the room prepared for them; the others adjourned to the dining room and sat to talk, drinking coffee.

Rissa asked of Hawkman's offworld stay. He waved a hand. "Dull, for the most part. Tending to business. Some of it's yours, Rissa—scan the tapes when you have time. But mostly dickering with Norden for *Valkyrie*, and he took hell and forever to make up his mind. I can't blame him; space was his life and he hated to leave it. But from my side . . ."

"Yes." Rissa nodded. "Bran and I, of course, have met Norden. If he were younger, I think he would have stayed with *Valkyrie* and joined Tregare."

Hawkman smiled. "I got that impression, too. But now— tell me the things that happened, that Bran Tregare only hinted at. The man—Peralta—?"

She told it. Sometimes Hawkman frowned; sometimes he shook his head. Finally; "My son's not known for being overly trusting, and I can't fault him this time, either. Who would expect *ship's* weapons crammed into an aircar?" Head thrown back, he laughed, then sobered. "But between you, you got him. Too bad, in a way—I mean, that he had to try it. A man like that . . ."

"I agree," said Rissa, "and Bran, also. His death is—a loss. But of course we had no choice."

"Course not," said Hawkman. He turned his head, listening. "An aircar coming—that'll be Bran Tregare?"

"Yes," said Rissa. "I will leave now and await him in our rooms."

• • •

UPSTAIRS, Tregare soon joined her. He was smiling, but when she asked he shook his head. "Wait—you'll see."

When they entered the dining room, the last to arrive, she saw what he had meant. At table with the two Hulzein couples were Ilse and Ivan; Ilse's left arm hung in a sling. Before Rissa could speak, Ilse said, "It's my own stupid fault, not Ivan's— I didn't know and I didn't ask. Sometimes I play a little rough in bed, and—"

"My reflexes got ahead of my brains. I *told* you I was sorry."

"He broke my wrist before I knew it. I'm lucky he was able to stop before he broke my *neck*." With her usable hand, she touched his shoulder. "Anyway—it won't happen again!"

"No," said Ivan. Then; "I'd thought to go with you, Rissa. But now—and Ilse wants me to train for First Hat on *Graf Spee*. So—"

Rissa moved to kiss him. "Of course, Ivan—this is best for you. And we all go to the same place."

Grinning, Ivan shrugged. "Yes—wherever that is."

Tregare spoke. "It's time you all—and some who aren't here today—knew my plans. All right—" He told of his scheme to take Stronghold, and then—perhaps—Earth itself.

Ivan banged a fist on the table. "It could work—Tregare, it could *work!*" He leaned forward. "From here, you can't find out what's what, Earthside. But with Stronghold taken—and I see no holes in *that* plan—you can sit and wait. Until the news from Earth points toward a good chance." He gestured. "But I'm not telling you anything, am I? You'd already figured it, right?"

"Sure I did," said Tregare. "But I'm glad you see it, too, and agree."

Ivan shook his shoulders free of tension in the way Rissa remembered. "I agree, all right. When do we leave?"

"Depends. But soon, in any case—don't get involved with any continued series on the entertainment channels."

Liesel had been unusually silent; now she spoke. "Hawkman. We've talked of going to Earth. Should we?"

"It's more can't than should," her husband said. "We don't have a ship yet—unless we go with Bran Tregare."

"No," said Liesel. "We—*I*—don't have time for that, not

at my bio-age. We have to go direct—or in freeze, at least. So I suppose we can't wait and buy a ship. But do we want to?''

"Let's wait and see," said Hawkman. "And on the chance, arrange signals with Bran."

"Signals?"

"If we go to Earth, we'll want to know whether it's friendly territory."

Conversation paused while food was served. Then Tregare said, "You'll know. Any Earth spaceport *I* take over, I'll run the UET students' underground fight song on all ships' frequencies, in the clear; every hour on the hour!"

And in incompatible keys he and Limmer sang; "And *that* is the reason, you can *plainly* see, why there's only one latrine in all of *U! E! T!*"

Hawkman laughed. "That should do it—shouldn't it, Liesel?"

"Yes. And Hawkman—if UET *were* still in charge—I think we have enough information to go in under false colors and get out again safely. Bran's done it and can advise us."

Tregare pushed his empty plate away. "You won't have to. If I get to Earth at all, UET won't have time to waste, checking your bona fides. That bunch will be too busy with its own problems."

Rissa frowned. "You are sure, Tregare? You have not spoken of this."

"I've thought of it, though." One hand made a fist. "The day I get to Earth in one piece, that's the day UET loses track of whether its butt's punched, bored, or clawed out by a wildcat!" He drained a glass of wine.

Rissa shook her head. "Tregare—is this fact or bombast?"

He grinned. "A little of both—sure. But I can make it work."

"I believe it," said Limmer.

"And I," said Ilse Krueger.

"Very well, Bran," Rissa said, "I only wished to be sure we do not, through overconfidence, lure our family and friends into trouble."

Tregare looked at her. "Before we leave, I'll distribute written plans to all concerned. All right?"

"Of course. It is only that we have drunk a considerable amount, and I—"

"I'll write it; you check it. Good enough?"

Rissa nodded and Hawkman said, "I like things put on paper, myself—it helps keep everyone on track. And now I'm tired. Liesel?" The two rose and the rest prepared to disperse. Ivan and Ilse left next; then Rissa and Tregare.

Upstairs, Rissa said, "Bran—I did not mean to say your thought is not good."

"You didn't. It's all right. But I'm bone-dead tired. Tomorrow, maybe?"

"Yes. Tomorrow. Good night, Bran."

NEXT morning Tregare was called away from breakfast to answer the viewscreen. He returned, grinning. "That was Deverel—with word from Zelde. *Inconnu* lands this evening or tomorrow morning, depending."

"Depending on what?" said Felcie. "Drive trouble? UET nosing around? Isn't space navigation more accurate than that? How—"

Tregare waved a hand. "Zelde's running on a least-fuel course, so she can skip the port and top off from the limited stock at Base Two. She's never landed there at night and would rather not."

"Rather cautious," said Ilse, "for someone who's going to command one of *your* ships."

"It's my ship she's being cautious about, and I agree." He turned to Liesel and motioned toward Sparline. "One thing—this means we're moving soon. We have to go to Base Two—and I'm not sure when or if we can get back here. So if we're going to see this younger-older sister of mine married, it had better be today."

"But we haven't time to *plan* it all!" Liesel's dismay was evident.

Sparline laughed. "What needs planning?" She spread her arms. "Our friends are here—what more do we need? If an impromptu wedding was good enough for Bran and Rissa . . ."

Ernol spoke. "She's right; we don't need anything fancy. Today's just fine."

Felcie giggled. "Let Derek perform the rites. He's in practice." They all laughed; the story was known.

Limmer shook his head. "I'd be honored, and that's truth. But it's Hawkman Moray's place to say the words for his daughter as he did for his son."

Rissa saw Hawkman's lips tremble as he smiled. "Thank you, Limmer. But I'll leave it to Sparline and Ernol." Brows raised, he looked at the two.

They nodded; Sparline said, "Derek's right, of course—we do need you, to say it all for us. Now—when do you want us ready—and where?"

"The sundeck on the roof," said Liesel, "and just before sunset. Will that do?" She looked around. "No objections? All right. *But*—" she added, "if you think you're getting out of anything, you're wrong. In a month or two we're going to have an official reception that will knock your eye out, with all the oligarchs standing in line to toady while they size up their new peer. I have that much coming, and I'm going to get it!"

Sparline patted Ernol's shoulder. "Don't worry—two months is a long time from now. We'll all be running your string with you, and I'll coach you how to handle the worse ones."

"And besides," said Hawkman, "by the time you two make your fashionably late entrance, we'll have the bigwigs full of wine and floating on drugsticks."

Rissa laughed. "I wish we could be here. But Stronghold will not wait."

"Nor Earth," said Bran Tregare.

AFTER a day of clear skies, clouds gathered, reaching bright, gaudy arms—orange, crimson and purple—up from the glowing horizon. The group stood, all but Hawkman facing the sunset. A cool breeze made Rissa shiver occasionally; she ignored her discomfort and listened carefully to Hawkman's words. When he had spoken them for herself and Bran, she had barely heard; parts of the ceremony she recalled, but less than half. Under her breath she repeated the responses as Sparline did—and with a side-glance she saw Tregare's lips move with Ernol's. At the end when Ernol and Sparline kissed, so did Bran and Rissa.

Kissing and embracing became contagious. After Rissa's turn with Ernol, she found herself caught by Hawkman, then her brother, then Limmer. As Tregare reached for her again, Liesel cried, "Wait a minute! If we're having an orgy here, we need some wine!"

Tregare laughed. "Or even if we're not! I'll get some." And catlike—a rather noisy cat, thought Rissa—he descended the stairs, two at a time.

"It *is* too pretty to go indoors," said Ilse Krueger, "but I need a wrap against this breeze." Rissa agreed and followed her. When she returned she found all but Ivan wearing additional clothing.

So in comfort now the group talked and drank, laughed and sang, until darkness and hunger drove them indoors. Dinner was late and leisurely; the remaining evening, until bedtimes, was brief.

ZELDE M'tana approached Number One when Base Two had entered darkness, and took orbit around the planet until morning. Caught in goodbyes that could not be hurried, Rissa and Tregare did not leave the Lodge until noon. Tregare took Limmer and Felcie in one aircar; after a time Rissa followed in the newer one, Ivan beside her and Ilse in the seat behind. As she approached the pass, she said, "Ivan? Do you wish to fly it?" He nodded; she switched control to him and he swung to enter the cleft.

He had little trouble with the turbulence and gauged his climb well. Rissa thought he swung too wide at the first turn of the dogleg, but he centered squarely on the second and brought the car through into clear air. "All right?" he said.

"Better than I did, my first time. And now—past the next ridge and to the left of the peak, yonder—then you can see the base ahead."

Ilse said, "You people are all crazy—you know that? You *scared* me back there, Ivan—and that takes some doing."

"I didn't intend to—I was just concentrating on getting through that dogleg."

"It is not an easy thing, at first," said Rissa.

"What I'm used to," said Ilse, "is up above, where there's more room. Aircars, no."

"This route," Rissa said, "is not usual for aircars. Few pilots could manage it."

"I believe that. This part—and peace be taken! How big *are* these hills?—this is more restful. Anyway—Tregare scared me too, yesterday—but at least I knew he'd done it before."

Ivan turned to grin at her. "And now you know I have, too."

Ilse tried to frown but laughed instead. "All right—now watch where the hell you're going, will you?"

Ivan slanted the car down between *Lefthand Thread* and *Carcharodon* to land beside Tregare's vehicle. "End of the line," he said. "All out." And they walked across the field —Ilse and Ivan to *Graf Spee*, Rissa past the other ships to *Inconnu*. She thought how different it was, since she last left this ship. Was she the same person? Probably not . . .

SHE climbed upship to the galley and found Tregare and Zelde M'tana. The woman turned toward her and held out a hand; Rissa moved to take it and was nearly smothered in embrace.

"Tari!" Now Zelde held her by the shoulders at arms' length, looking. "Only you're not, really, it turns out. Well, whoever . . . so you married the skipper, did you? And—Tregare's been telling me a lot in a hurry—fought a duel with Jimar Peralta—too bad he couldn't control his ambition—and earned your way to being Third Hat on here!" She squeezed the shoulders once, then released them.

"It was not quite as you said." Rissa made clear the different roles of Stagon dal Nardo and Jimar Peralta and, as Zelde nodded, said, "And you will command *Valkyrie*. Have you yet met Kile Ressider?"

"Oh, sure—we get along fine. He told it straight—first disappointed, then sold on the chance for a command at Stronghold, probably sooner than he'd have succeeded Norden in the ordinary way. I've gotta depend on Kile a lot—he knows the ship and I don't—so I made damn *sure* we're friends."

Did M'tana wink? Rissa could not be sure; she said, "I am glad all is to be well between you."

Tregare laughed. "Everybody gets along with Zelde. The easy way or the hard way—it's *their* choice."

"I learned that part from you, Tregare—you're a good teacher."

"The way I heard it, you kept things in line pretty well on *Chanticleer* while Parnell was falling apart, and after."

She shrugged. "You do what you have to. I was scared a lot."

"If you do the job," said Tregare, "nobody fusses how you felt while you did it."

Zelde grimaced but did not answer. Rissa said, "Tregare? Do you feed people on this ship, or has *Inconnu* run out of supplies?"

He laughed and ordered lunch served; the talk turned to immediate planning.

Now Rissa's days sped fast. She and Tregare lived aboard *Inconnu*, in the quarters they had shared with Chira. On *Carcharodon* and *No Return*, several turrets were modified to serve as practice positions. The work of arming *Valkyrie* and *Graf Spee* proceeded; now, with the crews experienced, it went much faster.

Rissa rode with Tregare when he took the scout across the Hills to return the truth field equipment. When they came back to Base Two, he delivered Arni Gustafson's greetings and regards to Felcie. On the same trip, scheduled with forethought, Rissa's third ovum went safely to the Hatchery, and Tregare made his "backup deposit."

Hilaire Gowdy came aboard *Inconnu* one day with a list of proposed officers for *No Return*. Her Second had been killed in Peralta's mutiny, and her Third had failed the truth field. Her candidates for those positions were upper-grade ratings who had been loyal in the fighting—but for First Officer she named Elrain Hardekamp, once Peralta's man.

"He's the best I've got, Tregare. But do you approve him?"

Tregare's brows lowered, then his face relaxed. "Yes, I remember—the first one I questioned. Well, the field said he's straight—and even without it I might've believed him. Sure, Gowdy, go ahead and make him First Hat."

When the woman left, Rissa said, "It comes together—does it not, Bran?"

He put an arm around her. "I think so—I really begin to think so."

"How much leeway have you left?"

"Not much—not a hell of a lot." He shook his head. "Peace be perpetrated—we've *got* to make it!"

THE next day Hawkman called; in the control room Rissa

watched the wavering picture as Tregare answered. "A ship landed—where did you say?"

Over the relayed circuit the voice came weak. "Three sightings. Near the Windy Lakes settlements it made a pass but didn't land. Then it did sit down, a little back from the coast at North Point—Rissa's peninsula. Several people are missing there. And now it's gone to ground somewhere beyond the Slab Jumbles."

Tregare's lips drew taut, white against his teeth. "Identification?"

She saw the indistinct head shake. "Nothing solid. The only witnesses who know anything about ships say it looked awfully small. But nobody—nobody that's still around to talk —saw it up close."

"UET?" Tregare's voice was almost a whisper. Then back to normal: "I heard talk—before we Escaped—they planned to try smaller ones. Cheaper, for some purposes—if the design worked. But in all these years I've heard no more, anywhere. And out *here*? No. I—"

"Then who, Bran?" Rissa could stand silent no longer.

"Who do you suppose?" He turned back to Hawkman. "I've got to check this. And damn it—I *can't* use one of my ships. The fuel, the work schedules—we'd miss deadline." He scowled. "The scout! It's not armed to match a real ship, but maybe I can dodge what I can't stand up to."

Hawkman paused, then said, "Yes. Anything I can do, Bran?"

It was Tregare's turn to hesitate, then he said, "Ask Dr. Estelle Marco at the Hatchery if she or some other competent medic can meet us at the port tomorrow and come along. I'll be there by—oh, call it mid-morning."

"I'll see to it. And—I forgot—Liesel and I looked over the plans you sent for contingencies at Earth. They're sound—we have no changes to suggest."

"Good. I'll be in touch when I can—before final liftoff, surely."

"I'm glad. And—that's you, Rissa, behind Bran?"

"Yes. Hello, Hawkman—my love to all of you."

"And ours to you. Well, I'll call Marco. Good-bye."

The picture dimmed. Rissa said, "It is the Shrakken?"

"Who else?" Tregare spread his hands.

"Why do you wish Dr. Marco to be with us?"

"*Us?* This one you're not going on!"

"As you often say, the hell I am not. Now, again—why Marco?"

Before he spoke, he shrugged. "Because something's funny about the Shrakken—and I don't mean chuckle. There's no fancy specialists here—shipboard *or* groundside—a plain medic's all we've got. But maybe she can take one of them apart and see what makes it tick."

"You would kill them?"

"*They've* killed, haven't they? But—" He shook his head. "Autopsies are the last resort; maybe we can do without them. But either way, I want Marco with us."

"Us? But, Bran—you said—"

"If you want to go, you'll go—one way or another. Might as well go together."

"It is pleasant to have an understanding husband." Then, "Bran! Not *here!*" Enjoying the game of playing helpless when both knew she was not, she waited until he released her. "You have calls to make, I know. I go to our quarters. Twenty minutes?"

When he arrived some minutes late, she ignored the lapse.

IN the night she woke, not knowing why. She heard Tregare's breathing; it was not that of a sleeper. "Bran? You are awake?"

"Yeah. Can't sleep."

"You are not ill?"

"No." She sensed the movement of his headshake. "It's just this thing tomorrow—the Shrakken. It's so damned *crucial*—if they're a real menace, maybe we have to stay here—all bets off—"

"Bran?" She reached for him. "Might I help, now?"

He laughed and came to hold her. "I don't know—you might, at that."

But in their embrace she felt him strain to achieve at all, and at the end she knew it had not gone well for him. Afterward she lay hoping to hear him breathe in the rhythms of sleep —but if he did, it was after she herself slept.

• • •

RISSA took the scout up next morning and flew it across the Big Hills, but Tregare—though he showed evident fatigue—took control for the landing, saying, "You're almost ready for that, but not quite."

Ivan was with them, and Hilaire Gowdy. The older woman's appearance surprised Rissa; while she might never be slim nor pretty, her weight loss gave her a healthy look. In her own strong-featured way, Rissa decided, Gowdy was becoming an attractive woman. Even the unruly hair was trimmed and brushed into relative neatness.

Rissa was caught staring; Gowdy grinned. "Let myself go something awful, hadn't I? That outspoken young chit with the truth gear brought me up short. Took a good look and didn't like it, so . . ."

"You must be very pleased now. I am happy for you."

"Oh, I have more to take off. But it gets easier."

As Tregare landed the scout, talk ceased. Rissa let the ramp out and down, and stepped onto it. She saw Estelle Marco get out of a groundcar, and waved. A younger woman—tall, carrying an equipment bag that seemed heavy, followed the doctor to and up the ramp.

"My assistant, Landa Cohoes," said Marco. Inside, Cohoes set the bag down; Rissa took charge of introductions.

Shaking Cohoes's hand, Tregare said, "You're both coming along?"

"If you don't mind," the doctor said. "One of you could carry this ton of junk for me, I suppose—but if I understood what Hawkman Moray was saying, another pair of skilled hands could help."

Tregare nodded. "Sure, that's good. Rissa—fill it in, will you, on the way? Might as well take off now, if we're all ready." With all seated and securely belted, he took the scout up.

As she talked, Rissa watched the two women's reactions. Marco occasionally nodded or grimaced; the other's grave expression did not change. Rissa could see the woman was past first youth but her skin was clear, her brown hair—worn long, coiled at the nape—untouched by gray. Finally Landa Cohoes said, "And these creatures have been seen—by humans—only twice?"

"Yes," said Rissa. "First by the Committee troops who —we are almost certain—killed them. Then by the settlers on Charleyhorse—where, as I said, *they* killed at least one."

Tregare said, "Limmer—one of my captains—saw them over a viewscreen, ship to ship. But not for long, and the picture wasn't very good."

"Are you sure they killed the woman at the colony?" said Marco.

"We're sure of damned little," said Tregare. "That's why —until we find out more, if we can—I don't want this world left undefended."

He took the scout high; now they passed over those unbelievable piles of stone, the Slab Jumbles. Beyond them Rissa saw a gleam of light, and Tregare shouted, "There it is! UET or Shrakken, we've found it!" The scout dropped low over the monstrous stones, and then alongside them toward the ground. Balancing the vessel on thrust that barely supported it, Tregare moved slowly to the last southernmost slab. Halfway along its great length, he grounded beside it.

To their left as they disembarked, the fallen monolith loomed high. Tregare, leading, turned to the others. "If this bucket weren't so noisy, we could've got closer. Try to land beside them, though—they'd take off—all I could do is shoot. So we have to sneak up on foot."

"And then what, Bran?"

"What you're good at, Rissa—play it by ear." He looked from one to another. "Except for our medics, we're all armed —right?"

Marco said, "We're armed, too, but Landa will be hampered by the equipment."

Ivan moved to take the bag but Hilaire Gowdy said, "No—let me. I'm only fair with guns, anyway." Ivan smiled and stepped aside as she shouldered it.

They set off—Tregare and Ivan ahead, Rissa guarding the rear. Occasionally Tregare gave further instructions. "If we can, we want to talk. If they shoot first—well, depends on the setup. If we can, get to cover and play it from there. If not— standard practice—get flat and shoot the piss out of them.

Until they quit or as long as *we* last—but I always bet on our side."

A little farther along. "Say they manage to take off. I run like hell back to the scout and chase—only thing I *can* do. They leave any behind, that's up to you—keep them alive if you can, but don't take any chances you don't have to."

"And then what, Bran?"

"Oh, sure, Rissa—this is no place to be stuck. Soon as I'm high enough, I'll call Hawkman—get a couple of aircars here, needed or not. Five vacant seats and the rest full of armed help."

Rissa frowned. "Bran—"

"What's wrong?"

"I wish we had conferred." He waited; she said, "If an aircar had made rendezvous and were here *now*—"

He turned, eyes widened. "Peace take me, *yes!* We could drop in quietly, surprise them—and me or someone in the scout, ready to go up if need be."

"And *without* your having to run like hell, Bran."

"Yeah, yeah—wait a minute." Then he shook his head. "No—we don't have the time. I'm sorry—we're stuck with things as they are. *Damn!* I couldn't sleep last night, and I miss it."

They reached the end of the towering slab; Tregare dropped to his belly and crawled to peer around a sharply angled corner. Rissa looked back; she saw bare rock and flat ground; the only clumps of boulders large enough to give cover to an enemy were outside the range of a quick rushing attack. She moved to join Tregare.

She looked. "Are you sure, Bran, we have not circumnavigated the Slab Jumbles?" For the ship ahead, perhaps a hundred meters distant, was almost a twin to Tregare's scout. But near it a dozen or so Shrakken sat or moved, pursuing their activities.

"Bran—what are they doing?"

"No way of knowing—the equipment's totally unfamiliar." Over his shoulder. "Ivan? Could you man the scout?"

"If Rissa's not ready to land it yet—and she's flown it some —it's too hot for me. Sorry."

"Then damn it, it's up to you and her to lead the parade— because I have to stay in position to run for it." And nearly a kilometer back, Rissa thought . . .

"I could fly it," said Gowdy.

"Sure. But—no offense—you'd take too long getting there."

"I could start now. If theirs goes up, I see it and follow."

Tregare hesitated. "All right—go ahead." Gowdy handed the medical kit to Cohoes and turned to jog back toward the scout.

Slowly, along the base of the great stone, they began to move—Ivan and Rissa ahead, Marco and Cohoes following, and Tregare behind. Lesser boulders, singly and in groups, spotted the plain and gave sparse cover. Still, Rissa was surprised at how closely they approached before one Shrakken's high-pitched cry brought all the aliens standing, staring at the intruders.

Rissa stood. "Please! We want to *talk*!" She held her gun behind her, out of sight—but Ivan had risen also, and his weapon was visible, pointing above the Shrakken but not by much. Again she wished for better advance planning—*this muddle is not like Tregare.* But, lack of sleep—she shrugged.

After a frozen moment, she repeated her cry. The Shrakken broke into a rapid gabble, all shouting at once—then, hit or miss, grabbing up equipment or leaving it, they ran for their ship. Now Rissa and Ivan ran also, both firing—but at the ground ahead, barring several Shrakken from their sanctuary.

Seeking refuge, the remaining aliens—those who had not reached their ship—scattered. Some vanished among boulder clumps, and two into the passageway between the first major slab and its neighbor.

Then Rissa heard and felt the Shrakken drive's hum build, and threw herself flat behind a boulder. Concussion from the violent takeoff jarred but did not injure her; she rose to see Ivan coming first to hands and knees, then standing. He shook his head and grinned. "Some blast—my ears are ringing."

Marco and Cohoes approached; the doctor said, "Tregare's sprinting for the scout ship. If Ms. Gowdy gets it off ahead of him, he'll be back. Otherwise she will."

"Yes," said Rissa. "Now—has any of us counted how many Shrakken are still here?"

Marco said, "Three out among those tumbled rocks, and two went into that—not a tunnel, exactly—where the one slab rests against the other. Five, in all."

"That's presuming," said Landa Cohoes, "that there aren't some others out somewhere that we didn't see."

Rissa shook her head. "All right—another approach, then. Did any see how many got *aboard* their ship?"

The consensus was five minimum, eight at most. "Then we can assume," said Rissa, "that we saw them all. For the ship is the size of Tregare's scout. Unless they spend their time stacked like cordwood, twelve is a reasonable number for it to carry."

Noise struck them; she looked to see Tregare—or was it Gowdy?—flash into the sky. Then she said, "We have our own job to do—catching one of the Shrakken for Tregare. How—?"

"This is my game," said Ivan, "I know the rules. Okay, Rissa?"

"Certainly—if you have the greater knowledge, then you must take charge."

"All right." He explained. "We're not going into that blind passage—too good a place for ambush. I didn't recognize any weapons, but we don't *know*. So we'll scout those clumps of rocks out in the open. Now here's how it works . . ."

Rissa and Estelle Marco guarded the open ground between the big slabs and the boulder groups so no Shrakken could cross it. Before Ivan and Landa set out to explore the rock-studded area, he said, "And remember—*always* be sure you're in sight of one other person, and the more the better."

At first, with the need to check on the whereabouts of others while also watching for any sign of aliens, the search was slow. Then Rissa caught the knack of it, ranging back and forth, getting cross-sights on a cluster of rocks and Ivan or Landa approached it from a different direction. But all signals were "negative."

Then she saw one! She signaled; Ivan sprinted over rough ground and shouted to the creature. It ran; Ivan pursued, stopping short—*how can he know without looking?*—of going out of Rissa's line of sight. Almost leisurely, he fired. Dust erupted at the Shrakken's feet and it fell, rolling. Curving his path so that Rissa never lost sight of him, he ran to it.

She started toward him—had he wounded the creature, or

avoided that?—when she heard a thin scream. She looked around—Marco and Cohoes were safe enough and looked as puzzled as she was.

The scream came again—full-throated this time, and rasping—and this time she sensed its direction. From around the huge slab, it sounded—from the direction they had come. Without thought, she began running. Ivan called to her, but she did not pause.

Turning the corner, Rissa looked and saw nothing. She slowed, peering to each side. Again the scream, and now it was to her left—from outlying boulders a distance away. She ran faster—then, realizing she might need breath to fight, slowed and took it.

Before she reached the clump, a Shrakken fled it. Momentarily she veered toward it, then resumed her course; Ivan already had his alien—and those screams had not been Shrakken! Slowing, she rounded the clump of boulders and reached her goal.

Hilaire Gowdy lay there—eyes bulging and upturned, hands twitching feebly, clothes torn and crotch running blood. The woman made a weak sound, almost a whispered scream. Then her eyes closed. Gasping, Rissa dropped to her knees—looking closely, she saw that Gowdy still breathed.

She shook her head and stood—what to do? A touch on her shoulder—she spun to face a Shrakken, standing, topping her by more than a head, bobbing lightly up and down as the long, thin hands reached toward her and withdrew again.

Shock! part of Rissa's mind calmly compared the reality to the pictures she had seen, while time slowed and another part of her prepared to kill—for this creature was—*Now! Danger!* —the Shrakken pursed its strange mouth and spat. Not a liquid—her involuntary gasp inhaled a vapor that smelled of musk.

Danger, indeed!—she struck, but her arm was as slow as time itself—numbness took her strength and the Shrakken pushed her down. She saw the upright segmented member— "a real hard-on," Tregare had said—it dripped viscous liquid tinged with red. At its base a bulge appeared and moved out along it.

And then the creature dropped onto her and—*pain!*—as the

Shrakken forced itself into her, her scream echoed the one she first had heard. And the next, and the next . . . but she could not move.

Nor could she think. She felt something torn from her, saw the Shrakken rise, turn in mid-air, and fall to ground in the fixed range of her vision. Where the segmented member had been, bright orange blood gushed and a short-tentacled ovoid thing—its color pulsating between pink and orange—emerged and fell to ground. The Shrakken cried out once, then shuddered and fell silent, limp.

Rissa's sight glazed; dimly she saw Ivan, brandishing a knife stained orange. His mouth moved, but she heard nothing. And then she saw nothing, and felt not even pain.

"PEACE take you, is she going to be *all right*? It's been two days—you must have *some* idea!" It was Tregare's voice, and though she could barely open her eyes, she recognized that she lay on a bunk in the scoutship. Rissa's instinctive defenses relaxed.

She assayed herself. She could not move, except a twitch of fingers—certainly she could not speak. But pain and numbness had lessened; she could wait for the rest of it.

She heard Marco say, ". . . time for the paralytic agent to wear off, and it's beginning to. As I said, I got the thing out of her before it could dig its roots in. I don't think I've mentioned—I wasn't so lucky with Ms. Gowdy. The egg, or larva or whatever it is, had gotten deeper, and attached solidly to the uterine wall. I had to do a hysterectomy to save her life."

Briefly she laughed, a dry sound that carried no hint of amusement. "I found a fibroid tumor that would have given trouble before too long, and Gowdy's past fertile anyway—so maybe, unwittingly, that obscene creature did her a favor."

Now it was Tregare who laughed. "Obscene? Earth has wasps that do about the same thing. But who would have thought it?" Peripherally, Rissa saw him shake his head. "The Shrakken was female, and the big hard-on an ovipositor."

"But why do they use *people*?" Dr. Marco.

"The way I get it—I've talked with one of them a little—when the instinct hits, they can't help it. The immature form has to eat to survive; they're driven to take whatever's handy.''

"But how can we have dealings with such creatures?"

Tregare cleared his throat. "We'll manage—we'll have to. Usually they use a drug to hold off ovulation when that's necessary, but this ship had run out. So the way it'll have to work is, they watch their people closely as they can, and we provide animals for when they need them. It's not pleasant, but life often isn't—or maybe you've noticed."

"I have, Tregare—I wish I hadn't. I'll go now. I want another look at the foot of the Shrakken your brother-in-law first brought down. The injury's not serious, but I'm interested in the way they heal. Never saw anything quite like it."

Hearing them leave, seeing what she could see while her head refused to move, Rissa considered what she had heard. After a time she relaxed and let sleep have its way.

The next day she woke able to move and speak—still slowed, but recovering rapidly. She sat propped against pillows while Tregare fed her and told her more.

". . . and I see how they'll help us take Stronghold. But, after what happened—do you want to meet them?"

"Of course I do." She smiled. "For one thing, I should like to know whether there is any way we might duplicate their zombie gas."

THE Shrakken had not surrendered easily. When Rissa next accompanied Tregare to Base Two, repairs were underway on their scoutship—but she could see how his projector had half-gutted it. She wondered how they had managed to land the craft.

"As soon as they were out of atmosphere, I holed them," Tregare said. "They had to duck back down for air, and for a while they followed orders pretty well. But they were suiting up, and made another break for it. That's when they got the works."

"And were many killed?"

"Afraid so—six on their scout, plus the one Ivan got groundside, out of fifteen total. But they don't seem to hold a grudge on it. They know we can't put up with the way they have to incubate their young sometimes, and they're willing to compromise. Not that they have much choice. . . ."

Approaching the full-sized Shrakken starship where it sat alongside *Graf Spee*, Rissa walked with ease and little pain. She thought, and said, "Compromise? On what terms?"

"You'll see. And listen close—they talk funny—put our words into their own grammar, I guess. You'll get the hang of it."

"For what use? Bran—what is it you wish me to do here?"

"Just listen, mostly—and talk with them, if you want. I trust your savvy."

She nodded and saw five Shrakken emerge from their ship. Without speaking, the aliens joined the procession as Tregare led the way to *Inconnu*. Waiting in that ship's galley were Limmer, Gowdy, and Ivan. Tregare motioned for the aliens to sit.

When all were seated, Rissa looked around at the disparate group, waiting to see who would speak first. No one did, so she looked to the Shrakken and said, "We know you as Shrakken. How are we known to you?"

One—the most vividly colored—answered, "Humans, call you yourselves. Say we—would we the deaths not had."

Rissa looked to Tregare; he made no move. She nodded and said, "Neither did we wish to kill—only to talk. But you—"

The alien moved its mouth; Rissa could not interpret the action. It said, "Sad we feel. But the egg need, control we not can. Death a time or other comes. This we not would want—"

Tregare spoke. "Stonzai—we already covered this. We give you freeze-chambers—for incubator animals *or* to hold one of you with the hot eggs. But you don't ever gut a human again. Right?"

In neither nod nor shake, the Shrakken's head moved; Rissa could not guess what was meant. "Try what you say do—to live and breed—all we can, is."

Tregare grinned. "Then you'll do as I've asked?"

Horizontally across the triangular eyes, Stonzai's eyelids twitched. "As we must will. Humans, you—much demand. But—you do mercy have."

At Tregare's nod, the Shrakken rose and left; the others followed. Rissa looked at Tregare. "You might tell me, Bran—what *have* you asked of them—and why?"

"Simple. We could use a decoy at Stronghold. They're it."

"They will do what you wish? You can trust them?"

He smiled. "Both yeses, I'm convinced. Now, then—what did *you* think of them?"

She shook her head. "I do not know enough to judge. The one seemed sincere; certainly their biology is not a matter of choice." She paused. "You have not told me, as yet—how did you coerce their *major* ship to join you here?"

Seeing Tregare's grin, she thought of what he had told of his early training. But he said only, "They didn't have a choice. That ship's weapons—camouflaged, by the way—are pea-shooters, compared to ours. About even with the projector on my scout. But mainly, they were low on fuel—no place they could go. So they gave up." He laughed. "When I got them refueled at the port, now *there* was a shindy for you."

"But the main point," said Rissa. "On that basis, you trust them to help you?"

"It's more than that. I don't know who they've been up against before, and that's fine with me—because they *expected* to be killed ten for one—and they're grateful I didn't do that, as a matter of course. You heard what Stonzai said about mercy?"

"Yes. But can you place trust in that saying?"

"Rissa—outside of you and my family and the truth field, I trust damned few. But like it or not I have to deal with a lot of others. And it doesn't bother me an awful lot."

Looking at him, she saw no signs of strain. "In that case, Bran, it does not bother me greatly, either."

He came to her. "It better not." He kissed her. "You knew the worst of me from the start." Again a kiss. "Didn't you?"

She pushed back enough to stand and face him. "And I am also learning the best. When I heal from the hurt the Shrakken gave me, we will pursue that matter further."

Tregare cupped her face in his hands. "I can wait. I don't like it, but I can."

TREGARE ordered four of the spare projectors mounted in the Shrakken ship. To Rissa, he explained, "The *Sharanj*—that's close to how they pronounce it—has to look like a real menace, chasing one of our ships into Stronghold. One with its weapons camouflaged, of course. Now, then—" He gestured with both hands. "Here's the rest of us in hot pursuit—*forcing* the alien ship down to land at the port. See how it works? UET's too busy—until it's too late—to give us much trouble about identifications."

"But—to arm the Shrakken—possibly against us, later?"

"Not exactly. Inside, the turrets are bare bulkheads. No traversing motors, no controls except the trigger switch. Power leads, sure—the things have to spit so's you can see it. But I'm installing fixed-tuned units—to *look* deadly, but way off effective frequencies. And I haven't explained how our heterodyne-tuning circuits work."

"I see. Yes, Bran, that is well planned."

He smiled. "If Stonzai does the job for us at Stronghold, I may make those turrets fully operational. I've hinted as much to her—and that's *more* bait, you see."

"Stonzai is their captain?"

"Not exactly—she speaks for *Sharanj*, is how she puts it. But from our standpoint it works the same."

"Bran—do you think the Shrakken might become our allies —not enemies as we had feared?"

"I think they *want* allies—that that's why their ship went to Earth. As for being enemies—well—" The Shrakken home worlds, he explained, lay more than half the width of the galactic arm from Earth, and slightly down it. Shrakken exploration and expansion had been more along the arm than across it—as had Earth's. So the two species were not in direct competition.

"—and won't be, for centuries. By then, relations should be pretty well established—maybe joint colonies, for that matter. With the drug to delay ovulation there'd be no problem. Bad luck nobody on *Sharanj* knows just what it is or how to produce it."

"And they are—how far from their own nearest world?" She saw Tregare shrug. "Bran—without freeze-chambers, how would they have managed on the home voyage? What could they have used?"

"Stonzai told me the answer to that one. First, as many animals as they could keep alive, aboard. And then—each other."

Rissa gasped. "Oh—the poor, poor creatures!"

"Yeah. You might say, pardon the pun, that it takes a lot of guts for them to go to space at all."

TIME and Tregare's temper grew short. Now there was little Rissa could do to help; the last-minute problems were not in her field of knowledge. She had no luck with her idea of duplicating the Shrakken paralytic vapor, for she could not procure a sample—none of the aliens was due to ovulate before departure deadline.

Belatedly she realized that her two identities would cause confusion in intership communications and—feeling shame-faced in some cases—made her true name known to those who knew her as Tari Obrigo. Vanois seemed put out, but Derek Limmer waved her apology aside. "Hiding, when it's out of necessity, is a hard habit to break. But I'm glad to know you—Rissa."

THE day before departure Hawkman flew the pass, bringing Liesel, Sparline and Ernol to the cabin. The six lunched together, crowding the small kitchen, and afterward sipped wine as they talked.

Tregare handed Hawkman an envelope. "Bernardez is over-due but I still think he'll get here. If he does, the *Hoover*'s your best bet for going to Earth—a ship that's kept cover with UET but known to our people, too. Here's your bona fides to deal with him—or with Malloy, if *he* turns up. Look them over."

Hawkman did so and nodded. "Yes—authorizing me to represent you—his instructions to arm the ship and camou-flage the weapons—but now—?"

"I'm leaving a technical cadre here. Four people, attached to you—if you don't mind—for logistics, and under your orders. They can rotate duty while they're waiting—here, the Lodge, or in town—but two here at all times. If Bernardez—or Malloy—doesn't show up in a reasonable time, the four will fit into your operation all right. They're volunteers."

"Yes." Hawkman looked again at the papers he held. "Then, let's see—if ready before the critical date, to go to Stronghold—"

"But I told you, Bran," said Liesel, "I've no *time* for such travel."

"Freeze-chambers," Tregare said, "The *Hoover*'s are always in good shape."

"—or if not," Hawkman went on, "to go directly to Earth. And the signals to look for, and—yes, the new codes for him to use." He looked up. "It's thorough."

"I'd hoped so," said Tregare. For a moment, he frowned. "The way to get along with Bernardez—it's the way you probably would, anyway. Tell him right away that your effective command doesn't mean you're looking over his shoulder all the time—that you rely on him for all the information you need and none that you don't. And you'll get it, too. But Bernardez works best when he's not nervous, and it makes him nervous to have somebody jogging his elbow."

"You're saying," said Sparline, "that this Bernardez is a dangerous man?"

Tregare laughed. "Hell, yes—to his enemies. Or he wouldn't have the *Hoover*."

"And you, Bran," said Rissa, "have *Inconnu*, and *Left-hand Thread*, and *No Return*, and—"

"—and Rissa Kerguelen," he said. "And that makes me most dangerous of all."

SHE laughed then, but Liesel, not smiling, said, "It's true— you two together make a greater force than you do separately. And that's saying a lot."

"As may be," said Rissa. She stood. "Anyone care for a walk?" Ernol and Sparline joined her; the rest declined. The three walked to the plateau's edge and looked down past the shadows to the lower Hills and the vast plain beyond. "The Big Hills!" said Rissa. "There is nothing like them. I hate to leave—them, and you."

Sparline gripped her arm. "And I hate it that you *must* leave. You and Bran—I'm just getting to know you both. And then maybe Liesel and Hawkman go, too." She shook her head. "If only Ernol and I could join you—but somebody has to mind the damned store!"

Ernol's hand clasped his wife's shoulder. "It's a good store and a good world. And they'll be back, I'm betting."

Sparline's mouth twisted. "Maybe when we're *old*, they will. All those years . . ."

Rissa spoke. "The long view, Sparline, remember? But I agree; it does take its toll." She turned and led them back along the rim of the plateau; when they reached the rear of it she stopped and pointed uphill. "The trail here—at this time of day, if we hurry, there is a view point—the plains will awe you."

She turned to walk, but Sparline caught her hand. "Not me—I'm not for climbing today, especially in a hurry. You two go ahead, but don't take too long. Even Hawkman wouldn't care to fly the pass in twilight, and six of us would sleep cramped in Bran's cabin." She squeezed Rissa's hand, smiled, and walked away.

Rissa's brows raised; Ernol nodded and they climbed the trail, breathing faster as they reached the viewsite. For a time they watched, as shadows crept out across the plain.

Then she turned to him. For a moment, until he smiled, she thought she would have to ask. And this time her joy matched his.

Each still holding the other, Ernol said, "I'm glad for you."

"I wished you to know—and this was the last chance. I feared I would have to merely tell you, but—"

"Sparline's guessed for some time. It's good she was right."

"Sparline is often right. As, for instance—concerning *you*."

Both laughed; they dressed and ran down the trail. They reached the cabin soon enough that goodbyes, when they came, were not unduly brief.

Too quickly, even so, came time for parting. "We'll be together again—"

"On Earth, and here, too—"

"It's not so long if you look at it right—"

"—and stay in freeze a lot—"

"Unfreezing's the best part—a new world—"

"—or the same one again—"

"The same *us*!"

"Oh, damn it, I'll *miss* you—"

"—and I you, but—"

"We love you—"

"If we don't get into the air soon," said Hawkman, "the four of us won't get home today." So the final round of kisses went quickly. And then Tregare and Rissa stood looking after the aircar.

"Oh, Bran! Will we ever see them again?"

WONDERING what had roused her, she came awake. Tregare? He breathed evenly enough, but . . .

"Bran?"

"You should be asleep."

"And you—but we are not." Her hand found his cheek. "Why?"

For a time he did not answer. Then, "When we lift tomorrow—ready or not, we're staking *all* of it."

"Of course. We have known that."

She felt his head shake. "For us, sure—and even for Earth. But it's just now got to me—we're risking the Hidden Worlds, too."

"I do not understand. What new danger?"

"UET's been playing it close to home—not ranging out here, much. I'd figured it was our raids, held them back. But—" His laugh held no humor. "Not to sound conceited, you see, it's not me or anything I *really* have that scares them—"

"Oh! As Ivan told—on Earth, the Underground rumors, But, Bran—" In sudden comprehension she fell silent.

"Yeah—you get it now. Those rumors—they only work *as long as I don't show up.* If we fail at Stronghold . . ." Shuddering, he sighed. "You see, Rissa? It's not just Stronghold, or even Earth. It's *all* the marbles!"

While she thought, her fingers kneaded his neck's rigid cords. "Of course, Bran—how could it be otherwise?" She paused. "Have you lost confidence in your plan? I have not."

"No. With what we have, it's as good as can be done. But . . ."

"Tregare! We have agreed that this *must* be tried, and who else could attempt it? So—do we go ahead?"

His arms gripped her. At first his laughter wrenched him, as though he sobbed—then it came freely. "Yes, Rissa—peace knows it, *yes!* I'll be all right."

And when at last he slept, in the moments before she herself found sleep, Rissa thought: *Whatever happens—here is where my life belongs.*